Gold, Guts and Glory

Acclaim for
Sweet Glory and *Train to Glory*
(Books 1 & 2 of *Glory: A Civil War Series)*

Sweet Glory

First-Place Winner of:

YA Fiction, 2009 Maryland Writers' Association
& Southwest Writers' Novel Contests

TV ME! Contest, 2013 Sarasota County Film
& Entertainment Office

Historical Fiction, 2018 Top Shelf Indie Book Awards

Bronze Medalist, 2016 Young Adult Fiction (General),
Readers' Favorite International Book Awards

"This book combines historical accuracy with romance and a suspenseful narrative that will keep readers hooked." ~*Publishers Weekly*

"A wonderful supplement to a school Civil War history lesson as well as an entertaining read any time for all ages." ~*Historical Novel Society*

"Kudos, Lisa, you've written something wonderful."
~*Author Ginger Simpson, historicalnovelreviewblogspot.com*

Train to Glory

2016:

First-Place Winner of Children's Literature,
Arizona Authors' Association's Literary Awards

Finalist, Arizona Book of the Year

Finalist, Dante Rossetti Award (Young Adult Fiction),
Chanticleer Book Reviews & Media

2017:

First-Place Winner of Chapter of Excellence
(Best First Chapter), Writers After Dark

Finalist, Young Adult Fiction,
Desert Rose (Romance Writers of America) Golden Quill Award

Finalist, Young Adult Fiction (Mystery),
Readers' Favorite International Book Awards

"Train to Glory is a fascinating novel that has adventure, romance, action, and intrigue and a cast of interesting well-defined characters…is a well-written story that readers will find thought provoking and informative."
~Michelle Stanley, Readers' Favorite Book Reviewer

"The prose is impeccable and the powerful descriptions paint a sizzling setting for readers to revel in. Fast paced and very entertaining, this book will come across as a great source of entertainment for many young and adult readers."
~Divine Zape, Readers' Favorite Book Reviewer

Also by Lisa Y. Potocar

Sweet Glory

Train to Glory

Gold, Guts and Glory

Gold, Guts and Glory

a novel

Award-Winning Author

LISA Y. POTOCAR

Gold, Guts and Glory

First Edition

Published by Lisa Y. Potocar, November 2021
www.lisapotocarauthor.com

Cover design by Paper and Sage
www.paperandsage.com

Interior design for print and digital formats by Cindy Jackson
www.whenweshare.com

Photography by Charles Lambert

Published in the United States of America

Print ISBN: 978-0-9990488-4-9
eISBN: 978-0-9990488-5-6

1. YA Fiction/Historical/United States/19th Century/Civil War/
Women's Equal Rights/Knights of the Golden Circle
2. YA Fiction/Historical/Romance
3. YA Fiction/Historical/Mystery

Dedication

To my husband, Jed, whom I can never thank enough for all of his support throughout my writing endeavors! Had he and I lived during Civil-War times, I know we would have made a highly effective husband-wife duo for the likes of the Pinkerton Agency.

Author's Personal Note

Dear Readers,

Here we are again!

I was thrilled when you expressed a desire for more of Jana Brady and Keeley Cassidy's story beyond both *Sweet Glory* and *Train to Glory* (Books 1 & 2 of *Glory: A Civil War Series*).

As I mentioned in my previous "Author's Personal Note," I had to ponder long and hard the plot for *Train to Glory*. It finally came to me when I learned that suffragists had suspended their crusade for women's equal rights during the American Civil War to funnel all of their energies into providing for the soldiers, especially in nursing. This to the chagrin of Susan B. Anthony who predicted their complacency would set them backward. And it did! In 1862, New York State repealed the parts of the Married Women's Property Act of 1860, which allowed a married woman to make decisions for her children and a widow to manage her late husband's estate. With the war winding down, who is there better to help re-ignite the cause for women's equality than a woman soldier? So, Susan B. Anthony, Elizabeth Cady Stanton, and other suffragists invite my primary character, Jana Brady, to travel across Upstate New York speaking about her soldiering, nursing, and spying during the war to prove: Women ought to hold the same rights to juggle everything a man can if they have a mind to it. To heighten the excitement of my story, I injected a heavy dose of intrigue into it surrounding Jana's kidnapping and love anew for Jana and Keeley through Keeley's amnesia.

Fortunate for me, the seedling of the idea for *Gold, Guts and Glory* struck me eighty percent of the way through the writing of *Train to Glory* as with this moment:

> *Jana didn't confide in Mr. Tanner that her only appeal for working for the Pinkerton Agency would be if she and Keeley didn't rekindle their love. Then, she'd need something exhilaratingly adventurous to get her through her grief. If, however, they did rekindle their love, and he found farming unappealing, maybe he'd consider becoming a detective. She smiled at the thought of them becoming the Pinkerton Agency's first husband-wife team.*

And, so, I give you now *Gold, Guts and Glory*, Book 3 of *Glory: A Civil War Series.* I truly hope you enjoy it!

Warm Regards,
Lisa Y. Potocar

Jana Brady wondered if Cupid's arrow could possibly embed in a heart deeper than hers. Settled on a picnic blanket at a wooded edge of the Brady homestead, she gazed upon her Irishman Keeley Cassidy, haloed by the early afternoon sun's radiant spray through the oak leaves. Jana yearned to run her finger down the dazzling dimple of his handsome profile. Instead, she contented herself with caressing the joined hearts of the Claddagh ring that he'd passed down to her from his late mam and listening to him read:

> Fast-anchor'd eternal O love! O woman I love!
> O bride! O wife! more resistless than I can tell, the thought of you!
> Then separate, as disembodied or another born,
> Ethereal, the last athletic reality, my consolation,
> I ascend, I float in the regions of your love O man,
> O sharer of my roving life.

Keeley closed Ma's autographed copy of Walt Whitman's *Leaves of Grass* and set it aside. He turned to her. The sparkling adoration for her in his emerald eyes sent Jana's soul soaring skyward to swing on a cottony cloud. "As the romantic words o' our wartime poet friend suggest, the thought o' our being together all o' our lives excites meself."

Wriggling closer to him and nestling her cheek upon his shoulder, Jana said, "It excites me too, Keeley."

He peeked around her in the direction where the Brady clan and their dear cavalry comrades, Leanne and Charlie, were too busy arranging the food and drink for Jana and Keeley's engagement picnic to notice them. Grinning in satisfaction, Keeley swept Jana up in his arms, nudged her chin up, and locked his lips on hers in a voracious kiss.

Bracing the hand blessed with his betrothal ring against his muscled chest and pulsating heart, Jana pushed away. "I'm sorry, Keeley," she said through gasps of breath, "I had to stop before I got lost in you forever."

"Are ye saying me kisses stoke yar passion for meself?"

She replied with a groan and angled her face into the breeze to fan the passionate flush upon her cheeks. If only their wedding was today. Ma was a miracle-worker, but even she couldn't have pulled off the grand affair she hoped for them with a little over two months left to orchestrate it after Jana and Keeley's return home in mid-March. She really would've loved for Jana to marry her soldier-sweetheart in May—her favorite time of year when the wildflowers are in bloom and Jana had turned the special age of twenty. Although Jana and Keeley had wished for that too, Jana would never regret having to delay their nuptials into the summer. The new friends they'd made and the adventure they had with old friends during Jana's tour of upstate New York speaking about her experiences as a cavalryman, nurse, and spy in the late war—by special request of suffragists Elizabeth Cady Stanton and Susan B. Anthony—were memories she would cherish forever.

Reading her mind, as he always could, Keeley said, "Sorry ye won't be finding out how good a lover I meself am tonight."

"Oh?" Jana elbowed his good bicep. She'd gotten in the habit of sitting or standing to his right to avoid bumping his left bicep. It was still tender from the bullet he'd taken shielding her from assassination at her last lecture in Albany. "And how many lovers have you had at your youthful age of twenty-four to know that?"

Keeley corralled her back in his embrace and sniffed her hair, which Jana was glad she'd washed that morning in Castile soap, specially scented in lavender just for him. In a sensual whisper, he said, "An Irishman never tells."

Opening her mouth to tease him further, Jana was cut short by the echoes of a carriage clattering down the valley.

When it forked right past the Brady homestead to traverse the newly scored lane up a modest knoll to Jana and Keeley's property and dowry from Ma and Pa, Keeley mumbled, "As yar pa would say: Who'd yar ma forget to invite and is madder than a hornet?"

"I can't imagine. Everyone's here and all accounted for."

Frowning at the interruption to their private interlude, which Ma had insisted they enjoy before their celebration got underway, Keeley said, "It seems, me lass, we're seconds away from finding out." He rose to his feet, shook his legs until the hems of his summer trousers spilled over his dress boots, and then helped Jana up.

Jana smoothed out the folds of her favorite red-and-purple floral day dress and held on to Keeley's arm as they hastened to where family and friends awaited the reining in of a velvety black Morgan at a respectable distance to avert a squall of dust.

The sunlight glanced off a silver shield-shaped badge pinned over the right lapel of the driver's long black traveling coat, momentarily blinding Jana.

While Jana's vision adjusted, Leanne stepped up alongside her. Crossing her arms over her chest, Leanne widened her stance and donned a playful smirk. "Well, well, well," she called out to the wagon handler, "if it ain't Duke Tanner. Thought we'd never see the likes of ya agin after we rounded up Jana's kidnappers on her speakin' trip."

Climbing down from the four-wheeled chaise with its calash top unfolded, the Pinkerton agent inspected Leanne from head to toe in her slouch hat, neatly pressed trousers, and spit-shined boots. He seemed especially preoccupied with her revolver, which was holstered to her waist belt and staring him down with her summer short coat removed. Tipping the brim of his black felt derby toward her, Duke returned a tongue-in-cheek smirk. "I see you're still toting your security blanket around, Leanne." He pivoted around, thwarting any retort by her, while he waited for his traveling companion to collapse her parasol and pull up her petticoats and skirt before assisting her to the ground.

Jana recognized the fancily clad woman immediately as the famous Kate Warne: first female detective, whom Allan Pinkerton hired after she convinced him that women make better spies than men because they can goad intelligence out of male braggarts and cozy up to their wives and sweethearts out of whom they could pump more secrets. She'd proven her mettle by uncovering the details of a plot to assassinate Abraham Lincoln on his way to his debut inaugural as president of the United States. Afterward, she'd safely escorted him to Washington City, disguised as her invalid brother. And Jana believed, if Kate had been in the Union capital after she'd helped capture those conspiring to harm Jana along her lecture tour, she would've prevented John Wilkes Booth from slaying President Lincoln. Clasping her hands, Jana whirled around. "What a wonderful surprise, Ma, for you to have invited Kate and Duke to our party."

Ma attempted to answer Jana, but only a chirp came out.

"Ah, I see." Jana turned back to shake their hands. "So, what brings you here?"

Kate's grimace lifted her boned cheeks higher and narrowed her puppy-dog eyes. "I'm afraid we've had the bad fortune of interrupting a momentous affair."

Doodling with the crocheted snood binding her sandy-colored hair at the nape of her neck, Ma said, "We definitely would've invited you to Jana and Keeley's engagement picnic if we'd known how to contact you."

Kate reached out and squeezed Ma's hand. "Please, don't give it a second thought, Julia."

After Pa led the way in further handshakes and pleasantries, Ma splayed her palms toward the buffet table, laden with baskets of freshly baked bread, platters of cold meats and cheeses, jars of pickled eggs and green bean salad, applesauce, and a frosted butter cake. "We were just about to eat and, as you can see, we have enough to feed a regiment. Please, join us."

Duke freed a gold timepiece from the hip pocket of his vest and studied its face before freeing it to dangle on its chain, hooked to the top buttonhole of his vest. "We appreciate the invitation, but, unfortunately, we cannot tarry long. We have a train to catch to Pinkerton headquarters in Chicago."

Kate added, "I'm truly sorry to delay your festivities further, but we must beg an audience with Jana and Keeley right away by order of President Andrew Johnson."

Everyone jerked to attention, standing stiff and still like the metal poles suspending the canvas canopy over the food table.

Withdrawing a cotton handkerchief from beneath the girded cuff of her sleeve, Jana blotted the beads of excitement budding across her forehead at the prospect of adventure.

"Our business with Jana and Keeley is highly confidential, but given our familiarity with you all"—Duke squinted at Jana's much younger sisters—"I don't see any harm in allowing present company privy to a general overview."

Lifting her chin with a huff, Eliza said, "Molly's practically a baby still and too young to understand anything to repeat it, but I'm old enough to be trusted with your secret, if that's what you're wondering, Mr. Tanner."

Duke winked. "Then, you're both in, and you may call me Duke."

Pa directed everyone to be seated on benches around the family's large old picnic table, which he and Keeley had carted up from the barn by wagon and Ma had beautified with a blue-and-white-checked cloth and a centerpiece of pink, white, and yellow wildflowers. To free up room for the newcomers, Pa scooped Molly onto his lap and Eliza rolled and stood up a sawed log for her perch. Ma finished pouring claret into wine goblets for Jana's twin sisters to dole out, and, once the three of them sat, Pa nodded for either Duke or Kate to begin.

Folding her gloved hands upon her lap, Kate said, "I'll make it short and simple. As I previously stated, we're here by order of President Andrew Johnson. He's cognizant of Jana's investigative prowess, and he's eager to recruit her and Keeley to track down a shipment of greenbacks, which President Lincoln had allocated to pay the soldiers fighting around the Mississippi River. It was secreted aboard a prisoner train bound for Elmira and stolen from it in the immediacy following the train's tragic wreck."

One big united gasp gashed the air.

"The train carrying Confederate captives to Elmira Prison, which collided with a coal train last July near Shohola, Pennsylvania?" Pa said, his voice booming with surprise.

"Hmm," Jana said, taking a sip of her wine. "I don't recall the Elmira *Gazette* or any other rag having reported anything about a lost Union treasury."

"Precisely," Kate said. "President Lincoln commanded it kept covert to avoid a rampant search."

"That's all we can divulge at this time," Duke said. "Jana and Keeley will be fully briefed in Washington...that is, if they accept this mission. A meeting has been scheduled for June 12th at 1:00 p.m. with President Johnson in his office at the Executive Mansion."

Keeley looked to Jana, and the subtle tilt of his head and upward curl at a corner of his lips portrayed his interest.

Jana, on the other hand, had difficulty refraining from bouncing all over her bench to the thrill of adventure. Like a dog waiting to be let loose for the hunt, she wanted badly to be on the next train.

With a clap of her hands, Rachel said to Rebecca, "Oh goodie, another adventure we can live vicariously through Jana."

"And now Keeley too," Rebecca added, her fair-skinned cheeks flushed equally as red as her twin's.

Leanne leaped to say, "Something tells me you're gonna need backup. Me and Charlie can help. He hasn't set up his photography studio yet, and I can git our younger brother to keep the books and a foreman to oversee the operations for my blacksmith shop while we're gone—same as I did when me and Charlie followed ya 'round for yer lectures, Jana. We'll head home to Buffalo tonight and git set up so we're ready to drop everything as soon as you're done with yer meeting with the president."

The magnification of Charlie's eyes behind his wire-rimmed spectacles practically colored his glass lenses azure. "Definitely, count us in."

"Thank you, Leanne and Charlie," Jana said. "Your support is always a welcome relief."

Eliza fiddled with her embroidered collar. "When I get out of these suffocating clothes and back into my riding britches, I'll go with you too," she said to Jana and Keeley, drawing a look of admiration from Leanne for—no doubt—her preference of male attire.

Scowling at Eliza, Ma said, "You'll be staying home. No nine-year-old child of mine is going to be traipsing about the country, even with Jana and Keeley chaperoning her." She swatted her hand at

Eliza's pouty lips. "Why am I even discussing this with you? It's not as though Jana and Keeley are going anywhere right now. They're breaking ground soon and will be too busy building a home to accept this investigation, right, Jana?"

Everyone swiveled toward Jana.

Noting Jana's squirming, Pa came to her rescue. "Now, Julia, let's leave the decision up to Jana and Keeley." He eyed Kate and Duke. "Why them for this expedition and not you?"

Ma rolled her eyes. "Really, Thomas, are you still pursuing this?"

"Now, Julia, they've come all this way. No harm in hearing them out, right, Jana and Keeley?"

Jana nodded for Keeley to answer, hopeful of his reply.

Shrugging, Keeley said, "Aye, I owe Kate and Duke as much after all they did to keep me Jana lass safe from harm during me absence from her orations around the state until I had recuperated from me brief memory loss."

Duke scratched the wind-blown tufts of his black hair behind his ear, displacing his hat a tittle. "Let's not forget, Keeley, in the end, you're the one who saved Jana and, unwittingly, her lecture-circuit patron from assassination."

After a few clucks of her tongue, Ma said, "Poor Wyatt. He was merely allotting the income prescribed by his father's will for his social-climbing mother, which, may I add, should've been plenty generous for one person to live and entertain on."

Duke scowled. "Incredibly, Mrs. McGriffin duped us all into believing some anti-woman's rights extremist was out to murder Jana when, all along, she was gunning for her son."

"A shame what greed does to derange people," Pa said.

Jana winced at the heart-wrenching memory of Keeley sprawled out on the portico of the state Capitol in Albany, dead—or so she'd thought—with what appeared to be blood oozing from his heart instead of his bicep.

Noticing Jana's reaction, Ma said, "Thank the sweet Lord she's tucked away in an insane asylum and her cohorts are locked in prison, where they can't hurt anyone anymore." She brushed an imaginary crumb from the tablecloth. "Anyway, that's all behind us now."

Duke, who'd also been observing Jana and discerned Ma's cue to change the subject, slapped his thighs. "Speaking of greed, it is imperative we resume our discussion of the stolen payroll. Kate and I are under a time crunch. Now, where were we?"

"Why not us for this investigation you asked, Thomas?" Kate said. "Allan Pinkerton cannot spare us. His agents are spread thin; they've been disbursed to the railroads to uncover sabotage by striking crews, protect against robberies, and investigate embezzlement, and I have a new force of female detectives to prepare for field work."

"Additionally," Duke said, "Allan Pinkerton remembered Jana was born and raised in Elmira, where the train was headed before its crash. He was convinced her familiarity with the terrain and contacts from the Brady's involvement in the Underground Railroad between Elmira and Pennsylvania were invaluable resources. He sold President Johnson on Jana and Keeley for the job." He raised his wine glass to Jana and Keeley. "And here we are, charged merely with bearing this incredible opportunity."

Rubbing his clean-shaven chin, Pa said, "Who'll be footing the bill for this endeavor? Jana and Keeley can't afford it." He gestured toward several enormous stacks of lumber enshrouded in canvas. "A good chunk of their soldiers' pay has already been invested in building materials for their homestead."

"In the form of paper currency, we have a princely stipend from the United States Treasury and *Erie Railway* to give them now. It should more than cover any traveling expenses they might incur during their sojourn. And"—Kate spiced her tone with intrigue—"if Jana and Keeley were to recoup the shipment, President Johnson will reward them a percentage of the spoils."

Guessing the question on the minds of Jana and everyone else by their curious expressions, Duke said, "We don't know the figure; President Johnson preferred to discuss it privately with Jana and Keeley."

Pa harrumphed. "Enough to reclaim the income tax President Lincoln levied on us for the damnable war?"

Kate's face lit up. "And then some, I'm certain. Its value is unknown; although, it's rumored to be upwards of two million dollars."

Gulping a big swallow of light red wine, which she'd been sipping, Jana nearly choked.

Keeley blinked in disbelief. "Wha…wha…wha—"

Pa interpreted Keeley's unfinished question. "What did you say? Two million dollars?"

An ardent bob of Kate's head in affirmation of her assertion loosened the pins holding her fashionable top hat in place. She grinned as she straightened them.

During the momentary silence, Jana estimated in her head: *Even one percent of the total sum would yield enough money for me and Keeley to build a palace and hand us and Ma and Pa a more comfortable living.*

Ma broke the quiet. "Such a considerable carrot tells me this caper entails danger."

With a nervous clearing of his throat, Duke said, "In the immediate aftermath of the train collision, five Rebel prisoners are estimated to have escaped while the guards focused first on ascertaining the extent of the wreckage and wounded before securing the perimeter and the army payroll. If I were one of the two guards, who believed no one but themselves knew of the treasury aboard the caboose, I also would have given priority to saving lives above all else. Unfortunately, it allotted enough time for the heist to occur. The weight of the large chest and its four money bags make it more than a solo job. Thus, Jana and Keeley could be pitted against two or more of the five escapees in hunting down the stolen treasury."

After having eluded death in a fiery cavalry battle, at the gallows for spying on the Confederacy, and from kidnappers and would-be assassins on her lecture circuit, a showdown with a few thieves failed to frighten Jana. Nevertheless, she hurried to change the subject before it did anyone else. "What if we don't find the money?"

"Then, there's still a handsome wage for your work, which will be negotiated with President Johnson at the conclusion of the job, if that's what you're asking," Kate said.

Duke shrugged. "Quite the incentive to find the fortune, isn't it?"

"We'll do it," Jana blurted.

All heads swung her way.

Following a frown of frustration for Jana's eyes only, Keeley faked nonchalance to her outburst and smiled at everyone else. Calmly, he rose from the picnic bench. "I know y'are in a hurry," he said to Duke and Kate, "but will ye kindly allow me Jana lass and meself a private moment to digest the matter?"

"Of course," Kate said.

Retrieving his watch, still dangling from its chain, and studying its face, Duke said, "Unfortunately, we can only give you thirty minutes before we'll need your answer."

"And while they're discussing the matter, you have enough time for some dinner," Ma said to Duke and Kate.

Jana heard their gleeful acceptance of Ma's invitation as Keeley led her out of sight and earshot of the partiers.

Leaning back against a towering stack of lumber, which dwarfed his height of six feet, Keeley crossed a leg over the other and his arms over his chest. "I love ye, me lass, with all o' me heart, and I'd go to the ends o' the earth with ye. But when were ye going to allow meself a stake in the decision?" he said in a bruised tone.

"Forgive my impulsiveness, Keeley. I don't know what came

over me."

Relaxing his pose and taking both of her hands in his, Keeley said, "I fell in love with ye because o' yar adventuresome spirit and yar courage to fight for the preservation o' the Union and woman's suffrage and equal rights. I don't expect ye to alter that in yarself. In fact, during the War o' the Rebellion, ye challenged meself to fight hard, not just for the soldier's pay, but to change America's prejudice against the *daft* Irishman to make the United States a place where I'd be proud to build me hearth and home. What I'm trying to say, me lass, and, as yar ma always says about us: we're two peas in a pod. Where plans or decisions affect the pod, don't ye think we two peas should make them together?"

Jana remembered back to the beginning of the war, when the federal government underappreciated the cavalry's importance and relegated them to scouting the enemy's position, guarding bridges, and carrying messages between officers. The troopers of Jana and Keeley's regiment were bickering and brawling out of boredom in being held back from battle. Keeley convinced them they were a band of brothers and their survival depended upon their acting as a family. He was applying this same concept to them as a couple. And he was right! Squeezing Keeley's hands, Jana said, "What does it matter where we are as long as we're together? What do you say about our going to Washington to at least learn more regarding this mission? We make a powerful duo. It seems our country needs your leadership skills and my tenacity and intuition to recapture the missing payroll. It's the chance of a lifetime, and we could use the money."

Keeley stared off longingly in the direction of where the high field grasses had been mowed to soon bear their hearth and home.

Reading his mind, Jana said, "Ma and Pa will gladly oversee the building of our house while we're away."

"I appreciate their willingness, me lass…I do. But we might not want to rush it. Part o' the thrill is in laying our foundation together."

Keeley's hands fell away from hers, and he faced her with an expression dulled with doubt that thrashed Jana's soul. "The more I think o' it, this trip will be the best thing for us. It'll give us some time alone, and how we get on will be the truest test o' the strength o' our union."

The breeze shifted direction, illuminating for Jana that, with one outburst, she'd complicated things between her and Keeley. She knew he was harboring a fear she'd choose adventure every time over settling into a life with him. The fruity claret soured on her tongue to a troublesome notion: *Will this venture pry open a new window into my true self and expose incompatibilities between us, too irreconcilable for us to sustain a future together?*

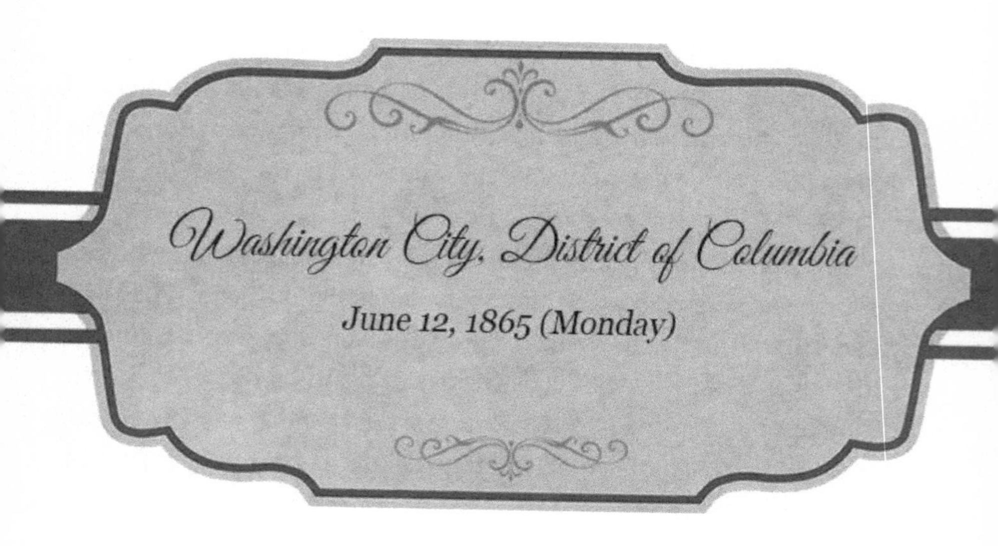

Jana hiked the dust ruffle of her plain mauve skirt up off the railed platform between train cars and dropped her free hand into Keeley's strong grasp for help in guiding her down the iron steps.

The last belch of steam from the locomotive evaporated all around them in the dewy, early-morning air as Jana and Keeley shuffled across the roofed platform arm-in-arm. Their echoing footfalls blended in with the jostling throngs arriving and departing on the tracks of the *Baltimore & Ohio Railroad*. Jana wondered how many times President Lincoln had come and gone from this Capitol-Hill station. His two most significant occasions were vastly incongruous: in 1861, upon his arrival for his first inauguration as the president of the United States and, in 1865, upon his departure to his final resting place in Springfield, Illinois. *Such a waste of genius,* Jana sadly thought, hard-pressed to name any of the preceding fifteen presidents of the United States, except George Washington, whose administrations could rival the encumbrances thrust upon him.

With Jana clutching her carpetbag and Keeley his leather valise for their overnight stay, they headed into the Italianate-style depot and crossed a grand hall to the ticket office.

Keeley stepped up to a counter and summoned an agent. "What might be the most direct route to Willard's Hotel, sir?"

Trolling forward on the casters of his chair, the clerk poked his hawkish nose through his barred window, and the pupils of his beady eyes tapered to tiny pin heads as he squinted at Jana. "Say, don't I know you, miss?"

"I don't see how," Jana said, dropping her carpetbag onto and facing the floor, pretending to tighten the mauve grosgrain ribbon that she'd wrapped in a bow around the low crown of her straw hat.

Keeley subtly sidestepped, inserting himself in front of Jana to shield the ticket agent's view of her. "Aye, me wife and meself have never been to Washington before now."

He lied on two accounts: about their marriage and their never having visited this city. Between her middle and pinky fingers, Jana twirled the antique gold Claddagh adorning her left ring finger. It was the only relic Keeley had of his mam and da who, along with his younger sisters, had perished in the Great Famine of Ireland. Although she and Keeley had postponed their wedding, Kate and Duke had suggested they act as a married couple to draw less attention to themselves as individuals, given especially Jana's fame. And, back in August 1862, when Jana, Keeley, Leanne, and Charlie were stationed at nearby Bladensburg, Maryland, they'd toured Washington after their superiors had rewarded them a furlough for successfully teaching the men of their regiment to use Pa's speedy and gentle method of breaking in their cavalry horses.

The brass buttons sewn into the railroad operative's coat sleeves clanked to the abrupt slap of his palms against the counter. "You're *the* woman soldier from New York. Your picture and accounts of your escapades have blazoned the newspapers here." He swiveled slightly in his chair and called over his shoulder, "Hey, everyone, come see—"

"Sir"—Keeley indulged in an intimidating growl, never before heard out of him by Jana—"ye've got me wife confused with another and, if ye don't want meself to lob off the tip o' yar prying nose, I suggest ye keep it to yarself." He parted his broadcloth waistcoat and wrapped his fingers around the handle of his cavalry knife, partially unsheathing it to prove he had the bluntest of blades to carry out his threat.

The startled clerk shrank in his swivel chair and propelled it backward out of Keeley's reach. Fetching a handkerchief from his breast pocket, he mopped the sheen of sweat on his forehead and face.

Re-sheathing his knife, Keeley leaned in close to the window and, in a mellowed tone, he said, "Ye see, me wife and meself are on our honeymoon, and we prefer to go about our way peacefully."

Keeley's reference to her as his wife plucked a sweet melody from Jana's heartstrings. How she wished it were true.

"I see," the clerk said, loosening the bow tie around the stand-up collar of his white shirt.

"Now, back to me question, if ye please," Keeley said.

"Uh...uh, yes," he stammered, "the best route to Willard's Hotel."

"Aye."

"Given your desire for anonymity, you might be better served to take a private hack."

"Public transportation will do," Keeley tersely said.

"Then, the *Washington and Georgetown Railroad* will set you right on the hotel's doorstep."

"Thank ye, kind sir, and a very good day to ye," Keeley said, browbeating the agent with a scowl to make him think twice about publicizing their presence.

The operative tipped his black cap with a shaky hand, blurring the legibility of the railroad emblem hobnailed to his hatband.

Hidden from the clerk's scrutiny, Jana and Keeley keeled over in laughter. They drew glimpses from the ladies sipping tea or embroidering in their parlor but went unnoticed by the raucous gentlemen slurping whiskey or ale and playing cards or tossing darts in their saloon—out of which tumbled a giant billow of cigar smoke. The stench added to Jana's nausea. She held her stomach to quell her hunger pangs as they stepped out front, and her eyes ran high up the depot's unique brick, stucco, and brownstone exterior to its four-sided clock tower. Noting the hour and minute hands at a quarter past 8:00 a.m., she said, "We have nearly five hours before our meeting with the president and plenty of latitude to check in at the hotel, freshen up, and have breakfast. I don't know about you, but I'm famished."

"Aye, meself too."

They easily located the line for the *Washington and Georgetown Railroad Company* among a cavalcade of streetcars parked curbside.

From the coins jingling around inside his trouser pocket, Keeley withdrew ten cents for their total fare. He handed it to the driver, and Jana and Keeley climbed aboard the small wooden car, squeezing onto a bench near the front.

Their transport filled to capacity quickly, and the conductor took his seat at the helm, slapping his reins against the rump of a muscled roan; it ambled southeastwardly away from the corner of New Jersey Avenue and C Street, along the inlaid street rails, and into the noxious odors blowing from the Washington City Canal—currently in use as a sewer and storm drain.

Jana soon forgot the tainted air with her attention diverted by a commanding view of the Capitol and home of Congress. "Oh, how lovely," she said, marveling at the completeness of its central feature. Only the cake-like tiers with their marbled columns were finished back when Jana and Keeley were last here together. Raising the dome had been suspended briefly during the war due to the Capitol building's service as a military barracks, hospital, and bakery. *Ironic,* Jana thought, *how the symbolic cap of our nation's unity was finally donned while our country was yet divided.*

Observing Jana's fascination with the bronze monument rising majestically above the dome, Keeley elbowed her. "If I didn't know any better, I'd say she was a tribute to yarself, me lass."

Jana felt her pride swell to his analogy. Ablaze under the sun in all of her bronze glory, the female warrior wore a feathered military helmet and a chiton secured by a broach and partially covered by a fringed Indian-like blanket draped over her left shoulder. In her right hand, she held the hilt of a sheathed sword; in her left, the laurel wreath of victory and a shield. At her base, Jana knew, was etched *E Pluribus Unum*: the Latin phrase for "Out of many one," which Ma had translated in one of her many homeschooled history lessons. It was a philosophical tactic employed by the country's forefathers to incite the colonies together and into rebellion against and independence from Great Britain. Until their conveyance swerved right to begin a northwesterly clattering slog along the rounded cobblestones of Pennsylvania Avenue, Jana's eyes remained glued to the statue, aptly named *Freedom Triumphant in War and Peace*. Ironically, she was chosen before the war by Confederate President Jefferson Davis when he was a U.S. senator.

Several blocks up on their right, Keeley pointed at Matthew Brady's National Art Gallery. "I fondly remember ye, meself, Leanne, and Charlie posing in our cavalry uniforms for a daguerreotype there."

From her carpetbag, Jana dug out the portrait and showed it to Keeley. "I keep this near me always as a good luck charm."

Keeley grinned. "If only ye'd want to keep meself pinned to ye always as yar good luck—," he was cut short when his attempt to hug Jana knocked the precious picture from her hand.

Reflexively, Jana slung her fingerless-gloved hand out and caught it before it flew out of the open window and off with the wind whisking up grit from the intersecting, unpaved roads. She chuckled at her own adeptness; her quick reactions had been useful many times, like when she'd snagged two hard-boiled eggs hurled at her simultaneously during the outset of her lecture in Buffalo. Appearing in her cavalry uniform had offended the hecklers, who had difficulty accepting women pioneering their way into men's roles; it had forced Jana's change in wardrobe to her Garibaldi or military-style dress for her remaining lectures in Seneca Falls, Johnstown, and Albany.

"That was close, me lass." He shuddered. "Reminds meself o' when I knocked the *Bible* from yar grip and all o' the numbered pieces o' Castle Thunder Prison's blueprint fell out o' its pages. I'll never forget nearly getting ye hung in yar attempt to smuggle in a diagram o' potential escape routes for meself and other Yankee inmates."

Jana re-stowed the daguerreotype and, with a jagged sigh, said, "I fear that ghastly moment will haunt us the rest of our lives. Thank the sweet Lord we dodged my worst nightmare of sending Miss Lizzie and her extensive spy ring to the gallows to be hung alongside me." She fell silent to pay homage to poor Pinkerton agent Timothy Webster, who hadn't escaped execution. Fortunate for Elizabeth Van Lew, a Southern socialite, Unionist, and Jana's mentor in spying, neither Jana nor Keeley had compromised their connection with her to Confederate authorities in her home city of Richmond, Virginia.

"Aye, and, as they're forever in yar debt, so am meself. If it weren't for ye, me lass, I might've died in Richmond's rat-infested prison."

A cynical notion popped into Jana's head and dizzied her. Lowering her voice below the clomping of the horse's hoofs and the groaning planks of their car, she said, "Do you really love me, Keeley? Or do you stay with me because you feel indebted to me?"

"Be assured, me lass"—Keeley flicked Jana an admonishing glance—"I fell in love with ye long before ye rescued meself and, if I didn't love ye, I would've repaid me gratitude to ye by now and moved on."

Jana chastised herself for bringing out an uncharacteristic

irritability in him, seemingly commonplace of late. "Forgive my jumpiness where our relationship is concerned. I have only myself to blame for the postponement of our nuptials."

"It takes two to cut an Irish reel," Keeley said in a gentler voice, "and I expected too much out o' ye too soon."

"Does that mean you still want me?" she asked.

He winked. "For now, me lass."

"I'm relieved because you mean the world to me." Jana pecked him on the cheek, not caring a hoot about rules for public etiquette. Then, she snuggled into his arm and basked in his spicy cologne as they rode along in a comfortable quiet.

The Kirkwood House at 12th Street came into view and shattered Jana's contentment. It was a gruesome reminder of the complex plot around President Lincoln's assassination. On that fateful night, incumbent Vice-President Johnson lived at the hotel. He might've been killed there, had it not been for co-conspirator George Atzerodt imbibing alcohol and losing his nerve to slay the unguarded Andrew Johnson while John Wilkes Booth shot down President Lincoln at Ford's Theater. As Jana recollected how the very next day, the Kirkwood hosted the swearing in of Andrew Johnson as the seventeenth president of the United States by Chief Justice Salmon P. Chase, their cab slowed to a crawl and stopped at the corner of 14th Street. She was glad to reach their destination so she could cast aside her morose ruminations.

After disembarking from their streetcar, Jana and Keeley were warmly welcomed to the sprawling six-story Willard's Hotel by a doorman. He directed them into the lavish lobby and to the clerk's desk.

Jana and Keeley registered as Mr. and Mrs. Keeley Cassidy. Although Keeley would've preferred for her to register as Mrs. Jana Brady Cassidy to maintain her independence and show of equality to him, they both wished to avoid recognition of Jana's name, given her fame. Afterward, they went straight to their third-floor room, booked under their pretense as a married couple.

In perusing their cozy quarters, Jana thought, *Wouldn't it be something if this was the same room where Julia Ward Howe composed the 'Battle Hymn of the Republic' to the melody of 'John Brown's Body?'* She imagined Julia writing her lyrics by, in her own words, "the gray of the morning twilight" streaming through the tall mullioned window across the polished writing desk and brass and glass inkwell with dip pen. Turning back to Keeley, she saw him surveying the sleeping accommodations with only a double poster bed.

"Ye take the bed, me lass, and I'll take the chair and footrest. If ye'll allow me one o' the two bed pillows, I'll use me coat as a blanket."

"That's chivalrous of you, Keeley, but"—she injected a mischievous twinkle in her eye—"I have a better idea."

His brows lifted. "Oh? I'm all ears, me lass."

"If we were to drape the top sheet over the diagonal bed posts to create a screen between us, we could share the bed. To give us equal room, I can sleep with my head at the top, and you with yours at the bottom."

"A titillating idea, me lass." Keeley grinned, showing a mouthful of pearly teeth. "But don't get any ideas about crossing battle lines in the night to forge an attack on meself."

Jana coquettishly batted her eyelashes at him. "Well, we wouldn't want to make ourselves enemies. Maybe we could skip the sheet." Frowning at the bed, she thought, *It's a shame we have to worry about it at all. But Ma would see right through me if we anticipated our wedding vows.* And she'd never lie to Ma or Pa again, as she'd done when she told them she'd been at the battlefront nursing instead of soldiering during the Great Rebellion. More importantly, she'd never want them to harbor ill will against Keeley.

"Better to keep the sheet, me lass. We can't have ye succumbing to me charms," Keeley quipped, followed by a frown at the bed too. "I'd never want to start off on the wrong foot with yar ma and pa, whom I've come to love as me own."

Feeling the same fluster warming her cheeks as she saw painting Keeley's, Jana hastened behind the dressing screen. She needed an immediate splash of water from the wash basin. After dousing her heated face and cleansing it and her neck in rose-scented soap, she changed her blouse, brushed and rearranged her hair in a crocheted snood at the nape of her neck, and donned her hat. Then, she pressed her palms against her cooled cheeks, sucked in a deep breath, and sailed into the room. As Keeley took his turn freshening up behind the partition, Jana re-robed in her short black bolero coat—her favorite style because it was easy to slip into with its three-quarter pagoda sleeves and without buttons or fasteners and because its waist-length rounded panels tapered away from each other and flaunted her fashionable black belt and white button-up blouse. Finally, she grabbed her gloves, just in case breakfast went overtime.

After locking up, Jana dropped their room's clunky skeleton key into her drawstring purse, and she and Keeley hurried downstairs. An aroma of meats, vegetables, and cakes stirred up Jana's taste buds and led her across the threshold of the dining room to the reception desk. Within ninety minutes of their arrival at the train station, they found themselves following the wagging coattails of the host as he led them across a patterned carpet and space ornamented in the rich crimson and gold colors of royalty. Halting before the last available table, he slid it out and back once Jana and Keeley were comfortable on the button-tufted settee. Their backs faced a tall window covered with wispy white sheers beneath a heavy valance and curtains tied back with matching material. From their seat, they could observe all comings and goings in the dining room.

The host returned to his reception stand and was replaced by their waiter, who introduced himself as Edward. He jotted down their beverage order and hustled away to retrieve it, giving Jana and Keeley a moment to study the extensive breakfast menu. When he returned, he poured coffee from a silver urn and water from a glass pitcher. "What else may I get you?"

Keeley nodded for Jana to place their order.

Raising her voice a decibel to be heard over the lively conversations, tinkle of silverware, and clatter of cups against saucers, Jana said, "We'll make it easy on you, Edward; we'll both have scrambled eggs, ham and red-eye gravy, fried onions and potatoes, and strawberries and cream."

"Very well," Edward said and retreated to the kitchen.

Grinning, Keeley said, "It's truly amazing how well ye know meself, me lass. I had me mind set on the same meal."

Jana reciprocated a grin and saluted him with her coffee cup, and they settled into perusing the guests around them until Edward appeared with their heaping plates of food.

Finished with their first course, Jana was spooning up a strawberry with a dollop of cream when she observed a young boy crossing the threshold into the dining room. He appeared undernourished by his pallid face and thin frame. When he removed his soiled and frayed derby, he freed flaxen curls and showed a wolf's rare gray eyes, one glaringly bruised.

The youngster stepped up to the reception desk and mouthed something to the host.

Frowning upon the unkempt youth, the host seemed reluctant to allow him into the dining room. He finally relented to the youngster's persistence, pointing him toward a table diagonal to Jana and Keeley's.

The haggard messenger fetched a piece of yellow foolscap from the pocket of his stained knickers and handed it to a lone diner, who set down his newspaper, read the missive, and began scanning the dining room. His dark, piercing eyes hesitated only once—on Jana.

To appear oblivious of his stare, Jana ratcheted up her sip of water to a healthy swallow as a ruse to angle her head back far enough to eclipse her own gaze through the large bowl of her glass.

After some words by the stylishly garbed gentleman, which were indecipherable with his mouth concealed behind his newspaper, the diner pawed around in a trouser pocket of his black brushed-wool business suit, withdrew some coins, and dropped them into the palm of his dusty-clothed errand boy.

The bedraggled boy beamed at his treasure. Before he scooted, he stole a glimpse of Jana over his shoulder.

Jana hid her mouth behind her napkin, pretending to dab at her lips to keep them from being read while she mentioned the curious affair to Keeley.

When Edward finished collecting payment from Jana's gawker, Keeley seized the opportunity to do some spying of his own. He snapped the fingers of his right hand high in the air to summon their fare. Edward's passage toward them established a fortuitous barrier, which Keeley subtly peeked around to get a good view of the snoop.

Edward set their bill before Keeley on the white linen tablecloth. "How was your meal?"

"Absolutely scrumptious," Jana said, pressing her palm against her stomach. "Our compliments to the cook."

After counting out the money into Edward's hand, Keeley said, "I have a question for ye, Edward, but I insist ye refrain from looking. Me wife and meself seem to recognize the gentlemen to whom ye just rendered his bill o' fare. Embarrassingly, we can't place him and we were wondering if ye might clear the matter up for us."

"Certainly. The gentleman is a real estate tycoon. His operation is prolific throughout the east, probably in your hometown also."

Keeley's head jerked back in surprise. "And how might ye know from where we hail?"

"People and politicians from all over the United States come here to eat. I study accents to guess where everyone is from. Your origin is obvious, sir. But the lady's dialect hints to western—or maybe south central—New York."

Jana's lips parted. "I'm impressed."

Edward chuckled. "Don't be. When your job is as repetitious as mine, you have to spruce it up. I get to know the origins, livelihoods, and hobbies of all of our repeat customers. Most people like to talk about themselves; although, there are some"—he gave a curt backward nod of his head—"like that gentleman, who are a bit more tight-lipped."

"Might ye share his name, Edward?"

"John Woodcock. Rumor has it he'll take a seat in the federal Congress as a temporary replacement for a senator from Pennsylvania who has a protracted illness. Not sure why he's here now. Congress isn't in session until December."

"Do you know where he resides?" Jana asked.

"I hear he comes from somewhere near Shohola…easy to remember since"—he groaned despairingly—"that's where the tragic train wreck occurred last year."

His assertion nearly bowled Jana over, but she managed to keep a stiff torso and subtly move her hand under the table to squeeze Keeley's. When he returned her squeeze, she knew they were thinking alike: Was John Woodcock's presence in Washington and his stolen glances of Jana pure coincidence?

After Edward bid them a good day and scurried away to help another party, John Woodcock rose from his table. He tucked his newspaper under his arm and started out of the dining room. Then, he pivoted on the heels of his shiny boots and bee-lined straight toward Jana and Keeley. With his mid-section—plumper than a potbellied stove—hovering over the edge of their tabletop, he measured Jana up with a contemptible smirk.

The hairs at the nape of Jana's neck rose like the hackles of a wary dog.

"Allow me to introduce myself," Woodcock said, extending his manicured corpulent-fingered hand to Keeley.

Since common courtesy dictated the lady of a party be addressed first and he'd intentionally bypassed Jana, Keeley snubbed his outstretched hand. "No need…me lass and meself know who y'are."

John Woodcock retracted his hand and stared down his pompous nose at Jana, in particular. "No matter, I know who you are too."

"Oh?" Jana said.

"You're the illustrious Miss Jana Brady, who—"

Jana cut him off. "You mean Mrs. Jana Brady Cassidy."

He eyed her Claddagh ring, then her, and sneered, "You mean Mrs. Keeley Cassidy, don't you?"

Throwing his shoulders back and tossing his chest out, Keeley said, "She means to call herself as she has, and it's none o' yar concern."

"Oh, but it is." Woodcock jutted out his prominent jaw and continued his churlish castigation of Jana. "I can't abide women butting their noses into a man's world where they don't belong—especially by playing detective."

Abruptly, Keeley rose and pushed the table out across the silky fibers of the carpet, forcing Woodcock to teeter backward a few of his large boot sizes.

Their movements drew the curiosity of nearby diners.

Tugging the hem of his coat and standing tall, Keeley leveled his wrathful eyes upon Woodcock. "If y'are intimating, sssir," he hissed, "about me Jana lass's landing her feet in the male domain through her soldiering and public speaking, ye better get on board. In many ways, women have proved themselves above us men through their fortitude in war. They're on a roll to carve out new roles for themselves, and not even the likes o' y'are are going to stop them. I meself applaud them."

The eavesdropping patrons clapped, and Jana smiled at Keeley's disciples.

With a snivel, John Woodcock waved a dismissive hand at them all, and he narrowed his icy eyes on Jana. "You think yourself high and mighty, *Mrs. Keeley Cassidy*. You're going to be sorry if you try reeling in bigger fish than you can dare fry." Woodcock spun around and, cockier than an overindulged rooster, swaggered out of the dining room.

His threat sent tingles of uneasiness up and down Jana's spine. What was he up to that it involved them? The politicians in the District of Columbia operated in a small radius, and she hoped President Johnson could shed some light on John Woodcock.

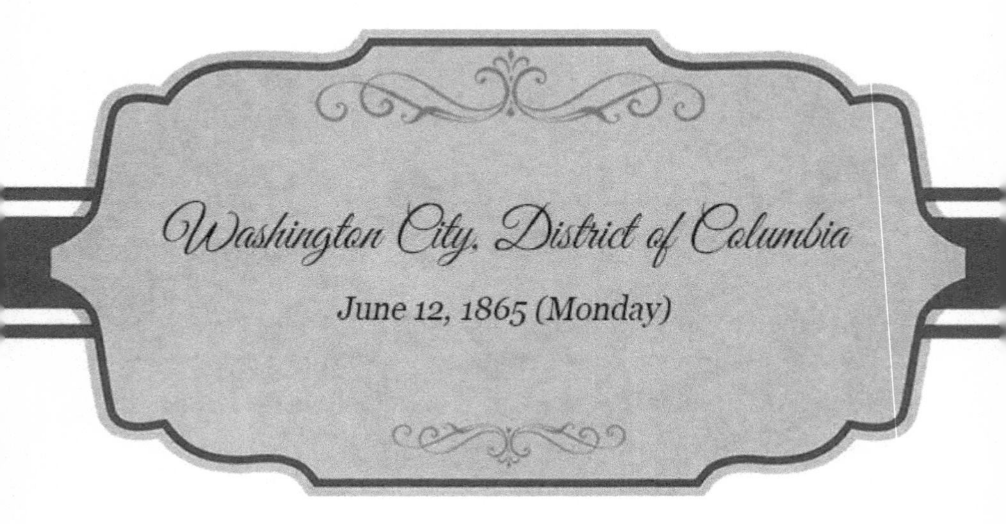

Jana rose from the breakfast table, feeling slightly shaky after their confrontation with the petulant John Woodcock.

Taking Jana's hand in his, Keeley gave it a reassuring squeeze and grasped it firmly as they breezed out of the breakfast room with all eyes upon them.

In the lobby, Jana noted the time of 11:00 a.m. on the Grandfather clock near the registration desk. "We have two hours before our meeting with President Johnson, and I could use some fresh air to compose myself."

Keeley wrinkled his nose. "Aye, it would be good to get the stink o' John Woodcock off us."

"How about a walk through Lafayette Square?"

"Aye, a great idea, me lass. It'll land us close to the White House so we won't be rushing to our meeting."

They took a few steps when Jana's brain bristled a warning for her to beware. Subtly, she scanned the room and caught Wolf Boy peeking at them from around an ornate marbled-granite column. Steering Keeley around toward the staircase, she positioned them with their backs to the little imp to circumvent his reading their lips.

She lowered her voice faintly over the hustle and bustle of hotel staff and patrons. "Forget the walk in the park for now. We're being watched by John Woodcock's young messenger. Let's catch Wolf Boy at his own game."

"What do ye have in mind, me lass?"

"If our ruse plays out as quickly as I think it will, we'll still have plenty of leeway to get to our meeting," Jana said, then outlined her plan.

After a stretch and a yawn, and retrieval of their room key from Jana, Keeley proceeded upstairs, pretending he was going to their room for a rest.

Jana exited outside to fake a leisurely stroll. Commencing down the sidewalk of Pennsylvania Avenue, she hooked left onto 14th Street. A snappy sidelong glance satisfied her that Wolf Boy was still following her. Before she hit F Street, she deviated left into the cobbled courtyard at the rear of Willard's Hotel. She was delighted to find it bedecked with bountiful places for Keeley to conceal himself. In the fruity-and-floral-scented air swirling around the courtyard from the flowers, shrubs, and plants, Jana smelled success. She rounded a fountain, where she discovered Keeley crouched behind its broad pedestal and beneath its deep basin. Unfalteringly, she continued her trek toward F Street until she heard a shriek. Retracing her steps to the granite fountain, she saw Wolf Boy trying to squirm out of Keeley's firm grip on the back of his shirt collar.

"What do you think you're doing, mister? Let me go!" Wolf Boy said in a child's shrilly pitch.

"Not until ye tell meself why y'are following me lass," Keeley said, pivoting the grimy youngster toward Jana.

Wolf Boy thrust out his jaw. "I don't have to tell you anything."

Looming over the lad, whose head barely rose to the height of his chest, Keeley snarled, "Ye'll find meself a worthy opponent, lad, and ye'll answer me question or else..."

Jana surmised Keeley had intentionally let his voice trail off to allow the boy a moment to envision the horrors a worthy opponent could do to him. Little did the mischievous sprite know, her betrothed hadn't a violent bone in his body, and Jana wanted to bust out laughing at Keeley's theatrics.

"Or else what?" Wolf Boy said, his previous impudent tone replaced with a fretful tweet.

Splashing the youngster with the crystal-clear water from the fountain, Jana glowered and said, "Your head will take a dip."

"Aye," Keeley said, marching him over to the fountain and bowing his head over the rim of the basin. Wolf Boy's oversized derby dove off his head and into the water. It floated amongst a garnish of mint leaves as Keeley touched the tiny tip of the youth's nose to the surface. "I hope ye can hold yar breath for a long time, lad."

Wolf Boy twisted around and reared his head back to see the muscled knots in Keeley's clenched jaws. After an audible gulp, he said, "I'll tell you what you want to know, if you promise to let me go afterward."

"If I think y'are lying, no amount o' pleading will keep meself from drowning ye."

Wolf Boy threw up his hands in surrender. "I don't want any trouble, mister. What do you want to know?"

Releasing him, Keeley splayed his stance, making himself impenetrable against any attempt by Wolf Boy to escape. "Again, lad, why are ye following me lass?"

"I was minding my own business, grubbing coins to feed myself from passengers at the railroad station, when a ticket agent flagged me down. He paid me to go to Willard's Hotel and deliver a note to a man who goes by the name of John Woodcock."

"What might this ticket agent look like?" Keeley asked.

"Hmmm," Wolf Boy said, staring off into nowhere until the flapping wings and flutelike song of a cinnamon-brown, spotted-bellied wood thrush flying overhead snagged his attention. His glistening eyes switched back to Keeley. "I know. He looked like a crow with black, beady eyes and big beak for a nose."

Jana and Keeley shared a knowing look: Wolf Boy's clerk had to be the same who'd paid Jana excessive attention at the train depot.

"I swear on my life, I don't know what the message said," Wolf Boy offered. "All I cared about was getting paid again by Mr. Woodcock, as the ticket agent promised I would. Then, Mr. Woodcock gave me more money to follow you around all day and report back to him later."

"Well, this is yar lucky day, lad." Keeley pawed around in his trouser pocket. Withdrawing a few coins, he raised Wolf Boy's hand up and dumped them into his soiled palm. "We appreciate yar honesty."

Wolf Boy yanked a cracked-leather pouch from the pocket of his knickers and filled and re-stashed it. Drawing his pencil-thin brows in together, he peered up at Keeley. "Hey, mister, you duped me."

Keeley's cheek twitched. "How so, lad?"

"You had me believing you were a brute."

"Are ye saying I meself am a good actor?" Keeley said chuckling.

Expelling a huge sigh, Wolf Boy replied, "I'd say."

Keeley tapped the youth's bicep with his fist. "I have a soft spot for orphans living on the streets...that is, if I've pegged ye right." Keeley's shoulders drooped and his eyes dulled with despair. "I've walked a mile in yar shoes, lad. Once upon a time, I was an orphan, living on the streets o' New York City."

"Really?" Wolf Boy said. "You seem to have done all right by yourself, mister. How'd you get off the streets?"

"I enlisted in the cavalry to save the good pay for building meself a hearth and home one day. That's when I met"—he smiled adoringly at Jana—"me lass. We fell in love, and, after the war, her family accepted meself into their clan. I'm one o' the luckiest people in the world."

Wolf Boy scowled at a loose pebble. Kicking it across the

courtyard with the tip of his holey brogan, through which his threadbare sock protruded, he said, "If only the war was still going on, I'd sign up too. I hear lots of ten-year-olds, like me, fought for the Union."

"Aye, although I hate the idea o' lads yar age soldiering, I imagine ye would've been sly enough to worm yar way into the army." Keeley shot his hand out to Wolf Boy. "By the way, me name's Keeley, and me lass's name's Jana. What's yars, lad?"

Wiping his hand on his coat, he shook Keeley's hand. "Someone found me as a baby dumped in an alley. They brought me to the orphanage, where I was given the name Alexander." He wrinkled his nose. "But I like Alex better. They never gave me a last name because they said I'd get one after I got adopted. They lied." He dropped his chin to his chest. "I never got adopted, and I wasn't going to stick around where no one cared a hoot about me. I figured I could do better on my own, so I ran away." His light gray eyes darkened to the color of steel as they narrowed in on Keeley, then Jana. "Nobody's going to take me back there either. Just as they've done before, they'll send me out to families who'll only use me to work on their farms or in their factories." His hand quaked as it went to his bruised eye. "I might be scared of the street bullies who steal my food, blankets, and money and kick me out of my shelters, but I'll suffer through their thievery and beatings and die of starvation before I'll ever go back to the orphanage."

Keeley winced and looked away from Alex, hiding the dew in his eyes and quiver in his lips.

Knowing Keeley was reliving the dreadful memory of his homelessness through this boy's sowed a sorrowfully heavy ache in Jana's chest, and she steered the conversation during his silence. "Don't worry, Alex, we're not here to take you anywhere."

Alex looked heavenward and mouthed a thank you.

"How long have you been on your own?" Jana asked.

"A couple of months. I figured, by now, I would've found a better home than the street alleys." He shrugged. "Maybe I've set my hopes too high," he said, sounding indifferent despite his frame wilting like the petals of the spring blooms littering the courtyard's cobbles.

Detecting a desire for family and home in his attempt to paint a picture of nonchalance, Jana yearned to wrap her arms around him and hold him there forever. She felt her heart expand at the sudden epiphany. *Why can't I?* She blurted with excitement, "What would you think about adopting my family as your own, Alex?"

Alex staggered backward and began teetering and tottering.

Keeley grabbed on to him before he fell into the fountain and sank below its bubbly surface next to his hat. Staring at Jana with wonderment while he addressed Alex, Keeley said, "Ye won't regret it, lad, and ye won't find a more loving lot than the Brady clan anywhere."

Alternating his dumfounded look between Jana and Keeley, Alex stuttered, "A f-f-family of m-m-my own?"

"That's right," Jana said.

"And I'd be adopting them, not the other way around?"

Smiling, Jana ardently bobbed her head. "It seems a bit more permanent that way, don't you think?"

Alex's tears gushed down his cheeks.

Jana opened her arms to him, and he hesitated before falling into her embrace. In the collapse of his bony body against hers, she felt him molting a lifetime of loneliness, and her own tears welled.

"No one's ever been this nice to me," Alex said between heart-wrenching sobs.

Sniffling and stroking his greasy curls, Jana said, "You better get used to it, Alex."

Keeley sniffled too and blinked away his tears. "Aye, lad, there's a world o' kindness where we hail from, and ye'll fit in well there."

Jana added, "If you choose to accept our offer."

Alex peeled his arms away from Jana. Swiping his soiled coat sleeve across his wet cheeks and runny nose, he said, "You wouldn't kid me, would you?"

Drawing a cross over her heart with her index finger, Jana said, "I couldn't be more serious."

Keeley placed his hands on Alex's shoulders and gave them a tender squeeze. "Now, lad, I hate to be abrupt, but me Jana lass and meself have some important business to take care o' and we must be on our way."

Jana nodded at a wrought-iron bench of floral scroll. "Why don't you sit there, and we'll return here in about two hours to collect you."

"But what do I do about Mr. Woodcock? He paid me to follow you and report on your whereabouts. I won't take his money and run." He crossed his arms over his chest. "I'm no thief."

His scruples reminded Jana of Keeley's. Rather than face his own guilt or ostracism by his peers for being a deserter, even though his amnesia gave him good cause, Keeley had navigated through warring factions in reaching the landing at White House, Virginia, to consult with his regimental surgeon about his prognosis and obtain from him an honorable discharge.

Ruffling his hair, Keeley said, "Yar integrity is exactly why ye'll fit in with me Jana lass, meself, and the Brady clan."

"Do you know where Mr. Woodcock is now?" Jana asked.

"He's in his room at Willard's, waiting for me."

"How about telling him you lost us," Jana said. "To show you're honorable, and you rouse no trouble from him, return the wage he paid you to follow us. You could conduct your business while we do ours, and we'll meet you back here in about two hours. We have lots to do to get you ready for our trip back to my family's farm."

"If I don't get back here before you do"—Alex blinked his eyes rapidly with worry—"don't leave without me."

"We never make promises we don't keep, lad," Keeley said.

As Alex started to go, he looked toward the fountain and turned a cold shoulder at his drowned derby. Then, he skipped away with his golden curls bouncing in the breeze.

Jana wondered if he'd decided to abandon his shabby headgear because it was a sore reminder of his sad life, which he'd just as soon forget.

Studying the timepiece he'd extracted from his vest pocket, Keeley said, "We have an hour to spare, me lass, and we only need five minutes to walk to the President's House."

"Nevertheless, we should get going. We might need extra time checking in. And maybe the president will appreciate our punctuality and admit us right away, so we can hurry back here in case Alex runs into trouble and needs backup," Jana said.

"Aye…sage advice. But before we go, me lass"—he gathered her hands up in his and raised her knuckles to his lips and kissed them—"I must tell ye, what ye did for the lad was the kindest gesture I've ever seen from anyone." With a dimpled grin, he tilted his head toward his right shoulder. "And since I know ye did it for meself, yar gesture makes it the second kindest ye've done for meself."

"Oh? What was the first?"

"Ye saved meself when ye fell in love with meself."

"And you saved me, Keeley, when you fell in love with me. I'll never have another lover, but"—she giggled—"I just might save a few more orphans, if that's all right with you."

"It's a beautiful Irish limerick to me ears, me lass."

Sobering, Jana said, "I know Ma and Pa will embrace Alex and raise him as their own, but what do you think about our taking over after we return from our venture…that is, if we accept it? Given your and Alex's parallel backgrounds, I believe you might have the best understanding of and influence over him during his transition into his new life."

"Are ye sure, me lass?" Keeley burst out, nearly breathless with excitement.

She brushed her hand down his cheek. "Except for my love for you, I've never been surer of anything else."

"Do ye think yar ma and pa will agree to it, considering we've never had the practice o' childrearing?"

"We've got to start somewhere, Keeley, and I think Ma and Pa will want us to do what makes us happy."

The sparkle in Keeley's emerald eyes was enhanced under the bright blue sky overhead. "Ye'll make a wonderful mother, me lass. I've witnessed yar gentle and nurturing treatment o' yar sisters."

"And you'll make a wonderful father, Keeley. I know because I've witnessed your gentler and more nurturing treatment of my sisters." Jana circled her arm around Keeley's and, as they hiked toward the President's House, she felt a buoyance in each of their treads. Euphoria radiated through her heart and soul at the prospect of her and Keeley raising Alex together. It was a huge commitment to mold a child who'd come to them half-grown, and she was surprised she wasn't frightened by it. Would she be as the time grew closer?

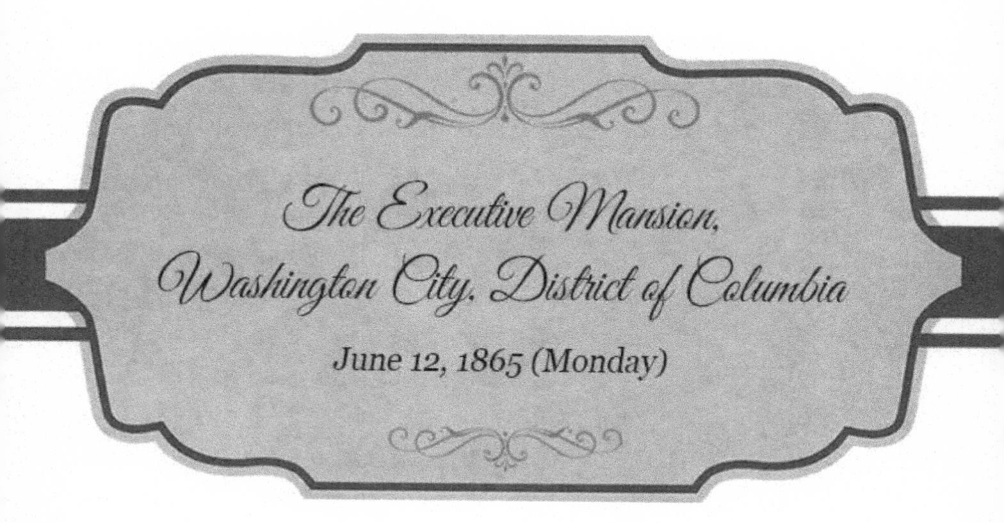

Jana and Keeley exited the hotel's courtyard left onto F Street and immediately faced the opulent Treasury Department, its entire eastern front along Pennsylvania Avenue ornamented in thirty gargantuan columns of granite. Who would've thought the decision to add a west wing to its east and central ones in 1855 would turn out to be vital? The loftier building had served well during the war, which had brought extra financial accountabilities, hence the need for a larger workforce, comprised mainly of women substituting for men off soldiering or occupied with the business or politics of war. Jana applauded the federal government for guaranteeing these female clerks their jobs post-war. Another victory for women pioneering their way into men's roles! Jana hoped that pricked John Woodcock's whole being worse than if he'd rolled in stinging nettles.

Taking a right onto and heading north along a short section of Pennsylvania Avenue, they left the United States Treasury behind and immediately passed the State Department, a depraved brick structure and mere shadow of its magnificent neighbor. Around its north side and continuing west on the broad stone sidewalk of

Pennsylvania Avenue, they finally reached the massive carriage and adjoining walk-in gates to the White House or People's House, as President Lincoln liked to refer to it. Jana admired Lincoln's conviction that "The people of the United States had bought the house and placed him in it to temporarily serve them, and they had the right to see the inside of it and him in it." He'd certainly upheld his oath, allowing himself to be besieged by scores of civilians every day, except the Sabbath, to dispense with their grievances, oblige them with his autograph, accept their gratitude, or engage with them in conversation or story-telling.

Across the avenue lay a public park enclosed by rails. Jana smiled to her recollection of her midnight stroll through Lafayette Square with Keeley, Leanne, and Charlie. Its gas-lit, brick paths meandered around the centrally located equestrian statue of Andrew Jackson, professed to be the first in the country cast in bronze and the first in the world to exhibit a horse balanced on its hind legs.

Jana and Keeley blended in with others strolling up the curved stone path along the semi-circular carriageway amidst wooded grounds of leafy and flowering trees.

A laborer in denim overalls moved aside and waited for everyone to pass before continuing to sweep the walkway while other groundskeepers raked the graveled drive or its inner lawn, graced by a bronze statue of Thomas Jefferson being washed of pigeon droppings—the latter a seemingly thankless job due to its interminability.

Climbing the steps of the North Portico and crossing through a set of its colossal white columns, Jana and Keeley stopped before the front door and pulled the bell, as they'd been instructed to do, while others walked right in.

A lanky, middle-aged gentleman, in a modest business suit, came out to greet them. Leaning in close to Jana and Keeley, he practically whispered through his clove-scented breath, "By the descriptions I've been given of you, I believe you are Miss Jana Brady and Mr. Keeley Cassidy, here for your appointment with President Johnson."

"Why, yes, your observation is to be commended." Jana also found it amazing that he'd addressed her and Keeley as unmarried; he'd obviously been entrusted with all or a portion of their caper. While he introduced himself as Thomas Pendel, chief doorkeeper of the White House, Jana scoured him from head to toe, awestruck.

Thomas chuckled. "Let me guess," he said to Jana, "you believe me to be the ghost of our late president."

"The resemblance is incredible," Jana said.

"Aye, and, if ye were to shave yar mustache and beard, I imagine ye'd truly be his twin," Keeley added.

Thomas's beam drew his angular cheeks up into ripe red apples. Maintaining his lowered voice, he said, "Don't let it get around...Mrs. Lincoln once sent me to painter William Morris Hunt in Boston to have me pose for a full-length portrait in President Lincoln's clothes."

"An historic accomplishment to share with your children and grandchildren," Jana said.

Bowing his head in sorrow, Thomas said, "Of greater honor, I got to know good ole Abe on our frequent walks to the War Department and elsewhere. If only I'd been guarding him at Ford's Theater on his ill-fated night instead of standing here. My training with the District of Columbia Metropolitan Police and keen eyes and ears might've helped me foil his assassination." He popped his head up and spat angry words. "I blame his death on two men: Secretary of War Edwin Stanton for denying Lincoln more than one guard outside his balcony and John Parker for abandoning his post at the intermission. Before he went off to the theater, I made Parker swear he'd redeem his reputation for shoddiness in his duties as a policeman and he'd stick to the president like glue. Why John didn't, he isn't saying. And any investigation into his neglect has been quashed beneath Edwin Stanton's rush to find Lincoln's murderers." He pounded a fist into the palm of his other hand. "Time and again, I warned President Lincoln against traipsing about Washington City alone or with just me as his chaperone, and he finally heeded my words, only to wind up dead."

"Y'are not to blame, sir, and ye should take solace in the fact ye were steadfast in yar guarding o' him during yar assignments."

Thomas's appalling revelations wedged Jana's heart in a vice-grip of sadness and put a slight tremble in her voice. "With John Wilkes Booth dead, we might never know the full extent of the conspiracy to murder President Lincoln and what magic he would've plucked out of his tall stovepipe hat to bring peace."

"Well, I know President Lincoln would want us to carry on." Thomas clicked the heels of his polished boots together. "A dictate of my job is to conduct you to the hostess of this mansion. Follow me, please." He led them through a high-ceilinged storm entrance of iron and glass and into a broad, rectilinear double-ceilinged vestibule. Thomas tarried there to allow Jana and Keeley's scrutiny after he gleaned from them that this was their maiden tour of the White House's interior. To their immediate right, visitors stood in line at a window, fronting a miniature room or, as Thomas called it, the porter's lodge. "Unlike you, they have to present me their calling cards, which I, in turn, present to the president or other occupants before I'll permit them beyond the vestibule."

Jana had once heard the grand foyer described as having more the flair of a bank lobby than a warm, welcoming entryway into a home. With its frescoed ceiling of layered crown molding, two ten-foot-high wall-mounted mirrors on the right and left rising up from marbled mantels, goliath chandelier, and heavy furniture and planters, she had to agree with the assessment.

Thomas gestured them onward, and they passed through a doorway in the middle of a floor-to-ceiling screen of frosted-glass panes framed in decorative cast iron and held up by ionic columns. It was old news that President Martin Van Buren had it installed during repairs to the President's House after the British burned it in 1814 during the War of 1812. The screen's purpose of reducing cold air drafting into the formal rooms beyond it probably benefitted President Lincoln the most with the outer door incessantly being opened by the comings and goings of visitors during his presidency. Entering into a broad transverse hallway, the doorkeeper cut a diagonal swath westward, past an enormously egg-shaped room of mostly blue décor, to the next smaller parlor, out of which the soft touch of a piano's keys drifted. On the threshold, Thomas announced Jana and Keeley's arrival and motioned them inward. Then, he bid them goodbye and marched off in the direction of his post.

Jana and Keeley stepped inside the spacious parlor and into a swirl of stale perfume and cologne. Since every home embodied the scent of its owners, Jana wondered if this was a vestige of Abraham Lincoln and his family. She thought sadly how this strongest sense of a great man and president would soon be erased by its new occupants. Gaping at the furniture, opulently upholstered in crimson satin and gold damask, a new sensation overtook Jana. It crawled under her skin and nipped at her worse than the chiggers she'd oftentimes been subjected to on the march or in camp with the cavalry. *For the second time today, we find ourselves basking in the color of blood. Is it coincidence or omen?* Then, her eyes met George Washington's, staring down upon her from his full-bodied portrait, which had to be the famed one Dolly Madison had ordered cut out of its heavy frame in 1814 for easier removal from the burning Executive Mansion and transport to a safe haven in Maryland. Washington's generalship in the American colonies' bloody War of Independence against Great Britain was a stark reminder to Jana that her mission to track down a shipment of lost Federal money paled in comparison to the blood both General Washington and she'd seen shed. It bolstered her courage for her and Keeley to accept President Johnson's undertaking.

Their hostess, who looked to be in her mid-thirties, slid off a rosewood bench before its matching grand piano, and her petite form practically floated across the carpet toward them. Rounding a white marble table, she offered a warm smile that transformed her serious expression. Extending her hands and wrapping one around Jana's in a stout grip and the other around Keeley's, she said in a soft-spoken voice, "How good of you to come, Miss Brady…Mr. Cassidy. I am Mrs. Martha Johnson Patterson. Please, call me Martha."

"Likewise, please, call us Jana and Keeley," Jana said, seeing in Martha's petite, rounded facial features a striking resemblance to Clara Barton, whom Jana and Keeley had worked alongside when they were assigned to nurse the wounded following the December 1862 battle at Fredericksburg, Virginia. Similar to Clara, she parted her dark hair down the center; dissimilar to Clara, who wore her light hair up in a braided crown, Martha let hers swing in a long-braided ringlet bound by a barrette. That and the timepiece she had dangling on a chain around her neck were the only pieces of jewelry gracing her.

Martha brushed off her apron over her simple every-day dress—unsurprisingly meticulously tailored, given her father's trade before he'd entered politics. "Please, excuse the disheveled state of me and this room." Waving her hand around at the worn rug, stained furniture upholstery, shredded draperies, peeling wallpaper, and chipped paint, she said, "It and the rest of this house got a good trampling under hundreds of thousands of visitors and decimation by keepsake hunters passing through during President Lincoln's time in residence here. As well as most recently when thousands of mourners came to pay their respects while his body lay in state in the East Room. My sister and I only just recently arrived and have begun tidying up."

"Don't ye have staff to help ye?" Keeley asked.

"Oh, yes, but back in Tennessee, my sister and I perform much of our own housekeeping, and we feel compelled to act accordingly in the house entrusted to us by the people of the United States." She expelled a withering sigh. "There are innumerable decisions to make about repairing and refurbishing this place. Given my mother's invalidity from tuberculosis, aggravated by her melancholy from the loss of a son and son-in-law during our late war, she does not have the privilege of acting the role of first lady—an obligation bequeathed to me as the eldest daughter."

"We're sure you'll do justice to this house and make our country and your mother and father proud," Jana said. She sensed, whereas other first ladies, especially Mary Todd Lincoln, needed to leave their mark of lavishness on the Executive Mansion's décor, Martha was genuinely concerned with spending conservatively in its preservation.

"Thank you, Jana. I shall do my best." She leaned in close to them and, in a lighthearted whisper, said, "Don't tell anyone, but I would rather be dusting, polishing, and milking the cows grazing near the south lawn than playing hostess for my father. I am neither inclined nor accustomed to such grandiose levees, dinner parties, and balls."

Jana snuffled. "I can identify with you on that point. If I were you, I'd be hiding out in the stable with the horses all day and night."

Chuckling, Keeley said, "And after we're married, might I be taking on the dusting and polishing while ye milk the cows and muck the stalls?"

Jana and Martha joined Keeley's laughter, truncated by Martha saying, "Speaking of making my father proud, I shall neglect to do so if I delay you further from your appointment with him." She studied the face of her clock-necklace. "Right about now, I am sure he is anticipating your arrival and will be happy to receive you fifteen minutes early." Brushing past Jana and Keeley, she motioned for them to follow her. She led them out of the Red Room and easterly along the main corridor.

Passing two pier tables, flanking the door jambs into the Blue Room, Jana succumbed to the sentries' temptations to rub their glossy, marble surfaces. She swiped her dusty palm off on her bodice coat sleeve and then brushed the motes from it.

They veered left and opposite the Green Room to confront a narrower staircase, situated between the vestibule and the East Room. The latter chamber was renowned for hosting eminent balls, parties, and receptions, and Jana's funneled glimpse into a segment of it framed by the door upheld its reputation for extravagance with its heavy, velvety wallpaper of crimson, garnet, and gold, velvet carpet, and giant gilt mirrors. As they climbed the business staircase, nowhere near as grand or sweeping as the ceremonial one Jana had spied on the west side and must ascend to the first family's private quarters, Jana felt the gaunt carpet threads of the creaky steps beneath her boot soles and the breaks in polish of the chunky, dark-wood bannister against her palm. The President's House appeared old and decrepit, certainly inconsistent with its age of sixty-five. *Poor Martha and her sister,* Jana thought. They had much refurbishing to tackle on a budget, sure to be the paltriest ever appropriated by Congress due to the insurmountable costs of war.

At the top of the second-story landing was a small windowless reception area, cocooned by the stairs and three closed doors. Noting Jana and Keeley curiously scanning the room, Martha said, "Have you never been in the President's House?"

They shook their heads.

Pointing to her right, Martha said, "Beyond that pocket door are the family's private quarters, which includes an impressive library the size and shape of the Blue Room beneath it." She rolled her eyes. "So much for their being private, though. The house staff told me that tourists and other callers managed to finagle their way into President and Mrs. Lincoln's bedrooms. It is a wonder President Lincoln stayed safe in this house with its doors and staircases sparsely guarded—if at all—and its doors open to all." Her gaze shifted straight ahead. "The president's anteroom lies beyond that doorway. It also is windowless, having become that way after President Lincoln had a partition put up to give himself a private passageway between his office and the family library so he would be invisible to the daily stalkers." She waved her hand left. "We shall take this entryway." She hoisted the hems of her skirts, headed up a few steps, and opened the door for Jana and Keeley to pass through into a broad wood-paneled and trampled carpeted area. "This is the waiting room. It adjoins offices for the president's private secretaries, other clerks, and some records. During the previous administration"—she pointed at a northward-facing door to their immediate left—"President Lincoln's private secretary, John George Nicolay, and Nicolay's assistant, John Hay, shared a bedroom within."

Soft rays of sunlight lured Jana's eyes up toward a lunette window, sunken into the roof and the room's solitary source of exterior light. Jana felt closer to it than she would have, had it been in the reception area since the floor of the waiting room was obviously raised to accommodate the extraordinary ceiling height of the East Room below.

"Marvelous, isn't it?" Martha said, cutting sharply right and tapping on the door, which she opened after no audible reply came from within.

On Martha's heels, Jana and Keeley crossed over the threshold into the chief executive's office.

Jana whiffed the unmistakable odor from the Red Room sifting through a tinge of gas from the chandelier and other gas-lit fixtures. It proved to her, Abraham Lincoln had indeed left his ghostly scent besides the mark of his tumultuous reign: books, papers, and maps littered an old mahogany writing desk capped by pigeonhole shelves crammed with letters and other documents. None of which, Jana believed, could've originated from Andrew Johnson this early in his administration. Especially since he had to use the reception room at the Treasury Department to conduct the country's business for five weeks into his presidency because of Mary Todd Lincoln's mourning over her slain husband delaying her departure from the White House.

"Father, allow me to introduce Miss Jana Brady and Mr. Keeley Cassidy," Martha said, drawing President Johnson away from his southward gaze through one of two tall, heavily draperied windows.

As he turned his somber expression toward them, Jana pondered what he'd been fixating upon when they'd entered:

> *Was it a stretch of the Potomac River, which, from its headwaters in West Virginia to its mouth at the Chesapeake Bay, divided the North and South and circumnavigated places of hard-fought battles, such as the single bloodiest day in 1862 at Antietam, Maryland, and, in crossing it, climaxed in pivotal battles, such as in 1863 at Gettysburg, Pennsylvania?*
>
> *Or the unfinished obelisk on the Mall commemorating George Washington?*
>
> *Perhaps the recently and partially burned red-stoned Smithsonian, anchoring the middle of the Mall?*
>
> *Or maybe the pillared mansion and its grounds across the Potomac River on Arlington Heights, which the federal government had confiscated from Confederate general Robert E. Lee's wife and descendant of Martha Washington, Mary Anna Custis Lee, during the war and continued to expand as a military cemetery?*

Jana realized her subconscious had invoked landmarks with construction and reconstruction in common. The first—entailing the tearing down of an impalpable fratricidal wall to make the country one big happy family—most certainly to be the biggest headache for President Johnson.

"Thank you, Martha," he said with barely a trace of his Southern roots in his inflection. He unclasped his large hands from behind his back and hurried his heavy strides toward Jana and Keeley. Shaking Jana's hand with a firm grasp, he then shook Keeley's with the same white-knuckled grip. "I appreciate your promptness in answering my summons, Miss Brady…Mr. Cassidy."

"To maintain the clandestine nature of your meeting, Father, I have instructed Tom to usher scheduled callers to the Red Room and to keep everyone else in the vestibule."

The president's smile at his daughter mingled gratitude with admiration.

"Now, before I leave to assure Mother's comfort," Martha said, "shall I call for some tea or lemonade?"

"I will leave the decision in your very capable hands, my dear."

Martha glided toward the south window and pulled a tasseled silk bell cord dangling from the plaster ceiling near the pigeon-holed desk blocking a tall door, which had to lead into Lincoln's private passageway, through the anteroom, to the family library. The high-backed secretary barricading the entryway seemed odd to Jana. Perhaps the passageway had become a pesky paradox to its purpose since it could also conceal would-be assassins. After all, Martha had minutes before mentioned her having heard of callers roaming the Lincolns' private chambers—by the sound of it—as freely as the cattle grazing on the south lawn.

As the president waited for Martha to exit the room, Jana noted the stark contrast between him and portrayals of Abraham Lincoln. She somehow doubted the late president's towering presence had intimidated his shorter and stockier vice-president, whom she'd heard could be obstinate and argumentative like a bulldog. His prominent forehead, enhanced by a hairline that curved around a jutting widow's peak, commanding nose, rounded, upturned chin, and plump, frowning lips certainly loaned credibility to the rumor. No matter, Jana would be the judge of the new commander in chief's merits based upon her own interaction with him.

The smartly dressed president straightened his bowtie, tugged at his coat sleeves, and Jana was thankful when he moved to the head of a long mahogany table in the middle of the room and gestured for them to sit on each side of him. The more casual furniture in the eastern half of the office looked feeble, and she didn't want to be the person who finally split the nap of either threadbare sofa or broke up one of the rickety chairs into kindling wood.

While the president took his seat, with his back to the windows, Keeley held Jana's cushioned chair out for her and made sure she was situated before he marched the long way around the table to his own seat. He'd doubtlessly and wisely chosen his route to stay within view of the president, in deference to any delayed paranoia President Johnson might be suffering from his would-be assassin having lurked in his shadows. Who could blame him? Although, if other accomplices who could be named in Lincoln's assassination and the planned murders of incumbents Vice-President Johnson, Secretary of State Seward, and General Grant were wise—like Mary Surratt's son John—they would've dodged Washington City by now. Lest they risk capture and execution by the nine military commissioners who were still weighing evidence and interviewing witnesses to help decide on the fate of the eight accused in the "Lincoln Conspiracy"—as Jana had come to call it, after once hearing it dubbed as such.

Jana rubbed the green baize fabric covering the tabletop and wondered if President Lincoln had made the last of the many ink stains upon its coarse woolen background. Her emotions were bittersweet: She felt honored to congregate around the table where President Lincoln had debated with his cabinet over political and war issues, including the Emancipation Proclamation. Where he'd received world leaders, military officers, and politicians of all stripes. And where he'd heard civilians pleading for the discharge of their only surviving male kin at the battlefront or pardon from execution for the desertion of a loved one. Yet, she felt a chasm of grief within her over his premature death. If they hadn't already, she sensed the citizens of the United States would also come to feel the void of Lincoln's competent and fatherly leadership. Especially once his killers were brought to justice and the realization that President Lincoln was lost to them forever hit home.

Poor President Johnson, he has some big shoes to fill, Jana thought. She felt sorry that he had to shoulder the oppressive burden thrust upon him by the assassination of President Lincoln, and she yearned to help him grow into those shoes, even if only partially, by recovering the army payroll. Was it realistic to think she and Keeley could pull off finding what thus far seemed to be the proverbial "needle in the haystack?"

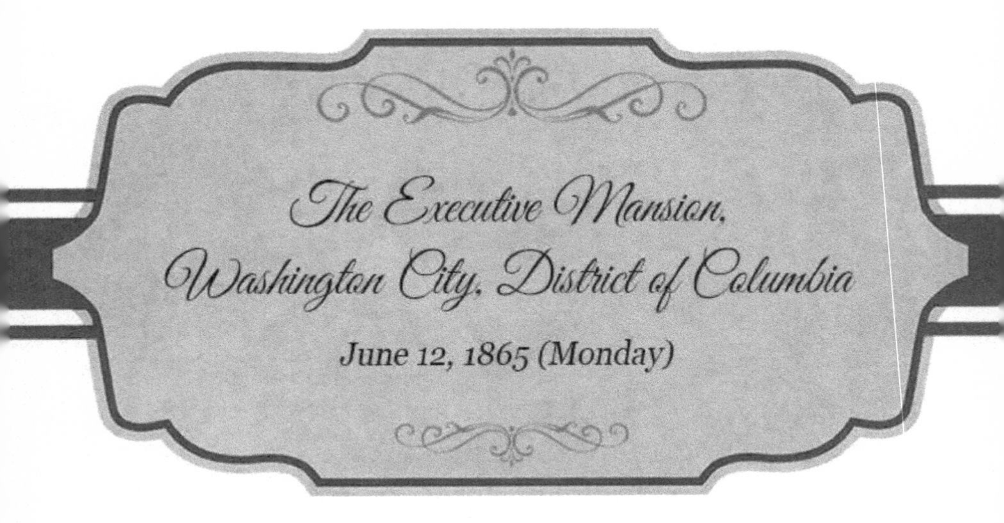

Jana looked up to find the president observing her.

As though he'd read into her thoughts about his leadership, President Johnson cast a weary, sidelong glance at the portrait of Andrew Jackson, hanging on the west wall above the fireplace's marble mantel.

Is President Johnson expecting the seventh president of the United States to magically dole out some advice for eradicating the federal debt? Jana wondered. Why not? To date, Andrew Jackson was the only president of the United States to balance a national debt of several million dollars (owed to the French government, Dutch bankers, and domestic creditors for their financial support during the War of Independence). Astutely, he'd accomplished it by selling federally owned lands out west and nullifying expenditures on infrastructure. Although Old Hickory had passed into his afterlife twenty years ago, his examples lived on. Perhaps fellow Tennessee-politician Johnson was drawing some guidance from them now.

The president's heavy-lidded eyes gravitated slightly downward from Andrew Jackson's portrait to a large clock on the mantel.

Since she and Keeley had entered the office, Jana noted few minutes having ticked away to the swing of the pendulum. She imagined a president had to adhere to a tight schedule from sunup to sundown; therefore, the clock was his best friend.

Again, he clasped his hands, this time over a piece of yellow foolscap, on which Jana observed a right-handed slant to the loopy cursive writing. Getting right down to business congruent with his beleaguered air, President Johnson said, "In this tumultuous time, the duty of this office weighs heavy upon my shoulders. I fear, with each step I take, my proposals for resolving the myriad of challenges facing our nation will be discredited by Radical Republicans who distrust me. For the life of me, I cannot fathom what more I need to do to prove my unwavering loyalty to the Union."

Jana suspected he was referencing his pre-war outspokenness against secession; his retention of his senatorial seat in the federal Congress when, post-secession, all other Southern politicians had vacated theirs; and his tireless toils during the war, from 1862 through 1864, to reestablish federal authority in Tennessee after President Lincoln appointed him military governor there.

President Johnson continued, "At least President Lincoln and Secretary of State Seward trusted me. I am eternally grateful for their choice in me to replace Vice-President Hannibal Hamlin as Lincoln's running mate for his second term of office."

"Aye, and, by the electoral and popular votes, I'd say Lincoln's and your switch from the Republican ticket to the National Unity Party ticket was a stroke o' genius in capturing the votes o' the Union Democrats."

Jana added, "Your party cunningly advertised that opposing sides could put aside their differences and capably work together for the good of the country."

"Both very true statements," President Johnson said. "Sadly, in President Lincoln's absence, I have no insulation. I am already hearing controversial whispers over my having ordered a military tribunal to decide the fate of those accused of murdering President Lincoln."

"Did you really have the choice, sir, of placing the conspirators in a civilian criminal court for a trial by jury?" Jana asked.

"Aye, the whole affair seems fitting o' a war crime." As Keeley qualified his theory, he counted them off on his fingers: "President Lincoln's assassination occurred while he was the commander in chief o' the Union Army. It was committed by those in rebellion against the United States o' America. It occurred within the boundaries o' the federal district, which, I would think, could be considered a garrison o' the Union Army, fortified as it was. And it occurred while the largest Confederate Army in the east under General Johnston had yet to surrender to General Sherman—even though General Lee had already surrendered the main army o' the Confederacy to General Grant."

"Not to mention," Jana added, "there were other Confederate departments scattered throughout the South that were and still are holding out." She spied a map of the West, un-spooled upon a wooden rack. "Actually, has Confederate general and Cherokee chief Stand Watie surrendered his Indian troops in the Choctaw Nations area yet?"

"Hopefully, soon," President Johnson said, then channeled the conversation back around to the trial. "One absolute, Secretary of War Stanton supports the military tribunal since he all but pushed me in that direction." He groaned. "Though, I fail to understand his rush to select the commissioners, who are sure to be biased. All nine are Union-Army officers whose commissions were approved by President Lincoln. Only one has legal training, so I imagine the other eight will be vulnerable to the biases of Judge Advocate General Joseph Holt and his assistant prosecutor who are sitting in on the tribunal and doubtlessly swaying the arguments toward execution."

Another prickly thorn in poor President Johnson's side, Jana thought.

The president's broad shoulders sagged. "I, however, refuse to argue this point with the Secretary of War. I must pick my battles wisely with him. Lord knows, as I have already alluded to, I am acrimoniously quarreling with him and other Radical Republicans over how best to achieve reunification of the Northern and Southern states. In fact, on the morning of Lincoln's assassination, Stanton presented a Congressional blueprint for Reconstruction to President Lincoln and his cabinet. Imposing military rule, black suffrage, and the requirement that a majority of white males within a seceding state's borders pledge an oath of loyalty before it can draft a new constitution, including the abolition of slavery, inaugurate a new government, and elect representatives to the federal Congress are unduly stiff prerequisites for readmission into the Union." He sat up straight and squared his shoulders. "It will only anger the former Confederate states and prolong the quick and amicable restoration of our country, which President Lincoln had envisioned by requiring only ten percent of a seceding state's voters on the rolls for the 1860 presidential election to swear an oath of allegiance to the United States and obeisance to its laws regarding the abolition of slavery before they can begin the process of readmission. I successfully implemented Lincoln's Ten-Percent Plan in Tennessee, as it was also done in Arkansas and Louisiana. The Republicans' outline smacks of dictatorship and ours is a republic. I believe my appointment of interim governors to oversee the overall process of readmission is adequate enough."

"If your cabinet and the federal Congress are worried about your being lenient with the South during Reconstruction because of your Southern roots," Jana said with a shrug, "I think your unprecedented one-hundred-thousand-dollar reward for Jefferson Davis's capture and the ex-Confederate president's ongoing imprisonment send a clear message you intend to be tough on it." It had to be eating him up inside to maintain his impartiality toward the South, knowing his strategies would impact his family, friends, neighbors, and former compatriots. *He might occupy the prestigious office of president of the United States, but could there be a more unenviable position in world leadership right now?* Jana wondered.

He scoffed. "Additionally, I intend to force each Confederate state to repeal their ordinance of secession before it can be readmitted into the Union. I will also take President Lincoln's temporary exclusion of high-ranking Confederate-Army officers and government officials from readmission two steps further by also excluding former federal officials, graduates of the military academies at West Point and Annapolis, and especially owners of taxable property worth more than twenty-thousand dollars who supported the rebellion or fought for the Confederacy. And by forcing these classes of Southerners to apply to me personally for a pardon and restoration of their political and voting rights."

"It seems, sir," Keeley said, "that permanently taking away the rights to vote or hold office o' those most responsible for fomenting the rebellion ought to be one strike in yar favor. Why wouldn't Radical Republicans jump on yar program to ban construed enemies o' the United States from ever again legislating in the federal Congress beside them?"

"Especially since my plan punishes the wealthiest of the planter class." He grimaced. "I know it sounds hypocritical since I freed the few slaves whom I owned, followed by all in Tennessee, only after President Lincoln's official declaration of his Emancipation Proclamation went into effect on January 1, 1863." President Johnson's frown slanted inwardly at himself, and he sounded sincere when he said, "I had a change of heart concerning slavery when I realized it was the major factor ripping our country apart."

A rap at the door was timely for deflecting his doleful remorse. Martha entered and hastened across the dark-green carpet with large buff-colored diamonds and floral accents.

The president adjourned the discussion while Martha instructed a kitchen maid to place an oblong silver tray in reach of her father and his guests.

After dismissing the domestic, Martha busied herself placing porcelain dessert plates, linen napkins, and glass goblets before the trio.

President Johnson picked up where he'd left off, the woefulness in his speech dissipating as he talked on. "It would be a coup for me to land on solid ground with the holdover cabinet from Lincoln's administration and Congress if I were to gift them the missing payroll. It is sorely needed to replenish the federal treasury with our national debt from the war having risen exponentially, and"—again, he glimpsed the clock, which read ten minutes beyond when he'd last checked it—"more critically, before the Thirty-Ninth United States Congress returns to session in early December."

It struck Jana: *His obsession with the clock probably has less to do with his keeping to a daily schedule and more to do with his rush to recoup the army payroll.* Was he praying to Father Time to be charitable?

When Martha finished pouring lemonade, she encouraged Jana and Keeley to help themselves to the sugar cookies and said, "Do you require anything else, Father?"

"No thank you, my dear. I don't know what I would do without you," President Johnson said to his daughter, who was already closing the door behind her.

The overwhelming aroma of vanilla made Jana's mouth water and sent her hand lunging for a cookie.

Smirking at her, Keeley seemed to be telegraphing, *How can ye possibly eat after a filling meal?*

Jana telegraphed back, *You should know better.* He was conscious of her hankering for sugar cookies. She could be stuffed to the gills on the main meal and, still, her palate would prevail for the sweet treat. Besides, she could always concentrate better when her taste buds were fully sated, and she sensed an intensification of their conference ahead. Biting into the warm, chewy, savory cookie, she resisted an unladylike utterance of delight.

Keeley's attention averted to the president. "What more can ye tell me Jana lass and meself about our mission?"

Raking a harried hand through the leftward part in his graying, dark hair, the middle-aged president dove into his narrative. "As we all are well aware, the closure of the three federal mints in the rebellious states of North Carolina, Georgia, and Louisiana at the outset of the war and the Philadelphia Mint's lack of production by the end of 1861 caused a hoarding of coins by the general population and their shrinkage in circulation. This forced the Treasury Department to print greenbacks to pay for the war. President Lincoln earmarked two million dollars to replenish the payrolls for the soldiers fighting around the Mississippi River." He cleared his throat.

During his pause, Jana and Keeley flicked each other a look of subdued bliss. Jana was pretty sure Keeley was also remembering Kate Warne's claim to their reaping a percentage of the spoils.

The president continued, "With the Confederate Army retreating perilously close to Washington on July 12th, 1864, after the battle at Fort Stevens, one of the capital's strongholds, Lincoln feared lingering Rebel scouts could seize and use the payroll to help reinvigorate the Confederacy's coffers and dying cause. He concocted a brilliant plan for the precious cargo to travel a circuitous route northeast, out of harm's way: It was placed aboard a train in Jersey City, New Jersey, being readied to carry Rebel prisoners, arriving by steamer up the Atlantic Coast from the overcrowded prison at Point Lookout, Maryland, to the newly built prison in Elmira, New York." He huffed. "If not for the unfortunate train collision, the ploy would have worked. Knowledge of the payroll aboard the caboose was entrusted to only two soldiers from the Federal War Department's Veteran Reserve Corps. All of the other guards were left to think nothing more than supplies for Elmira Prison were being freighted in the large unmarked chest. The two guards, who were privy to the classified information, survived the train wreck, and, when they were detained and grilled, they were adamant they had nothing to do with stealing the payroll and were too busy detailing the extent of damage and wounded and saving lives to garrison the perimeter against escapes. All of this has been corroborated by witnesses at the scene. Anyway—," the president's breath caught and he coughed.

"Here, sir." Jana slid his lemonade closer to him.

He swigged half of his glass before setting it down. Then, with his linen napkin, he wiped the liquid beading in the vertical groove between his nose and upper lip. "Thank you, Miss Brady."

"You're most welcome, sir."

"Recently," President Johnson continued, "President Lincoln had one of his appointed U.S. marshals check their assets. He confirmed that neither of the veteran guards had derived a sudden influx of wealth. Therefore, a more likely scenario is that a few or all five of the Rebel prisoners, who are believed to have escaped, learned about the army payroll aboard, and they miraculously hauled it away or hid it until they could exhume it at a safer time. The administrators of the *Erie Railway* allege their investigator searched the area and turned up no clues as to its whereabouts."

Licking crumbs away from her lips, Jana said, "Why do you say *allege*, sir?"

"The investigation by the *Erie-Railway* agent was conducted rather swiftly for my fancy. I am sympathetic to the tremendous pressure he must have been under to return to and secure his job. He was dealing with laborers striking for fairer wages proportionate to increased profits gained by the railroad's transport of coal. Any stoppages would have impacted the Union Army's mobility, and it would have forced the federal government to usurp control of the railroad for its continued operation by the military—same as was enforced upon the *Pennsylvania and Reading Railroad*. Unfortunately,

Pinkerton agents and Union officers, with their trained eyes for such reconnaissance, were swamped with the business and espionage of war and unable to commit to the initial search."

Sliding his chair closer to the table, Keeley said, "If I may be so bold to ask, and before me Jana lass and meself are sent on a wild-goose chase, how are ye sure there was federal money aboard the prisoner train?"

"I thought you might ask," President Johnson said. After smoothing out the creases of the starchy paper before him, he slid it midway between Jana and Keeley. The order was clearly written in the same hand as the signature of President Lincoln.

"Has anyone thought to interrogate Jefferson Davis?" Before the president could answer, Jana continued to say, "Maybe he learned of the theft and sent his minions to confiscate it from the train robbers for help in, to repeat your words, reviving the Confederacy's coffers and its dying cause. And maybe he'd be willing to relinquish it in exchange for an abridged imprisonment at Fort Monroe." She'd love to get something on the Confederate president; she still harbored a grudge against him for rejecting her exoneration from execution a year ago this past May and for putting her through the nightmares of having to escape the gallows and nearly suffocating in a coffin. Smothering a smirk, Jana thought, *His nationwide ridicule as a coward for attempting to escape from the 4th Michigan Cavalry dressed in his wife's shawl will have to do.* Her mockery of Jefferson Davis fell far from hypocritical contrasted with her insisting upon Keeley's dressing as a woman on his way to attaining an honorable discharge from his regimental surgeon. As an outwardly appearing able-bodied man, Keeley could've been conscripted into either army; his bumbling around on the battlefield in an amnesic state would do no good for himself and his allies. President Davis had donned female attire out of cowardice, to evade facing up to his treason against the United States of America.

"The War Department has questioned him a few times, and he

stands firm in his ignorance of any missing federal payroll, but, of course, he would. However"—President Johnson arched a shaggy eyebrow at her—"I am impressed with your analytical aptitude, Miss Brady. I trust you and Mr. Cassidy are the right sleuths to get to the bottom of this heist."

Keeley's cautious side suppressed Jana's surge of pride. "How dangerous might this investigation be to me Jana lass and meself? I sense we're being thrown into a wolf's den."

"I will not lie to you." The president's cheeks puffed up and deflated with a hiss of air, reminding Jana of Professor Lowe's enormous gas balloon, used by the Union Army for aerial spying on the Rebel-troop positions and strengths. "As I mentioned before, once President Lincoln issued an order to print money in defense of the Union, a handful of government employees would have participated in its execution."

"And loose lips sink ships," Jana thought aloud.

"Yes, and, unfortunately"—the president's expression plunged into despair—"greed and power for personal or political gain have historically trumped loyalty and patriotism."

Jana pondered the profiteers who'd grown fat from their manufacturing of shoddy shoes and uniforms and defective armaments, the former exposing the soldiers to harsh temperatures when they crumbled to nothing, the latter exposing the soldiers to backfiring mechanisms. Both had caused too many unnecessary deaths. The cookie's vanilla flavor soured in her mouth. Her desire to spit it out was supplanted with the satisfying image of one form, representing all of the gluttonous and corrupt profiteers, shot down before a firing squad.

"There is something more you need to know." The president began squirming in his chair. "President Lincoln feared he was fighting a two-front war against the Confederacy and its arm—the secret society known as the Knights of the Golden Circle. Are you aware of the KGC?"

"Yes," Jana said, "its manifesto comprises visions of expanding slavery beyond the eleven seceding states through border and western states and territories of the United States and Mexico, Central America, and the West Indies, including Cuba."

Keeley posed, "Pre-war, didn't Southerners dually represented in the KGC and federal Congress try to get resolutions passed in Congress for the annexation o' many o' the lands me Jana lass just named as protectorates o' the United States?"

"Ah, yes," President Johnson said. "Mercifully, they failed. If either resolution had been voted in, the power of the wealthy slave-holding class would have burgeoned to the degree of non-extrication. As it was, they eventually recruited Copperheads opposed to war and sympathetic to the South, thereby promulgating its poison into the bordering states of Kentucky and Missouri and the northern states of Ohio, Illinois, Indiana, Michigan, Wisconsin, and Iowa." He leaned his forehead into the fingers of his right hand and massaged its deep furrows. "What I am about to tell you is not general knowledge, and I would rather it not spread like wildfire and incite mass hysteria."

"Anything you tell us, President Johnson, will never leave this room," Jana said.

"Not through us. Ye can count on it," Keeley added.

"Even so, I feel you deserve full disclosure to benefit your decision to either accept or decline my assignment." President Johnson's eyes nervously twitched as he glanced toward the waiting room, as though he mistrusted that no one had slipped upstairs. Then, he crossed his arms over the tabletop, leaned in close to Jana and Keeley, and lowered his voice to say, "According to a report from Judge Advocate General Holt—as you know, our highest-ranking officer over military justice and law—to Secretary of War Stanton in late 1864, intelligence amassed from inside the previously mentioned states estimates five-hundred-thousand Northerners to be KGC members. The vast majority is equipped with arms and trained for battle."

Alarmed by the high number, Jana's eyes froze with Keeley's. *Could we really be contesting the KGC in the quest for the army payroll?*

"And Judge Holt's figure *excludes* enlistments from the Southern faction," the president said, with an anguished expression. "God only knows the strength and the wealth of this subversive organization, which is claimed to be all-seeing and which Judge Advocate General Holt asserts is the culprit behind our fratricidal conflict and possibly Lincoln's assassination. As of late, the KGC has become too quiet for comfort."

Crossing his legs and arms, Keeley said, "I'm not suggesting Jefferson Davis had anything to do with Lincoln's murder, but me Jana lass and meself have heard whispers he's a major influencer in the KGC. If he's managed to get hold o' the stolen Union payroll, might his incarceration have slowed down the movement o' it a wee bit so we might better track it?"

"Yes." He pounded his fist on the tabletop, and, oblivious of his rattling the silver tray, agitating the lemonade in the pitcher and goblets, and thrusting Jana and Keeley back into the curved oak slats of their chairs, he continued, "We cannot hold Jefferson Davis forever, hence the urgency in reclaiming the Union payroll before his release and allocation of it for a second rebellion." He scowled. "During the war, the Union intercepted a schooner outfitted by the KGC to pirate gold and commerce being shipped east from the Pacific Coast. I fear the society has burrowed farther underground to plot other unscrupulous methods of accumulating wealth."

Such as train robberies? Jana wondered, recollecting Duke Tanner's assertion about the post-war reassignments of the Pinkerton agents to the railroads. Was the Pinkerton Agency aware it could be impeding the KGC from amassing wealth through those means? Re-focusing on the president, she asked, "What about a Confederate treasury? Has the Union confiscated it?"

"Its loss is another bane for bolstering the federal treasury. None has been discovered in Richmond or other key southern cities. Nor was there any with Jefferson Davis or his high-ranking officials during their captures. When questioned about it, Davis maintained the Confederate treasury was completely depleted. Secretary of War Stanton and I refuse to believe it, and Stanton seems obsessed with finding it. I am sure Davis has devoted sycophants hiding it where we will never find it."

"Might John Woodcock be a henchman o' the KGC?" Keeley asked.

Stiffening, the president said, "What do you know of him?"

"Nothing before today," Jana replied and proceeded to update him on their encounter with and suspicions of him.

"With his many political connections in Washington," the president said, "it is highly plausible he has crossed paths with members of the KGC and has been recruited by them. His personal goal of wealth and power is certainly aligned with theirs, and it is fairly well established he is bankrupt from bad real estate ventures. In fact, that carpetbagger has badgered me a few times unsuccessfully about the federal government partnering with him on a diversity of investments in the South during Reconstruction to capitalize on its hard times. As a minor stockholder in the *Erie Railway*, he reaps a meagre allowance nowhere near enough for a man accustomed to a life of prosperity. I would not discount he has accepted a bid by the KGC for a sizeable reward to find and conceal the Union payroll until it can be delivered into the hands of the upper echelons of delinquents."

"Do ye really think an organization born o' Southern roots would be coldhearted enough to make use o' a Union payroll from a catastrophe in which so many o' their own were killed?" Keeley said, aiming a scornful look out the window at the South.

In a matter-of-fact tone, Jana said, "If the KGC were to view the expenditure of the payroll as vindication for their dead, then, why not?"

"Again, I feel compelled to provide for your consumption all of the particulars of this investigation." President Johnson propped his forearms against the tabletop, laced his fingers together, and rolled his thumbs around each other. Although he gazed at Jana and Keeley with beseeching eyes, he said, "I will understand if you wish to decline my request."

After Keeley ardently nodded his assent to see this objective through, Jana lifted her chin and said, "Three generations of Bradys have taught me to fight for my country no matter the cost to myself, and I intend to carry on, alongside Keeley, who's as keenly patriotic of his adopted land. Although, I'm not convinced the KGC is involved, and we've dealt with amateur thieves before."

Keeley grinned, silently communicating his understanding of her meaning and their shared memory: They, alongside Leanne, had cleverly chased off two Yankee deserters harassing Versella Stock Barney, Keeley's Southern caretaker after he stumbled into her homestead following the battle at Trevilian Station, Virginia, with amnesia from the blow of a rifle butt to his head.

The rolling of the president's thumbs came to an abrupt halt, and he perked up. "Does this mean you are accepting my assignment?" Following a nod from both Jana and Keeley, President Johnson said to Jana, "Of course, Mr. Cassidy is ineligible for a pension as he has no disability from his service, but yours is a unique case, Miss Brady, and I intend to acquire one for you for your outstanding wartime contributions, such as was awarded to Deborah Sampson for her military service in the Continental Army of our War of Independence."

Jana and Keeley stared speechlessly at each other.

Recovering her tongue, Jana said, "It's one thing to get paid for my soldiering, but I expect no extra remuneration for serving my country, sir."

President Johnson donned a stern face and put up a staying hand, making himself an impenetrable bulwark. "I shall not waver upon this, Miss Brady. Will twenty-five dollars a month do?"

Placing her hand over her heart, Jana said, "I guess there's nothing else to do than to accept your generosity with my gratitude."

"Good. Now that we have the matter settled, I need your investigation to be concluded by the first of November." He cleared his throat. "Just so you are not encumbered by the winter months in returning the treasury to Washington and before Congress convenes in early December." The president pushed back in his chair and stood up. "You have your work cut out for you." Before he dismissed them entirely, he tendered Jana an envelope for both her and Keeley, stamped closed by the United States Treasury's seal.

Awed by its sanctioned connotation, Jana rubbed the tip of her index finger over the raised wax of the outer rim, which was inscribed with the Latin abbreviation for the "The Seal of the Treasury of North America," and then along the inner circle, which included a chevron of thirteen stars (for the original states) in between a balancing scale (for justice) at the top and a key (for official authority) at the bottom. The seal, dating back to 1775 and symbolizing the united effort by the colonies to fund the Revolutionary War, preceded the birth of the Department of the Treasury in 1789.

"Inside is a promissory for you and Mr. Cassidy to procure five percent of the amount of the salvaged payroll," President Johnson said.

Keeley's jaw dropped, and Jana wondered if she'd heard right to her own dropped jaw.

Smiling at their dumbfounded expressions, the president said, "I thought, at the very least, you deserved a commission equivalent to the reward for Confederate President Jefferson Davis' capture." He leaned forward and set his palms on the tabletop. "Now, if there is anything else you might need, you know where to find me."

Jana regained her faculties to say, "There is one last thing, sir. I really think Keeley and I are going to need reinforcements. May we call in two of our most trustworthy and loyal cavalry comrades?"

"Yes. . .if it means getting the job done on time, and they will also be compensated. Shall I have some money taken out of the Treasury for any costs you anticipate they might incur?"

"No, the generous stipend that we've already received for our travel expenses should more than cover theirs too, and you can settle up on their wages for the job upon completion when we can provide you with more accurate figures for their time and involvement," Jana said.

"Very well, but, if at any point you find yourselves thin on funds, please, do not hesitate to wire for more. I will find the means to get it to you as soon as possible." The president drew his brows together and narrowed his stern eyes at them. "However, you and they must understand this operation demands the utmost secrecy. Outside of Allan Pinkerton and his two agents, who have vowed to forget they have ever heard of this mission, only the Secretary of the Treasury knows of it since you have been temporarily designated as agents under his direct supervision; thus, you are on the Treasury Department's payroll. If you were to fail to recoup the army payroll, I cannot have it publicized I wasted federal money on a losing proposition."

"Why not use agents of the United States Treasury or the Union Army's Bureau of Military Information? Weren't both pretty effective at penetrating the South to conduct espionage during the war?" Jana asked.

"Apart from most Treasury agents having returned to their original duties in the investigation of counterfeiting and other financial crimes, some have had their disguises compromised while others have disappeared or been imprisoned after they were exposed as double agents. Hugh McCulloch has only been Secretary of the Treasury for three months, barely enough time for him to come to know and trust the agents under his aegis. Thus, he agreed with my decision to hire outside of the existing pool. As far as the BMI stands, following General Lee's surrender, its intelligence activities were disbanded and replaced with the paroling of Rebels."

"Aren't ye worried about other dubious parties, who are under yar administration and might be competing with me Jana lass and meself for the lost treasury, tattling on ye about yar appropriation o' our wages without Congressional approval?" Keeley said.

"Unless they are itching to live out their days in Old Capitol Prison, they will wish to avoid trumpeting my covert arrangement as it will only expose their own traitorous scheming against the federal government. Since we remain under extraordinary circumstances with some units in the South still in rebellion against us, I will expand my wartime executive power to appropriate money where I see fit, just as President Lincoln did." Again, President Johnson's eyes nervously twitched, this time, as he glanced toward the anteroom, as though he was expecting it to be filled with members of his cabinet, congressmen, or other important dignitaries, and he lowered his voice to strictly emphasize, "Thus, I demand that you deliver the payroll directly to me. I do not want another single person, including the Secretary of the Treasury, aware of your discovery."

Jana knit her eyebrows together at the oddity of his order. Why the secrecy? Could he have designs of his own on the army payroll?

Appearing to notice her bafflement, President Johnson cleared his throat. "I will need some time to assess where it can be best used upon its return. As the saying goes, and I am sure you understand, 'Too many cooks in the kitchen spoil the broth,'" he said, sounding contrite.

"Ye have our word," Keeley said, "we'll be discreet, and me Jana lass and meself can vouch for our comrades' discretion too."

Contemplating his demand for secrecy, Jana said, "How about Keeley and I develop a cipher system for encoding and decoding our communications with you? We could have it done before we leave Washington and personally deliver it to Thomas Pendel for your eyes only."

"That is a splendid idea, Miss Brady. You may direct all of your correspondences from the field to Secretary of the Treasury McCulloch. Although I would value updates from the field, I fear you will have to go out of your way to find a telegraph, and I wish to avoid unduly encumbering your investigation. Thus, the better procedure would be to wire me only if it is an emergency."

"You seem worried, Mr. President, about our meeting your deadline. Don't be. I intend to finish long before its expiration." Realizing she'd just made a unilateral statement without regard to Keeley's input, Jana rushed to say, "Fall is Keeley's and my favorite season—when Elmira is still vibrant and colorful; I have my heart set on marrying Keeley then, and I think he reciprocates the notion."

With an easy nod at Jana, Keeley said, "Aye, and there's the matter o' building our hearth and home around an adopted child." A shard of sunlight through the upper sash of the southeast window accentuated the gleam in his eyes.

Jana beamed back at him. Her sixth sense told her, she and Keeley were on the right path to merging their different philosophies of adventure; however, she'd remain cautiously optimistic. Their journey together was still in its infancy.

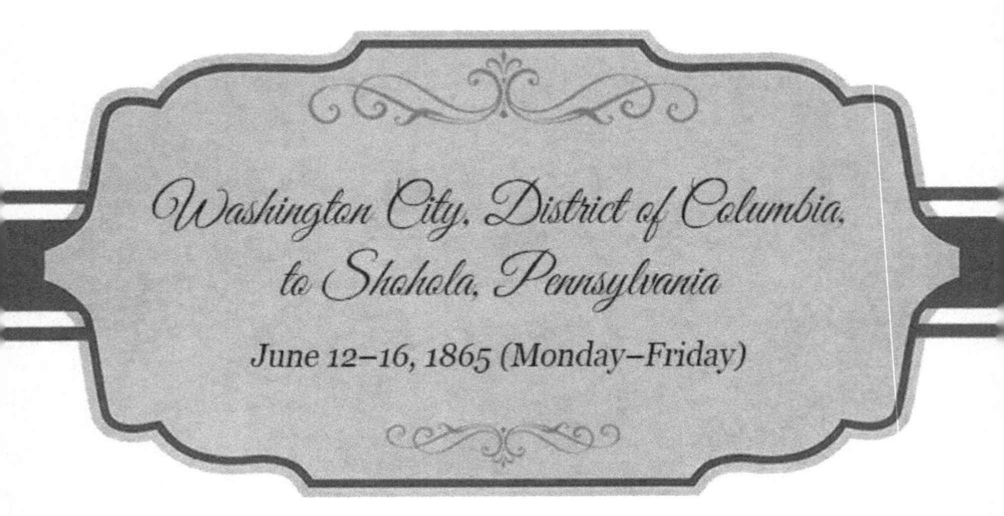

Jana and Keeley returned to the courtyard in under two hours and found Alex pacing before the wrought-iron bench, his tattered brogans threatening to fall apart with every step.

Perking up to their arrival, Alex was quick to report, "Mr. Woodcock was fuming mad at me for losing you. The scrooge pocketed the money he promised me for following you, but that was the least of my worries." He peered over his shoulder as though he fretted an attack. "I was afraid he was going to throw me out of his window, and I high-tailed it as soon as I got free of his grip on me." He pointed to a gash in his coat sleeve. "See what he did to me."

"Good work, lad. Mr. Woodcock's ire proves ye were convincing about losing us," Keeley said.

"But I got to tell you, two grouchy strong men passed me in the hall. The one with a limp shoved me aside"—he thrust out his soiled palms—"and I wasn't even in his way. Anyway, as I started downstairs, I saw them knocking on Mr. Woodcock's door." He shuddered. "I'm glad I'd already left Mr. Woodcock's room when they showed up."

Over Alex's head, Jana and Keeley swapped looks of concern; they appeared to be on the same page in figuring Woodcock was hiring men to trail them.

"Could you describe the two brutes a little better?" Jana said.

"The one who limped had only whiskers, and he might've even been bald. The other had a head and face full of hair, blacker than midnight."

Jana placed her arm around Alex's bony shoulders. "Come tomorrow, you'll never have to worry about bad men and bullies anymore." She cast him a calm and reassuring smile. "Now, let's go get you a proper meal and some new clothes."

In their coming and going from the hotel to shop, Jana, Keeley, and Alex used the service stairs to dodge John Woodcock and his potentially prowling goons, and they ordered food from the dining room and ate in their room. Then, there was the matter of sleeping arrangements. Knowing Alex would learn of their unmarried status when he got to Elmira, Jana and Keeley had to tell him that they were posing as husband and wife and sharing a room for reasons they had to keep secret. He understood, and Jana had a cot sent up to their room for her use, and Keeley and Alex shared the bed.

Jana and Keeley waited for Alex to fall asleep to avoid rousing his curiosity while they devised their cipher system for President Johnson. It was less sophisticated than Miss Lizzie's, but more complex than a coded statement, such as: *Ma caring for Pa's wounds at Washington City. She needs help*. This could easily be translated to: *Jana and Keeley were heading to Washington City and they needed backup*. Plus, this kind of coding contained endless possibilities for words and required extensive development and training time, which they didn't have. Theirs was written as follows:

> RULES FOR ENCODING:
>
> Each un-capitalized letter of the Latin alphabet equals two letters up (a = c; y & z wrap around to a & b, respectively). For example, write *handy* as: *jcpfa*.

> Where the same letter occurs consecutively, capitalize and write the second letter as a Roman numeral (I = 1; V = 5; X = 10) based upon that letter's numerical position in the Latin alphabet. For example, write *egg* as *giVII* (e = g; g = i; g = VII).
>
> Putting it all together, write *we need help* as: *yg pgVf jgnr.*
>
> RULES FOR DECODING:
>
> Reverse the instructions for encoding; thus, *yg* in the above example would be: y = w and g = e to spell *we.*

They sealed it inside an envelope, and, by the dark of night, Keeley slipped out of the hotel and to the White House, where he hand-delivered their cipher to Thomas Pendel for President Johnson's eyes only.

Early the next morning, Jana and Keeley arrived at the *Baltimore & Ohio Railroad* depot with Alex, who marched tall and proud in his store-bought shirt, light coat, knickers, hat, and brogans. While Keeley purchased three tickets for the 6:00 a.m. train and sent a telegram to Elmira to alert Jana's parents of their late-evening arrival on June 14th and new companion, Jana and Alex stayed out of sight of the hawkish railroad agent. They wished to avoid him seeing the three of them together and John Woodcock's learning of the boy's deception. Although, Jana believed Woodcock would deem his former errand boy irrelevant.

Alex enjoyed his train travel. He declared his favorite part of the trip, above the beautiful sights, was the three of them getting to know each other better. He pummeled them with scads of questions about themselves, the Bradys, and the farm. One of his first: "As I told you before, I've been shuffled around to a few families, and the kids hated having me around, even if I was only there for hard labor. Do you think your sisters will too?"

After Jana and Keeley shared a look of sympathy, Jana said, "I'll let Keeley answer your question since he was in your boat with my sisters at one time."

"Don't worry yarself, lad. Ye've got the advantage. They didn't have a brother growing up, and now they'll have two. They're going to embrace ye at first sight as they did meself." He ruffled Alex's washed and wavy locks. "Ye'll see."

Come night, with nothing but darkness outside of the train's plate-glass window, Alex curled up in his skimpy space between Jana and Keeley, nestled his head into Jana's arm, propped his legs across Keeley's lap, and fell into a restful sleep by the sound of his soft, easy snores.

Jana and Keeley smiled at each other, and Jana knew he was also thinking: *How could we have avoided already falling in love with him?* Turning her smile down at Alex, Jana felt her heart fluttering. She wondered if she was feeling the affection of a mother or sibling toward this sleeping boy with the face of an angel and a world of hurt already having encumbered his young life. She figured it would take several close interactions with him on the home front to find out, and she was disappointed at being hampered from getting started right away. When her mind conjured up her favorite mottos: *things happen for a reason* and *timing is everything*, she relaxed every muscle in her body, resigned to letting matters evolve as they will.

Although Alex was also disappointed to learn Jana and Keeley would be leaving him behind for some time, he got used to the idea with every picture Jana and Keeley painted of the lovely Bradys and his new home. His worries fled on the wings of the chirpy night crickets when the Bradys showed up at the Elmira depot for their arrival at 9:00 p.m. and cheered them off the train.

Jana knew she could count on her family to roll out the red carpet and treat Alex like royalty: Pa shook his hand, Ma assured him that he'd have his own bed, Rachel and Rebecca offered to introduce him to other boys his age, Eliza promised to take him horseback riding and hunting, and a wide-eyed Molly (awake well beyond her bedtime) gifted him her rag doll, which Alex graciously accepted.

Following the crack of dawn on June 16th, Jana and Keeley were back at the Elmira depot to catch the train to Shohola, Pennsylvania.

"All aboard!" the conductor cried out at 7:45 a.m.

After the Bradys and Alex wished them a safe and prosperous journey, Jana and Keeley embarked the rearmost wooden car of eight and dropped into the last upholstered bench, away from the other passengers so they could more freely discuss their assignment.

The conductor took their and everyone else's tickets in their car, then exited through the forward door, onto a connecting platform, and into the back door of the next car. Presumably, he'd finished collecting tickets when the train started its chug out of the depot at 8:00 a.m. sharp.

Jana and Keeley focused mostly on Alex as they waved goodbye to him and their family. They had discussed feeling torn between staying home to care for him and proceeding with their mission. But they agreed it wouldn't be fair to rescind their promise to President Johnson to search for the army payroll. Besides, Alex was in the best of hands, and he'd already settled in and taken to doing chores alongside Pa.

Ma and Pa were elated with Jana and Keeley's decision to legally adopt Alex after they were married; however, they cautioned against telling Alex until they arrived home safely, especially when they heard about the extra danger in there potentially being more than one party in the hunt for the lost treasury. Ma emphasized that it would do no good for Alex's mental health to get his hopes up to gaining parents, only to lose them. Ma and Pa also hated to see Jana and Keeley go, but they understood. After all of their preaching about fighting for one's country at the sacrifice of one's self, Ma and Pa knew they'd be hypocrites to try talking Jana and Keeley out of going.

When the Bradys and Alex disappeared from sight, Jana dropped a paper bag, which Ma had filled with slices of cake on the space between her and Keeley. Then, she removed and set her straw hat atop her large carpetbag between her feet. Heaving a huge sigh, she said, "The past five days have been a whirlwind."

"Aye, we accomplished a fair amount," Keeley said, referring to their roundtrip between Elmira and Washington, taking Alex under their wings and getting him acclimated to his new surroundings, packing clothes and toiletries, and combing through the archives of the Elmira *Advertiser* for news about the Shohola catastrophe.

Their last bit of business at home had involved telegraphing Leanne and Charlie, requesting their backup. They weren't exactly sure where their investigation in Shohola would lead since the prisoners aboard the train had fought mostly in regiments from Virginia, North Carolina, and Georgia, so Washington seemed the best rendezvous point for quickest access to all three states and the safest place to send telegrams. They assigned Leanne and Charlie a particular boarding house, where Jana and Keeley's telegrams would be delivered, and a date of arrival no sooner or later than June 19th, when Jana and Keeley figured to have their investigation in Shohola wrapped up. Suspicious of telegraph operators along the way, who could be bribed by those trailing her and Keeley to divulge the contents of their dispatches, Jana and Keeley asked Pa to meet Leanne and Charlie's train during its brief stop at the Elmira depot and personally hand them the same cryptograph they'd invented for President Johnson, along with a request that they commit it to memory, then destroy it. Pa would also give Leanne and Charlie money out of Jana and Keeley's generous stipend from President

Johnson and the *Erie Railway* for their travel and boarding expenses.

Patting Keeley's hand, Jana said, "There's no rest for the weary. We should get started examining our assemblage of newspaper correspondences. We need to outline our field investigation before we reach Shohola."

"Aye, we can't afford to waste time when we get there."

Huddling together, they took turns silently reading through each of the mimeographed correspondences of the Philadelphia *Inquirer*, New York *Tribune,* and Philadelphia *Daily Age* and a transcript alleged to have originated from the Port Jervis *Tri-States Union*. Then, they developed a brief summary of the train wreck, which, with his more legible handwriting, Keeley scratched out within a notepad of yellow-lined foolscap:

> On July 15, 1864, at approximately 2:50 p.m., about one-and-a-half miles above the sleepy village of Shohola, Pennsylvania, an eastbound fifty-car coal train and a westbound seventeen-car prisoner train collided on the single tracks of the *Erie Railway*. The tragic wreck occurred at King and Fuller's Cut—the severest curve in the region, where the visibility was reduced to fifty feet on either side—making it impossible for two trains traveling at a combined speed of thirty-miles-per-hour to apply their brakes in time to avoid the crash.
>
> Per trafficking rules for railroading along single tracks, a branch line (in this case, the coal train) was to be detained at a junction (in this case, Lackawaxen, Pennsylvania) until *both* a signal train (regularly scheduled train flying signal flags for an "extra" behind it) and the "extra" (train with special right-of-way status—in this case, the prisoner train) passed by. Due to a few delays, the "extra" or prisoner train ran four hours late behind its signal train.

Next, and, muted by the rumble of their train car along the single-track mainline of the *Erie Railway* to eavesdroppers, they began a more intensive study of their archival research. Jana transcribed highpoints that sprang off the pages of their newspaper articles for Keeley to jot down in his pad of paper. They finished the process one-third of the way into their eight-hour trip, which had already included a few stops for water and wood at primary and secondary stations and, thankfully, only one whistle stop for the embarkation of passengers who flagged down a passing train from a small shed in a remote area.

Assembling the sheaf of newspapers from the pleats of her gingham skirt, Jana refolded and stowed them in her carpetbag. "I need a respite," she said, pressing her hands against her roiling stomach.

Keeley hooked an eyebrow. "The color o' yar cheeks is alternating between the green and white o' yar checked skirt, me lass. Are ye ill?"

"I'm a little queasy from riding and reading."

"Ye might feel better if ye were to have a nibble o' the lemon cake yar ma sent along." He tucked his pencil in his breast pocket, then stretched and yawned. "I meself could use a boost o' energy after all o' our studying."

"I think you're right." Jana fished two generous slices from the crackly paper bag and doled them out. Before she bit into hers, she mustered up a teasing twinkle in her eye. "I last felt this nauseous riding the train between my lectures in Buffalo and Seneca Falls after I read your letter to me over and over and over again, until I had it committed to my memory."

Keeley slapped his hand over his mouth to avert a spray of food. "So, y'are saying I made ye sick?"

Elbowing him, Jana said, "No, dummy. Your letter gave me hope that, through your amnesia, you were falling in love with me again."

"As ye know I did. And me love for ye has grown deeper since the recovery o' me memory." He pinned her beneath a flirtatious grin. "Speaking o' memory, how's yars? Do ye remember the words o' me letter?"

"I do." Jana licked crumbs from her lips and closed her eyes. When the letter spilled out of a file in her mind and onto the black backdrop of her eyelids, she recited:

> Dear Jana Lass,
>
> When I feel the love that yar ma, pa, and sisters have for ye, I wish I was with ye guiding yar safe return to them. Yar ma and pa insist on me staying home, where the air seems favorable to me health, though. But I want ye to know that all ye need to do is send up a smoke signal, and I'll be by yar side faster than an artilleryman can pull a lanyard to fire his cannon.
>
> Fond regards,
> Keeley

Concluding her narration, Jana opened her eyes, lifted her chin, and sniffed the air. "So there. If that doesn't prove my love for you, Keeley Cassidy, I don't know what will."

They shared a laugh before falling silent to gobble their treats. Swaying with their car's roll over tracks conforming to the severely meandering Delaware River southeastward along the New York-Pennsylvania border, they rested their heads against each other and appreciated the landscape sliding past their window. Rugged rocky crags, backed largely by a wilderness of scrub pine and oak trees, yielded to fields of rye, oat, wheat, and corn or pastures with grazing cows. Once they were treated to a bald eagle's launch from a pine branch and skyward soar; another time to a herd of white-tailed doe loping into the woods with their spotted young.

With only a few hours left until arrival at their destination, Jana broke their lull. "I'm feeling much better and"—she brushed cake crumbs from her lap—"as much as it pains me to detach my eyes from Mother Nature's bounties, we have lots of work to do to narrow our field visits and interviews."

"Aye, I wondered how long it'd take the hound in ye to pick back up the scent," Keeley said, retrieving his pencil from his pocket and notepad from his wool-trousered lap.

In dissecting their notes, four categorical questions emerged. Beneath each, Jana and Keeley assigned all of their highpoints, along with extrapolations. Then, they sat back to review Keeley's artistic canvass of scribbles, made under the duress of their jittery train car:

1. Was *Erie-Railway* Dispatcher Douglas "Duffy" Kent Negligent or Criminal?

    He was unequivocally responsible for clearing the coal train through the junction.

    Purportedly, he'd shown up at his post reeking of alcohol. Although the presiding jury blamed the railroad for having re-hired this notorious drunk a few times, it exposed Duffy's weakness, and he fled from his community's ostracism and hasn't been seen since.

    Case for Negligence: If Duffy was inebriated, did he confuse himself or did someone else confuse him about the prisoner train having already passed through the junction behind its signal train?

    Case for Criminality: Did he feign inebriation by pouring alcohol on himself to capitalize on his reputation as a drunk after someone promised him wealth to clear the coal train through or to look the other way while someone else did it?

Looking up from their notes and drawing Keeley's eyes to hers, Jana said, "Either case above could explain why Duffy Kent omitted sending a telegraph to the dispatcher in Shohola reporting he'd waved the coal train through the junction."

"Aye, and why Duffy attended another party hours after the crash. Either he was truly ignorant o' his tragic deed and unable to abstain from the lure o' alcohol or he was acting both parts as a repeat performance at his post on the fateful day to cover up his criminal behavior."

After Keeley recorded their supporting remarks, they proceeded to the next question:

2. "Was the Coal Train in a Hurry?" (Title of one of the articles in the Philadelphia *Press* of July 18, 1864).

    A few days prior to the train wreck, the federal government, in an unprecedented move, seized the *Philadelphia & Reading Railroad* for the vital shipment of coal to the war effort when the *P&R* and its striking crews failed to come to a resolution over wage increases.

    The *Erie Railway* was experiencing the same grumblings from their employees. Any strikes and resultant government takeover would seriously jeopardize the railroad's bountiful gains from its shipment of coal on its branch line (from mines in Honesdale, Pennsylvania, to the eastern ports of Philadelphia and New York).

"As the article suggests," Jana said, "do you really think the *Erie Railway* would've been desperate enough to pressure its dispatchers or engineers into observing a dangerously new policy of gambling on beating any potential oncoming train as far as it could along its single tracks?"

"I can't say, me lass, but, in the railroad's defense, the prisoner train was delayed four hours behind its signal train. That, combined with common dispatch errors o' nightmarishly heavy traffic from daily scheduled and unscheduled public, freight, and coal trains competing for the same single tracks, makes it conceivable for even a competent dispatcher to err in reporting a signal train and its extra as having already passed through a junction."

"A very strong case for the collision truly being nothing more than an accident," Jana said. While Keeley again recorded their supporting remarks, Jana slipped out of her bolero coat and opened the bottom sash of their window and leaned her face into the airflow. "I better have you read the rest of our notes to me. I feel a little flushed, and my sickness from the motion is coming on again."

"Why don't we take another break, me lass?"

"Thanks for your concern, but"—Jana reclined her head into the lustrous nap of their velvet-covered seat and stared at the stationary bench ahead of them—"with your help, I'm perfectly capable of pressing on."

Keeley read their next question and postulations aloud:

3. Was Coal-Train Engineer Sam Hoitt Part of Some Bigger Conspiracy?

   The only survivor of his and the opposing engine crews, Sam contended he'd spotted the prisoner train in the nick of time for him to jump before impact, but too late for him to warn his fire-and-brake-men.

   He later testified he was never told about the presence of an opposing prisoner train along the single tracks.

   He could've been in collusion with Duffy and someone else, who'd promised both him and Duffy great wealth to cause the collision.

"The latter point would support Sam Hoitt's keener watch than his crewmen for another train coming around a sharp bend," Jana said, keeping her face angled toward the flow of air spiked with burning wood from the steam locomotive.

"Aye, and it seems testimony by his conductor to corroborate Hoitt's claim he was never told about the opposing prisoner train heading toward his when he stopped at Lackawaxen Junction is conspicuously absent." Again, Keeley recorded their supporting remarks and continued his narration:

> 4. Did Several Delays Along the Tracks Create Opportunities for Mischief?
>
> In Jersey City (New Jersey), where the greenbacks were secreted in the caboose and the prisoners boarded their extra, a delay of an hour and a half occurred while the captain of the guards returned to the steamer, which had shipped the prisoners up the Atlantic from the overcrowded prison at Point Lookout, Maryland, to hunt down three escapees. And, in Port Jervis (New York), the train stopped for water and wood to fuel the steam locomotive.
>
> During these layovers, curiosity seekers turned out to commune with the prisoners aboard their train.

"Could these delays have given some villain, who was tracking the army payroll and knowledgeable of the *Erie Railway's* routes and schedules for both its main-and-branch lines, ample time to plot a collision between the coal-and-prisoner trains?" Jana posed.

"Aye, and the lengthy delay in Jersey City could've given a villain ample time to recruit Rebel prisoners in the robbery. Any soldier would feel fortunate after he learns that the train he's riding is destined to collide with another and that the odds o' his escaping death riding in his rearward car are much higher than his dying from disease, malnutrition, or exposure to the elements in prison."

Jana pondered a soldier's fear of imprisonment. A wretched stain on her home city's otherwise unblemished history would eternally be the deaths of nearly three thousand out of a little over twelve thousand Rebels incarcerated at Elmira Prison in the one year of its existence. This 24.5% mortality rate was just shy of the highest of 28.7% for the infamous Andersonville Prison in Georgia. *It's no wonder the Rebel inmates had dubbed Elmira Prison "Hellmira."*

Continuing his thought, Keeley said, "And, for risking his life, even the scrupulous soldier could easily be convinced: Why not add to me fortune by allowing meself a slice o' a treasury I'm being asked to steal?"

Keeley recorded their final supporting remarks, and Jana noted aloud, "All of our postulations bring us right back around to John Woodcock."

"Aye, his state of bankruptcy, connections to Shohola and the *Erie Railway*, and his reaction at the hotel tell meself he's somehow involved in the theft."

"He would've definitely had access to the dispatcher and coal-train engineer, and he could've enticed them with a percentage of the bounty to nudge the accident along." Jana chewed on her bottom lip. "I hate to believe in such a malicious plot, but, if it turns out to be true, I can't see one man orchestrating such a sophisticated sequence of events. I suppose John Woodcock could be a puppet of the KGC. After all, Judge Advocate General Holt affirmed there were at least five-hundred-thousand Northerners within the secret society; some of them could be chameleons in positions of authority within the federal government and the *Erie Railway*."

"It was unsettling for meself to believe the KGC could be coldhearted enough to make use o' a Union payroll from a train wreck that killed so many o' its own soldiers. Now, ye expect meself to consider it could've coordinated a collision condoning a mass murdering o' its own people?" Keeley frowned, the skin of his brow puckering. "That surpasses all o' me wildest nightmares. But"—he scanned the train car, his eyes grazing the fancy hats of each dapperly dressed gentlemen—"as President Johnson said, 'greed and power for personal or political gain have historically trumped loyalty and patriotism.'"

"To your point, maybe the KGC wouldn't condone a mass murdering of their own, but they know John Woodcock did, and now they're blackmailing him into giving up the payroll."

"That's an interesting twist, me lass, and I'd much rather believe that o' the KGC than their having plotted to murder their own for it."

"Or there could be a far less malicious and simple explanation," Jana said. "Maybe a few of the prisoners overheard the guards talking about the payroll, and they acted alone in the heist. And maybe John Woodcock knew of the payroll through his political connections, but he lacked designs on it until he learned of the crash. After which, he sent feelers out about the fate of the treasury, and now he's merely tracking it, just as we are."

"Or, if he's at the helm o' the sabotage, regardless o' whether or not he's in thick with the KGC, he's hired two goons to track us. That means the escaped prisoners have—"

Jana interjected. "Double-crossed him."

"Aye, and there's one other distressing element. If Woodcock isn't in thick with the KGC and not in the business o' sabotage, I'll wager, if he knew o' the army payroll, so did the all-seeing KGC. We could be battling three separate parties for the money, and we still don't know how many o' the five Rebel escapees we're up against."

"Given the bulkiness of the money chest," Jana said, "there has to be at least two prisoners involved."

In unison with their move out of the junction at Lackawaxen, Keeley said, "We accepted this mission fully aware o' its dangers, but we might want to brace ourselves for a fight from more than one angle."

Speaking of bracing themselves, Jana sat up rigid and Keeley followed suit as they prepared to meet the most dangerous fragment of the *Erie Railway's* few tracks in Pennsylvania, laid between the majority of its route through New York, starting at Piermont on the Hudson River and terminating in Buffalo. Until now, Jana had never appreciated the extreme risk to her life in riding this section of the railroad. But...after her and Keeley's thorough examination of the Shohola train wreck, Jana realized just how much her life was in the hands of the engineer. She prayed there wasn't a beguiling chest of two million dollars aboard their train.

Jana stared off into no man's land, trying to empty her mind of all thoughts and fears.

Ten tense minutes passed.

Whoo, whoooooo…whoo, whoooooo…whoo, whooooooo! The urgency behind the whistle's blare and the squealing of the brakes to slow the train considerably from twenty miles per hour conveyed the engineer was taking every possible precaution to avoid a repeat of the greatest train disaster during the war and historically as far as Jana knew.

Upon the locomotive's tug into the harrowing convex *S* of King and Fuller's Cut (named for the construction contractors), Jana's morbid prophecy of tipping over and tumbling down the embankment into the river rattled her. She slammed her window shut. *As though that will help anything in a crash*, she thought. Then, she leaned into Keeley's open arm and toward the opposite side of their coach in its embrace of the shaggy cliff of trees and brush.

Keeley peeked around her and whistled. "Now there's a sheer drop-off down to the river to oblige a fast and furious roll o' a chest weighted down with money bags."

Jana squeezed her eyes tight to block out the vexing view. Against the shadowy stage of her eyelids, a ghoulish re-creation of the wreck—evoked by accounts within their newspaper articles—played out: The upended locomotives of the prisoner and coal trains appearing as two behemoth Cyclopes leaning against each other, sapped of energy from their bloody clash and glowering at one another through their solo pilot lanterns. The prisoner train's tender flipped onto its head, crushing the engineer and fireman to death beneath its load of cordwood. The forward-most boxcar jammed into a space of less than six feet, all but one of its thirty-eight occupants squished together and sent to heaven as sardines in a tin. The next sixteen cars down the line chopped up into matchsticks or severely damaged, and their victims strewn trackside or mangled, impaled, or beheaded between their passageways or on their iron rods and timbers.

Opening her eyes and hoping to erase the images, Jana continued to be haunted by the journalistic accounts. She cringed to the heart-wrenching sounds described of the collision: The initial impact likened to the boom of a mighty cannon. The moans, shrieks, and wails of the wounded and dying captives, guards, and trainmen forced her to re-live the cries of soldiers whom she'd once evacuated from the battlefield. Vigorously rubbing her arms to ease her shivers of dread, Jana wondered if she'd ever shed the venomous memories of war.

Keeley tightened his hug around her, easing her distress.

Bowing her head to avoid his scrutiny, Jana said, "The war might be over, but there's much healing to do as a country before we can be whole again." She began twirling a mother-of-pearl button on her cotton blouse. "It's not just the thrill adventure has over me, Keeley."

He lifted her chin with the pulsating tip of his forefinger and locked his apprehensive eyes into hers. "What are ye saying, me lass?"

Matching the intensity of his stare, Jana said, "I answered President Lincoln's call to fight for the preservation of the Union and the abolition of slavery. I begged to spy in Richmond to help free you and other Yankee prisoners. I answered the suffragists' call to help advance the cause for woman's equal rights. Now, I fear I've dragged you into following me in answering President Johnson's call to recoup a Union payroll, which might put us in extreme peril." She paused to contemplate her next words carefully so as not to hurt him.

"Go on, me lass."

"I don't know if I'll ever be able to resist the call to fight for my country, no matter the cost to myself. As you've heard me say ad nauseam, it's been sown into my nature by three generations of Bradys, but the roots run deeper from the development of my own convictions." Digging her nails into her palms, she tried putting a lid on her simmering rage to keep it from boiling over. "Part of it means bringing those to justice who'd intentionally harm others in pursuit of personal or political gain." Jana thought of Leanne—always inclined to take on bullies. If she and Keeley were to confirm evildoers had cost the lives of so many innocent men in the Shohola train wreck, Jana wondered what she'd do when she caught up with them. Would she be able to control herself from taking matters into her own hands and stringing them up to a tree?

"I admire yar convictions, me lass, but. . ." his voice trailed off, and his prominent Adam's apple skittered up and down to his apparent desire to swallow his next utterance.

"But what?"

Looking away, he said in a near whisper, "I'd never get in the way o' them, me lass."

Would he move out of the way of them, though? Jana wondered to the mournful inflection in his tone. Her cheek smarted, as if to a slap across her face, warning she could die a lonely, old spinster. Could she give up a life with Keeley to save the world? Her instincts confirmed this trip was definitely as much about her own self-enlightenment as it was tracking the money and rounding up the bad guys. She rested her head against the plate glass of her window, tired of her morbid thoughts.

Thankfully, their train chugged through King and Fuller's Cut without incident and, a few minutes later, slid to a stop before Shohola's small depot close to its scheduled arrival of 4:00 p.m.

While baggage handlers gathered their trunks and loaded them onto a carriage, Jana and Keeley stole glances around the platform. They were relieved when no one paid them excessive interest.

The wagoner transported them a short distance to the three-story Shohola Glen Hotel, where, as they'd done at Willard's Hotel, they registered as Mr. and Mrs. Keeley Cassidy. Upon Jana's inquiry of the clerk, they were disappointed to learn of "Uncle" Chauncey Thomas's absence; the hotel's owner might've been able to provide some clues into their probe through conversations he'd had with the wounded prisoners and guards whom he'd cared for at his place. Unfortunately, she and Keeley would be long gone by the time he returned from his business trip. However, they were delighted at their sleeping quarters, which included a bed large enough for them to share and hang a bedsheet diagonally between them, as they'd planned to do at Willard's in Washington until Alex's overnight stay with them changed it. They freshened up and went downstairs to one of the second-floor dining rooms. Since it was void of other diners, the youthful waiter let them sit anywhere. They chose a table away from the window and hall, where they were risk free of being overheard or having their lips read.

Their server seated them, then whisked away with their order of beef stew, boiled potatoes, cornbread, and custard.

When he returned and was pouring their water and wine, Keeley nodded for Jana to take the reins of their inquiry.

"My husband and I have only just arrived here, but Shohola

strikes us as a peaceful place."

"Odd you should mention it. The Lenni Lenape Indians' name for Shohola is *Place of Peace*."

Jana couldn't help thinking, *A year ago, Shohola was anything but a place of peace.* "Are you from around here?" she asked their waiter.

His face lit up as though she was his very first customer to have an interest in him beyond his service. "I am. Born and raised on a farm within the township, about two miles upriver."

Keeley piped in. "Anywhere near where the two trains collided last year?"

"Too close for comfort." He paled. "Although Farmer Vogt and his son were the first to witness the collision from high up on a hill where they were cutting rye, my family and I were amongst the first to respond, once we identified the earsplitting crash and quaking earth for what it was."

On the one hand, Jana felt their waiter's pain; on the other, she was excited by her sense he had something important to impart.

"I'm sorry, lad, if me question has caused ye distress."

Shuddering, he said, "I wished I'd been old enough to be off fighting so I wouldn't have witnessed the ghastly aftereffects."

"I don't mean to diminish what ye witnessed, lad, but imagine the wounded and dying from the train wreck lying together in one tragic heap and magnify it by a hundred and ye get the aftermath of battle. Only add watching yar family and friends mowed down right in front o' ye day after day. Be glad ye weren't old enough to fight."

Staring out through a window, their waiter seemed to speak his next thought aloud. "I guess the grass isn't always greener on the other side." His soft brown eyes returned to them. "My mother always tells me that, and I reckon I get what she means now."

Keeley smiled. "Ye'll find over time, the bad memories lose their bite."

Nodding his head in gratitude, the youth peeked over the shoulder of his homespun coat and shirt. "I'd better get to the kitchen in case the cook needs help."

"Wait," Jana said. "We're interested in seeing the gravesite of those who died in the collision. Would you be able to point us there?" To his inquisitive look, her mind spun for a plausible explanation. It struck gold. "One of the guards was an uncle of mine." Jana forced her lips into a quiver and dabbed her fake tears with her linen table napkin. "We were very close, and I'd like to pay my respects."

"Oh, I'm truly sorry for your loss, ma'am."

"Thank you. I need to make sense of this horrible tragedy for my own healing. You understand, don't you?"

"I do, and I can take you to the gravesite, if you'd like."

Determined to keep their server from learning their business, Jana said, "I'm sure you're busy. We could rent a wagon and mule from the livery, if—"

He cut her off. "I have permission to cross Farmer Vogt's property, and you might be interested in a stop beforehand to learn about a vigil to the crude cemetery." When he saw he'd piqued Jana and Keeley's interest, he said, "I'll let Tobias Müller tell you all about it. I don't have to work at the inn tomorrow"—he frowned—"but I do on the farm. After our interview with Mr. Müller, I'll have to leave you trackside with instructions to the burial site and return later to pick you up."

Jana sighed in silent relief to have him out of their way for their search. "Don't worry about us. You should be where you're needed most."

"Aye, we'll be fine, lad."

"How about I come to call around 7:00 a.m.?"

"That would be wonderful," Jana said.

"If we're to be traveling companions, lad, we might want to introduce ourselves," Keeley said. "We're Mr. and Mrs. Cassidy, but ye may call us Keeley and Jana."

Their waiter bowed. "It's a pleasure to meet you. I'm Franz

Wilheim, and you may call me Franz." Eyeing Jana's attire, he said to her, "You might want to wear something you don't mind getting roughed up. You'll be trudging through briars and bogs."

"Anticipating as much, I have a suitable outfit, and we'll be ready and waiting," Jana said, trying to keep herself from bouncing off her chair to the tin ceiling.

When they returned to their room, Jana donned a cotton nightgown, which bared the skin of her neck only, and Keeley donned his calf-length nightshirt. They were too tired and lazy to hang a bedsheet between them so they crawled into bed, with Jana situated beneath the sheet and quilt and Keeley beneath the quilt but atop the sheet.

"It's a most twisted arrangement, me lass"—he grinned flirtatiously as he brushed strands of her unbound tresses away from her cheek and kissed it—"but it'll guard against any temptations in the wee hours o' the night." With a groan, he fluffed up and propped his head on his feather pillow, snuggled as close to her as possible, and closed his eyes.

Keeley's quiet breathing told Jana that he'd somehow managed to fall fast asleep, even while her mind still raced over the prospect of discovery tomorrow. She matched her breath to his and luxuriated in the heat emanating from his body. *I'm so glad he's here with me*, she thought as she drifted into a slumber.

Jana awakened to the soft tangerine light of dawn sifting into their room around the edges of the unfurled window shade. She was surprised to feel more rested than she ought to with her tossing and turning all through the night. Rolling over, she found Keeley's eyes smiling at her.

"Good morning, me love." He cradled her, kissed her forehead, and gazed upon her with a yearning to swallow her up.

A passionate blaze inside Jana sent her to the brink of encouraging him onward, and she was glad when, with an agonizing sigh, he spun away from her and sprang out of bed. While he shuffled about the room, collecting his toiletries and clothes, Jana ogled his muscular calves, visible below his long nightshirt.

He turned and gave her a wink when he caught her staring.

Although she laughed, she failed to blush. By sheer necessity, during her days marching with the cavalry, she'd lost her modesty after baring her butt to her cavalry comrades while toileting—once even to Keeley when he followed her into the woods in an attempt to validate he was falling in love with a woman. Unfortunate for him, but fortunate for her, in a squat, she'd easily hidden her feminine part.

Keeley yielded the dressing screen and washstand to Jana, who chose to wear a blouse and skirt down to the dining room to avoid quizzical looks or interrogations over the masculine costume she'd don for their outing that day.

After a tasty breakfast of Johnnie cakes, pork sausage, mixed berries, and Jana's favorite brand of *Folger's* coffee, they returned to their room so Jana could change.

Slinging the strap of his water-filled canteen over his shoulder, Keeley eyed Jana's britches, coat, hat, and riding boots. "So, we're back to playing a man, are we, me lass? No more hugs or kisses for ye until y'are back in women's attire. It's bad enough yar pa ribs meself sometimes about falling in love with ye when ye were dressed as a soldier, but I won't have outsiders questioning me sexual preferences."

Jana giggled. "You must know by now, Pa teases you because he's fond of you. Anyway, I came prepared as I see you did for battling the bogs, briars, and rough roads." She holstered her Colt onto her belt and buttoned up her summer riding coat to hide it, whereas Keeley kept his visible to discourage any transgressions. Pulling her hat low over her face, she followed Keeley closely down the stairs and outside. Their footsteps echoed as they crossed a sprawling front porch, its floorboards forming a roof over the ground level, where the tavern was located.

Keeley leaned his forearm against a square column at the landing of the steps. "What do ye suppose the day might bring, me lass?"

To Franz's arrival in his creaky wagon, Jana rubbed her hands together vigorously and said, "I hope an army payroll."

"Aye, and we're on the brink o' finding out, me lass."

Franz called out, "Good morning." He started to tip his hat at them, then hesitated when he glimpsed Jana's outfit.

Jana held her elbows out to show her patches. "I told you I had the right clothes to wrestle the wilderness."

"Aye, she's me little tomboy." Keeley's cheeks reddened and his lips pinched together as he strained not to laugh. He composed himself long enough to say, "Her ma and pa paid meself handsomely to take her off their hands. Regretfully, I have to ask them for a bigger dowry since she eats more than meself."

Jana backhanded his good arm, and she and Franz joined his laughter.

To their waning hoots, Franz said, "You two make a happy couple. I hope I find someone who fits me as perfectly as"—he held up his gloved hands—"these do my hands."

"That's very kind of you to say, Franz," Jana said to her and Keeley's exchange of reverent regard.

Keeley sobered to say, "Speaking o' food, lad, if ye think we'll be out too late for supper, should we ask the cook to put something aside for us?"

Jana flashed him a smile that telegraphed: *Go ahead and rib me about my appetite, but I know you're truly concerned about me.* She silently gave thanks for having Keeley in her life, and she'd never let go of him without a huge fight.

"We'll be back long before the last dining hour." Franz pointed his thumb at a wicker basket on the wagon bed. "My ma felt badly about my having to skip guiding you, so she packed you a dinner hearty enough to tide you over until breakfast tomorrow morning."

Touching her heart, Jana said, "That's awfully sweet of her, and we're grateful for your support too."

"Aye, please, be sure to pass along our gratitude to yar ma," Keeley said.

"If your stay here happens to get extended, you'll find folks around here are very charitable. In fact, my ma and many other women from Shohola and Barryville, across the river in New York, came by the dozens bringing milk, bread, cake, tea, coffee, and sheets and other cloth to make into bandages to minister to the maimed from the train wreck. Some donated their last loaf of bread or slab of meat." He peeked around them at the hotel and chuckled. "Although he has the bad fortune of being an Englishman, we Germans respect Uncle Chauncey for his having opened his hotel, home, and store to the wounded and dying. And his ongoing charity keeps this community strong."

"Unfortunately, we must be on our way tomorrow, but we'll definitely consider returning some day when we have more time to tour your beautiful community," Jana said.

Franz gestured Jana and Keeley aboard. Releasing the screechy wagon brake, he clicked his cheek simultaneously with a gentle flick of the reins across the mule's sorrel rump to set it into a brisk trot.

Over the clippity-clop of the mule's hoofs against the dewy but hard surface, Jana said, "Do you know anything about Duffy Kent, the railroad dispatcher who passed the coal train through to colliding with the prisoner train?"

"I didn't know him personally, but he had a bad reputation as a drunkard. In fact, he was run out of town after a jury determined he was intoxicated *again* at his post and the likely cause of the crash, even though they held the *Erie Railway* liable for re-hiring him a few times." Franz only corroborated what Jana and Keeley had gleaned from their newspaper articles.

Jana said, "Do you know if the residents of this area would consider him spiteful?"

"Maybe carefree and foolhardy in his fancy for parties, but I don't ever recall anyone referring to him as spiteful."

Following Jana's line of questioning, Keeley said, "Do ye know anything o' the character o' the coal-train engineer, Sam Hoitt?"

"No, but he must be respectable."

"Why do ye say that, lad?"

"No man who'd risk blowing himself up to try saving his fireman and then the engineer and fireman of the prisoner train would compromise the lives of others, just to transport his coal to its ports on time."

Jana smiled at Franz. "I appreciate your entertaining our questions. It's all part of my coming to terms with the tragedy."

"Think nothing of it. I'm happy to oblige in any way I can, so ask away."

"I can't think of anything else right now," Jana said, settling back against the backboard of their bench to enjoy the ride along the country road, which wound through woods of leafy-and-needled trees and open lands robed in healthy stalks of corn, rye, oat, and wheat.

After curving northward, Franz steered the mule across an uncovered wooden bridge over a narrow brook, and, a short distance later, he slowed the wagon. The aroma of wash soap skipped with the nimble breeze to greet Jana's nostrils seconds before Franz parked on the south side of a modest clapboard house.

A matronly woman rose on her toes to peer over the bedsheet she'd just pinned to her clothesline, stretched taut for, at least, a hundred yards between the house and a pine tree. She greeted Franz with a smile, plumping up her already cherubic cheeks. Before he could reply, she was inviting her callers in for coffee and freshly baked donuts.

Franz nodded toward her large tin tub teeming with laundry. "We appreciate your generous offer, Mrs. Müller, but we don't want to interrupt your wash, and these good folks' time is limited. They'd like to speak with Mr. Müller about the train collision a year ago before we're off on other urgent business. Is he handy?"

Mrs. Müller sidestepped the dripping bedsheet and stood where they could more fully see her. Drying her hands on her apron, tightly cinched around her pudgy mid-section, she looked toward the growing fields. "Just as he and our sons were doing last year when the trains collided, they are out tending to the crops. Maybe I can help you."

Following introductions, Franz explained Jana's wish to visit her uncle's grave. Then, he said, "With the war behind us, and it not being a secret anymore, I told them nothing more than you sheltered a prisoner who escaped from the train wreck. They're interested in hearing all about him, and especially his nightly ritual. Since it's your story, I thought it would be best if they heard it straight from the horse's mouth."

Mrs. Müller's fingers disappeared beneath the ruffle of her cloth bonnet as she scratched her temple. "As you suspected, Mr. Müller's a better storyteller than me. If you're pressed for time, though, I'll do my best."

"I have no doubt you will, Mrs. Müller," Franz said.

Blowing a tuft of her dark tresses, which had escaped from her bonnet, she beamed as she dove into her narration. "Shortly after Mr. Müller and I returned from aiding the wounded souls from the collision, we discovered an escaped prisoner hiding out in our barn. He said he'd been riding in the last car before the caboose. Fortunate for him, he escaped injury. Although he was homesick, he stayed on and helped us through the fall harvest." She stared past them in a southerly direction. "Such a nice young man, always willing to lend a hand." Switching her eyes back to them, she said, "And sensitive too. His guilt over having survived the train wreck drove him to the burial ground nightly to honor his fallen comrades."

Jana felt Keeley's slight torque in unison with hers. Was he also wondering if the Müller's transient farmhand was one of the thieves?

Fortunately, neither Mrs. Müller nor Franz noticed their reaction with Mrs. Müller prattling on. "Every night, we'd look out the window and see him racing to the graveyard, a lantern swinging in one hand, flowers in his other." She pointed northward, toward the railroad tracks. "Why I bet you can still see the path he beat down on John Vogt's property to the river."

"Can you tell us the name and address of your refugee?" Jana asked.

Mrs. Müller's brows furled like the bedsheet waving in the wind.

Whether she was confused by Jana's question or incongruity between Jana's costume and sex, Jana quickly said, "It would give me great pleasure to write and thank him for his care and vigilance over the dead, especially my uncle who was a guard on the prisoner train."

She shrugged. "I don't see why not. His name's Jedediah Fernsby. He was with the 13th Virginia Infantry Regiment. I don't have his address, but Jed—that's what he preferred we call him—said he lived in Louisa County."

When Keeley flinched, Jana moved her hand imperceptibly to Keeley's, resting on the bench between them, and gave it a light squeeze. He squeezed back to signal they were thinking alike: Could Keeley's caretaker and their friend Versella Stock Barney, also from Louisa County, know Jed Fernsby?

"That's all there is to tell," Mrs. Müller said. "Are you sure you won't come in and sit a spell?"

"No, ma'am, we really should be on our way," Franz said.

"We've taken up enough of your time. I appreciate your tidings." Jana projected a sad mien. "It's a comfort to know my uncle had someone encouraging his spirit into the afterlife with well wishes and flowers."

Franz took up the reins to signal their departure.

"Wait!" Mrs. Müller tapped her forehead. "I almost forgot the best part."

While Keeley followed Jana's earlier cue to sit emotionless, Jana sat on her hands to keep herself from fidgeting with impatience for the lucrative news she sensed was about to be gained.

Mrs. Müller continued, "After Jed left, we learned from the Fischers that the Rebel escapee, whom they sheltered, borrowed their fishing boat to paddle downriver each night. He also alleged a need to visit the burial trench and pay his respects to his fallen comrades. He and Jed must've become friends—probably journeyed back to the South together since they left Shohola at the same time." She slammed her fists on her pudgy hips. "Why Jed would take up with a fella who'd bite the hand of those who hid, housed, and fed him is beyond me. Without a goodbye, the ungrateful man stole the Fischer's boat. Fortunately, it was found a few miles downriver and returned."

"Do you happen to know his name and where he was from?" Jana cleared her throat. "Again, so I can write and thank him too."

Mrs. Müller's voice chilled. "Why on earth would you write such a scoundrel?"

Keeley spoke up, "I meself was imprisoned in Richmond during the war, ma'am, and I can tell ye a man will do just about anything to get home to his loved ones." He half-smiled, half grimaced. "Stealing a fishing boat seems a minor infraction, don't ye think?"

Her icy tone melted. "When you put it that way, young man, I reckon you're right."

Jana marveled at Keeley's power of persuasion. He could probably convince a bank robber to give up a livelihood of thievery to become a man of the cloth. Perhaps he'd have a chance to wave his magic wand during their forthcoming escapades.

Maintaining his charm, Keeley said, "Back to me wife's question. Might ye have a name for the other escaped prisoner?"

Franz answered for her. "Fulton Jibbs."

"That's it," Mrs. Müller said, bobbing her head.

"Did this Fulton Jibbs also serve in the 13th Virginia?" Jana asked.

"I assume so," Franz said. "The Fischers and Fulton suppered with us a few times, and Fulton claimed to be from Louisa County too."

Jana felt the subtle jab of Keeley's elbow in her side on cue with her thought, "*We've no doubt just nailed at least two of our culprits.* Why the *Erie-Railway* investigator overlooked prisoners living in the area made perfectly good sense to Jana—the big-hearted Germans had done a cracking job concealing them. If these charitable people ever discovered their Rebel refugees had used them to get to the money, they might do Jana the favor of stringing them up to a tree, high up on their German Hill.

"If that's all you have for us, Mrs. Müller, we'll be on our way," Franz said.

Waggling her index finger at Franz, she said, "Don't think this qualifies as a visit, young man. Come back soon and bring your ma."

"I promise, Mrs. Müller."

She swept Jana and Keeley up in her good-natured smile. "And if you're ever in town, don't be afraid to stop in."

"Thank you, Mrs. Müller," Jana said, and Keeley added his own utterance of gratitude.

Franz tipped his hat at the kindly woman and resumed their trip.

From their reigning seat high on the hill, Jana and Keeley could see the railroad tracks.

Franz followed their eyes and pointed down to an intervening hill, where the tracks disappeared. "That's King and Fuller's Cut, where the trains collided. John Vogt and his son have a wider view of the tracks where they are now checking their crops, same place as they were a year ago when they saw the collision in the making and were helpless to do anything about it."

"Aye, I don't envy their nightmares."

Jana attempted to extrapolate the expanse of track involved in the accident from the prisoner train alone. Scanning the area, starting from the middle of the cut back to where she estimated the seventeenth car would've landed, she jerked upright at the same time the front wheel dipped into a rut and pitched them about. It masked her movement to her epiphany about the location of the stolen payroll, and she began chewing on her cheek as she mulled it over.

Franz interrupted Jana's thoughts, stopping her short of bloodying the inside of her mouth. "There's one more thing Mrs. Müller forgot to tell you."

"Oh?" Jana said.

"A farmer, who lives below the suspension bridge, had his wagon and mule stolen from his barn, near the time of Jed and Fulton's departure. The wagon had a false bottom, special for carrying escaping slaves through the Underground Railroad."

Jana recollected her and Keeley's wagon ride when they were escaping Richmond, Virginia, after her near hanging. Although they'd spent quality time huddled together beneath a false floor, they constantly feared Jana's being caught and returned to the gallows; Miss Lizzie outdid her own genius when she had the floor covered in manure to deter any military official from stopping them to closely examine the wagon bed's contents.

"Why would they need a wagon with a false bottom?" Franz asked. "What would be so important for them to hide?"

Jana shrugged and nonchalantly said, "In their desperation to get home, they undoubtedly snatched the first wagon they happened upon."

"That's true," Franz said, reining in the mule near a farmhouse, situated close to the railroad tracks.

Breathing a silent sigh of relief, Jana was glad her explanation seemed to have squelched further curiosity on his behalf.

"We've reached the Vogt's place and where you get off," Franz said, pulling the wagon's brake and perusing the homestead and seeing no one about. "It's a shame John and his son are working the fields. Maybe they could've added a few details to the story."

"I'm completely satisfied with your and Mrs. Müller's information. I can't imagine there's anything else to tell," Jana said.

Franz started out of the wagon, and Keeley said, "We can

manage from here, lad."

Upon Jana and Keeley's disembarkation, Franz handed his mother's picnic basket down to them and gave them directions to the gravesite. "I'll meet you back here around 4:00 p.m. Do you have a timepiece to keep track of the hour?"

Jana shot Keeley a silent warning to play along with her whim. "About that," she said to Franz, "how far is it to Shohola from here?"

"A mile and a half along the train tracks."

"Since it's only thirty minutes by foot, would you mind if Keeley and I walked back to the hotel? It's such a beautiful day, and I, at least, could use the exercise."

"Ah, I see," Franz said. "I don't blame you for wanting some quiet time with your grief after you've bid your uncle a proper farewell."

"Yes, thank you for understanding, Franz," Jana said.

Peering at Keeley's canteen, Franz said, "I assume you're all set with water, but, if you run out, Farmer Vogt won't mind you drawing some from his well. You'll find a tin cup in my ma's picnic basket for you to share."

"Speaking of your ma's picnic basket, how should we get it back to you when we're through with it later?" Jana said.

"Drop it at the registration desk. The clerk on duty will hold it for me in the office. I'm not sure I'll see you tomorrow, so I'll say goodbye now." He tipped his hat at them. "I wish you the best in your endeavors. Please, be careful with your footing down the steep embankment. I wouldn't want you to go tumbling down it into the river and get seriously hurt."

"We appreciate the advice, Franz. We'll be careful," Jana said, praying her promise had a stiff backbone behind it and their trip didn't come to an end before it got started.

Jana and Keeley watched Franz disappear around the bend as they trekked toward the railroad tracks.

"Now, me lass, tell meself the point o' our walking back to the hotel. Not that I mind the extra exercise."

"It dawned on me," Jana said, "the money was stowed in the very last car, which would've come to a crashing halt seventeen car lengths below the cut from where the locomotives careened into one another. With the guards' worrying more about establishing the extent of damage and saving lives than securing the payroll and the perimeter against escapes, the bandits would've had only enough time to hide their loot near where they removed it from the train. Later, I highly doubt they would've transferred such a burdensome load this far upriver, out of the way of their home-and-south-bound route, and in the vicinity of the resting place, where they'd risk mourners, snoops, or spirit seekers stumbling upon it."

Keeley frowned at himself. "I never would've thought o' that."

"Don't fret, Keeley, it comes from months of training. In spying, Miss Lizzie taught me to pay equal attention to the smallest of trivialities."

"Ye never cease to amaze meself. It's no wonder Allan Pinkerton and President Johnson have put their faith in ye. All the same, we're here, so don't ye think we ought to comb the area around the gravesite? Jed and Fulton might've thought to stash the money right under everyone's noses, same as ye faked yar death from a heart attack, on yar gallows, in front o' a swarm o' rabid Southerners."

"And, should anyone ask us for a description of the site before we leave town, we need to be convincing. Though, I fear the greenbacks are gone," Jana said despairingly.

"Aye, the boat and false-bottomed wagon seem to suggest that."

"We better get moving; we have a lot of ground to cover."

Jana and Keeley hesitated at the tracks, looking and listening for an oncoming train. Safely crossing to the grassy berm opposite, they were excited to find a worn footpath. They followed it to the core of King and Fuller's Cut and up and over the high railroad embankment. Shimmying down the steep slope, their boot soles rustled up remnants of last fall's dried leaves and earthen rot. The stench put a morbid thought about the dead into Jana's head. Would she find them hovering over their final resting place, motioning for her and Keeley to lend them a hand into the afterlife with song and praise? That they were cheated out of the tradition of their loved ones by their sides cut deeply into Jana's heart. She was glad when only the wooden sentries of the graveyard showed themselves beneath the dense canopy of trees.

"I hope, me lass, that we're not looking upon the effects o', as President Johnson put it, 'greed and power trumping patriotism.'"

Kneeling between the common marker for the forty-eight fallen Confederates and the first marker of seventeen for the Union guards, Jana pressed her palms against both slabs of splintery wood. To the dead, she said, "We vow to put closure to your senseless deaths by sorting out the mystery around your train wreck and, if applicable, bringing the wicked to justice."

"Aye, we'll do just that, me lass."

Abandoning the Confederate burial trench and individual graves for the Union guards, Jana and Keeley split up so they could search a wider berth around it. They gave up after an hour and no evidence of manmade intrusion upon the forest materialized. Retracing their steps up the hill, they heard the rumble of an oncoming train along the tracks. Its brakes squealed as it slowed, and its shrill whistle blew to warn of its presence on the south side of King and Fuller's Cut. Jana and Keeley ducked below the railroad embankment to soften the noises of the locomotive on their eardrums and to avoid rousing curiosity and gossip over their presence. As the freight train passed, the ground trembled beneath them with a great force, which Jana figured to be unquestionably miniscule compared to the colliding of two trains.

The rear car disappeared around the deadly pass, and Jana and Keeley resumed a slow slog along the trampled path, paying strict attention as they got closer to where they estimated the caboose of the prisoner train had lain bruised and battered. Approximately a twentieth of a mile back toward Shohola, they were elated to see a trampled path hooking up and over the railroad embankment, and they followed it all the way down until it ended above the river. Again, she and Keeley split up to search a wider berth on each side of the path.

Jana wandered the south side, using her gloved hands to bushwhack her way up the acute slope in rambling switchbacks. When her pant leg snagged on a briar, she lost her footing and stumbled over a stone slab, landing hard with a thud. "Ouch!" she said before her face smooshed into the ground. She rolled over and sat up, spitting out pine needles and leaves. Once her vision cleared, she scanned the area. A large boulder seemed too perfectly shaped for and unnaturally propped up against the opening into a small cave. She hopped up and brushed off her denim trousers, eager to explore.

Following a path of scrubs, either crushed or with their branches sheared off, Jana reached the rocky sentry within minutes. She knelt before it, sweeping debris away from the surface of something wedged beneath it. Her pulse sprang into a full gallop when she recognized the faded green corner of some paper denomination of legal tender, which Congress had sanctioned printing by the United States Treasury in February 1862 to help pay the soldiers and finance the war. She let out a whoop and then a whistle to summon Keeley.

"Where are ye, me lass?" he called out, his voice muffled by the distance between them.

"About forty paces in on my side of the path, halfway between the river and the railroad embankment."

Reaching her side, Keeley said, "What have ye, me lass?"

She pointed to the piece of paper.

Keeley squatted before the rock. When he finished examining the bill, he looked up with a wide grin and pumped his fist. "I believe ye've located the hiding place, me lass."

"Help me move this barrier," Jana said.

Keeley scrambled to his feet, and Jana inched over, giving him room to place his palms against the rock beside hers.

"Ready?" Jana said.

"Aye, on the count o' three, a deep breath and push."

Lighter than they thought, the stony sentry lifted upon their initial surge, and they easily ousted and sent it rolling down the embankment. It crushed scrubs and rebounded off trees before it dove into the river with a hulking splash.

Jana picked up the fifty-dollar bill and flipped it over. The front side bore the profile of Alexander Hamilton, the very first Secretary of the Treasury and founder of the nation's financial system. She ogled the greenback, giddy over the hope of finding the rest.

With room for them both, Jana and Keeley wriggled inside the shallow, musty-aired grotto. Enough light filtered into the domed, dusky space for them to see an unmarked wooden chest—most likely the culprit behind the trail of destroyed scrubs, which Jana guessed had been hastened from the train and over the railroad embankment and sent rolling down the hill. Did it hold the army payroll? Her hopes swelled when she saw the iron padlock still clinging to its hasp. Her hopes were dashed when, upon closer inspection of its back, they found the rear hinges wedged off the lid and hanging loose on the box nails.

Keeley slowly lifted the lid, peeked in, and collapsed onto his haunches. "Empty, me lass, but"—he pointed to several denominations of bills littering the floor behind the chest—"we've recouped a wee bit o' the stash."

With a crestfallen sigh, Jana said, "I might've died of shock if we'd found the entire army payroll intact. At least we're on the right track." Alongside Keeley, she began raking in the bills.

A twig snapped.

Jana froze. "Did you hear that?" she whispered, extracting her Colt from beneath her coat.

"Aye," Keeley whispered and un-holstered his gun too.

They crawled to the mouth of the cave and scanned the area in three directions and as far as the naked eye could see. When neither man nor beast showed itself, they rose to their feet and peeked over the mossy roof in time to see someone skedaddling up the hill.

"Guard the grotto," Keeley said, flying off in hot pursuit and scattering the birds in a nervous squawk as he disappeared up and over the railroad embankment.

Slowly, Jana orbited her spot, looking and listening carefully for unnatural movements.

A shot rang out.

Jana's fright hammered her chest, and she found herself blindly sprinting up the hill on her wobbly legs. She almost slammed into Keeley on his way over the railroad embankment. "Are you all right?" she asked between gasps for breath. To his nod, she holstered her revolver and bent over, holding her kneecaps to help steady her legs and slow her breathing.

Rubbing her back, Keeley said through his own pants, "It was actually meself who instigated the shot. I thought I could freeze our intruder, but he had too good o' jump on meself to be fazed by me bullet hitting him. For a big burly man, he's incredibly nimble."

Jana straightened and threw her arms around Keeley. "If I can help it, I'm not letting you tackle danger all by yourself ever again."

"And ye'll only be out o' me sight if it means keeping ye safe, me lass."

Pulling away from him, Jana said, "By your description of the burly man and his being nimble, he was no Mr. Woodcock."

Keeley wiped sweat from his forehead, face, and neck with his handkerchief. "Aye, but right before our snoop disappeared down the tracks toward Shohola, I caught a glimpse o' him. He had a head full o' hair, blacker than midnight, and he met up with another, who had a limp. Both match Alex's descriptions o' the goons who knocked on Woodcock's room at Willard's."

"Now," Jana said, "we pretty much have proof that John Woodcock is having us followed and capitalizing on our search."

"Aye, and it's certain his goons are off to report the fate o' the payroll to Woodcock."

They shimmied back down the hill, and Keeley posted himself outside the cave while Jana crawled back inside and raked in the bills. Tallying the lone five-hundred-dollar bill with the ones, twos, fives, tens, twenties, and hundreds, Jana reported a total of eight-hundred-and twenty-five dollars, adding, "Jed and Fulton must've been in a real hurry to leave this much behind."

"Aye, and, if we don't reclaim any more o' the loot, we're owed five percent o' this." Keeley clicked his cheek. "A stipend o' forty-one dollars and a twenty-five-cent silver piece isn't bad for the work we've done this far. And if ye don't mind, me lass"—he wadded up the bills and buttoned them up in his coat pocket—"I'll keep these on meself in case we're ambushed. As ye know through yar near hanging, the war has stripped some men o' their chivalry, and I'd rather meself than yarself be frisked."

"It seems our work here is done," Jana said, eying the wicker basket upon her stomach's growl.

"Aye, and, o' course, ye've built yarself up an appetite." He chuckled. "I admit, I meself have too."

Moving to higher ground where they had a panoramic view of the woods, they reviewed the case while they chomped on bread, cheese, dried beef, and strawberries.

"About the railroad dispatcher," Jana said, "I believe he was drunk at his post, but I also believe Franz's testament that Duffy Kent is purely misguided as opposed to spiteful. If there was any malice behind the train wreck, I'm convinced someone manipulated him into thinking the prisoner train had already rolled through behind its signal train and that he'd sent a warning to the dispatcher at Shohola of it. Afterward, Duffy either disappeared because he was being ostracized by his community or he was paid by someone, such as John Woodcock, to disappear or both."

"Aye, and, if I meself had shady dealings with the likes o' a Duffy Kent, I'd want him out o' the picture right away. I'd be afraid the next time he got intoxicated and was under pressure, he'd spill all o' his beans, including the whereabouts o' his prized whiskey still."

Sucking on a juicy strawberry, Jana said, "I think we can also rule out involvement by Sam Hoitt, purely by the coal-train engineer's saintly attempt to rescue others knowing he could've been killed in the process."

"Aye, and, in Sam's case, he's a professional engineer. He would know where the dangerous parts o' the tracks are and be on constant vigil for the nose o' another train's cowcatcher coming around the corner. Plus, his seat in the cab gives him the advantage o' observing the hazard evolving with only a split-second to warn his fire-and-brake-men."

"So, we agree Duffy Kent and Sam Hoitt are non-entities?"

"Aye. What's our next move, me lass?"

"Assuming the Rebel thieves were home-bound to Virginia with their plunder, there are too many escape routes they could've taken between here and there."

"Aye, so the better strategy would be to work backward to sniff out their trail. And, if we're thinking alike, a trip to our old stomping grounds and a telegraph to warn our dear friend Versella Stock Barney o' our visit are in order," Keeley said, staring hard and long southward.

Jana knew he was apprehensive about the danger of traveling through the South with General Lee only having surrendered the Confederacy a little over two months before. Even as she charged her tone with optimism to say, "We'll stick to public transportation all the way since it'll be faster and safer," Jana had her own reservations about what they'd face in the vicinity of Trevilian Station. Not far from there at Brandy Station, she'd taken a bullet in the arm and lost Keeley to capture; then, very near there, a year later, she'd almost lost Keeley to his amnesia. She cringed inwardly. Where that area was concerned, would her luck be tested once more?

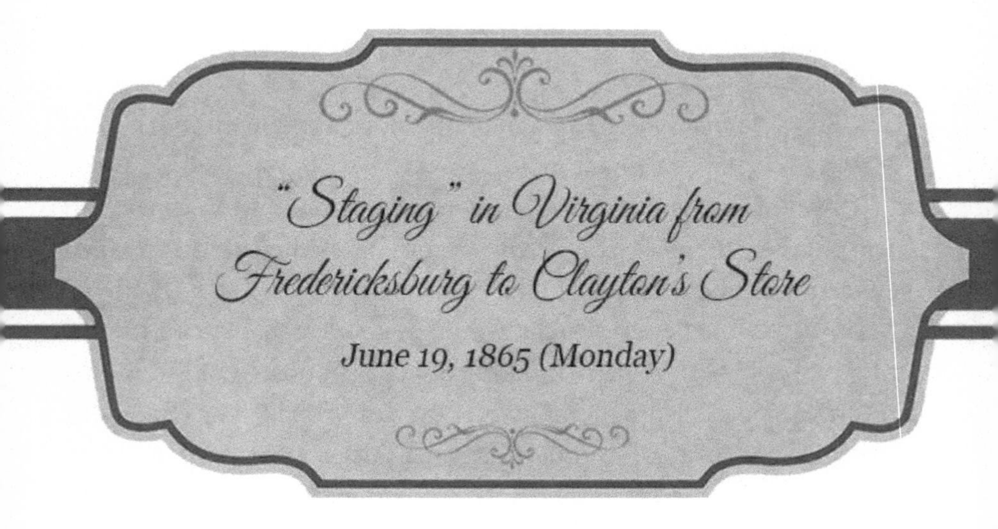

Jana awakened to a frantic buck of their cabin and catapult of her cheek off Keeley's shoulder.

"Hang in there, Mr. and Mrs. Cassidy. It's coming upon noon and our halfway mark," their driver hollered loud enough to be heard over the clatter of the iron-rimmed wheels rolling over a country road, roughed up by two armies tramping over it during the four years of war, including her and Keeley's own regiment a few times.

Jana sank into the distressed leather of her bench, thankful that the rutted road was the source of her rude awakening and not Rebel guerillas surrounding their coach. She would've preferred a comfier, safer, and faster ride on the train most of the way to Versella's, but the tracks and rolling stock of the *Orange and Alexandria Railroad*, a major link between the North and South, had been alternately demolished by Rebels and Yankees throughout the war.

Pushing the oiled-leather shade away from the outer frame of the window, Keeley leaned a safe distance out of the coach and hollered loud enough to be heard from his position, opposite the driver, "Thank ye for the update, Henry."

"Oh my, it's awfully bright out there." Jana buried her bleary eyes in the crook of her arm until she heard a swish, signaling Keeley's release of the rolled-down blind shielding them from the red-clay dust of the Fredericksburg Stage Road and Virginia's heat for the past five hours.

"Aye," Keeley said, rapidly blinking his eyes to adjust to the changes in light.

Jana opened her mouth wide in a protracted yawn. Fearing her jaws might freeze in place, she snapped them closed. "How long was I asleep?" She stretched her skirted legs across the middle bench, glad to have the luxury in the absence of other passengers aboard. Because of their mad race for the treasury and resulting desire to bypass most of the relay stations required of travelers for brief respites and dining, she and Keeley had rented out the entire Concord.

"Since the last swing station, a wee bit more than two hours ago. I meself fell dead to the world shortly thereafter. That is, until a bludgeoning from yar head"—he rubbed his whiskered chin—"assaulted meself."

"Ohhh, poor lad." Jana grinned at Keeley. "Did I hurt you badly?"

He pinched his lips together, but failed to hide the smirk behind them. "Not to worry, me lass, I've popped me jaw into place, and yar whack is all but forgotten. But I might want to move over, out o' the reach o' yar noggin."

Jana poked his rib with her elbow. "Very funny." She sobered. "It was chivalrous of you to give me the least jarring seat below the driver, but I think we should trade spots for the second half of our trip."

"Ye know very well, me lass, I'll not sacrifice yar comfort over me own. Besides, I rather like being jostled about."

With sunlight streaming in upon his handsome face, Jana noted Keeley's groggy eyes. He appeared as exhausted as she felt, and she heaved a long weary sigh. "I'm beginning to wonder about our decision to travel four hundred miles in two days without layovers."

"Are ye saying ye didn't get good sleep over the past thirty hours with people bustling about us to make their rail connections? Or riding the trains with their unrelenting stops? Or chugging down the Potomac River on a steamer? Or jouncing along rutted roads in stagecoaches?"

"If you call a few catnaps here and there good sleep, then I got a ton."

They shared a laugh.

"The peace of mind we got in sticking to public transportation, especially through the South, outweighs our virtual sleeplessness," Jana said.

Keeley shifted toward Jana. Enveloping her in his arm, he nuzzled her hair over her temple. "I'll take the coachman's advice and hang on to ye. We wouldn't want ye flying out o' the window, now would we?"

Jana wriggled into him. "Any excuse to cuddle is good enough for me."

After another hour of rocking on the creaky leather braces of their chamber, Jana and Keeley heard Henry call, "Whoa," and the stagecoach lurched to a stop. They were tossed about a little more as Henry climbed down from his seat.

Henry opened the door on Jana's side. "We're at the next swing station, folks. Feel free to walk around while the horses are being changed."

In the characteristically thick drawl of the deeper South, which Jana had assumed the day before after they'd breached the Mason and Dixon's Line into the former Confederate territory, Jana said to Henry, "Would it be all right with y'all, Henry, if we were to lay over he-ah a spell to allow us a picnic and y'all a rest?"

"A fine idea, me lass," Keeley said in his native brogue, requiring no modification because of the proliferation of Irish throughout the

United States.

Henry happily agreed and loaned them his wool blanket.

Obeying Henry's suggestion to stay within a stone's throw of the stagecoach, Jana and Keeley spread their blanket out upon the prickly grass beneath the shade of a stately oak and its cascading garlands of Spanish moss.

Henry saw to changing the four horses. Then, climbing up onto his seat, he tilted his hat over his face and reclined his head against the upper rail around the roof of the stagecoach and corral for the trunks.

From her carpetbag, Jana retrieved a paper bag filled with blueberries and biscuits, which they'd bought at the last relay station, and a northern newspaper, which they'd picked up along the way.

"Ladies first." Keeley held out his canteen, covered in a cotton-and-wool cloth dampened to keep the water cool—a trick they'd learned in the cavalry.

After Jana and Keeley took a few swigs, they polished off the blueberries, which, one by one, burst their fruity sweetness as Jana squished them between her teeth. Then, they dug into the flaky, buttery biscuits. In between swallows, Jana unfolded and smoothed the newspaper out across the pleats of her skirt with her free hand and read aloud the headline for the front-cover story, dated June 18th: "Rebel Raider Colonel John Singleton Mosby Surrenders!"

Keeley leaned in close to her for ease in reading the article along with her.

In summary, it reported:

> Mosby had disbanded his rangers from the 43rd Virginia battalion on April 21st, even though he intended to continue the fight with the Confederacy. Prior to his reaching General Joseph E. Johnston's army in North Carolina, Johnston surrendered to Union General William T. Sherman, so Mosby turned for home. The rescinding of

> the five-thousand-dollar bounty for his arrest had prompted his surrender on June 17th. Mosby was allowed to keep his sword and horse and return home, but only after he laid down his arms and pledged to abide by federal law—the same generous terms of parole extended by General Grant to General Lee and his Army of Northern Virginia on April 9th and General Sherman to General Johnston and his armies on April 26th.

"Thank goodness," Jana said, shuddering, "we don't have to worry about that savage skulking around this annex of his wartime playground."

"Aye, I wouldn't want to run into the likes o' him. He's not above murder to get what he wants," Keeley said, referring to Mosby's execution of three Union soldiers in retaliation for the execution of seven of his rangers.

The crack of a branch from the woods across the road sent Jana's biscuit flying from her grasp and Keeley upright.

Craning her neck, Jana spied two ruffians ducking behind oaks. "Did you get a good look at them too?"

"Aye, and one had a face full o' hair black as midnight, and the other might be bald, just as Alex described the brutes who knocked on John Woodcock's door at Willard's Hotel. What should we do about them, me lass?"

Before Keeley could answer, they heard a stampede of horses' hoofs heading their way.

The racket jarred Henry awake. He retrieved his rifle from under his bench and laid it across his lap simultaneously with the arrival of a band of four shoddy riders, who kicked up a cloud of dust as they reined in and surrounded the coach.

One of the gang called up to Henry, "Where ya headed?"

"Clayton's Store," Henry said, a ripple of unease in his tone.

Sensing worse trouble from these men than, for now, the two

watching them from the woods, Jana tasted bile creeping up into her throat.

Keeley, his face creased with alarm, squeezed Jana's hand tight enough to leach the color from it.

Feeling her Claddagh ring chafing her finger, Jana yanked her hand away from his, removed and dropped the precious memento down the shaft of her left riding boot, and wiggled her ankle until it settled beneath the arch of her foot. She whispered, "If they're looking to rob us, let them rummage through our trunks; they won't find the secret compartments, and, as far as I'm concerned"—she patted her embroidered carpetbag—"they can have the decoy money I keep in here."

With a barbed tongue, the spokesman of the scraggly party said, "Carryin' any Yanks we can string up to a tree?"

His horsemen sneered.

Keeley loosened the cravat around his neck, and a nervous perspiration trickled down Jana's spine, dampening the camisole beneath her corset. Their worst nightmare in roving through the South during these hostile times had come true. Could these men be remnants of John Singleton Mosby's guerillas? It was possible their leader's surrender was too ripe for his ex-rangers to know about it.

Unsnapping the flap of his holster, Keeley freed his Colt for quick access beneath his unbuttoned coat.

Jana coaxed her derringer up and out of her boot shaft by its glossy pearl grip and tucked it into her right skirt pocket.

Stuffing his cheek with a plug of tobacco, Henry casually said, "With war over, I've been transferring Virginians back home for weeks now. I assume the folks riding my stage are more of the same and eager to be reunited with their loved ones."

Bless him for buying us time to hatch a plan, Jana thought.

The guerilla leader nodded toward Jana and Keeley. "That 'em over there?"

While Jana's mind spun for some scheme to get them out of their predicament, Henry evaded answering him and instead fibbed, "I just signaled my passengers for our departure. If I don't keep to my schedule, gentlemen, I could lose—"

He was cut off by an uproar of chortles. One voice rose above the din. "I don't see no gentlemen 'round here. Do ya, Captain?"

The leader ignored his underling and growled at Henry, "We'll just head on over there and have a little chat with yer patrons, and you'll be on yer way in no time—with or without 'em."

"The war's over, you know. Why not move on?" Henry said.

"Ain't to us. So, if ya don't mind, we'll have that little powwow now."

"I reckon there's nothing I can do or say to stop you."

Simultaneous with Henry's retort, Jana finally harvested a seedling of subterfuge. In a rushed whisper, she commanded Keeley to act mute, as he'd done on his way to see his regimental surgeon about his amnesia and honorable discharge. Then, he'd executed the ploy to hide his masculine voice behind his disguise as a woman, lest he be unmasked as an able-bodied man and face imprisonment as a deserter or conscription by either army; now, she hoped to use it as a weapon to melt the ice around any chivalry left in the hearts of these rogues. Unless the Confederate government had stripped it from them, as it had done unto itself through its decree to hang women caught in traitorous deeds against it. Jana was a prime example of their hypocrisy in gallantry when they sent her to the gallows. Licking away the salty droplets of sweat beading on her upper lip, Jana clambered to her feet.

Keeley stood too, but slightly behind Jana.

Extracting her fan from her left skirt pocket, Jana went on the offensive. "Would y'all stop jabbering and get on with it." She vigorously fanned herself. "It's hot out he-ah, and I'd like to resume our ride inside the coolness of our carriage."

The captain urged his horse on and motioned for one of his men to follow.

As they reined their snorting horses in before her, Jana focused mainly on the captain whose gaunt, ashen cheeks and bony frame betrayed his emaciated state. He and his minion were former Confederate soldiers, who had yet to shed their filthy and frayed homespun butternut uniforms. The small bugle stamped into the front of their hats, as opposed to crossed sabers for cavalry, signified they were infantry. Jana's anxiety receded some; at least they weren't dealing with the men disbanded from John Mosby's 43rd Virginia Cavalry. She inhaled a deep breath behind her fan to feed her brain the necessary oxygen it required for a battle of wits.

Over the riders' squeaking saddles, the captain tipped his kepi at Jana and said, "Ma'am."

Jana slapped her fan over her heart. "Oh my de-ah Lawd, y'all have the richest amber-colored eyes I ever did see." She lied. They were frightening with their probing black pupils, and his upturned eyes blended with his tapered face and long pointy nose to remind Jana of the gray foxes that she and Pa had chased away from their henhouse a few times. She clucked her tongue. "Why, it's a shame to hide them and y'all's handsome face behind a tangled mass of hair."

Gray Fox's cheeks flushed, and he glared at his scrawnier inferior, warning he'd gnash into his sallow flesh and strip it away from his bones with any heckling from him.

Miss Lizzie had taught Jana to conquer the enemy by plying them with custard, compliments, politically agreeable conversation, or a combination thereof. Jana had no sweet treat to offer Gray Fox, so she hoped her reference to his good looks had begun to soften him up for the third ploy, which she'd pack with political partiality toward the South—same as she'd done a year ago in getting past the guard into the hospital of Castle Thunder Prison in order to guide Keeley and other Union soldiers to freedom.

Gray Fox recast his gaze upon Jana, the flush in his cheeks dwindling. Clearing his throat and reviving his authoritative tone, he said, "Where ya headed, ma'am?"

"Why, home to South Carolina. From what I he-ah, that despicable Union General Sherman tore up our beloved state." She batted her eyelashes and flapped her fan faster to give the impression she might faint. "I just might lie down and die if we were to find our home in ashes."

"Ain't ya a good distance out of yer way?"

"We're lying over a spell near Louisa Court House to visit a woman who tended to my brother after the battle the-ah." Leaning to one side, she allowed Gray Fox a peek at Keeley. Out of her peripheral vision, she saw Keeley salute a comrade in arms. She could kiss him for following her lead in plying the enemy with reverence.

"What's wrong with him? Seems mighty yeller of a strappin' feller to hide behind a lady."

"He's got amnesia from, of all things"—she shook her head and rolled her eyes—"a *friendly* rifle butt to the he-ad in a dismounted charge with his cavalry regiment." Before Gray Fox forced her to pluck a wrong number for Keeley's regiment out of the blue sky, Jana rushed to say, "And it caused him to go mute." She had no idea if that could happen from a bash to the head, but she bet neither he nor his men did either. "None of the doctors who've treated him understand it, and, since his afflictions have persisted for almost a ye-ah now, they fe-ah he'll never regain his memory or speech." She quivered her lips and peered pitifully at Keeley over her shoulder. "It's truly dreadful. But I suppose, I should be grateful he's alive and otherwise healthy."

"Ain't that the truth," he said, his expression turning grim. "I can't march a mile in yer brother's boots. I ain't got one scratch from a bullet or shrapnel on me. But"—he crossed and dropped his reins over the skeletal withers of his horse and rubbed his eyes with his weathered knuckles—"I ain't ever gonna git rid of the nightmares of watchin' family and friends bein' shot down, stabbed to death, or blown to bits."

Although Jana could empathize with his hauntings, he'd exposed his weakness, and she'd capitalize on it. "Then, why on earth would y'all tempt fate or add to your nightmares?" She feigned a terrified shudder and fanned herself. "I'd hate to think your follies could still get y'all or your men killed. All along our route from Maryland, we've seen Yankee cavalry patrolling for the likes of"—she slung his own intentions for her and Keeley, had they been Yankees, back at him—"renegade Rebels to string up to a tree." She crossed empathic eyes upon them. "Y'all be assured, our cause is lost and there's no bouncing back. No one came out of war unscathed. Look at my brother he-ah and what we might face upon our return home. I'll bet y'all have family who need you home to help mend fences. Do y'all even know if they've survived the war?" She let them ruminate on her question before turning and gesturing for Keeley to pick up and hand her the northern newspaper. It still reeked of printing ink and crinkled in her hands as she unfolded it to display the front page. "As y'all can see, even the tenacious John Mosby has surrendered. They say he's returned home, and I'd venture to say he's already back to lawyering and being productive in society as we all must do."

"Let me see it." Gray Fox reached down and snatched the paper Jana offered him. Perusing the front page, he said, "Ain't no picture of Colonel Mosby in this report, and I can't read. How do I know you're tellin' the truth?"

Timidly, Gray Fox's comrade said, "I can read, Captain." After he was handed the newspaper and he mouthed through his reading of the article, he looked up and shrugged. "She ain't lyin.'"

Gray Fox's shoulders fell limper than the humid air, and he stroked his chest-length beard in his good long silence. "I reckon it's time we was gittin' home. We're pretty near out of ammunition and too hungry to fight any Yanks."

The emaciated condition of these men's horses registered with Jana for the first time. The poor animals were obviously starving and dispirited, evidenced by their ribs poking out around their saddles and their heads bowed low, almost to their knobby knees. Fanning herself again, Jana said with conviction, "Even if out of necessity, I'm glad y'all have concluded to capitulate. The South needs capable men, such as y'all, to help it rise from the cinders of rebellion and stand proud again. We Southerners have one thing in our favor: One of us is running the federal White House. I ardently believe Andrew Johnson won't forget us during Reconstruction."

"I hope you're right, ma'am." Gray Fox tipped his hat at her. "Good luck to ya and yer brother."

Jana swiped the back of her hand across her forehead. "I'll pray for y'all to thrive in our destitute times."

The captain and his man slowly turned their horses around and started away.

To her second epiphany within minutes, Jana called out, "Oh, Captain."

He reined in his horse and swiveled in his saddle. "Yes, ma'am?"

"I know this might sound hypocritical, but if y'all are on the lookout for wayward Yankees, I do believe there are some following us. I saw them"—Jana pointed her fan toward the woods across the road—"right about the-ah. They might be looking to rob us. We can't have that when we can barely feed ourselves." Frantically fanning herself, she said, "But, please, y'all promise me right now, chivalry is not de-ad in the South and y'all won't go stringing them up to a tree. Just relieve them of their money and run."

Right on cue, twigs and underbrush snapped underfoot and the two men turned tail and fled.

Gray Fox smirked, his yellow teeth bared through his thick mustache. "We're on it, ma'am, and, if they git smart-mouthed, I ain't promisin' we won't hang 'em." Then, he spurred his horse into a lethargic gallop and his men followed him to the edge of the woods, where they dismounted and sped away in as hot a pursuit of the Yankees as their enfeebled limbs could carry them.

Jana had noted a limp in one of the scaredy-cats, and she remarked upon it to Keeley.

As they collected their things, Keeley said, "Aye, it further supports Alex's description o' one o' Woodcock's goons, and it would seem the pair o' them has managed to follow us from Shohola to here. Let's hope they're the only ones trailing us, and our newfound Rebel friend and his band o' impoverished men chase them more than a wee bit off course."

Henry shook his head at Jana when she and Keeley reached the stagecoach. "You have a tremendous knack for acting, Mrs. Cassidy."

Keeley's broad chest inflated and deflated to his billowing sigh. "Aye, me beautiful wife does indeed."

"We could've wound up in a three-way shootout," Henry said, blotting his forehead with a handkerchief. "I'm grateful to you for digging us out of trouble."

"We're grateful to y'all for playing along with our deception. Since Mr. Cassidy he-ah arranged our travel with y'all, y'all know he's neither mute nor suffering from amnesia."

"I stand by the stagecoach company's oath to keep their passengers safe." He leaned toward the opposite side of the stage and spat tobacco. "So be it if it includes going along with fanciful stories." He looked over his shoulder to where Gray Fox and his men had tethered their horses and said with a nervous chuckle, "We best get moving before our interlopers spring some equally agreeable ruse as yours, Mrs. Cassidy, on our outlaws to reroute them back to us." He waited for Jana and Keeley to confirm they were comfortably seated, and then he released the screechy brake, cracked the whip, and set the horses in motion.

Stealing Jana's hand into his with a buoyant squeeze, Keeley said, "Yar improvisation, me lass, is exceptional."

"You aren't so bad yourself. Your salute was perfect, and it somehow gave me the idea to resurrect your amnesia to go along with your being mute." She kissed him on the cheek. "We make a great team."

"Aye, our acting might not surpass Edwin Booth's reputation for greatness on the stage, but I'll bet it does his evil brother's," he said, referring to Lincoln-assassinator John Wilkes Booth.

"Shall we take up acting as a career when we've finished our detective work, Mr. Cassidy?"

Simultaneously, Keeley swept out his free arm and leaned sideways in a half-bow. "Our audience awaits us, me lass."

"Let's pray it excludes any more renegades like Gray Fox and his gang and John Woodcock's goons."

They united in semi-nervous titters, and Jana knew Keeley was also wondering if their encounter with Gray Fox would be the least of their worries.

A sudden disturbing notion, borne out of her own words to Gray Fox about President Johnson's remembering the South during Reconstruction, struck Jana. *The president claims the Secretary of War is obsessed with the lost payroll. Could he be making a case against Stanton to deflect his own obsession with it for his own gain—personal, political, or both?* President Johnson had demanded she and Keeley deliver the lost payroll directly to him without anyone else's knowledge of it. Once they did, neither they nor the Secretary of the Treasury would be the wiser regarding his disbursement of it. Were they truly headed into a nest of cobras charmed by the president himself? Or was she suffering from an overwrought imagination stemming from her fatigue?

"Staging" in Virginia on the Fredericksburg Road to Clayton's Store

June 19, 1865 (Monday)

Jana caressed the embroidered flowers of her cloth carpetbag, slumped on the bench beside her, trying to quiet her nagging thought that President Johnson might want the army payroll for his own personal or political gain. Up until now, she'd chosen to chalk up the heist of the Union payroll to a couple of thieves and a lunatic striving to maintain his wealth and status in society. She creased her forehead in uncertainty.

"What's got ye bugged, me lass?"

She divulged her disconcerting theory about the president.

Stiffening against the vertical leather folds of their backrest, Keeley said, "His desperation to get hold o' it does seem a wee bit odd. Not to mention, amongst the four Union leaders reportedly targeted for assassination, President Johnson is the only Southerner, and his killer lost his nerve. General Grant prevented his own assassination by his sudden and fortuitous departure from Washington City."

"The South misjudged that Lincoln would abolish slavery as soon as he took office. If only it had considered his proposal of gradual emancipation with compensation for the extermination of its slave labor, perhaps the North and South could've avoided war." Jana shook her head in dismay at the hundreds of thousands of Americans lost to war. "Who's to say the Confederacy didn't misjudge that Lincoln, in post-war Reconstruction, would begrudge the South by placing harsh demands upon it, commensurate with the plan spearheaded by Secretary of War Stanton and backed by the majority of Radical Republicans in Congress?" Solemnly gazing at Keeley, she said, "So, a change of command was in order, with Johnson ordaining himself the perfect candidate to lead the United States into Reconstruction in order to soften any enforcement of strict rules against his beloved South. Or maybe he's a puppet of the Confederacy, KGC, or both to fulfill the lofty goal."

"Aye, at his core, President Johnson's still a Southerner and the South would be banking on that—just as ye intimated to Gray Fox."

"He might be vilified in the South over his anti-secession sentiments and support of the Union, but President Johnson was a proponent of slavery, and he kept his slaves up until Lincoln issued his Emancipation Proclamation in January 1863." Jana concentrated on the diamond-shaped pattern in the soft, leather trim over the rear, forward-facing seat for help in organizing her thoughts. "Maybe he favors ongoing oppression of freedmen. His injection of the missing payroll into the South's economy could make the South a little more obstinate to the North's demands while putting Johnson back in the South's good graces."

"Are ye saying President Johnson was either lured back into the ideals o' the Confederacy by his own prejudice against the freedmen or by those who see him as malleable when it comes to policymaking over the freedmen's future treatment?"

Jana felt her whole face crimping with disgust. "Frederick Douglass once espoused he saw a loathing for his race in Vice-President Andrew Johnson's eyes. As the Hebrew prophet Jeremiah questions in the *Old Testament*, 'Can the leopard change its spots?'"

"Come to think o' it, President Johnson only admitted to loathing slavery because it was ripping our country apart, and he seemed genuine in his declaration. But maybe he loathes the freedmen as a race o' people."

"Given his unrelenting toils as military governor of Tennessee, it seems absurd to think he'd participate in anything that would undermine his restoration of federal authority and peace there." Jana drummed her fingertips against the leather armrest of her windowsill until her mind flipped to show the opposite side of the coin. "President Johnson griped about his cabinet and Congress distrusting *him*, but his non-disclosure of our investigation to all but one of his cabinet members tells me, he distrusts *them* too."

"Why do ye think he does, me lass?"

"Well—," Jana's vocal cords vibrated to a bounce of their coach. She waited for both to stabilize, then said, "If we're to buy into President Johnson's sincerity about supplementing the North's economy with the stolen treasury and his truly having been a target of assassination, who else from President Lincoln's cabinet would've benefitted from his death?"

Keeley frowned. "I hate to admit me ignorance, but I don't know the exact line o' succession to the presidency. Do ye happen to know, me lass?"

Flicking her index finger skyward, Jana said, "I do, thanks to Ma's history lessons." She paused momentarily to consider the incumbents and their political attachments.

"And? Don't keep meself in suspense," Keeley said chuckling.

"Per the Presidential Succession Act of 1792, in the case of a double vacancy in the offices of president and vice-president, the president pro tempore of the Senate is first in line, followed by the speaker of the House of Representatives. Both of those men, Senator Lafayette Foster from Connecticut and Congressman Schuyler

Colfax from Indiana, respectively, are Radical Republicans and staunch abolitionists." Jana threw out her palms. "I can't imagine the president pro tempore having anything to gain from both Lincoln's and Johnson's deaths as he's a temporary presidential replacement, minimally for two months, while the Secretary of State notifies the governors of each state to call a special election to fill the vacancies. And I seriously doubt Senator Foster would've been electable over the most visible of Lincoln's cabinet members, who, I'm sure, would've had designs on becoming president of the United States."

"Aye, and those cabinet members would've appealed to the voters because o' their maximal experience in managing the federal government during the worst o' times."

"Thank goodness, Secretary of State Seward is recuperating from his grave wounds, but he'll be ill for quite some time. So, his attackers have successfully removed him from consideration for the presidency as they'd obviously intended. That leaves"—Jana paused, then counted off on her fingers—"the Secretaries of Treasury, War, Navy, Interior, and Agriculture and the Attorney and Post Office Generals. Of them, I would think Treasury, War, and Attorney General are the most important posts. At least, the Continental Congress thought they were when they created them first in 1789 for George Washington's cabinet."

Draping his legs over the middle bench and reclining his head back into the palms of his laced fingers, Keeley stared up at the leather ceiling. "Might we nullify Hugh McCulloch from consideration since he only became Secretary o' the Treasury one month before Lincoln's death? It's barely enough time for him to plot or involve himself in anything sinister, and President Johnson trusts him."

"Yes, but we must consider Salmon Chase, who was Secretary of the Treasury for almost the entire duration of Lincoln's first term. It's fairly well known his relationship with Lincoln was strained because of Chase's indignation at losing the 1860 Republican nomination for president to Lincoln. However, it seems farfetched of Chase, a lawyer who's known for his many charitable defenses of fugitive slaves and help in forming the Free Soil Party—including coining its motto: Free Soil, Free Labor, and Free Men—and who, overall, shared Lincoln's convictions, to murder anyone for his personal or political gain. Whether or not he still covets becoming president of the United States, I doubt he would've wanted to upset the apple cart under President Lincoln's competent leadership."

"Aye, and why would he risk losing his appointment by President Lincoln as chief justice o' the United States Supreme Court to run for president, especially when it proved unsuccessful for him before? If I meself were in his shoes, I'd want to avoid putting meself in the undesirable position o' having to claw me way back into the offices o' the federal government."

Picking lint off the three-quarter bell sleeve of her black bolero coat, Jana freed it and watched it spiral down to the scuffed varnish of the creaking floor. "So, we're down to the Secretary of War and Attorney General."

"I meself am not demeaning the importance o' the Attorney General to President Lincoln's administration, but I don't see the role o' chief law enforcement officer o' the United States over court cases and legal matters as critical to wartime decision-making compared to the Secretary o' War. If I meself were plotting to murder President Lincoln and some o' his cabinet, Edward Bates would be low on me list."

"I agree. President Lincoln and Secretary of War Stanton were the two most responsible for spearheading the Confederacy's defeat. I can understand assassins targeting President Lincoln, Vice-President Johnson, and General Grant, but why target Secretary of State over Secretary of War?" Jana reasoned out her own hypothetical question. "Secretary of State Seward supported war against foreign powers, especially Great Britain and France, if they tried to supply the Confederacy with ships, troops, and arms. The Union's making foes of those countries drives them right into the Confederacy's goals of achieving recognition and reward as a separate country. Even more unnerving, Stanton was apparently at home in Washington City when he learned of Lincoln's wound, Seward's attack, and the plots against Johnson and Grant. I don't recall hearing anything about an attack against him."

Sitting up straight, Keeley gawked at Jana. "Are ye saying Stanton was bought out by the Confederacy to conspire against Lincoln?"

"Or maybe the KGC, the Confederacy's instrument," Jana said.

"Why might he align himself with the Confederacy or its secret society? He seems to hate both and want to punish them for inciting war."

"Because he hated Lincoln's lenient plan to reunite the country. . .maybe as much as he hates the South. Stanton showed his shrewdness in war. Perhaps he used the KGC for their clandestine nature and resourcefulness." On the burnished, black surface of her rolled-down shade, Jana pictured Secretary of War Stanton's scheming face. She glared at it. "Once the knights of the KGC helped him get rid of Lincoln, he could turn on them—he's in the best position to dispose of any evidence or witnesses linking him to the KGC and Lincoln's assassinators. Remember, he oversaw the hunt for John Wilkes Booth, Confederate President Jefferson Davis, and the Confederate treasury. And he's currently overseeing the prosecution of the eight accused of Lincoln's murder. With Lincoln out of the way and any complicity on his part squashed, he's free to seek a presidential nomination and resume recruiting the incumbent Radical Republicans of Congress in his vengeful tide against the South."

"If that's true, how do ye explain why Stanton would want to assassinate General Grant and the others in Lincoln's cabinet?"

"Very simply"—Jana removed her eyes from her conjured image

of Stanton and peered up at Keeley—"either Stanton didn't care how far the KGC went as long as they got rid of Lincoln or he was kept in the dark about the other targets."

Keeley scratched the tuft of hair above his ear. "Our newfound friend and chief doorkeeper of the White House, Thomas Pendel, blames Secretary o' War Stanton for denying Lincoln more than one guard outside o' his balcony and assigning Lincoln a policeman who had a dodgy reputation in his job. Even so, why would John Parker have left his post during intermission, knowing he could land himself in jail, or worse, be executed for it?"

"Maybe Parker was charged to disappear by the one man who ordered him to guard President Lincoln: Secretary of War Stanton who, in his position of power, could easily rake over any trail of evidence to Parker and himself."

"Or might someone have produced Parker an order forged in Stanton's hand?"

"Possibly," Jana said. "But why would Stanton be eager to cover up proof of his innocence as he seems to be doing now?"

Their coach violently lurched, throwing Keeley sideways and Jana across his lap.

Keeley righted himself while keeping Jana steady and caressing her back with long soothing strokes. "Are ye all right, me lass?"

"I'm fine"—she giggled—"but feel free to keep rubbing my back."

With an amused snort, he said, "Ye know, if ye wanted to sit on me lap, all ye had to do was say so."

"Very funny." Jana pushed up and away from his lap and reclaimed her own seat.

Slipping his arm around her and holding her tight, he said, "It might be better if ye were to stick close to meself where I can keep ye safe from harm."

"A very wise idea, me lad, and now that we have that settled, where were we?"

"Ye asked meself why Secretary o' War Stanton might want to cover up a forgery o' his signature and proof that he didn't release John Parker from his post outside o' President Lincoln's theater box."

Jana raised her eyebrows at him, keen for his reply.

"If I meself were Secretary o' War Stanton, and I'd picked a notorious bungling fool to guard President Lincoln, whether or not forgery was involved, I'd want to cover it up, else I meself look more like the bungling fool." He clicked his cheek. "I wouldn't want me stellar record in the management o' war to be obliterated by the assassination o' a president whom I swore to protect."

"Or maybe Stanton's covering up the fact that he paid someone to forge his signature and to disappear afterward to hide his complicity in the conspiracy." Jana tucked stray strands of her hair under her crocheted snood. "Let's not forget, Stanton rushed President Johnson to convene a military tribunal, and he's taken charge of overseeing its prosecution. It could be a tactic to divert widespread curiosity over Parker's having abandoned his post to the hearing."

"I'd say he's accomplished it with the trial having blown up into quite the bit o' sensationalism."

"Also, President Johnson questions Stanton's assignment of biased commissioners and his promoting Judge Advocate General Holt and his assistant prosecutor to argue their points in favor of execution."

Wiggling his right foot upon the middle bench, Keeley said, "In conclusion, it seems we're saying Stanton convened a court o' highly prejudicial military and political officials, who he knew would come to a swift decision to get rid o' anyone or any evidence proving his co-conspiracy. That's a pretty chilling hypothesis, me lass."

"Yes, but it's something we should carefully consider as we continue our quest. He's a very powerful and respected man. With the KGC's sponsorship, he becomes a formidable figure." Jana's eyes widened. "I just remembered something of significance. President Johnson indicated President Lincoln had one of his U.S. marshals check into the activities of the veterans of the Federal War Department's Reserve Corps, who were guarding the Union payroll on the prisoner train, to ascertain if they'd come into sudden wealth. That seems to suggest President Lincoln was suspicious of their being paid to turn their heads and look the other way during the theft. And since they were under Stanton's command, could that suggest President Lincoln was suspicious of Stanton's collusion in the criminal act?"

"Aye, but why might Stanton need the money?"

"To throw the KGC a bone for its silence in his part in the conspiracy to assassinate President Lincoln?" Jana said hypothetically.

"I meself would like to believe the guards o' the Veteran Reserve Corps were honorable, but they could be hoarding their compensation until it's safe to use it." With a forceful huff, Keeley's lemon and blueberry breath permeated the leathery, hickory air within their berth. "Our late war has certainly brought out the worst in many men."

Rubbing her tired eyes with the knuckles of her index fingers, Jana said, "We've certainly had a lot to process over the past few days."

"Aye, John Woodcock and his thugs, double-crossing Rebel prisoners, the KGC, and a gang o' guerillas. We better net as many winks as possible to prepare for the next phase o' our trip. It could wind up in a showdown with all o' the connivers at once."

Their coach lurched again.

This time, they braced each other from toppling over.

"Pardon the pun, me lass, but it would seem our venture is turning out to be a wild, wild ride." Keeley's bleary eyes grimaced at her. "Would ye be opposed to our aborting the mission if we found it was spiraling out o' our control?"

Jana squiggled deeper into Keeley's embrace. An image of Alex popped into her head and stunted her immediate reply. Although Alex was unaware of her and Keeley's commitment to adopt him, Jana knew. She surprised herself when she blurted, "If I had only myself to consider, I wouldn't think twice about sacrificing my life for my country." Jana traced her fingertips down Keeley's stubbly jawline. "But now I have two lives I place above my own—yours and Alex's—and I won't do anything to hurt either of you." And she meant it, even as she yearned to finish what they'd started. She patted his hand and stared up at him in earnest. "Let's put our heads together with Leanne's and Charlie's to outwit them all."

He nodded and, shortly afterward, they both dozed off.

Keeley's bodily twitches disrupted Jana's sleep. She speculated that his mind was spinning from their unsettling conversation and that he was worrying over what began as a simple chase ending in a four-way shootout. For the sake of making it home to Alex, Jana closed her fatigued eyes in hopes of catching a few good winks to be mentally and physically sharp in the forthcoming days.

Jana and Keeley simultaneously uttered a prayer of thanks when three hours after their provocation with Gray Fox, Henry called out, "Whoa!" and announced their early-evening termination at Clayton's Store.

Upon the immediate cessation of their cabin's swing, Jana pushed the oiled curtain away from the window and poked her head out. Sucking in a big breath of fresh air, she choked on the silt kicked up by their transport and collapsed onto her seat in a coughing fit.

"Here, me lass." Keeley unscrewed the lid from his canteen and held its tinny-tasting pewter mouth against her lips.

Jana tilted her head back, letting the cool water trickle down her throat to coat her tickle. Regaining her voice, she said with a sheepish grin, "Now, that was an idiotic thing to do."

Poker-faced, Keeley said, "Aye, I have to agree, me lass."

Jana's eyebrows shot up to his gentle but uncharacteristic rebuke.

"I say that, me lass, because ye nearly choked to death." His dimples burst out to his big smile. "And, if ye had, how might I have managed the recovery o' the army payroll all by meself?"

They shared a hearty laugh.

With her heart full of love for him, Jana gazed up into his doting eyes, feeling grateful for his levity in softening her embarrassment.

Keeley kissed her forehead. "I love ye with all o' me heart too, me lass."

When the dust had settled outside, Henry opened their door and helped Jana and Keeley down the stirrup-like iron rung.

Jana spied a lone man sitting on the top porch step beneath a wooden sign for Clayton's Store.

Springing up from his perch, he brushed off the seat of his work pants and came darting toward them with litheness unexpected of a large, hearty man. "I expect you're Jana and Keeley," he said, his rich voice between a tenor and baritone.

Keeley peered up at the man, a good three inches taller than his height of six feet. "Aye, and who might ye be that ye know us?"

"I'm Isaiah Stock Barney." Smiling at their puzzlement, he clarified, "My wife, Jess, and I recently changed our surname from Hale to Stock Barney to honor both Versella's maiden name and Harold's family name in gratitude of their kindnesses to us over the years."

Apart from this enlightenment, Jana and Keeley knew the rest of the Hale's story: On their journey north, after their master was killed in battle and their mistress freed them, the Hales stumbled into the Barney homestead, tired and hungry. The Barneys needed help on their farm, and the Hales needed a new home. It was a match made in heaven. The Barneys gifted the Hales a parcel of land on which to build their house and a promise to share equally in the profits from all of the crops and livestock they raised and sold together.

Within earshot of Henry, Jana maintained her Southern accent. "We've not met Harold yet to know his reception to y'all's change of surname, but I'm sure Versella was over the moon with y'all's tribute. She made it abundantly cle-ah to us that she considered y'all and your family part of hers right away."

Isaiah beamed. "We felt their immediate embrace into their family, and you guessed Versella's reaction right, which Harold mirrored." Sticking out his muscled hand and enthusiastically shaking each of their hands, he said, "I hope you don't mind my informal address of you. Versella told me it would be all right to call you by your given names."

"Aye, and we prefer ye do."

With introductions concluded, Isaiah, Keeley, and Henry transferred the trunks from the roof of the stagecoach to the bed of Isaiah's mule-drawn wagon, where Jana, Keeley, and Henry bid each other goodbye.

During the farewells, Isaiah subtly winked at Jana. Apparently, he'd both picked up on her phony Southern drawl and been apprised of her past disguises by a little birdie named Versella.

Henry climbed aboard his coach. Out of courtesy of his larger transport leaving a tornado of dust in its wake, he held up his horses until Jana, Keeley, and Isaiah squished together onto the single bench of Isaiah's wagon and Isaiah took up the reins and steered them several hundred yards down the Marquis Road.

Leaning forward to see around Jana, Keeley spoke over the clippity-clop of the mule's hoofs and the clatter and creak of the wagon's wheels and boards. "I can't tell ye how nice it is to finally to meet ye, Isaiah. Versella told us so many wonderful things about ye and yar family."

Jana added, "We were disappointed to have missed meeting you all and Versella's sister by only minutes last year when we stopped by Iva's homestead to warn you that Versella was all alone. But we were greatly relieved to know you'd all be reunited with Versella on the very day we left her."

"I meself am glad we missed ye." Keeley's cheeks flushed orange to match the bonneted-heads of the wildflowers growing roadside and tossing in the draught created by their farm dray. "I'm sure ye've been told all about me Jana lass and Versella's ruse to have meself dress as a woman on our way to seeing me regimental surgeon about me amnesia. For me own good, it was a prudent thing to do as me outwardly appearance as an able-bodied man could've gotten meself imprisoned as a deserter by or conscripted into either army in me unfit condition. Still, I'd rather ye meet meself now as a man than last year as a woman."

"There's no shame in putting on a dress to survive," Isaiah said, giving Keeley a heartfelt look. "I would've put on a dress to escape enslavement if I hadn't feared me and my family being caught and sold to separate owners and worse existences."

"I appreciate yar sentiment, Isaiah," Keeley said, "and, now that ye put it that way, meself having to dress as a woman is but a wee inconvenience to the oppressiveness o' yar past life on the plantation."

"Dreadful circumstances reflective of our tumultuous times," Jana said, noting the permanent brackets around Isaiah's mouth and lines across his broad forehead.

With a solemn expression, Isaiah stared off between the mule's ears. His silence seemed eternal until he finally turned back to Jana and Keeley. "Actually," he said, his spirit lifting slightly, "Master and Mistress allowed me and Jess to 'jump the broom' in marriage and gave us work in the Big House, where Mistress taught us to read and write and proper speech in the same way she'd learned it from the Pennsylvania Dutch."

"Ah," Jana said, "that explains your northern accent."

"Yes, and, for their acts of kindness, I'm grateful to Master and Mistress. Still, I always dreamed of freedom for me and my family, and…" his voice trailed off to tears welling in his eyes. Then, he inhaled deeply. "Sometimes, this new life of ours steals my breath away."

"We couldn't be happier for you and your family, Isaiah," Jana said, and Keeley nodded agreement.

While he automatically steered the mule, Isaiah peered at Jana. "Speaking of gratitude, we're all grateful to you and Leanne for helping Keeley rescue Versella from those Yankee bandits last year. Wish I'd been a fly on the henhouse wall to see it. Though, Versella tells the story vividly enough."

Jana shuddered along with the floorboards beneath her boot soles. "I'd hate to think what would've happened to Versella and Keeley if we'd arrived later than we had."

"Me too," Isaiah said, mopping his sweaty forehead with his handkerchief and re-focusing on the road ahead. "Speaking of Versella, she wanted to come fetch you herself, but she and Jess are home readying for your arrival."

"What about Versella's husband and two sons?" Jana gulped hard. "Did they survive the war?"

"Yes, but only Harold has come home. Fortunately, he wasn't wounded and he's recovering well from pneumonia." Isaiah's knuckles whitened as he balled his hands around the reins. "I get angry every time I think of Southerners who fought against their will for slavery and died in battle or from their wounds or disease. Although Harold is a staunch abolitionist, he believes in states' rights. But he detested fighting for a cause he thought could be settled more peaceably, especially if non-slave owners had a bigger voice in leading the South alongside the wealthy planters. The deaths of so many, from both sides of the war, deepened Harold's sentiments against slavery but softened his convictions for states' rights—but only where the entire country is concerned." Isaiah glanced heavenward. "Thank the good Lord Harold wasn't conscripted until late '62, when the Confederacy changed the maximum age from thirty-five to forty-five. It cut his soldiering to two-and-a-half years of starvation, long marches, and sleeping on the cold ground at his advanced age."

"Did he get good medical care in the army?" Jana asked.

"He was cared for in Richmond at a military hospital, touted as the largest in the world, by a competent and compassionate nurse and administrator from South Carolina. He praises the widowed and childless Phoebe Yates Levy Pember as his angel of mercy, second to Versella, of course. Unfortunately, Harold was forced to evacuate too early from the hospital before the Yankees seized control of it on April 3rd."

Jana was acquainted with the sprawling hospital compound on Chimborazo Hill. With its ninety medical wards; bake houses; kitchens; ice houses; soap house; stable; guard house; chapel; bathhouse; carpenter, blacksmith and apothecary shops; and five dead houses, it was no wonder its size was celebrated. Also, its surgeon-in-chief, James B. McCaw, was heralded for his progressive thinking. During construction, he'd mandated wide avenues between the wards and for each to have ample windows and doors for circulating fresh air as a sanitary measure for the speedy rehabilitation of his patients. The hospital had played into Miss Lizzie's deception for Jana's disguise as a Southerner married to a captured Yankee. She had Jana create trust around Richmond so that, ultimately, she'd be allowed into the Castle Thunder Prison's hospital to visit Keeley. She'd accomplished it by collecting clothing and other fabrics from the belles of society and delivering them to Chimborazo Hospital to be torn up into bandages. Under this guise, Jana had smuggled in a blueprint of escape for Keeley and other Yankee soldiers.

"Unfortunately," Isaiah groaned, "his long passage home, mostly on foot, has preyed upon his health and slowed his full recuperation."

"He's fortunate to have survived illness," Jana said. "The Union estimates that for every one of their soldiers who were killed in action or died from a battle wound, three died of disease or illness as the result of starvation or exposure to the elements."

"When ye consider the idea o' conquering one's foe is to kill and maim through weapons o' destruction, it's an ironic twist o' fate that many more died o' disease and illness," Keeley said.

Jana thought, *If only the hotheaded politicians had left it up to us women to resolve the conflict.* From the beginning of time, women were fiercely protective lionesses over their kin and country, and Jana trusted her sex would never have allowed the schism between the North and South to get as far as a nationwide barroom brawl, which cost hundreds of thousands of lives, decimated the land, and incurred immense debt. She envisioned the only weapon women having wielded to preserve the Union was the same their forefathers had wielded to incite the original thirteen colonies into banding together as a nation and freeing themselves of British tyranny: the Latin phrase *E Pluribus Unum* or "Out of many one." In following these words, gracing the Great Seal of the United States since an enactment by Congress in 1782, Jana further envisioned women calmly and capably compromising over bringing the agrarian South and industrialized North together to grow and manufacture cotton, rice, tobacco, and indigo without slave labor.

"A Liberty Head Double Eagle Twenty Dollar gold coin for yar thoughts, me lass."

Before she could answer, a bugling bay averted the trio's attention.

A hound dog, the size of a small pony, came on an all-out tear up a wooded lane. As it circled the wagon, its long bays ebbed to more excitable yips.

Isaiah reined in the mule and brought the wagon to a stop. "Hello, Drummer," he called out.

The dog skidded to a stop and reared up, anchoring his large front pads on the scooped floor beneath their feet.

Reaching down, Isaiah tickled the scruff of Drummer's white, furry neck, and he leaned back to give the dog a clear view of his passengers. "Hey, boy, meet Jana and Keeley."

Drummer appeared to interpret Isaiah's command as his needing to have a closer inspection of the newcomers because he abandoned his station, trotted astern, leaped up onto the wagon bed, squeezed between Jana's and Keeley's trunks, and came up behind them. Whipping his white, cord-like tail, he got Jana and Keeley giggling when he took turns sniffing their necks with his tacky nose and licking their cheeks with his fine, sandpapery tongue.

When he began gently pawing their forearms and staring them down with furrowed brows and beseeching, big, brown eyes, Jana said to Isaiah, "What do you suppose he wants?"

"To take you home with him?" Isaiah scratched into his tightly coiled hair over his temple. "I've never seen him take to strangers this fast. If you're in need of a dog, I'm sure his breeder would offer you a reasonable price for him. He's the last of his litter from nearly two years ago, and it would be nice for Drummer to land as good a home"—the late-afternoon sun reflected a mischievous glint in his eyes—"as his brother before him did."

Smiling at Isaiah with a glimmer of anticipation in her eye, Jana said, "If only a dog wouldn't slow us down, we might consider adopting him right now." The notion of getting a dog for Alex when they returned home hit her. Perhaps the two of them could help each other adjust to a new home more quickly.

Keeley might've been reading Jana's mind when he said, "He seems friendly enough for a family pet." He peered at Jana. "If it's not too far out o' our way, maybe we'll fetch Drummer before we head home."

"Yes, if possible." Jana smiled at Keeley while she patted Drummer's white, bristly shoulder.

"He's got beautiful markings," Keeley said, studying his reddish-brown head, ears, and rump and the black saddle on his back, all distinguished against a snowy-white background.

"What breed of dog is he, Isaiah?" Jana asked.

"A Treeing Walker Coonhound, descendant of the English foxhound brought overseas to Virginia in the late seventeen hundreds. His breed was mixed with the Tennessee Lead sometime afterward, but it resembles more the English foxhound in looks and skill for the hunt. Walkers tree coons, mountain lions, bears, and, obviously"—Isaiah chuckled—"strangers they take a liking to." When Drummer persisted in his affections toward Jana and Keeley, Isaiah waggled his thumb rearward and said, "All right, Drummer, get down and go on home now."

Drummer's tail fell flaccid, but he obeyed.

As they watched him saunter down the lane with his head bowed low, Jana said, "I feel awful sending him away."

"He'll be fine, and it's time we were getting home ourselves." Isaiah snapped the reins and prodded the mule into a trot.

The wagon rolled and bumped along the wooded road through the air scented with the sweet fragrances of pines and wildflowers and earthy odors of oaks and tall grasses. The smells brought Jana back to the fields and woods at home, where she'd spent the bulk of her childhood climbing trees, wading barefoot through creeks, practicing with her slingshot, and hunting with Pa. A shiver of excitement to show Alex her stomping grounds rerouted her back to the moment and her forthcoming visit with Versella. "I hope Versella isn't fussing over us and sacrificing her nursing of Harold," she said to Isaiah.

A robin with a worm dangling from its mouth flitted overhead and swooped into a tree, prompting Isaiah to say, "Does a mother bird fuss over her chicks?"

They all hooted at the coincidence.

"Speaking of roosting," Isaiah said, "it's hard to believe it's been four years since the big drinking gourd in the sky led us to Versella and Harold." He reclined into the backboard. "Jess and I often wonder what more we could possibly want beyond our happy lives."

Jana raised her hand in jest. "I know." When both Isaiah and Keeley arched their eyebrows at her, she sobered to say, "How about equality for everyone in our country no matter their makeup?"

"Aye, I couldn't agree more. Although, for me nationality, at least, it seems the chains o' our perceived ineptitude are starting to loosen," Keeley said, referring to the Irish's newfound respect as a result of their fierce fighting in the War o' the Rebellion alongside those who'd subjugated them to menial labor and impoverished existences since their migration to the United States.

"We might be free now, but I'm afraid we black folk will have a long uphill battle in overcoming prejudice against us," Isaiah said dolefully.

"It's a shame any of us have to prove our equality." Jana felt the familiar shackles of suppression growing tight around her, attempting to silence her from having a complete say in matters affecting herself and her country—all because she was a woman. "Aren't we all *people* begat from the same beginning just as black and white and male and female lambs are born out of the same ewe?" She crossed her arms over her chest and huffed. "In fact, per the Constitution, anyone born or naturalized in the United States is a citizen. There's especially no disparity between sexes and who has the right to vote, hold office, and sit on juries, and I aim to jump on the bandwagon with those battling to prove it. Maybe next time there's a heated debate threatening to divide our country we'll all have a voice."

"Amen," Isaiah and Keeley said in unison.

Jana stared at the road ahead and pondered equality for her sex in particular. Since the birth of the United States, an interminable number of women had been daring in the defense and development of their country. Not to mention they'd been relied upon by their male kin for social, political, and economic advice. Jana and an army of contemporary women had followed in their footsteps, proving their mettle and merit during the Great Rebellion. They'd very capably busted out of their traditional roles inside the home as wives, mothers, and homemakers and outside the home as teachers, governesses, laundresses, and maids to master nursing, doctoring, spying, managing farms, plantations, factories, shops, and hospitals, working as government clerks and Pinkerton agents, ministering, and organizing charity for the relief of soldiers. All for the comfort of their male kin away at war. What more did they have to do to prove themselves worthy of the same rights and privileges as men? Recapturing the lost treasury was apt to be a nationwide spectacle. Could Jana hope to add another feather in the inexhaustible plume of the woman's cap?

The Barney Farm, Near Louisa Court House, Virginia

June 19, 1865 (Monday)

The swerve of the wagon snagged Jana from her silent laments about the woman's denigration in the United States. Her mood flipped and she crossed her ankles to bind her jittery legs from launching her out of the wagon and out-running the mule over the remaining distance to their dear friend Versella.

A long minute later, the wooded lane opened into a broad clearing. Since last July, the oaks had recovered from their flaccidity and discoloration under a drought and were green and thriving, but the whitewashed coats of the farmhouse, henhouse, and barn had chipped and dulled more. And the enormous cauldron and its paddle, which Versella had been employing to launder clothes when Jana and Leanne first happened upon her, stood idle.

Jana's eyes shot to the second-story window, remembering how Versella had given her and Leanne a subtle backward nod to signal the barrel of a rifle aimed at her through a part in the curtains. Even after Jana and Leanne had rescued her from the Yankee deserters stealing her food, dread continued to choke the atmosphere through everyone's anxiety over war and Keeley's amnesia and Jana's worries about her and Keeley's future together. Now, an air of peacefulness pacified the place as a middle-aged man gently rocked beneath the roof of the front porch, smiling upon a boy spinning tops and a girl combing her doll's hair.

The commotion of their conveyance captured the porch dweller's attention. His lips curled up into a smile around the stem of a smokeless pipe clamped between his teeth.

"That's Harold," Isaiah said, "and, as I'm sure you've figured out, the children belong to—"

He was cut off by their shouts, "Papa's here, Papa's here," and a long bugling bay, which preceded the streak of a large coonhound out of the barn. His long galloping stride covered an acre of land between them within a blink of an eye.

Alongside Keeley's gape at the dog, Jana stammered, "How…how…how could Drummer have beaten us here?"

Isaiah's mischievous gleam from minutes before flared, and he keeled over his reins laughing.

Jana tapped her index finger against her chin. "Oh, I see," she said to Isaiah. "He's Drummer's brother and the next to the last of his litter who, you mentioned, landed a good home."

"Aye, and it would seem that good home is with ye Barneys."

Through spits and sputters of laughter, Isaiah said, "Forgive me for wanting to see your astonishment when it dawned on you that Versella pursued Leanne's suggestion to get a dog, which she did upon your immediate departure last year."

"Ye managed to accomplish yar shocker…ye did," Keeley said. "I can't believe it. He appears to be an exact replica o' Drummer."

"Even his and Drummer's bays are identical," Jana said, referring to his initial long, bugling bay to warn of their presence and his choppier, more excitable yips now as he circled the wagon and his prey.

"Aye, is there anything that sets the two o' them apart?"

"The black saddle on Drummer's back drapes down further over the ribs, and Drummer's a little taller." After showering the coonhound with praises for his alertness, Isaiah changed his tone to that of master. "Enough barking now, Bugle. Jana and Keeley are friends."

Bugle fell silent and into a glide alongside the wagon. He held his reddish head high and pointed his tail skyward to his self-proclaimed duty as their escort.

"Bugle?" Jana questioned. "His name's perfectly suited to the distinctive blare in his bay."

Isaiah cocked his head at her and smiled. "That's exactly how Bugle's name came to Versella, and it made her giddy to think it honors her dear Yankee cavalry friends."

At the mention of his name, Bugle craned his long neck up at Isaiah and broke out in anxious yips.

"All right, Bugle, go on back to the barn and guard Calico and her newborn kittens."

As he dashed off, Jana admired his sleek frame and powerful muscles, and Keeley said, "If we were ever to get a dog, me lass, I'd definitely like a Treeing Walker Coonhound."

"Me too," Jana said.

Isaiah pulled the reins and brought the mule to a stop in unison with the screech of the front door busting open on its rusty hinges and slamming against the outer wall. The ambush startled Harold, who would've tipped over backward in his chair had it not been for the wall breaking his fall.

Versella steadied Harold in his rocker. Then, she gathered her skirts midway up her shins, her gangly arms forming wings and flapping fast as she flew down the stairs toward them. Clinging to the floorboard on Keeley's side, she said, "I thought I'd never lay eyes on my dear Irishman and heroine ever again. Now, y'all come on down here right now so I can get a closer look at y'all." She stepped sideways to give them room to disembark, and they'd barely landed on solid ground before she snared them in her arms.

In squeezing Versella tight, Jana whiffed a sweet, doughy aroma that got her salivary glands watering for Versella's good cooking.

Hugging Versella too, Keeley said, "Me Jana lass and meself are happy to be here with ye now, Versella."

"Ohhh...I'm tickled y'all have come to see your old friend so soon." Versella released Jana and Keeley and dabbed the teardrops in her whiskey-colored eyes with her long apron. Pressing her warm palms against each of their cheeks, she stared deep into Keeley's eyes. "I'm ecstatic y'all have recovered from your amnesia"—she switched her gaze to Jana—"and y'all are engaged."

Before Jana could reply, Harold came ambling up beside Versella.

Versella turned to face her husband. Blowing a wisp of her coal-black hair from her eyes, she muttered, "I told y'all to stay put, Harold."

Tapping his ornately carved cane against the red-clay ground, Harold said, "My darling Versella, I needed to exercise my joints—as y'all are always harping on me to do—and I was eager to greet our guests."

"Since y'all are here now," Versella said, "allow me to introduce Jana Brady and Keeley Cassidy."

Harold straightened up from his stoop, approximating Keeley's height. Reaching out and shaking Jana's hand, he grinned and said, "Since Versella didn't clarify who's who, I'm guessing y'all are Jana." He shook Keeley's outstretched hand. "And y'all must be Keeley."

With a swat of her hand, Versella said to Jana and Keeley, "Don't y'all mind him. He's always the court jester." She faced Harold. "Y'all behave now or I'll send y'all to your room without any supper."

Everyone laughed, including the two children, standing erect at Isaiah's hips like little wooden soldiers.

The boy tugged on Isaiah's coat sleeve, and Isaiah hopped to introducing his ten-year-old son Ben and eight-year-old daughter Chloe.

Wiping his palm on and smudging his tan trousers, Ben extended his hand, and his enthusiastic shake of each's hands emulated his papa's. "It's an honor to meet you…er…uh…miss…mister."

"Please, call us Jana and Keeley," Jana said.

Smiling shyly at Jana and Keeley, Chloe continued to cling to her papa's coat sleeve while playing with the cotton fabric of her calf-length skirt.

"They sure have brought us mountains of joy over the years," Versella said, gazing adoringly at Isaiah and his offspring.

Harold echoed her sentiment, adding, "I only wish I hadn't been cheated out of a few of their growing years."

"Well, y'all are here now"—Versella pinched his ashen cheek—"and every day we thank the good Lord for it."

"Amen," Isaiah said, motioning Ben toward the wagon bed to help him unload the trunks and waving off Keeley's protest at being left out.

Sweeping her hand toward the house, Versella said to Jana and Keeley, "Come now, let's get y'all settled." She turned to Harold. "I think y'all have had enough fresh air for one day." To a tiny wheeze from Harold, she placed her fist on her hip. "Have y'all been practicing taking deep breaths?"

"Yes, yes, yes." Harold extracted his tobacco-less pipe from his trouser pocket, put it in his mouth, and took a long drag on it. Upon exhalation, he winked at Jana and Keeley. "I've met generals less bossy than Versella." Sobering, he said, "She won't allow me tobacco in my pipe until my lungs clear, but she allows me to puff on it. She thinks it'll strengthen my breathing, and I think it's actually working."

"Aye, and, if I were ye, Harold, I'd let her act the part o' general." Keeley rubbed the side of his head, where the nasty bump and bruise from the rifle butt to his head were long gone and nothing more than a bad memory. "She did wonders for me health in bossing meself around."

After Isaiah and Ben delivered Jana's and Keeley's trunks to their rooms, Versella shooed her guests upstairs to freshen up while she returned to the kitchen.

Jana welcomed a spot bath by means of the cool water from the bedside basin, a soft cloth, and wintergreen-scented soap. After she donned a fresh blouse to go with her traveling skirt, she liberated her tresses from its snood, brushed them toward the nape of her neck, and clipped them in a brass barrette. Last, she re-tucked her derringer in her boot shaft. Her kidnapping during her lecture circuit around New York State had taught her a potent lesson about concealing a handgun on her at all times, when it was called for—like now with her and Keeley currently being stalked.

With a clean-shaven face and also smelling of wintergreen, Keeley waited for her on the second-story landing. He'd ditched his coat, but his Colt was holstered to his belt. He gestured for her to lead the way down the creaky stairs and into the kitchen.

Harold was seated at the head of a large trestle table, cheering Chloe on as she counted out the forks, knives, and spoons she placed around the eight dinner plates Ben was setting down ahead of her. Upon Jana and Keeley's arrival, she paused at eighteen.

"Please, don't let us stop you, Chloe," Jana said.

A slender but muscular woman slid piping hot biscuits from the oven and set the metal baking sheet atop the cookstove. With her golden brown face flushed from the heat of the stove, she whirled around toward Jana and Keeley and said, "Oh, please, do." She rolled her dark-chocolate eyes in jest. "She's already counted to a hundred twice before she started counting the silverware." Removing and hanging her oven mitts on a wall hook, she breezed over to Jana and Keeley, and, with a warm, welcoming smile, she reached out to shake their hands. "I'm Jess. It's lovely to finally meet you both."

Jana clasped Jess' hands. "We're delighted to meet you too."

"How was your trip?" Jess asked.

"Thank you for asking. There were a few ruts in the road, but we managed to survive them," Jana said, sparing her and everyone else the details of their encounter with Gray Fox.

"Well, I hope you're hungry. We've prepared a feast." Jess zipped over to the sink, from which she fetched strained macaroni, dumped it into a serving bowl on a small work table, and began buttering and grating cheese over it.

"Please, y'all, have a seat," Versella called over her shoulder to Jana and Keeley as she bent over the other two burners of her cookstove, alternating between stirring collard greens and whisking gravy, in a large heavy-lidded cast-iron pot in which the pork Isaiah was carving on a side table had probably been roasted over the fireplace grate.

Familiar with Versella's kitchen and unaccustomed to watching while those around them worked, Jana and Keeley rolled up their sleeves and washed their hands.

Keeley retrieved a wicker basket from a wall shelf and separated the biscuits into it and covered them with a cloth that he'd retrieved from the sideboard drawer of a rustic china cabinet.

Discovering a filled pitcher on a buffet, Jana poured milk into the glasses on the table and held a gravy boat for Versella to ladle the thickened juice from the meat into it.

With everyone seated and all the food passed around, Versella looked between Jana, Keeley, and Harold. "Why don't y'all trade some happier anecdotes from your soldiering days? Lord knows we hear enough of the horrors, and I don't want y'all dwelling on those tonight."

Jana and Keeley deferred to Harold first since he was their host.

To Jana and Keeley, he said, "As I'm sure y'all can confirm, even in the midst of war, there were lighter moments, thankfully. I can think of plenty, but here's one that comes to my mind first." He reclined against his ladder-backed chair and dove into his story. "One winter, the Union and Confederate picket lines were close enough for the guards to trade conversation, coffee, tobacco, and newspapers. To break up the boredom, the Yanks challenged us Rebs to a game of"—he picked up his biscuit and pretended to pitch it—"baseball. The highest-ranking officer of each side picked the teams from their respective encampments, and then they watched as we Rebs routed you Yanks twenty to twelve. It was all great fun until our players started preening like peacocks and mocking the Yanks about the final score prophesying our winning the war." He grunted. "Pretty embarrassing, considering we lost the war."

Keeley offered Jana the floor next, and she recounted an incident surrounding another game popular in winter encampment. "Once, by permission of our superiors, Keeley, Leanne, Charlie, and I were heading out to the countryside to hunt and forage food. With money at stake, some of our comrades were chasing down a greased pig. One of the gamblers took his misfortune of missing the pig out on me by christening me 'Nancy Boy' in front of my friends and scores of others hanging about." She grimaced. "I hated to do it, but, in order for me to maintain my disguise, I had to defend myself as any man would against the insult. So, I swung out of my saddle and, without one punch thrown, and, as I'd once seen Leanne do to a bully, I swept my heckler's legs out from under him, hopped on his back, and pinched his ear until he screamed an apology."

When everyone laughed, then looked to Keeley for his story, he said, "For me tale, I'll piggyback on me Jana lass's. As I later learned, her show was more for meself than anyone else. She sensed me awareness o' her disguise and me romantic feelings for her. But because she was uncertain about meself turning protective and tattling on her to get her discharged from the army, she refrained from revealing her secret. O' course, me courageous lass"—he shot Jana a look of admiration—"wanted to stay and fight alongside meself, Leanne, and Charlie."

Harold sighed and his shoulders slumped. "Camaraderie was certainly a major staple in making war more bearable."

Versella reached over and patted her husband's hand.

Rising from the table, Harold looked at Jana and Keeley, in particular, when he said, "I'm sorry to leave your company early tonight, but my bed calls."

"Please, think nothing of it," Jana said. "We're just glad we finally got to spend some time with you."

"Aye, and it's quite understandable. It took meself a long time to recuperate from the ill effects o' me eight-month imprisonment in Richmond."

While Versella and Isaiah helped Harold up to bed, Jana, Keeley, Jess, Ben, and Chloe scoured the kitchen. When Versella and Isaiah returned downstairs, Isaiah and his family left for home, a quick walk behind Versella and Harold's house, and Versella, Jana, and Keeley retreated to the parlor.

Darkness had fallen, requiring Keeley to turn the knobs to ignite the oiled wicks of the matching torchieres atop the fireplace mantel and light a path for Versella to set a server of tea on the sofa table and for all to find their seats.

As Versella poured the tea, steam from the teapot's spout swirled about and filled the air with an apple-and-floral fragrance.

Jana scanned the cozy room. The furniture and their arrangement were as she remembered from before, but the emotion was quite different. Then, Jana and Keeley had sat opposite each other nervously getting reacquainted through his amnesia while Jana despaired over their love being lost forever; now, they squeezed in tight together on the russet-and-white-striped sofa.

Plopping onto the floral chair across from them, Versella said, "I can't thank y'all enough for your kindness in sending me letters over the past year, keeping me apprised of your lives together." She rapped twice on her armrests with her open palms. "But do tell me why y'all have ventured into the South with war barely over and travel here difficult." She picked up her cup and saucer, squiggled into her chair, and began sipping her tea, signaling that she had all night to hear their story.

Jana and Keeley swapped turns relating their assignment and chronicling the details of their covert work thus far. Although they knew they could trust Versella, they kept their promise to President Johnson and told her only that they were working for the federal government.

When they described their discoveries in Shohola, Versella set her cup on its saucer and both on the table with a clatter. She slapped her thighs and said, "I've got some interesting news, sure to help y'all on your way."

Jana and Keeley moved in unison to the edge of their cushion to better hear Versella over the cacophony of cicadas chirping outside the open windows.

"I'm unfamiliar with any Jibbses, but, as monumental coincidences go, we know the Fernsbys. Not well mind y'all, but they attend our church. When their middle son Jed stumbled home about eight months ago, a rumor went around of his having amassed wealth after he'd survived a train wreck." Versella raised her hand and wriggled her long fingers at Jana and Keeley. "Would y'all allow me a brief digression before I disclose to y'all what I know will interest y'all the most?"

With her cup pressed against her lips, Jana blurted into her tea, "Of course," and the blast of steam from her breathy reply intensified the warmth of her cheeks, already flushed with excitement.

Versella continued, "After most of the soldiers from our area returned home from war, our local minister beckoned his flock back to Sunday sermons. I'm sure y'all understand, it's a long day for Harold, but he insists upon attending to pray for his fallen comrades and for his fortune in having survived the war. At the end of the service, Harold and I always linger on our pew so we don't hold up the departing congregation." She leaned forward, her voice filling with intrigue as she spoke. "One Sabbath, we witnessed Mrs. Fernsby pinching her son's ear until he uttered a penance, which included the words: stolen federal money and *Orange and Alexandria Railroad.*"

Jana piped in. "Are you sure you heard those exact words?"

"I couldn't be surer, y'all." Versella's face lit up, shining brighter than the full moon beaming down upon her through the mullioned window and creating a halo around her head.

Jana set down her teacup and reached over and squeezed Keeley's hand, bracing herself for Versella's forthcoming intelligence, apt to be a meatier morsel.

"Apparently feeling compelled to confess her further knowledge of duplicity, Mrs. Fernsby reprimanded Jed about his having accepted what she termed *blood money*, and she demanded he donate it to the needy. Next, she said, 'Over my dead body will y'all accompany your crony to Brandy Station for guidance in salvaging the money for some delinquents.'"

"Brandy Station?" Jana repeated, her senses reawakened to the unforgiving battle of June 9, 1863: man and beast screaming as they were dismembered, disemboweled, or decapitated by artillery shot or slashed up by a saber; an empire of flies swarming and feasting upon the remains; blood and decay boiled by a scorching sun into a caustic stew which assailed the nostrils, throat, and stomach. Worst of all, Jana, Keeley, Leanne, and Charlie had to sit on their mounts and watch it all before their impending charge up Fleetwood Hill into the razor-like jaws of Confederate artillery, waiting to pounce upon them, gnaw on their flesh, and spit out their bones. It was a miracle that she and her friends had made it out alive. She dug her nails into Keeley's palm and shuddered at the notion of their having to revisit that devil's playground.

Keeley wrapped his arm around her and lightly caressed her bicep, scarred from the bullet she'd taken on that day.

Versella reached for the teapot. "Would y'all like some more tea to calm your nerves, Jana?"

Placing her hand over roiling stomach, Jana said, "No, thank you. I just need a moment. I'm fine, really."

"Y'all take all the respite y'all need before we proceed." She shook her head and frowned. "Why, it just breaks my heart every time I hear my dear Harold shouting battle cries in his sleep."

"Aye, I can't help think we'll never really be rid o' our nightmares. But, while I'm awake, I meself intend to practice deflecting me frights to cheerful thoughts."

"I'll pray for y'all to conquer even your nightmares," Versella said.

Jana resolved to follow Keeley's advice to himself; she'd start now by pulling them all out of the solemn abyss into which she'd sunk them. Sucking in a deep breath, she said, "I'm ready to leave our battle memories behind, and I'm eager to hear what else you learned about Jed Fernsby, Versella."

"All right, if y'all are sure y'all are fine." With a nod from Jana, Versella picked up where she'd left off. "Dear Lord, what came next was sheer lunacy. Just like this"—Versella crimped her face in rage and shook her fists—"Jed lunged at his mother and screamed, 'You should've kept quiet, Mama. Now, I've got to go right your wrong before the all-seeing knights who made me hide the money and leave a map to its location have me killed.' Consequently, he ran past us out of the church, and, apparently, his parents haven't heard from their son since."

"How long ago might this have happened?" Keeley asked.

"A week ago yesterday," Versella said.

Jana slumped into the supple sofa cushion, stewing over Jed's having, at least, a week's jump on them.

Ignorant of Jana's gloom with her head bowed, Versella extracted a handkerchief from beneath her sleeve cuff and twirled it around her fingers. "I hope for Mr. and Mrs. Fernsby's sake, Jed's patched up his errant doings with the knights of whom he spoke and isn't lying dead somewhere. I can't imagine losing a child—no matter their age—as countless mothers did in the war." She dabbed her eyes, lifted her chin, and smiled. "Enough of my melancholy. Let's focus on happier things, such as my delight to announce my sons are courting and bringing their intendeds home to meet me and Harold any day now."

Toasting Versella with her teacup, Jana said, "Now, that's cause for celebration."

"Aye, it is at that." Keeley raised his teacup too.

Versella sighed wearily. "Just as I couldn't stop y'all from heading south last year, I suppose I can't talk y'all out of this mission." Jana felt her torso stiffening, and her and Keeley's silence forced Versella to say, "Could y'all at least wait for Leanne and Charlie to come to your aid?"

Rushing her words, Jana said, "Time is of the essence. Jed and the other Rebel thief, Fulton Jibbs, have a huge jump on us."

Versella frowned.

Jana hoped to appease her by saying, "We have Leanne and Charlie waiting in reserve at a boarding house in Washington City. Assuming the telegraph is operating in Louisa Court House since we got one through to you, we promise to send them a telegram from there, summoning them to Brandy Station."

"Isn't Louisa Court House out of your way?" Before they could reply, Versella said, "I insist y'all let me handle sending your telegram."

Jana knew she meant to do it herself as her own guarantee that it got done and Jana and Keeley had reliable backup.

"We might have to visit the courthouse anyway," Keeley said.

"Oh?" Versella and Jana said in concert.

Keeley explained, "If Fulton Jibbs resides in Louisa County, the courthouse should have records o' its residents and their addresses. We might want to scout out if Jed has gone to the Jibbs' homestead to round up Fulton. Or perhaps, even better, they're still there and we can talk them into giving up the treasury."

"Good thinking, Keeley," Jana said.

With a roll of her eyes, Versella said, "As much as I hate encouraging your daring venture, I have a few ideas to expedite your investigation. Come early morning, I'll send Isaiah out to speak with the minister of our church. He's preached elsewhere around Louisa County, and I'll bet he can tell y'all where to locate the Jibbses. Since he's duty-bound by confidentiality, he won't ask for an explanation to Isaiah's inquiry if Isaiah offers none."

A deep-throated and persistent baying pierced the night air.

Instinctively, Jana snatched her derringer from her boot shaft, and Keeley yanked his pistol out of his holster.

Cocking her ear toward the window, Versella listened for a few seconds. "Don't y'all worry; Bugle's probably treed a raccoon. It's nearly a nightly occur—"

She was cut off by a crash in the bushes outside and heavy footfalls retreating down the lane to the Barney homestead.

Bugle's bays grew louder as he approached from the vicinity of the barn, where the sound of a rifle exploded.

To Versella's horror-stricken face, Jana and Keeley hurled themselves up from the sofa.

"Go upstairs, Versella, and assure Harold all is well," Jana said, keeping her voice calm.

Although she eyed Jana hesitantly, Versella hoisted her skirts and scrambled up the creaky steps of the central staircase.

Keeley had already advanced to the front entryway. When he

heard Isaiah snap, "Come back, Bugle," he whipped open the front door, stepped out onto the porch, and called over his shoulder as he ran off, "Secure the inside, me lass."

Stationing herself before the front window, Jana felt her heart beating faster than the skedaddling of galloping hoofs. The moon's luminosity accentuated the silhouettes of Bugle, Isaiah, and Keeley, in order, chasing after a lone horse and rider. As the hide-and-seekers disappeared down the lane, the sudden silence of the night was deafening, as though the critters were holding their breaths to assess the danger. Then, an urgent *whoo, who, who, who, whoo* of a barn owl thrummed Jana's eardrums. Its hoot, oddly communicative, like the telegraph's series of dots and dashes, signaled he was alert to danger. After a short breather, the raptor's softer sequence of hoots seemed to convey she had nothing to worry about. Given its high vantage point and exceptionally good night vision, Jana trusted the owl's assessment. Still, she yearned to be out there in the thick of action, but she remained at the window. There was no way she'd abandon Versella to tend to Harold and fend off another intruder all alone.

When the cavaliers returned, Keeley declared he'd caught a glimpse of the same bearded man who'd been spying on him and Jana hours before.

Isaiah corroborated Keeley's description of the interloper and added, "I was out in the barn, checking on Calico and her kittens when Bugle began his baying. Thinking he'd sniffed out a raccoon, I tried quieting him from waking up Harold and the children, but he seemed more agitated than usual." He shook his head and frowned. "If I'd let Bugle loose sooner and made my shot closer to the eavesdropper to stop him in his tracks, we might've caught him."

"You did all you could, Isaiah." With a huff, Jana stomped her foot and said to Keeley, "How on earth did Woodcock's goons manage to elude Gray Fox and his guerillas?"

"I don't know, me lass, but, once they did, it was easy for them to catch up to us; they had the advantage o' speed, riding horseback over our slower travel by stagecoach."

Isaiah volunteered himself and Bugle to walk the premises throughout the night so Jana and Keeley could have, at least, one good-night's sleep for their forthcoming journey.

"I know I speak for Keeley too when I say we'll be embarking upon our trip as early as possible come morning." To Keeley's emphatic nod, Jana continued, "We refuse to subject you kind people to harm due to our presence, and we'll not argue the point."

"Then, I'll be on my way to the barn to fetch Bugle. Be sure to say goodbye before you leave," Isaiah called over his shoulder as he was turning the front doorknob.

"Wait, Isaiah," Versella said, coming down the creaky stairs. "We could use your help bright and early in the morning to go to our church and ask the minister if he knows of a family named Jibbs."

After eagerly agreeing to do it, Isaiah slipped out into the moonlit night.

Versella suggested Jana and Keeley reconvene with her in the parlor to discuss their plans for departure. Once they were reseated, she placed her hand over her heart. "Thank the good Lord for Bugle's vigilance. He surely lives up to a dog's reputation as man's best friend." Abruptly, she threw her arms out. "Speaking of Bugle, I'm going to instruct Isaiah to fetch his brother for y'all from his breeder on his way to church tomorrow." She winked. "I hear he has a meaner streak toward trespassers and a keener sniffer than Bugle."

Along with Keeley, Jana raised her eyebrows in surprise.

"I'll feel much better if y'all have a dog along for your protection."

Jana broke out in uncontrollable giggles, which exorcised a few pangs of her guilt over having exposed the Barneys to danger. Between fits, she managed to squeak out, "It looks like we'll be getting our dog much sooner than we'd anticipated, Keeley."

Jana's merriment was infectious, and Versella and Keeley joined her in laughter.

When the jollity waned, a scheme began to take shape in Jana's brain. "Where do the Fernsbys live?" she asked Versella.

"A short distance north of here and the church," Versella said.

"What are ye thinking, me lass?"

"Maybe we could get our hands on a piece of Jed Fernsby's clothing for Drummer to help track Jed. But how could we accomplish that without blowing our cover?"

"Hmm." Versella rested her elbows on the arms of her chair and her chin on her steepled fingers. "I've got it," she exclaimed, her hands plummeting to her lap and her cheeks flushed with excitement. "Yesterday, our minister requested donations for those in our area whose homes were pilfered and ravaged during the war. As y'all know, we had the good fortune of dodging devastation. Because of that, I volunteered to take up the collection. So, I'll give Isaiah our charitable articles and send him to the Fernsby's farm first to gather theirs. On his way back, he can drop everything off at the church and speak with the minister and then pick up Drummer."

"What if none of Jed's clothing is amongst the Fernsby's offerings?" Jana asked.

"My note will stipulate clothing is needed as much as food, and it will strongly suggest their sample cover the different sizes of each of their three sons. Let's hope that does the trick for y'all."

Gawping at Versella, Keeley said, "Is there any end to yar care and generosity?"

"Now that y'all mention it, it seems y'all are going to need a wagon and mule for your journey. We have an extra ensemble for y'all to borrow."

"Actually," Jana said, "I was thinking we should travel by horseback and ride with only an extra set of clothes and what we absolutely need for cooking and camping out. . .that is, if it's all right for you to temporarily store our trunks and anything else we can't carry with us in your barn."

"Why, of course, it's all right. In fact, it's the best excuse I have for holding y'all hostage to a return visit."

Frowning, Jana said, "We have another giant hurdle to overcome. I'm sure two good mounts are going to be hard to lease from the liveries around here, and I imagine the locals had most of theirs stolen by cavalrymen in need of replacements after their horses were killed in action or hobbled from overuse."

Keeley and Versella grinned at each other.

"What secret are you two harboring?" Jana asked.

Versella said, "Y'all and Leanne would've missed spotting them the last time y'all were here since we had them squirreled away in a wooded corral, but we have several good cavalry horses. We inherited them after we found them wandering rider-less after the battle around Trevilian Station. I doubt either army will ever come to repossess them, so y'all can have them. They came fully outfitted with blankets, saddles, saddlebags, hand axes, feedbags, cooking supplies—you name it—just about everything y'all will need for your trip."

"In case we have to ditch them in favor of taking safer transportation back to Washington City before we can get back here, we can pay you a fair price for them," Jana said.

Versella clucked her tongue. "Nonsense! We obtained them at no cost, and I'll brook no argument from y'all on that account. Consider them a wedding present."

"Fine, but about the clothing and other items we must leave behind," Jana looked to Keeley for his assenting nod before she said, "you'll have Isaiah take them to the church tomorrow and have them donated to the needy." When Versella started to protest, Jana regurgitated Versella's words. "We'll brook no argument about our contribution or any other expense, such as for Drummer and the telegram to Leanne and Charlie."

Versella's cheeks plumped up to her smile. "It's a deal." She held her hand out and shook Jana's, then followed up with, "So, it's settled. Come early morning, y'all will pick out your horses and pack up. Keeley knows where to find everything. I'll ride south to address your telegram, and Isaiah will head north to conduct his business. Let's all plan to converge where the Marquis Road intersects the top of our lane. We need to avoid Bugle reuniting with Drummer and delaying y'all."

"Do you think Drummer will follow us after a short introduction?" Jana asked.

"I'm sure of it. Bugle's kind loves and needs love. Because his breeder's in the business of selling coonhounds, he and his family act as aloof as humanly possible toward their litters to encourage an instant attachment to their new masters. I can tell y'all it worked for our and Bugle's immediate bonding."

Maybe that explains Drummer's excessive affections toward us, Jana thought. "I don't know much about Treeing Walker Coonhounds, but do they have good speed and stamina to keep up with a rigorous ride?"

"Yes," Versella said with gusto. "In fact, the Treeing Walker Coonhound requires lots of daily exercise for body and mind. Y'all are getting a good dog."

"Now that we have all o' that settled, there's but one wee issue yet to be resolved." When both women gave him a quizzical look, Keeley said, "The telegram to Leanne and Charlie needs to be in code. How will ye explain the need for secrecy to the dispatcher without rousing his suspicion?"

With a flick of her hand, Versella said, "Must I remind y'all about my participation in smuggling morphine between Washington City and the Rebel hospitals?"

Jana recollected Versella's sending them with a box of morphine on their way south to see Keeley's regimental surgeon about his amnesia. If they'd been stopped by either army, they would've resorted to lying about their bringing the pain-killer to their respective wounded and being ordered to hand deliver it to the proper medical authorities.

"And how do y'all suppose my incriminating messages went through the telegraph to my contact in Washington City?" Versella paused, allowing the answer to sink in.

"Ah"—Jana bobbed her head—"in code."

Impishly grinning, Versella said, "Any coded telegram I write will not be questioned by our local telegrapher since he was a willing accomplice in our smuggling ring. And, if I don't offer, he'll refrain from asking about the change in my cryptograph and the content of my message. For your protection also, I'll have our dispatcher send it to our trustworthy telegraph office in Washington City and order the recipient to rush and personally deliver the note from y'all to Leanne and Charlie at their lodging."

Versella reminded Jana of spymaster Miss Lizzie, in terms of her always having her tracks covered. She swore the halo around their angel's head had amplified in luster. As she was wishing she and Keeley could be as giving towards her, a notion struck Jana. They definitely could be. Now, Jana had a noble incentive to recoup the stolen treasury, and she was one-hundred-percent certain Keeley would agree to dole out some of their spoils to Versella. The extra money could help her get medical care for Harold and hire out repairs for their homestead. She dreamed of making their lives easier, and she wished she could get going right now, but there was a lot to accomplish before they took up the chase. She prayed they weren't too late to catch Jed Fernsby and Fulton Jibbs.

On the Road to Brandy Station, Virginia

June 20, 1865 (Tuesday)

The Barney homestead flurried with activity at the crack of dawn. After a hearty breakfast of porridge, toast, and jam, Jess insisted upon cleaning up the kitchen while everyone scattered to prepare for Jana and Keeley's departure: Versella rode her mare to Louisa Court House to send out Jana and Keeley's coded telegram to Leanne and Charlie; Isaiah took the wagon and mule to collect clothing from the Fernsbys, intelligence from the church minister, and Drummer; and Jana and Keeley rounded up, saddled, and accessorized their horses.

As planned, Jana and Keeley met Versella and Isaiah around 9:00 a.m. at the intersection of the lane to Versella's homestead and the Marquis Road.

Jana was worried about it taking time for Drummer to adjust to them, but he remembered them from yesterday and responded with licks to their pets and hugs.

Before Jana and Keeley bid their dear friends sweet adieu, Versella made them promise to return for a longer visit and to bring Leanne and Charlie along.

Armed with bountiful fodder for themselves, their new Treeing

Walker Coonhound, and the horses and directions to the Jibbs' homestead, they spurred their mounts up the road at a brisk gallop to test their dog's speed and concentration. Drummer immediately passed one test: He stuck with Jana and Keeley as they raced past the lane to his breeder's home.

The dewy morning air and the sense of freedom Jana felt from riding horseback brought a flush of exuberance to her cheeks. She yearned to free her tresses from their clips beneath her men's hat, but the thought of wrestling with a tangled mass at the end of a hard day's ride barred her from uncaging them.

Within five minutes, they reached the crossroads at Clayton's Store and their stage stop from the previous day. They reined in their mounts before a wooden road sign and studied the four markings: southwest to Trevilian Station, south to Louisa Court House, northeast to Fredericksburg, and north to Culpeper Court House. Lightly spurring their horses into a walk, they chose the latter direction, and, for the health of their horses' hoofs and joints, they planned to end their day at thirty miles or three hours, whichever came first.

Jana marveled at Drummer's vigor. His cheeks barely pumped as he strutted along. "I understand the *tap…tap…tap* of his large pads against the ground sounding like a drum as he runs, but I can't quite adapt to his name."

"Aye, Drummer doesn't seem fitting to our having him along, and the drums were the call for infantrymen. I can't bring meself to steal the name Bugle, so we need a name more fitting o' us."

"Through constant repetition, do you think we could get him used to another name pretty fast?"

"Aye, he took to our affections immediately and followed us willingly, so there's hope for his hasty acclimation to a change o' title."

"What shall we call our gentle giant?" Since Keeley was good at coming up with names, Jana left him alone to ponder it. He'd blessed Jana's cavalry horse with the Gaelic name for "battle maiden" because of Maiti's aptitude for forming up to the call of the bugle more speedily than any cavalry horse and her zeal to take the lead in a charge.

Keeley sprang up in his hooded stirrups. "How about Tracker?"

Jana twisted toward him on her creaking saddle. "That's perfect."

Reclining back against the curved cantle of his saddle, Keeley smiled with satisfaction. "Aye, although it might be the primary reason we consented to adopting him, Versella would argue he was meant to perform magic for our protection and the name Merlin might be better suited."

Jana called out to Drummer by his new designation and, when he failed to respond, she said, "It's a shame Merlin wasn't here right now to cast a spell over him."

"Aye, I still can't believe how much he looks like his brother, and I might need a spell cast over meself to keep from calling him Bugle."

"Me too. But there *is* one big difference between the two hounds."

"And what might that be, me lass?"

Jana drew her shoulders inward in a self-hug and squealed with delight. "Tracker belongs to us, and we're free to fall in love with him."

Shaking his head with a toothy grin, Keeley retorted, "By a wee prick o' his arrow upon our hearts, it would seem Cupid has already brought about our love at first sight."

Jana snapped her fingers to summon Tracker to her. He came and, due to his height, she barely had to lean over to scratch the white, bristly fur between his ears, thinly shrouding his large skull. She repeated several times, "Good boy, Tracker."

"Now that we've settled the matter o' our coonhound's name"—

Keeley surveyed Jana's men's trousers and coat, especially the bulge beneath her coat where her Colt was holstered—"are we back to calling ye Johnnie?"

"Jana will do. It'll be harder to hide my gender with just the two of us than it was amongst a regiment of cavalrymen. Besides"—she coquettishly batted her eyelashes at him—"we might need to snuggle tonight. . . that is, to keep warm. If we're happened upon, it'll be better if I'm seen as a woman. So, I'll act the part of a tomboy."

"Act?" Keeley playfully snorted.

After a roll of her eyes at Keeley, Jana suggested they light a flame under their horses' hoofs. "Come, Tracker," she called out and was elated when their Treeing Walker wagged his big brown eyes and long white tail at her.

They resumed a swift gallop, partway retracing the route of their stagecoach from yesterday. Tracker's powerfully churning hindquarters and spindly legs allowed him to keep pace. Approximately thirty-minutes later, they again slowed their mounts to a walk. After crossing a narrow bridge over the gurgling water of a broad rocky creek, they began counting the homesteads on their left. They followed the minister's instructions and veered westward into the third lane, its width generous enough to accommodate Jana, Keeley, and Tracker abreast of each other.

Jana noticed fresh hoof prints in the dampened clay heading back toward the road, and she remarked upon it to Keeley. To his silence, she found him riveted by something else, and she followed his eyes straight ahead. Until now, their obsession to reach their goal had blinded them to the landscape, sandwiched between the eastward coastal plain and the westward mountains. The magnificence of the fertile-green rolling hills backed by the majestic Blue Ridge Mountains took her breath away. The buildings of the small farming compound, toward which they advanced, appeared as blights upon the sprawling plateau.

Looking to Jana with yearning in his eyes, Keeley reached out for her hand.

She obliged the gesture, reveling in his tender grasp.

"It's what I picture o' our hearth and home, me lass, and I meself am excited to think we might be getting to raising it much sooner than we thought."

Jana's heart flitted happily about like the monarch butterflies in and out of the roadside bushes. "I too dream of the day when we'll have our own slice of heaven."

After a gentle squeeze, Keeley released her hand and clicked his cheek, nudging his horse into a trot.

Jana and Tracker caught up to him in a barnyard, where they scattered a dozen chickens out of their path.

Whether Tracker had been previously dulled to the jitteriness of fowl from his former barnyard experiences or he was exhausted, he avoided a chase. He plopped down on his haunches between Jana and Keeley and continually sniffed the air and scanned their surrounds.

Over the frantic clucking, a woman's voice called out from within the henhouse, "I'm so happy you've come…" her voice trailed off at the sight of foreigners. She skidded to a stop, and the basket on her arm swung in a wide arc, nearly toppling its bountiful eggs. "Oh, I was hoping y'all were my oldest son come home."

Jana's spirit summersaulted at her promising news. Had they found the Jibbses? Sensing her excitement, her gelding snorted and bounced his head, drawing the woman's unwanted attention toward her. Jana pulled her hat low over her face to avoid a lengthy inquisition about the mismatch of her clothes to her gender. Facing downward, she patted the lathered neck of her chestnut to calm him.

Fortunately, the woman's green eyes appeared to be looking straight through Jana in her obsession to straighten her plain straw hat. "Do forgive my ragged state." She shook hay from her faded homespun skirt. "We don't get many visitors around here."

Still holding his reins, Keeley crossed his hands over the curved pommel of his saddle in a relaxed manner and made a show of looking around. He and Jana had agreed beforehand upon his doing the interviewing to avoid Jana's voice being heard. "Are ye all alone with yar chores, ma'am?"

She pointed her thumb over her shoulder. "Mr. Jibbs—my husband, of course—and my younger son are out sowing the summer crops and my two daughters are in the barn mucking it out and milking the cow."

Jana and Keeley shared a sidelong glance to her affirmation of being a Jibbs.

"Before ye sighted us, ye thought we were an older son come home." Keeley faked a hard gulp. "I hope he hasn't perished in the war."

"Oh no, thank the good Lord." She stared off in the distance. "Though, I can't imagine what Fuji's infantry comrade needed from him that he'd give Jed priority over us."

Jana and Keeley arched their eyebrows at her, and Keeley said, "Fuji? Isn't that Japanese?"

Mrs. Jibbs giggled. "Yes. Our son's real name is Fulton. We call him Fuji because ever since he read about U.S. expeditions to Japan, he's been obsessed with going there and especially climbing Mount Fuji." She shrugged. "Anyway, Jed's mission for them had to be really important; it's not like our Fuji to leave us during the planting months." A motherly affection radiated through her smile. "Y'all don't mistake me now; my oldest son has a heart of gold. He stuck around for almost ten days after his friend's arrival to put us in good stead with the chores. He even made his friend pitch in." Exhaling a great sigh, she said, "I reckon we've gotten used to taking up his slack with his having been away soldiering the past four years."

"It's fortunate he made it home at all from the war with so many dead. And, if yar fortune continues, Mrs. Jibbs, he won't be gone long."

"I hope y'all are right. He only just left within the hour, but I already keenly feel his absence. Unfortunately, a mother hen like me always worries about her chicks."

Jana noted Keeley's subtle shift in his saddle, and she guessed he was trying to subdue his elation over Fuji and Jed's trifling lead on them.

Swatting her free hand, Mrs. Jibbs said, "I don't know why I'm unloading my woes on perfect strangers. Y'all must think I'm a gossip."

"Not at all," Keeley said. "I meself find it's often easier to talk to strangers."

"I appreciate your understanding. Now, what can I do for y'all?"

"Well, ma'am, we're heading home from soldiering ourselves, and—"

Mrs. Jibbs interrupted. "Where's home?"

"A little north o' Leesburg."

Jana presumed Keeley had plucked the place of their first skirmish with their cavalry regiment out of the air for two reasons: to eliminate the possibility of Mrs. Jibbs' having friends, family, and acquaintances in common with it being a three-day ride north of her farm and in case he had to describe it.

"Fellow Virginians, huh?" The hue of the woman's irises grew less visible as they narrowed in on Jana. "Did y'all fight too, young lady?" She must've noticed the parting of Jana's lips at the brusqueness of her question, and, before she allowed Jana an answer, she said, "Excuse me for saying, but your beautiful auburn locks and feminine face don't belong to a man."

Suddenly conscientious of wisps of her tresses tickling her neck, Jana refrained from reaching up. She didn't want to give the impression she was trying to hide something by tucking them up into her hat. Keeping her wits about her, Jana invented a ruse, requiring her to mimic Keeley's accent. "Our mam and da are progressive-thinkers. They raised meself and me brother here and our younger sister to share in the men's and women's work on the farm and to battle injustices no matter the cost to our lives. If we women had but a wee say in things, our country might never have come to blows." Jana lifted her shoulders. "I meself fought to prove we women are every bit as intelligent, skilled, and courageous as men and we deserve the same rights as them." She aimed what she hoped Mrs. Jibbs would construe as sisterly affection at Keeley. "Also, I was confident there was none more capable than meself to watch me brother's back."

She smiled at Jana. "I admire your grit. Another Belle Boyd, y'all are."

Because Jana and Keeley had brandished themselves as Virginians, Mrs. Jibbs offered no further narrative of Belle Boyd. None was required. The fashionable Maria Isabella "Belle" Boyd was famous or infamous, depending on which side of the Mason and Dixon's Line you lived. She was definitely a thorn in the Union Army's buttock. At age seventeen, she killed a drunken Union soldier, who was bullying her and her mother with lecherous language. She was exonerated, but she earned two incarcerations at Old Capitol Prison in Washington for spying on behalf of Confederate general Thomas "Stonewall" Jackson around the Shenandoah Mountains, near her hometown of Martinsburg, Virginia—before that portion of the state became West Virginia, Jana realized, on this very day in 1863. Jana knew Belle Boyd better by her other nicknames: La Belle Rebelle and the Siren of the Shenandoah.

"Aye, me sister is every bit as courageous as our Belle Boyd. She shielded meself from a bullet or two and did some spying herself."

"Well, now, that's something," she said to Jana. "I reckon the future will hold lots of tales of women's bravery in the war."

Before she could start another conversation, Keeley faked an uneasy squirming in his saddle. "Moments ago, ma'am, ye asked what ye could do for us, and we'll understand if ye can't oblige it." He ogled her basket. "Might ye be able to spare a few o' yar eggs for us and our dog's supper tonight?"

"Since y'all asked instead of stealing it from us as both Johnnie Reb and Billy Yank did during the war, I'll do better than that. Why don't y'all stay for dinner?"

"We appreciate yar generous offer, ma'am, but we need to make hay while we have daylight"—he peered at the dimming sky—"and before the rain hits hard." He frowned. "Ye see, our da died while we were at war, and our mam has but only one daughter at home to help with chores. We're itching to get back to her as soon as possible."

She smiled. "How can I argue with y'all after I lamented about my absentee son?" Lifting the hems of her skirts with her unencumbered hand and starting away, she nodded toward an iron ring driven into the bark of a mature oak tree. "Tie your horses up and let them graze on the lush grass while y'all head to the barn for some fresh milk and I gather eggs, fresh biscuits, and smoked meat for y'all."

Keeley removed his hat and placed it over his heart. "Y'are a Godsend, ma'am."

After packing away their forage and mounting up, Jana and Keeley prepared to leave when Mrs. Jibbs stopped them.

"It seems y'all are traveling the same road as my Fuji, and y'all just might catch up to him since your horses are in better shape. I know my Fuji, and he won't run a horse into the ground even to save his own life." She eyed them sorrowfully. "If y'all do happen upon him, send him his mother's love and wish for a speedy return."

"Aye, ma'am, we'll be sure to do that. However, might ye give us a wee description o' him and his friend so we might recognize them if we see them?"

Mrs. Jibbs rolled her eyes at herself. "That was daft of me to forget. Many say my Fuji looks more like me than his father with his brown, curly hair and green eyes. And his friend has blond hair and brown eyes. My Fuji is real tall and his friend is not much shorter."

"Again, thank ye, ma'am." Keeley tipped his hat to her, steered his horse around, and led Jana and Tracker back to the main road.

Far out of Mrs. Jibbs' earshot, Jana said, "You're one sly fox, Keeley. You managed to siphon information from Mrs. Jibbs without rousing her suspicion and another meal for us and Tracker."

As Ma always did when she was forced to fib, he gazed heavenward and said with forlornness, "Forgive us for lying to the charitable woman. I hope it doesn't come to our having to harm her son."

"You read my mind. We were painted a cruel picture of Fuji Jibbs in Shohola. Based upon his mother's goodness and Fuji's own guarantee of his family's comfort before he eloped with Jed, I can't picture Fuji Jibbs as a rotten egg."

"Aye, but desperate situations make desperate people. Who's to say, if we were in his shoes, we wouldn't have cut a deal to avoid death from imprisonment and cash in while we were at it to make our poor farming families comfortable the rest o' their lives."

"I sense we'll discover what Fuji Jibbs is all about soon enough."

"For now, me lass, let's set our sights on gaining on our pair o' artful dodgers."

Jana whistled. "Come, Tracker." She was amazed when he dropped in alongside her.

After a half-hour delay at the Jibbs' homestead, Jana and Keeley resumed their northward route. They alternated their horses' gaits between walking, trotting, cantering, and galloping upon the rutted road until an hour later a gusting wind slowed them entirely to a walk.

A fresh, earthy aroma charging the air and bleak clouds hovering over the mountain ridges spelled Mother Nature's mood swinging from cheerful to wrathful. It compelled Jana and Keeley to shorten their trip shy of the thirty miles they'd planned for the day.

Jana's disappointment was placated by two notions: The weather had to be stunting Fuji and Jed's progress too, and the delay would give Leanne and Charlie a chance to make up the extra hour they required to reach Brandy Station concurrently with her and Keeley.

At least twenty minutes lapsed after they'd crossed the intersection of the turnpike to Fredericksburg when they happened upon an abandoned and dilapidated one-room shack. They realized their good fortune when they found a working fireplace inside.

The dusky noontime sky and distant rumble of thunder set Jana and Keeley in motion.

Keeley disappeared into the nearby woods with his hand axe and Tracker sauntering beside him.

In between Keeley's coming and going a few times with a load of logs, Jana hid their satchels of greenbacks beneath some loose floor boards inside the shanty, and she watered the horses in a nearby stream, knotted long ropes around their bridles to give them room to graze on the tall grass or seek shelter beneath a spacious overhang at the front of the shelter, and stripped them down. Next, she brought their saddles and other equipment inside to keep dry. Beside the stone fireplace, she discovered a large ash pail, which she rinsed and filled in the stream and set out as a provisional watering trough. Last, she treated each gelding to a handful of oats mixed with dried corn as a nutritional supplement to the grass. Their gluttonous smacks ended simultaneously with what Jana hoped was Keeley's last whack of his axe with the weather worsening.

An ominous bolt of lightning blazed across the sky, and, when an ear-splitting clap of thunder followed in its immediate wake, Jana bent into the wind and hastened to intercept Keeley and Tracker, who was dragging a spindly branch to break up into kindling by his massive jaws.

Breathlessly, Keeley said, "Might ye manage these, me lass, while I fetch the last o' our fuel?"

"Of course," Jana said, accepting his armload of logs and carting them into the cabin.

Thankfully, Keeley took shelter a split second before he and his unwieldy heap of wood were caught in a deluge.

The gusting wind pelted the rain against their refuge with a vengeance, rattling the window panes and tin roof. It hampered Jana and Keeley from speaking without yelling, so they unrolled and sprawled out on their rubberized cavalry blankets, seizing the opportunity to catch up on their dearth of sleep.

Unaffected by the noise and flashes of lightning, Tracker curled up between Jana and Keeley and into a tight ball, appearing more the size of a large puppy than a full-grown hound. Aside from occasional nickers during the ensuing hours as one storm after another rumbled through, their geldings seemed unafraid too.

Sometime before twilight, after having dozed in and out like a bear in hibernation, Jana awakened to a soft spray of sunlight warming her cheeks. She stretched and yawned, rousing Keeley and Tracker. Rising to her feet, she went to the front door and opened it. "Oh my, come see the glorious rainbow," she called out over the sound of excess rainwater dripping off the roof and spattering the ground.

Keeley joined her in the frame of the doorway, and Tracker scooted past them into the calm to foray outside. Wrapping his arm around her, he said, "Back in me homeland, we believe leprechauns place a pot o' gold at the end o' each rainbow. Might it be a portent o' good things to come?"

"I think it is," Jana said, excitedly. "Notice"—she pointed northeastwardly—"that half of the rainbow stands right about where Brandy Station is located."

They stared at the rainbow until the brilliant colors of red, orange, yellow, green, blue, indigo, and violet blurred into one another, and Jana's growling stomach signaled suppertime.

Jana whistled and called out for Tracker, who came bounding into the cabin.

Keeley arranged dry twigs and logs beneath an old cooking grate and threw a sulfur match onto them, setting them into a roaring and crackling blaze.

Over a lowered flame, Jana warmed smoked bacon in their small fry pan, removed the sizzling slabs to their mess plates, and then scrambled nearly a dozen eggs in the pork grease for her, Keeley, and Tracker to share.

Before the natural light dwindled, Keeley trudged to the stream and cleaned their fry pan, tin plates, and utensils, and he filled their canteens and a four-cup tin coffeepot with water. Well after sunset, he re-stoked the fire and placed the pot on the grate.

Tracker merrily gnawed on a beef bone, and Keeley sat cross-legged watching Jana brew coffee. "Reminds me o' our fondest days with the cavalry, sitting around the campfire with Leanne, Charlie, and our other messmates, cooking, reminiscing about home, and singing."

"Those times were truly the bright spots of war," Jana said as she removed the boiling water from the flame and allowed it to sit a minute before she stirred four wooden tablespoons of coffee grounds into it. After two minutes, she stirred in a cup of cold water and waited another two minutes for it to sink the grounds to the bottom of the pot and for it to be ready to pour. She and Keeley agreed that, although the coffee was tepid, it hit the spot. Each had just about finished theirs when the horses began wildly whinnying and grunting.

Tracker sprang up and to the door, his nose wiggling as he sniffed the air wafting in through the drafty door jambs. Then, he began baying.

Jana and Keeley leaped to their feet and unsheathed their Colts.

Jana's racing heart pulsed in her neck. Could it be Woodcock's goons out there? She felt like a sitting duck with the four windows affording a view of them from every angle.

When the horses and Tracker continued their agitation, Keeley advanced to the front window and peeked out. "The starry sky is o' no use in pinpointing the source o' the animals' worry."

On cue, they heard the growl of a bear, likely lured to their site by the aroma of their fried food drifting out in the chimney smoke.

Jana's mind reeled back to when she was fifteen years old and out hunting with Pa. A black bear had reared up on Pa and was about to swipe the back of his head with its razor-sharp claws; Jana killed it with one shot straight through the heart. Before Jana could remind Keeley of that story and to caution him about a hungry bear, he cocked his Colt's hammer and dislodged the latch of and kicked open the door.

Still baying, Tracker whizzed past him.

Keeley followed on his heels, calling out, "Stay here, me lass, and guard our valuables."

Terrified of Keeley's inexperience in handling a bear, Jana sped after him through the lingering musky scent shed by the wild animal. Tracker's bays and the moon's pale light guided her, but her progress was slowed by the slick ground and having to bushwhack through underbrush and unsnag her coat sleeves from a few thorns. Still, she was closing in on the trio of man and beast.

Yelp!

Pop!

Tracker's cry and the gunshot brought Jana to a petrified standstill. The ensuing silence was deafening.

Tracker began yipping and Keeley's pleas for him to come away acted as beacons, leading Jana straight to them and where Tracker was clawing the scaly bark of a pine tree in his attempts to climb up after the bear.

To Jana's sudden presence beside him, Keeley jumped. "I thought ye were another bear, come to his mate's rescue."

"I'm sorry. I didn't mean to scare you." Between gasps for breath, Jana said, "I heard a yelp, then a gunshot. Are you and Tracker all right?"

"Aye, but it was a wee bit hazardous at one point."

"What do you mean? What happened?"

"The bear turned on Tracker, preparing to claw him. After I shot at it, Tracker chased it up the tree."

"Did you injure the bear?"

"It didn't cry out as though I had, and it climbed the tree without difficulty."

Jana held her tongue from giving Keeley a lashing over his perilous act of shooting into the dark. Her first priority was to remove Tracker from further confrontation with the bear. She extracted a handkerchief from her trouser pocket and lassoed it around Tracker's neck, all the while eyeing the bear for any defensive movement from his perch on a thick branch. Dragging Tracker down and away from the tree, Jana patted his head. "Good boy, Tracker. Now, come along and get your bone."

Amazingly, he was easily swayed and allowed Jana to lead him away.

Keeley fell in behind them after Jana passed him with a huff. When they were a good distance from the bear, he said, "Did I do something to ire ye, me lass?"

Jana swung around to face him, forcing him to stop. "You shot at the bear while he was entangled with Tracker? In the darkness, how could you be so sure you were aiming at the bear and not Tracker? Or the timing of your shot didn't coincide with a defensive move on Tracker's behalf, putting him in the bullet's trajectory? Or your bullet didn't ricochet off a tree and injure you, Keeley?"

Bowing his head in shame, Keeley said, "Aye, it was an impetuous act out o' fear for our coonhound."

"Perhaps a shot at the moon would've been just as effective for breaking them up." Not wishing to belabor the point, Jana tugged Tracker along by his makeshift collar as she went to Keeley and hugged him. "I'm just glad you and Tracker are all right." With a forgiving laugh, she said, "It's unlike you to be so impulsive, Keeley. I hope I'm not rubbing off on you."

Keeley humbly chuckled. "Next time, I'll try to keep a cool head and not leave ye behind on a matter affecting our pod."

"Now you see, Keeley, it isn't always easy to do. But let's put it behind us and move on." In the coming days, it was almost certain that they'd have to confront some or all of the factions vying for the treasury. Jana hoped she and Keeley could practice their preaching to each other because she sensed they were headed into turbulent water; paddling together would be the only way they could get through.

Jana and Keeley awakened before sunrise, completely rested after their liberal catnaps throughout the stormy day before. Using the time wisely until they could set off, they cooked breakfast for themselves and Tracker and fed the horses. Then, they strung up Jana's rubber blanket as a divider for spot bathing. Under a silvery moon, they went to the stream to fill their coffeepot for brushing their teeth and the provisional trough they borrowed from the horses for bathing.

After warming the ash bucket over the fire, Keeley offered Jana the first shift for bathing.

Jana wetted a flannel washcloth and lathered it up with a cake of *Proctor & Gamble's* lightly scented lye-and-wood ash soap—a luxury the Union Army had contracted for and Jana remembered their quartermaster sergeant doling out. Fortunate for Jana and Keeley, who'd thought to bring everything else but soap with them, it was amongst the other accessories found on the cavalry horses Versella had inherited.

As she finished her bath and started dressing, Keeley began a discussion of their ensuing strategy. "From what Versella tells us, it would seem Brandy Station plays some part in the stolen treasury, whether it's the hiding place for it or it holds a map to it."

Jana pondered its role as she pulled on her denim trousers. Watching the vapor rising from her bath water reminded her of the lazy swirl of steam that follows the initial belch from the stack of a locomotive after it had berthed. She jolted up. "The treasury is hidden somewhere along the tracks of the *Orange and Alexandria Railroad*, and Brandy Station holds the map. I'm sure of it."

"Why not the other way around, me lass?"

Fully robed after fastening the last button of her riding trousers, Jana rounded the divider. "Because Versella was adamant she and Harold overheard Mrs. Fernsby directly link 'stolen treasury and *Orange and Alexandria Railroad*.' And she identified Brandy Station as Jed's destination for 'guidance in salvaging the money for some delinquents' in a separate breath."

"Aye, it stands to reason." Keeley rose and took his turn behind the panel. Over a splash of water, he said, "It would seem inefficient to hide the missing payroll in Brandy Station, then backtrack up the *O&A* to hide the map." He paused for a few seconds. "But what if Fuji and Jed have already left Brandy Station by the time we get there? Might we be looking for a needle in a haystack as far as finding the map goes?"

While Jana mulled it over, she fetched her toothbrush from her small leather pouch and twirled its horse-hair bristles around in the coffeepot, shook out the excess water from them, and lightly dipped them in a small circular tin of Dr. Samuel Stockton White's cherry-flavored dental powder. She rinsed her mouth out with water in her coffee mug and spat out the excess paste onto the fire embers, which spat back at her with a hiss. "Maybe not," she said. "Jed disclosed that they drew—*not carved*—the map, so it would have to be under cover, protected from rain, sleet, or snow smudging it."

"Aye, and they wouldn't draw it out in plain sight, such as on the wall o' the train depot or some other bustling business, where it would pose problems for recovery later."

"For the same reason, they wouldn't risk drawing it in a private residence—even if it was vacated at the time—knowing the owners would re-inhabit their properties post-war. So, we've just narrowed our search considerably to abandoned buildings and places where the public congregates sparingly, such as a church."

"From what I meself remember o' Brandy Station, there are relatively few buildings within the village fitting our criteria. That might make the map easier to find."

"Let's not forget," Jana said, "once we familiarize Tracker with Jed's scent, hopefully, he'll sniff out his trail."

Keeley momentarily poked his head around the curtain. "There's still but one wee thing that doesn't make sense to meself. Why wouldn't Jed and Fuji have just drawn the map on paper and taken it with them for the KGC to fetch from them later?"

Jana focused on the fading fire. "Well...what do we know about the KGC?"

Burying his face in his washcloth and scrubbing it before ducking behind the curtain, Keeley's utterance was muffled but audible. "Like the Freemasons, they're a mysterious lot, who communicate by secret handshakes and coded messages."

"Precisely! If I were as paranoid as they are about protecting my possessions, I'd only want one map in circulation—and not drawn on paper—to lessen the odds of it falling into the wrong hands or of multiple copies of it being made from the original."

"Again, to me point about Jed and Fuji having already left Brandy Station upon our arrival, what will we do if we find the map and it's coded?"

"I guess we'll have to follow the tracks of the *Orange and Alexandria* and hope Tracker's nose comes in handy."

After he finished bathing, dressing, and brushing his teeth,

Keeley added the last few logs to the fire and sat down close to Jana.

Jana locked her hand around his and squeezed it. "If we were to find the army payroll, we stand to earn a king's ransom of one hundred thousand dollars. What would you think of our gifting some of our commission to the Barneys for their kindness and generosity?"

With a sharp intake of breath, Keeley stared at her with astonishment. "I've been meaning to speak to ye about the very notion. What do ye think o' twenty thousand dollars?" He clicked his cheek. "Eighty thousand dollars is still a king's ransom for us."

Jana threw her arms around him and kissed his cherry-tasting lips. "Your compassion and kindness is exactly why I love you so much."

Gently pinching her nose, he said, "Aye, and yar compassion and kindness is exactly why I love ye so much, me lass. I wish we could loaf here in each other's arms for a wee bit longer, but, unfortunately, there's work to be done before we ride out at sunrise." He gave her a tight squeeze and kissed her forehead. Then, he sprang to his feet and helped her up.

Jana and Keeley saddled and packed their horses under the moon's glimmer and the firelight fanning outward through the begrimed windows. At first glint of dawn's rosy fingertips stretching skyward, they swung into their saddles and headed north into a wind that was refreshingly cool and unencumbering to their progress. They rode abreast of each other and Tracker on the soggy road so all could avoid being slopped with mud plunged up and slung aft by the hoofs of a lead horse. Fortunately, the farther north they went the higher the sun rose, and its warmth combined with the wind to dry the road.

Not long underway, they reached the Rapidan River at Raccoon Ford, a scorched shell of its once thriving existence.

Jana scanned the heaps of charred remains on both sides of the river and sorrowfully pondered the lives uprooted from the torching of the village by Yankees upon their departure in 1863. From previous crossings here while on the march with her regiment, Jana remembered carding, grist, and saw mills, shops for tailoring the spun and woven fabric into clothing, carriage-making, and blacksmithing, a post office of the United States, a general store, a shoe and boot factory, and numerous farms and plantations. Sadly, a mill and brick plantation kitchen were all that endured.

A bridge to cross over from Orange to Culpeper County was missing, so Jana and Keeley spurred their mounts into the river, swollen by the previous day's downpours. As they waded through water up to their horses' underbellies, Jana and Keeley clung to the curved pommels of their McClellan saddles while they bent their legs up and back to avoid their boots getting soaked to their stockings. Their geldings were able to get good footing as they reared up and sprang up onto the grassy embankment.

To Tracker's agitated bays, Jana and Keeley swiveled in their saddles to see him frantically pacing the opposite embankment with his jowls quivering and his forehead wrinkled over his brows. No amount of gentle pleas could coax him to them.

"It seems our Tracker is afraid o' the water. Any idea how we might get him to swim across, me lass?"

"Yes." Jana seized the long rope she'd used for tethering her horse at the shack. "Unfortunately, it involves *both* of us re-crossing the river."

Tracker's bays terminated to Jana and Keeley's reappearance, and he skipped around them, his tail whipping with glee.

Dismounting, Jana fashioned a noose with her rope and pulled it taut around his long neck. Then, she remounted and tightened up the give on the rope between her and Tracker to keep him at her flank. She instructed Keeley to station himself behind Tracker and to begin his advancement into the river simultaneously with hers.

Tracker tried to resist, but the tug of Jana's horse and the nudge of Keeley's overpowered him. Splashing into the river, he paddled to the other side and clawed his way up the embankment. With all back on solid ground, Tracker shook the water from his fur, and, when Jana unleashed him, he dropped to the ground, rolled onto his spine, and kicked his spindly legs as he toweled himself off on the grass.

With a contented expression, Keeley nudged his horse up close to Jana's. "Nice work, me lass." He leaned over in his saddle and offered her his canteen.

"I couldn't have done it without you," Jana said, feeling the touch of Keeley's thigh against hers. Her pulse raced and her breathing sped up. She fanned her flushing cheeks with her gloved hand. "Is it me or does it suddenly seem hotter out here?" She swigged some water before passing Keeley his canteen.

Swiping his coat sleeve across his beaded forehead, he said, "Aye, it does seem a wee bit hotter, but"—he grinned at her—"the sun and exercise might not be all to blame."

Laughing, they urged their horses onward into the cooling wind. By staggering their pace between a trot, canter, and gallop, they arrived at Culpeper Court House a little over an hour after leaving Raccoon Ford. They walked their horses up the main street to muffle their noise, out of respect for it being a quarter past 7:00 a.m. and the quiet of the town. Along their route, they passed a saloon, a mere two blocks from the sanctioned edifices for the county courthouse, with its brick portico and wooden tower topped by a weather vane, the jail, and a Baptist church. All three consumed the entire block on the north side of Davis Street between Main and its eastwardly parallel street.

Jana's eyes lingered on the jail, sandwiched between the other two buildings, and she smirked at her fleeting vision of its being used to incarcerate whatever thieves they might round up from their caper.

Their brief ride through the county seat showed the whipping it had taken, especially during the cavalry battle of September 1863. Jana and Keeley were absent from it, she in a field hospital healing from her bullet wound and he in prison. But Jana had been within range to hear immediate reports of its outcome: Twelve guns of Union Major General Hugh Judson Kilpatrick's Light Horse Artillery had shelled the railroad depot and the streets and buildings nearby, and further damage was done by ricocheting bullets as the Confederates retreated. The mutilation was still evident, as well as the wear and tear from the unbroken occupation of the town by sizeable troops of Yankees and Rebels throughout the war added to its ragged façade. Even now, Union soldiers patrolled the area to keep peace between former slave owners and freedmen and secessionists and Northern sympathizers. Fortunately, Jana and Keeley passed through without being stopped.

Striking country road again, they alternated their geldings' gaits between a gallop and a canter, and they traversed the seven miles to Brandy Station in thirty minutes. They reined in their horses to a walk, keeping to the north side of the train tracks and a keen eye out for the ideal spot to house a map. After having passed a few buildings, including the train depot, with Union soldiers busy about the premises, Jana and Keeley reached a crossroads and stopped.

Tracker dropped to his haunches, barely panting from the exercise and on high alert to their surroundings.

As Jana and Keeley were discussing their next move, the echoes of galloping horses' hoofs met their ears.

Pivoting left in her saddle, Jana angled the wide brim of her riding hat down over her right eye to slash the sun's glare. She spied two riders heading south toward them.

Keeley retrieved his field glasses from the bag behind his saddle, raised them to his eyes, and took a good long look. Lowering them, he turned in his squeaky saddle and beamed at Jana. "It would seem our mates have arrived in the nick o' time."

Jana waved her arms over her head, signaling her and Keeley's presence to Leanne and Charlie. While they waited on their friends, Jana straightened in her saddle, and her eyes gravitated up the gently sloping Fleetwood Hill. It rose in tiers of wide-open grassy fields eastward from an extensive ridge like an emerald quilt laid out with rumples in its fabric. To her naked eyes, its patchwork of forests and fields appeared to have transformed itself back to its former beauty and to have all but forgotten their tattering as the most-abused parcel of land by both armies with their marches, encampments, and fiery spars upon it. Jana hoped she could take a lesson from this glorious countryside and flush from her memory the bloodbath of two years ago and what was being called the largest cavalry battle ever fought on North American soil. Although the Sixth Pennsylvania Cavalry had suffered the heaviest casualties in their charge across an open field higher up on Fleetwood Hill at Major Robert Beckham's guns, Jana's regiment suffered heavily too in their charge against an extension of Major General Jeb Stuart's Light Horse Artillery on Fleetwood's southern knoll. If the Tenth New York's casualties amounted to 6 killed, 2 mortally wounded, and 60 missing, the Sixth Pennsylvania's numbers had to be staggering. More gruesomely, Jana wondered how many men from both regiments had gone missing because they'd been blown to bits and were unidentifiable upon burial. She was relieved to be separated from her morbid thoughts by Leanne and Charlie's arrival.

The foursome dismounted. Before they had a chance to greet each other properly with hugs or handshakes, Tracker unexpectedly reared up, gently landed his paws on Leanne's chest, and knocked her to the ground. Straddling her, he bowed his head and licked her face.

Giggling, Leanne reached up and scrubbed the fur under his ears. "And who're ya, ya handsome devil?"

"Tracker," Keeley said in an admonishing tone as he extricated him from Leanne by the flabby scruff of his neck.

When Charlie bent over to offer Leanne a hand up, Tracker squirmed free of Keeley's grasp, bounced onto Charlie's back, and began licking his neck.

Now Keeley extricated Tracker from a chortling Charlie. "Sorry, me mates, I don't know what's gotten into our furry lad."

"I do," Jana said, helping Leanne to her feet. "He recognizes good people and wants them to know it." Then, she quickly illuminated for Leanne and Charlie how they'd come by Tracker.

"How d'ya like that? Versella actually obliged my suggestion to git a dog," Leanne said, grinning with satisfaction as she rescued her slouch hat, beat it against her gloved hand to expel the dirt, and replaced it on her head.

Sliding his wire-rimmed spectacles up onto the bridge of his nose, Charlie inspected Tracker while Keeley said with pride, "Me Jana lass and meself have already had the privilege o' seeing our Treeing Walker Coonhound chase a bear up a tree, and we've got high hopes o' him sniffing out the Rebel thieves who stole the money from the prisoner train."

Leanne's steel-gray eyes homed in on Jana, who was rocking on her heels, and she came to her rescue. "Since yer telegram sounded urgent, tell us what ya need us to do."

"Unfortunately," Jana said, "there's no time to brief you on our entire investigation. All we can tell you now is that we're tracking two Rebel prisoners who stole the army payroll from the Shohola train wreck. We're pretty sure they're working with the Knights of the Golden Circle, and—," Jana cut herself short to Leanne and Charlie's unified gasp.

"I take it ye both have heard o' the KGC," Keeley said.

Leanne and Charlie nodded.

Jana continued, "Additionally, we're being tracked by two goons hired by a bankrupt real estate tycoon and temporary U.S. senator by the name of John Woodcock. We're unclear whether or not he's affiliated with the KGC. If he's acting alone, we could wind up in a four-way showdown—that is, if the KGC has caught wind of the Rebel thieves having compromised the whereabouts of the treasury and it turns against them."

"We could really use yar help, mates, to find the map and payroll and maybe fend off a few brutes."

Jana chimed in. "We'll understand if the potential for extreme danger scares you off."

Leanne crossed her arms over her chest. "The KGC's involvement might've taken me by surprise, but none of it scares me off. So, ya can count me in."

To Jana, Charlie said, "Half the battle is in knowing whom we're up against, unlike we did of your kidnappers and would-be assassins on your late lecture tour around New York State." Charlie glanced at the southern base of Fleetwood Hill. "Over there, we cavalrymen proved our mettle against the superior Confederate cavalry, and, on this same ground, we'll prove our mettle against a gaggle of thieves. So, count me in too."

"That's the way, Charlie," Leanne said, bestowing him a look of adoration. She'd forever be grateful to him for adopting her and her mother into his family after Leanne had rescued her ma from her abusive pa.

"As me Jana lass alluded to, time is o' the essence. The Rebel thieves have but a wee jump on us to retrieve the map, which we've deduced was drawn here in Brandy Station and points to the treasury hidden somewhere north o' here, along the *Orange and Alexandria Railroad*."

Rubbing her gloved hands vigorously together, Leanne said, "Where do we git started?"

Jana said, "We need to search for an abandoned building or place where the townsfolk congregate sparingly, such as a church, and we believe our best bets are in the village center."

In a rush of enthusiasm, Charlie said, "We know the perfect place."

"Huh?" Jana and Keeley said in unison.

Charlie explained, "We've actually already been to the village center. Not finding you there, we rode back up to where our regiment fought to get a closer glimpse of it at peace and from where we could overlook the road from Culpeper Court House to Brandy Station."

"Aye, yar arrival seemed awfully coincidental to ours."

"Here's another coincidence for you," Charlie said. "We turned around where the main street through the village ends, and there was an abandoned building nearby that looked more like a home than a shop or business."

Leanne's face flushed with the thrill of the hunt. "What're we waitin' for? Let's go."

"Wait," Jana said when Leanne started toward her horse. "We have to be cautious. If Jed and Fuji are there, we need to take them by surprise."

"Just before the abandoned house, there's a southwardly intersecting road to the main street," Charlie said. "Why don't we leave our horses tied up near the corner and sneak over to our target?"

"Good idea, lad," Keeley said.

"Follow me." Leanne swung into her saddle and, with her friends barely astride their steeds, she trotted her horse to the crossroads, reined left, and set off in a gallop. In less than a quarter of a mile, she reined in at the next crossroads, dismounted, and tethered her horse to a tree with Jana, Keeley, and Charlie following her lead.

Before they set off, Jana fetched the scrap of fabric she'd sheared from Jed's trousers and gave Tracker a whiff of it, and Keeley fashioned a collar for Tracker out of his handkerchief and held on to him as the party of five crept along, ducking behind the sparsity of trees.

Charlie led the way to the side of the white frame house.

Positive their prowling had gone unnoticed when no one appeared in the first-or-second-story windows, they were about to tread out into the open when the whinny of a horse met their ears.

They all drew their Colts.

Lifting his nose to the air and sniffing, Tracker tore out of

Keeley's grasp and into a baying gallop, with Keeley racing after him.

"Guard the back door," Jana bellowed at Leanne and Charlie and sprinted after Keeley and Tracker. The tall, dewy blades of grass, growing wild along the side of the house, swished angrily and thwacked Jana's riding pants as she bushwhacked her way through them. Rounding the corner of the house, she spied two horses hitched to a post trackside before she caught up to Keeley, who stood before a gaping front door.

Over their heavy breathing, they heard Tracker's shrill yips tumbling down from the second story. They crept inside, to the base of the stairs, and listened.

A trembly male voice said, "Shoot the damn dog before he rips me to shreds."

Keeley whipped around to Jana and mouthed, "Follow meself up after I get to the top." Hugging the plaster wall, where the steps were always less traveled and creaky, Keeley crept up the narrow staircase and disappeared around the landing. She heard the echo of his revolver's hammer cocking and him say, "Don't do it, lads. Ye kill me dog, and I'll kill ye. I've seen a lifetime o' bloodshed and I'm tired o' it, but I'll do what it takes to protect me own."

Sticking to Keeley's path up the stairs, Jana crouched on the floor and peeked around the wall. She had a slim view around Keeley, who stood in the doorway of the room overlooking the road. Tracker had a fair-haired man, whose gun lay nearby, pinned supine on the dusty floor. A tall, dark-haired man had his gun trained on Tracker while he stared down the barrel of Keeley's. Taking a gamble, Jana called out, "Don't do it, Fuji."

Fuji jerked in surprise.

In one fluid motion, Keeley lunged forward, nabbed Fuji's gun out of his hand, and kicked Jed's across the musty room. Dust motes swirled around Jed and Tracker, sending Jed into a sneezing fit.

An unsympathetic Tracker bared his teeth, and his growls

escalated in ferocity to each of Jed's movements.

"Good boy, Tracker," Keeley called out. "Enough growling now."

With her Colt still in her hand, Jana scrambled to her feet, moved cautiously to Keeley's side, and gave Fuji a genuine smile. "Your mother, the lovely Mrs. Jibbs, sends her love and wish for your speedy return."

"How. . .how. . .how do you know my mother?" he stammered.

"We've been tracking you and Jed ever since we learned of your thievery in Shohola," Jana said. "We tried to catch up with you at your homestead, but you'd already left."

Removing his hat, Fuji raked a shaky hand through his short, curly, brown hair. "My mother knows nothing yet about my doings in Shohola or why I came here. Please, tell me you didn't tell her."

Keeley said, "No, lad, but ye might want to cooperate with us or she'll soon learn about yar debauchery and imprisonment."

"Who are you and what are you doing here?" Fuji said, his eyes probing Jana and Keeley.

Keeley answered his first question. "We're former Union cavalry, and we've worked with the Pinkerton Agency. Wouldn't ye agree those roles give us some pretty good credentials for scouting and investigative work?"

Obeying President Johnson's demand for secrecy and carrying on Keeley's elusiveness in naming him as their employer, Jana answered his second question. "We've been hired to return the army payroll in your possession to the federal government."

So as not to rile Tracker, who was still straddling him and panting in his face, Jed lay stiller than the wide floor planks beneath him and whispered, "I swear, Fuji, no one but my ma, pa, and the minister of my church knew I was off to make sure the money we stole was still hidden."

"Oh, shut up, Jed," Fuji retorted. "I know full well you would've come clean with me if you'd told anybody else, besides the other three, about our business."

Jana snapped her fingers. "Come, Tracker."

Before he freed Jed and moseyed to Jana's side, Tracker growled in Jed's face. It was as though he was warning him that, with one false move, he wouldn't hesitate to wield his sharp fangs and mighty jaws against him.

Jed eyed Tracker as he rose slowly to his feet and brushed the dust from his coat and trousers.

"Jed and I figured"—Fuji's tall, muscular frame slouched two inches to bring him down to Keeley's height of six feet—"we'd left too many breadcrumbs behind in Shohola, and others, like you, would find us."

"By *others*, do you mean members of the KGC?" Jana said.

Fuji shot up straighter and speedier than a bullet fired skyward. "How do you know about the KGC contacting us?"

"Let's just say, lad"—Keeley smirked—"we're as all-seeing as yar knights are."

"Members of the KGC *forced* me and Jed to surrender the money to them. And then they bullied us into service as their field agents to hide it. They said they'd kill us if it went missing!"

"Why didn't those who contacted you just take the money from you and hide it themselves?" Jana said.

"The KGC wanted the treasury brought home to the South. Since we'd proven our cunning in stealing and hiding the money in Shohola and were familiar with this territory, they trusted us for the second phase of the job. They gave me and Jed a general area where to squirrel the money but the exact spot where to draw the map, including the symbols to use in coding it. Then, they instructed us to take ten thousand greenbacks apiece from the loot and to forget our ever knowing about it." The muscles of Fuji's jaws tensed. "So, you understand why we can't give up the map."

"Well, lads, we know ye didn't use this house as a place to hole up overnight. Ye only had an hour jump on us from yar farm, and ye couldn't have made it this far in one day through the bad weather without laming yar horses. So, ye came here expressly to retrieve the map, and we don't need yar help to find it. However, it seems we might need yar service to decode it."

The floorboards behind Jana and Keeley screeched. "I might as well kill ya now," Leanne said, the cock of her gun's hammer resonating around the empty room. "You're gonna be dead ducks when we leave ya for the KGC, who's hot on our heels." Her potential bluff hit its mark, causing a terror-stricken Fuji to falter backward a few steps.

Keeley nodded back at Leanne. "Meet the third o' four troopers in our party. They"—he waggled his thumb between Leanne and Jana—"are also former Union troopers, and both lasses fought more fiercely than all o' the men in our regiment combined."

"And, by the way," Jana said, "it's no skin off our bones if we don't recoup the payroll. But it is yours. Just by virtue that you've come here to secure the treasury tells the KGC that your lips are loose and you can no longer be trusted with their secret."

Grinning roguishly, Leanne said, "Which one of ya wants to be put out of yer misery first? I don't mind killin' another Rebel to add to my long list of 'em."

Keeley simultaneously clicked his cheek and half-shrugged. "If ye'll work with us, lads, we can spare ye from death and maybe imprisonment or, at least, lighten yar sentence. But we need yar decision now."

Fuji's bronzed face wrinkled up like a bulldog's. "How can you guarantee all of that?"

Jana said, "I'm pretty confident we can convince our employer to expose the KGC as the thieves and you and Jed as the heroes who stripped them of their coffer." Jana and Keeley had knowledge of the army payroll in their back pocket. If President Johnson was a secret member of the KGC, and he tendered the treasury to it, Jana and Keeley would expose his treachery.

In a low voice as he eyed Tracker, Jed said, "Why would you make us heroes and not take the credit for yourselves?"

"Because we don't want to be in the limelight and you need to be," Jana said. She knew for a fact that neither she nor Keeley cared a hoot about it, and Leanne and Charlie couldn't afford to leave a trail of crumbs for Leanne's abusive father to follow to her and her mother. Plus, Jana had already had her fair share of the limelight through her military escapades and as a crusader for the woman's rights movement. "The KGC won't touch you after you've been made heroes. You might be ostracized in your community for returning money to the federal government, but, at least, you'll be alive."

"And I'll wager, if ye were to use some o' yar reward to help rebuild yar communities, they would soon forget yar sins," Keeley said.

"Even if you could convince your boss to let us go free, he's sure to take our rewards away from us," Fuji said.

Jana looked to Keeley, and, appearing to read her mind, he nodded his approval for her to say, "If you'll help us reclaim the treasury, we'll guarantee your reward by taking it out of our commission."

Fuji's and Jed's mouths fell agape.

"So, what's it gonna be, boys?" Leanne said. "We're wastin' valuable time."

After sharing a silent exchange, Fuji and Jed agreed to help.

Fuji stiffened with pride. "Just so you're clear, we're not bad guys. We only stole the money to support our poor farming families and"—he peered at Keeley—"communities."

"And just so we're clear," Jana said, "are we to understand you learned of the payroll aboard your train and stole it on your own volition? Not because someone recruited you during your layover in Jersey City or Port Jervis to steal it in the aftermath of an intentional collision between your and another train—that is, if you survived?"

Jed's expression contorted into confusion and horror.

With the veins in his neck bulging, Fuji sputtered, "I-I-I think I can speak for Jed too when I say, we would've taken our chances surviving the train wreck or imprisonment before we agreed to something as fiendish as that."

Jana felt tremendously relieved to learn there was nothing more sinister behind the train wreck than petty thievery. "We really need to move," she said. "Lead us to the map."

Holstering her revolver, Leanne barked, "I still consider ya scoundrels untrustworthy, and I'm gonna keep my gun hand at the ready and a close eye on ya. One wrong move and I won't hesitate to put a bullet between yer eyeballs."

Fuji raised his hands in surrender. "You won't have to worry about me."

Still warily watching Tracker, Jed slowly raised his hands too. "Or me either."

Tracker growled at Jed.

"If your dog doesn't rip me apart first," Jed said fretfully.

Patting Tracker's rump, Jana said, "Sit, Tracker." Then, she peered at Fuji. "Go ahead and retrieve the map. He won't bother you."

Fuji spun on his heels and hustled toward the outer back corner of the room.

The plastered wall—thus far concealed behind Fuji and unnoticed by Jana—revealed an impressive mural of scrawl.

When Jed noticed Jana, Keeley, and Leanne gawping at it, he said, "A thing of beauty, isn't it?" He raised and circled his index finger. "Look around. All of the walls in this room and others up here are covered with autographs, lists of units, caricatures and other drawings, slogans, and bantering between opposing armies. I'm assuming they were created while this house served alternately as a Confederate hospital and headquarters for various Union officers throughout the war."

Kneeling on the floor with his head bowed toward the base molding, Fuji called over his shoulder, "We found the autograph of Confederate cavalry general Jeb Stuart around here somewhere."

"Interestingly, some of the doodles were done in coal from the fireplace on this floor, while others, like our map, were done in pencil," Jed said, sounding like a tour guide. "Fuji, himself, is an artist; he drew our map."

Fuji promptly transposed the intricate scribbles of the map onto parchment paper, and Keeley swiped it out of the Rebel artist's hand and folded and stuffed it down the shaft of his boot.

Offering her handkerchief to Fuji, Jana ordered him to smear the original until it was illegible.

Before they exited the room, Leanne took control of Jed's and Fuji's guns, and Keeley patted them both down to assure they possessed no other weapons.

Jana was the last to leave the room, and she paused a second to admire the inscriptions flanking the door casings. She yearned to sign the wall too, but this was no time for frivolities. Descending the stairs, she thought of how she would've left her mark. She most definitely would've inscribed: Soldier, Nurse, Spy Johnnie Brodie, Tenth New York Volunteer Cavalry Regiment (alias Jana Brady of Elmira, New York). Beneath that, she would've written: Glory Be to Women, Equal Rights for All!

On the road again, the six treasure seekers and Tracker passed by where Jana, Keeley, Leanne, and Charlie had fought with their regiment.

Suddenly, Jana saw their battleground in a different light. No more would she shrink in repulsion from thoughts of that gruesome day. Instead, she'd remind herself that she, Leanne, and maybe other women disguised as cavalrymen or light artillerymen had made a gallant stand at Brandy Station, fighting as fiercely as the men beside them and proving to the world their courage and capabilities. Jana had the urge to stand up in her stirrups, wave a saber about, and shout, "Glory Be to Women, Equal Rights for All!"

Jana and Keeley led the entourage in a gallop up the hilly road parallel to the tracks of the *Orange and Alexandria Railroad*, Leanne and Charlie brought up the rear, and Tracker galloped alongside Jed. They had the Rebel thieves hemmed in on all but one side to hinder their escapes.

Approximately eight minutes into their jaunt, the road wound up and through a dense woodlot, its canopy of shade trees giving them much-needed relief from the relentless mid-morning sun.

Fuji cried out, "Whoa!"

Jed pointed to his right at a large, pillared boulder defending the head of a barely visible trail. "There's our marker."

"It's a very narrow footpath with low-hanging branches, so we'll have to walk our horses through in single formation," Fuji said, and everyone obeyed his call to dismount.

Leanne withdrew her Colt and waggled it between Fuji and Jed. Nodding at Jana, she said, "She'll lead the way with ya two next and me behind ya."

Fuji shrugged. "Why would we run when you're giving us a

chance to dodge death at the hands of the KGC and imprisonment by the federal government and"—he nodded at Jana and Keeley—"your friends are kindly covering our rewards by taking it out of their own pay?"

"Besides," Jed said, "you took our guns, so we can't turn on you and run once we find the money."

Jana aimed a staying hand at Fuji and Jed. "Let's keep our focus." Gathering her soft leather reins and drawing them over her gelding's head, she led him past the boulder into the forest. The roosting birds out-sang the rush of wind through the trees in their merry cheeps and chirps. It was as though they were excited to welcome Jana and company to a picnic at their summer home. *If only it were a picnic*, Jana thought to a foreboding stitch in her side.

Springing past Jana, Tracker held his nose high into the pine-scented air as he guided his pack along.

The party had trudged a couple hundred feet in when Fuji halted them a second time. "We go from here without our mounts since we need to veer off trail." After everyone hitched their horses to trees, he turned to Keeley. Holding out a calloused palm, he wriggled his long fingers toward himself and said, "I need the map."

Keeley withdrew the crackling parchment from his boot shaft and relinquished it to him.

Conferring with Jana, Keeley, and Leanne, Charlie said, "Should I stand watch here for any potential intruders?"

"If ye don't mind missing the treasure hunt, lad, it's not a bad idea."

"Keep yer gun at the ready so ya can git off a warning shot to us," Leanne said, prompting Jana and Keeley to un-holster theirs.

Charlie rolled his eyes at her. "Yes, sis."

"Let's move," Jana said, "before we have unwanted company."

Fuji scuttled away from his horse and paused before a felled pine, its trunk naturally broken into three chunks and stacked upon each other like tiles of tumbled dominoes. He vaulted over the middle section and spun around, squatting before and scrutinizing it.

They assembled around Fuji, peering over his shoulder to see an arrow carved into the reddish-orange bark of the elderly Virginia pine.

When Fuji interpreted the downward point of the arrow as a northeasterly direction, Leanne's forehead furrowed. "Doesn't make a lick of sense we're gonna go north when the arrow points south."

"If the arrow were on the opposite side of the log, we'd be going south," Fuji said, rising to his feet. "Anyway, this is our starting point." He unfolded the map, spread it across his thigh, and ironed out its creases with his large hand. Then, he nodded at Jed. "I'll decipher the symbols and you pace them off, just like we did before."

Given this was her first thrilling experience with a bona fide treasure map, Jana sidled up close to Fuji, intent on following the symbols and keys to their coinciding actions.

Fuji began by instructing Jed to count twenty long strides to match twenty tiny dots heading away from the felled tree's arrow.

Stopping before a black oak, Jed moved aside to make room for Fuji, who traced his fingers along the notches of a doubly curved snake; its head lying north, its rattle south. It would've been difficult for anyone to spot the carving through the tree's verdant branches and upon its striated bark, which mimicked the reptile's scaly skin.

Again, Jana peered over Fuji's shoulder at the map to see the snake laid out exactly as it was on the tree. However, the map more clearly showed the snake's rattle pointing north toward its head.

As though he'd read her mind, Fuji tapped the rattle and said, "We move from here to the head." Then, he instructed Jed to count twenty strides from the snake's rattle east toward the railroad tracks and along the snake's first curve to its apex. There, they found a round, flat stone, no bigger than a stack of five medium-sized Johnnie cakes. Fuji turned it over to reveal an arrow chiseled into its surface and matching the symbol on the map. Its tip pointed back toward the road. This time, Fuji instructed Jed to count forty strides west toward the road to the apex of the snake's second curve, where they found an exact stone replica of the previous marker. Again, Fuji rolled it over to reveal an arrow with its tip pointing back toward the railroad tracks. As Jed began to count the last twenty strides in that direction, a disorderly crashing through the underbrush stopped them all dead in their tracks.

Tracker began baying and sped off after the sound.

With lightning speed, Jana, Keeley, and Leanne ducked behind trees.

"Get down," Jana ordered Fuji and Jed, who dropped prone on the needled-and-leafy carpet.

Everyone blew a sigh of relief when Tracker chased a white-tailed deer past them.

Jana thought better of commanding their coonhound back. It would double their commotion and risk betraying their position, and it was doubtful Tracker would even hear her over his own baying and rush of wind through the trees. Plus, his continuing commotion could be advantageous to diverting other treasure hunters away from them.

After pushing themselves up off the ground and brushing debris from their coats and trousers, Fuji and Jed picked up where they'd left off. Jed finished taking the final steps of the snake, and Fuji pointed to the final marker on the map: greenbacks clamped between the snake's fangs. They stopped before a log, its circumference thrice the size of Fuji's girth, the largest in their party. Each knelt before a hollowed end and heaved out two twenty-pound burlap sacks.

Again, Leanne waggled her gun between Fuji and Jed. "Open the bags and prove we ain't been duped."

They obeyed, and Jana, Keeley, and Leanne bent over the bags, gazing wide-eyed at wads of greenbacks of various denominations.

The clicks of gun hammers resonated around the forest.

All heads wrenched toward the source of the ominous sound.

Woodcock's goons stepped out from behind the white oaks, their guns trained on the group. The one with a head and rugged face full of hair, dark as midnight, leered at Jana. "Thought you were so smart setting those Southern idiots on us back on the stage road."

Stricken with shame for having allowed these two oxen to nimbly creep up on them, Jana groaned at herself while noting Keeley's and Leanne's tormented expressions.

Beardy trained his gun on Leanne and snapped, "You first, toss your gun over."

Leanne hesitated, and Jana knew she was contemplating gunning him down. Scowling, she chucked her gun, intentionally short of Beardy's station.

Beardy then ordered the rest of his foes to shed their revolvers too.

Slow and deliberate, Jed raised his trembling hands in surrender. "Those three"—he nodded at Jana, Keeley, and Leanne—"stripped me and my friend of our weapons."

Fuji slowly parted the flaps of his waistcoat to show his empty holster. "Trust me, my friend and I are on your side."

Lowering his arms, Jed followed Fuji's lead in parting his coat and proving his holster was also void of a gun.

With a sidewise smirk at his bald compatriot, Beardy said, "Well, well, well, we've got ourselves a gang now."

Leanne's hands balled up into white-knuckled fists. Glaring at Fuji and Jed, she said, "Ya double-crossin' yella bellies. If I git the chance, I'm gonna wring yer fat heads off yer fat necks."

"You won't get the chance." Beardy sniggered. "We got orders to bury all evidence, including people."

Baldy mocked, "And our two mutineers will dig the grave or be thrown in with the rest."

Hearing their ambivalence to murder on their acerbic tongues, Jana numbed with terror.

"You two," Beardy said to Fuji and Jed, "strip those two of their guns."

Taking a deep breath, Jana willed herself out of her daze in order to outwit Woodcock's goons; they must've bypassed Charlie from the direction they'd come. If only she could get a warning shot off to her cavalry friend.

Jed started toward Jana, but Fuji sidestepped him, choosing to deal with Jana. With his back to the guerillas, he swept her up in a remorseful look.

Gambling on winning him over, Jana whispered, "Make your ma proud. Trip with my gun and take a shot into the underbrush." She coughed to cover up the sound of her clammy thumb cocking back her Colt's hammer before she passed her gun to him.

"Hurry it up, you two. We ain't got all day," Beardy shouted at Jed and Fuji.

Jed robbed Keeley of his gun and pitched it near where Leanne's gun lazed.

"Your turn," Beardy said to Fuji.

Before Fuji about-faced, Jana noted the heat of his conflict flushing his angular cheeks. He was the key to their rescue. She licked away the nervous sweat dribbling off her upper lip. Which side would he choose?

"Nice and easy," Beardy said, studying Fuji as he shuffled toward him.

Jana caught Keeley's and Leanne's eyes and subtly nodded at Fuji first and their guns second, hoping to prepare them for potential pandemonium.

Keeley blinked his acknowledgement, Leanne splayed her fingers by her side, and both followed Jana's lead in watching Fuji.

Each step Fuji took toward Beardy thumped Jana's eardrums crueler than the one before.

Tripping over a root, Fuji pitched headlong through the air and landed prone upon the ground, simultaneously firing a bullet over Baldy's head.

The crack of the gun raised a myriad of squawks from the nesting birds and sent them scattering, stunning Beardy and Baldy.

Tracker's bay slashed the air as he leaped into the fray. From behind, he tackled Baldy, whose gun flung from his grasp and landed near the squared toe of Jed's riding boot.

Keeley and Leanne dropped to their knees and lunged for their Colts; Leanne rescued hers first, drawing Beardy's attention.

Jed was slow to seize the weapon at his feet and come to her aid.

A split-second before Beardy put a bullet in Leanne, Charlie rose up behind him and jabbed the barrel of his gun into the base of the man's skull. "Do it and you're dead." He wrested Beardy's gun away from him, un-cocked the hammer, and lobbed it into the bushes. Gripping a fistful of his captive's collar, Charlie shoved him into the ring and flattened him out face down on the ground.

Jed rescued the revolver within his reach and aimed it at Tracker's trophy, earning a wag from the coonhound.

Sneering at the delinquents, Keeley said, "I'd say the tide has changed, wouldn't ye agree, chaps?"

Rising from the ground, Fuji grinned at Leanne. "Still gonna wring my fat head off my fat neck?"

Leanne returned his grin. "Not today."

"How on earth did you get here so fast, Charlie?" Jana said. "Fuji barely fired my pistol to warn you of our predicament."

"I heard these two cantering down the road. When they stopped shy of my post, I figured I'd better scout the situation. Then, Tracker came tearing out of the woods. His absence from your and Keeley's sides equally alarmed me." Charlie's azure eyes shone with admiration at the coonhound. "He's a smart dog. I led him along by his handkerchief collar, and he seemed to sense the need for quiet through my stealth. Thanks to the wind and these two dolts intently following your voices, they failed to hear a few snaps of twigs beneath our treads. When the time was right, I set Tracker loose, and he chose his adversary, leaving me with the other."

Beardy and Baldy were glowering admonishingly at each other.

Jana guessed they'd been watching them from the heights and were now beating themselves up over miscalculating the number of their crew. To compile their agony, she said to Charlie, "Thanks for being on high alert and always watching our backs."

Beardy shifted, and Leanne brutally burrowed her boot in his back enough for the hobnails of her sole to pierce his clothes and permanently brand his skin. "Now that we've rounded up these vermin, let's do to 'em what they were gonna do to us. Only, how fittin' would it be to stuff 'em into each end of the log in place of the sacks of money? That way, we ain't gotta dig a trench."

Because of her pa's abuse, Leanne hated bullies in the worst way, but Jana knew she'd never kill anyone other than in self-defense. With a threatening glare at Beardy, Jana said, "Better yet, let's torture them into telling us what we want to know. Afterward, we'll leave their bloodied selves behind for the vultures to pick over." She tilted her head back and let loose a high-pitched cackle, rivalling the one conjured up in her nightmares of the cannibalistic witch from the Brothers Grimm's story of *Hansel and Gretel*.

"You're bluffing," Beardy said.

Leanne bent over, grabbed his hair, and mashed his face into the ground.

Beardy bucked his head back and spat out grit. "That's child's play," he jeered.

Leanne socked him in the mouth and split open his lips. Then, she kicked him in the ribs and made him shriek.

With an upward curl of his lip, Keeley snarled, "Y'are messing with the wrong crowd. We might not look the type, but me cavalry mates and meself have done to Rebels what John Singleton Mosby did to siphon intelligence out o' Union soldiers. We have no scruples in doing the same to ye clowns, and"—he nodded at Jana—"as the lass said, leaving ye to die."

Kicking Beardy harder in his sore spot, Leanne said, "Sit up and git talkin,' ya dirty louse."

Beardy obeyed, hugging his ribs to shield them from another kick. Through gasps of breath, he grunted, "What do you want to know?"

"We know John Woodcock hired you to track us, but who hired him?" Jana said.

Beardy wheezed and coughed. "He was acting alone."

"How do ye know for sure?" Keeley asked.

"Because he swore the two-million-dollar treasury would be divvied up between him, me, and my friend here." In a slightly antagonistic tone and risking another kick by Leanne, Beardy said, "Doesn't sound to me like there's anyone else involved."

From what Jana could recall from the terrifying moments after Beardy and Baldy ambushed them, Fuji and Jed didn't seem to show any recognition of either man. Still, she asked Fuji and Jed, "Are these men the members of the KGC who hassled you?"

"No," they replied in unison.

The mention of the KGC flashed fear across the villains' faces.

Continuing her interview of Fuji and Jed, Jana said, "Do you have any reason to believe the KGC knows you came here to secure the money?"

Fuji said, "We only came after Jed's ma spouted off about it. He was paranoid about others having overheard her and come to search for it. I wasn't convinced, but, as I said before, the KGC is holding us responsible if it goes missing. So, it was worth our checking it out."

"Since these crooks and their boss aren't affiliated with the KGC, that means there could be knights from the all-seeing society watching over their loot and us right now," Jana said. "I hate to sound paranoid, but let's get out of here."

Frowning, Fuji said, "But they know who Jed and I are and where to find us."

"Don't fret, lad. They won't come after us now with Union soldiers patrolling the area, and, for yar help, we made a deal with ye to keep ye and yar families safe from the KGC's wrath. We'll put our plan in motion within a couple o' days, and they won't bother ye again."

Jana felt as sanguine as Keeley sounded that they could come through with their promises to Fuji and Jed, including their evading imprisonment. They held all of the cards with the army payroll in their possession, and they'd hold on to it until they had proof from President Johnson that he'd agree to their demands. They'd soon find out which way the wind blew with the president's loyalty.

Jana and company tied their captives' wrists, plunked them in their saddles, and got underway, marshalling them back to Culpeper Court House. Given Beardy and Baldy's intent to kill them, Jana would've loved to have indulged Leanne's fancy of forcing the felons into a trot behind their horses the entire seven miles under a searing sun, but she was anxious about toting nearly two million dollars. Although, thankfully, the four money sacks, which Jana, Keeley, Leanne, and Charlie had draped over their horses' withers, were inconspicuous as to their contents. For all anyone knew, they were carrying grains for their horses.

Just shy of noon, Jana and Keeley, along with friends and foes, arrived in the war-ravaged Culpeper Court House. They set Fuji and Jed free under two conditions. First, they made them swear to be charitable with their newfound fortune.

Expounding upon Keeley's earlier suggestion, Jana said, "Your community's acceptance of your charity immediately upon your return home will certainly insulate you from the KGC's wrath—maybe even more than what our superior can do for you."

"Aye, and yar family, friends, and neighbors will not want to feed the hand that feeds them to the wolves, and I'll wager the KGC will not attack their southern compatriots to get to ye."

"Whatever you do, though," Jana said, "avoid disclosing the source of your reward until we're certain our employer has executed our plan to expose the KGC. Give us five days, including today, then look for a telegram from us at Louisa Court House." Rather than give them her and Keeley's cipher—she never knew if they'd ever need it again—Jana outlined the simple coded message they'd send: *Yes to K. 2 Days to News. No to I.* Translated as: *Yes to exposing the KGC. Two days to hit the newspapers. No imprisonment.* "If the reverse is decided, there'll be no telegram from us, and our boss, no doubt, will have a military contingent waiting in Louisa Court House for your arrest."

Dreading their inability to visit Versella for a long time, Jana and Keeley's second condition involved entrusting Fuji and Jed to personally deliver twenty thousand dollars to her, along with their letter of appreciation for all of her charity.

Leanne narrowed her steel-gray eyes on Fuji and Jed. "Ya've got 'til sundown three days from now to git the money to Versella. Just like the KGC, we've got eyes in the backs of our heads, and we'll know if ya've swindled our dear friend out of her money. Then, I'm gonna dish out worse to ya than the KGC and make sure ya spend the rest of yer lives in a rat-infested prison."

Fuji raised his hands in surrender. "I told you before, we're not bad guys. We'll make sure she gets her money."

"By the way, other than his first name"—Jed nodded at Charlie—"we never did catch the rest of your names."

"It's best you never know them, so you can never slip about our participation," Jana said. "However, if you were ever to have an emergency involving us, we've given Versella permission to contact us on your behalf. Also, in our letter to her, we've asked her to never divulge our names to you or relative to our caper." Jana squinted at

Fuji and Jed. "Just in case curiosity gets the best of you, we've omitted signing our letter to Versella."

After parting ways with Fuji and Jed, Jana and Keeley left the money in Leanne and Charlie's charge. Then, they forced Beardy and Baldy into the courthouse by gunpoint and checked in with the Union officer, who had jurisdiction over a wide military berth in this part of the South to keep law and order, especially where a division between pro-slavery secessionists and freedmen and Northern sympathizers was concerned. At first, Jana and Keeley were enraged at his refusal to jail their prisoners without proof of their treachery—all because Beardy and Baldy declared their loyalty to the Union by reciting details of battles in which they'd fought and because they figured Jana's and Keeley's hands were tied in divulging any part of the plot surrounding the army payroll.

In succumbing to the realizations that she and Keeley were unable to show any credentials and it was their word against Beardy and Baldy's, Jana said to the post commander, "We can put this debate to rest if you'll allow us the use of your telegraph to send a message to Secretary of the Treasury McCulloch."

The officer's eyebrows rose, and his curiosity precipitated his permission.

Employing her and Keeley's cryptograph, Jana had the operator wire the following message to the Secretary of the Treasury to be directed to President Johnson: *jgcfkpi vq ycujkpivqp ekva. fkurqucn qh rtkuqpgtu? ctXVIIIguv lqjp yqXVfeqem! lcpc cpf mgVnga.* Translated as: *Heading to Washington City. Disposal of prisoners? Arrest John Woodcock! Jana and Keeley.*

Within a half-hour, the telegraph sounder tapped out a long series of dots and dashes, and the military officer ogled Jana and Keeley when the operator handed him a telegram signed by President Johnson *and* Secretary of War Stanton. He jumped to obeying the orders of the commander in chief and his army superior in locking up Beardy and Baldy and the army payroll and equipping a cavalry escort for Jana, Keeley, Leanne, Charlie, and their prisoners for their journey the next day to Washington.

Jana and Keeley were taken aback by President Johnson's candor about the army payroll to the Secretary of War. Maybe he'd told him to diminish their bickering. Or maybe he and Edwin Stanton were in cahoots to distribute the payroll to the KGC, and President Johnson had feigned discordance between him and Stanton to put Jana and Keeley off their scent. Either way, three layers of the president's cabinet were now aware of the payroll. They needed that check-and-balance to coerce President Johnson into obliging their plan of baring the KGC as thieves and thwarting Fuji's and Jed's imprisonments. His refusal to do so would reveal his and Stanton's treachery, and Jana and Keeley had no fear about exposing them and forcing the KGC's silence.

After a meal, hot bath, and good night's sleep in a local hotel, Jana, Keeley, Leanne, Charlie, and Tracker rose bright and early the next morning. The foursome ate breakfast in their fresh trousers and shirts that each had wisely carried with them, leaving their soiled clothing behind for the hotel to launder and offer to the needy. As they retrieved their horses from the stable, they were met by their squad of uniformed cavalrymen: a captain driving the wagon beside his lieutenant riding shotgun and two privates astride their horses.

Fittingly, Jana realized, Beardy and Baldy were confined atop a false wagon bottom, taunted by nearly two million dollars stowed beneath them. Rightly so, they were ornery and desperate as they tried worming out their wrist-and-ankle shackles and chains. Even if the prisoners could miraculously free themselves, they wouldn't get past Tracker, who trotted alongside the wagon, keeping a vigilant eye on them.

Jana, Keeley, Leanne, and Charlie thoroughly enjoyed their ride together, especially sitting around a campfire cooking, reminiscing about their wartime activities, and conversing about their current lives. It resurrected fond memories of their camaraderie in the cavalry.

The two full days passed by quickly and, thankfully, uneventfully, especially with Union patrols all about them and Yankee soldiers flocking to their new posts to help keep law and order in the South.

On the third day, Jana, Keeley, Leanne, and Charlie cheered when the dome of the Capitol building reared above the tree-line. Its crowning female warrior glistened under a voluptuous late-morning sun in the foreground of a clear cobalt sky. She beckoned them across the Long Bridge, between Arlington, Virginia, and Washington City, over the calm, shimmery water of the Potomac River.

Per President Johnson and Secretary of War Stanton's order, Jana and Keeley's unit left their prisoners in the gated courtyard of the imposing Old Capitol Prison under the commandant's supervision. Then, Jana commanded their cavalry escort directly to the President's House. She was anxious to wash her hands of the intimidating cache of money.

Leanne and Charlie remained in their saddles while Jana and Keeley climbed the steps of the North Portico and crossed beneath the giant white pillars to the door.

Removing their hats and slapping the dust out of them against their denim riding trousers, Jana and Keeley revealed their grimy faces to the doorkeeper.

Thomas Pendel's eyes lit up, and he smiled at them in reverence. Reaching out and giving Jana and Keeley hearty handshakes, he said, "I've been expecting you, Miss Brady, Mr. Cassidy. President Johnson is abuzz about your having accomplished your mission with alacrity. I've never seen him in a state of good humor for an extended period of time, such as he's been for the past three days."

Jana blew a sigh of relief. "And we're never so happy to be under your watch again, Thomas."

Peeking around Jana and Keeley toward Leanne, Charlie, and their uniformed escort, Thomas stroked his wandering mustache and soft-bearded chin. Business-like, he said, "I'm sure you're eager to dispose of your precious cargo."

Jana raised her eyebrows at him. "You know what we're carrying?"

"My reputation for loyalty to President Lincoln"—he puffed up with pride to his full towering height—"has earned me President Johnson's trust."

President Johnson's disclosure of the army payroll to the doorkeeper furthered Jana's faith in his innocence of KGC affiliation or anything underhanded for his own personal or political gain. She sensed she and Keeley stood a good chance of his obliging their requests.

"Now, to avoid public scrutiny," Thomas said, "hoof and wheel it around to the south entrance, slip into the cellar, and take the first set of stairs on the right, roughly below the grand East Room, up to the second floor. Martha will receive you outside the president's office."

Riding around to the east side of the Executive Mansion, just beyond the extension opposite the notable Conservatory, Jana noted other aspects of the grounds for the servants' daily operations in basking the president and his family in comfort: outhouses, carriage-house, woodshed, and stable. A westward breeze hailed from the northwest garden, scenting the air with flowering trees and peaches and strawberries. Jana could virtually taste the succulent fruits on the sweet spot of her tongue, and she yearned for some after the past few days' fare of eggs and smoked bacon. They ran into very few staff bustling about on this Sabbath, presumably because many were off observing their religious preferences. The whole carefree atmosphere impressed Jana more as a country manor than the mansion of a nation's president.

When they pulled up to the cellar entrance, Jana, Keeley, Leanne, and Charlie swung out of their saddles.

The captain offered his service and that of his cavalrymen to lug the sacks from the wagon and inside.

Before any of their escort made a move from the wagon or their horses, Jana said, "Thank you, Captain, but I think we can manage from here. However"—she glanced at Tracker, who'd jumped up onto the false bottom of the wagon bed after they'd unloaded their prisoners—"would you kindly watch our dog while we meet with President Johnson?"

"We'd be happy to," the captain said, turning around to tickle Tracker's ear.

Jana, Keeley, Leanne, and Charlie each removed a burlap sack from the wagon and flung it over their shoulder. As they entered the cellar, they joked about their odd appearance as one-humped camels entering the basement of the White House. Deep into the hallway, past the servants' quarters, they crossed over an invisible line from the stink of mildew to an aroma of freshly baking goods wafting out of the kitchen at the other end. Following Thomas's instructions to the letter, they found the staircase and tramped up it slowly and awkwardly under their burdensome loads.

True to Thomas's word, a gleeful Martha met them outside the president's office.

Feeling the heat of her embarrassment blotting her cheeks, Jana said, "Forgive our untidiness, Martha. We've come directly from the road. We hope President Johnson won't be offended."

Playfully swatting her hand, Martha replied, "I think nothing of it, and neither will he." Her eyes switched between Jana and Keeley. "He has come to expect nothing less of you than a tenacity to fulfill your duty in whatever manner you deem suitable." She glanced at

Leanne and Charlie. "And who might you be for me to adequately make your acquaintances to my father?"

Jana introduced Leanne and Charlie and explained their association to her and Keeley.

When Leanne started to set her sack down, Martha said, "Please, there is no need for a handshake." She giggled. "I do not wish for you to lift that weighty sack yet one more time and tweak a muscle." Then, she turned, opened the door, and announced their presence as she breezed across the threshold into her father's office.

They found President Johnson standing in a tailored suit gazing out the south window, exactly as Jana and Keeley had upon their first meeting with him. Unlike before, his hands were unclasped and dangling loosely at his sides. When he spun around, Jana noted a rosy tinge in his cheeks and a spirited light in his brown eyes. His facial features appeared more as a playful pup than the stern adult bulldog Jana had first seen in him.

Treading airily across the green carpet of diamond-and-floral accents, the president reached out to shake Jana's and Keeley's hands.

Jana and Keeley, in turn, obliged his outstretched hand after they set down their pudgy sacks and swiped their soiled hands across the breasts of their dusty coats.

"I had faith in your accomplishing my assignment, but your expeditiousness is incredulous," President Johnson said.

Leanne and Charlie, who'd been gawking at the room and the president, snapped out of their reverence when Martha said, "Father, I believe you have not had the privilege of meeting Leanne and Charlie Watson. They are Jana and Keeley's cavalry comrades and close friends, and they assisted in your assignment."

"I am grateful for your service to country and me," the president said, shaking Leanne's and Charlie's hands after they shed their loads and wiped their hands on their coats. He skimmed over each of his four troopers. "I suspect it will be short-lived, but, for the time being, you have rendered me a hero within the federal government, and it shall not go unnoticed with the people of our republic."

Keeley hooked a questioning eyebrow at Jana.

With a subtle shake of her head, Jana telegraphed her preference to wait for a better opening to discuss heroics with the president.

President Johnson motioned them toward the same mahogany table in the center of the room. "Please, make yourselves comfortable." Once they were all situated, he peered at Jana and chuckled. "Shall we have Martha send up the sugar cookies we had specially made for you?"

Jana collapsed back into the curved splat of her chair, shocked that the president had noticed her affinity toward the sweet treat during their introductory meeting. Her cheeks flushed, and she awkwardly giggled.

Well aware of Jana's ravenous appetite and affinity for sugar cookies, Keeley, Leanne, and Charlie ribbed Jana about it, leading the way for President Johnson's kindhearted laugh to put Jana at ease.

Martha interrupted the merriment. "I will also have some lemonade brought up," she said and exited the room.

With one more test for the president to fully enclose her circle of trust in him, Jana clinched her hands together upon her lap and squared her eyes on him. "Before our debriefing, I have one question for you, sir: What changed your mind about keeping our mission a secret with your cabinet?"

He shrugged his plump lips. "I thought better of my beginning with my cabinet on a reputation for surreptitiousness or, as some might perceive, underhandedness."

"That was probably a wise decision," Jana said, now more than ever convinced he was completely innocent of affiliation with the KGC.

"Now"—the president thrust out his palms—"I would love to hear the details of your field work."

Halfway into their debriefing, Martha returned with a house servant, whom she dismissed after the domestic set a silver tray of fresh lemonade and glasses on the table.

Jana paused in her recitation, waiting for Martha to slide a second tray of cookies central to everyone, pass around plates and napkins, and fill glasses to the rim with lemonade.

Finished, Martha said, "Do you require anything else, Father?"

"No thank you, my darling."

After Martha closed the door behind her, Jana picked up where they'd left off in their story, and Keeley, Leanne, and Charlie continued to alternately chime in with bits and pieces. Jana was sure to include Tracker's rescue in her telling, and she concluded by stressing the KGC's connection to the theft and John Woodcock's order to have his goons murder them all.

The president raised his glass in salute, especially at Jana and Keeley. "Praise to your most thorough approach to and execution and resolution of my challenging assignment." He took a sip of his lemonade and set his glass down. After wiping his mouth on his napkin, he said, "Speaking of resolution, John Woodcock and his goons bartered for lighter sentences by confessing their sins. Still, they will serve lengthy imprisonments for their traitorous deeds against the federal government and attempted murders."

Jana, Keeley, Leanne, and Charlie clapped.

When their applause abated, President Johnson eyed Jana's empty plate. "What? No sugar cookie yet, Miss Brady?"

Jana began twirling her silky linen napkin around her fingers.

Furrowing his bushy brows, President Johnson said, "It seems something of monumental importance is troubling you, Miss Brady. Please, be candid."

Jana started, "I made a promise—"

Keeley interjected. "*We* made the promise, me lass. Ye'll not shoulder the burden on yar own."

Smiling at Keeley for his thoughtfulness, Jana continued, "And we need a huge favor from you to keep it, sir."

"By all means, proceed," President Johnson said, crossing his arms and leaning them on the tabletop.

Jana outlined her and Keeley's blueprint for dealing with the KGC and Fuji and Jed, including omitting Fuji and Jed's collusion in the original theft. Additionally, she stressed to President Johnson that in order to give Fuji and Jed full credit for salvaging the treasury and insulation from the KGC's wrath, she, Keeley, Leanne, and Charlie must be spared from publicity.

President Johnson's voice wavered between disappointment and sympathy as he said, "I understand, but it is a shame the people of the United States shall forever be ignorant of your staunch patriotism, and we could all use a humbling dose of your examples right now."

"Thank you for acknowledging that, sir," Jana said. "However, the idea of two men, who fought for the Confederacy, putting aside their hostilities toward the Union and helping to sew the tattered edges of our country back together again might be a more healing dose. Don't you agree?"

With a sigh, the president said, "Yes, Miss Brady, and most eloquently stated."

"Whether or not ye decide to pardon our Rebel partners"—Keeley pushed out his chest—"me Jana lass and meself made a command decision to allow them their reward from the KGC for their help in reclaiming the payroll, and ye may take their twenty thousand dollars out o' our commission."

"Also," Jana said, "Secretary of the Treasury McCulloch will find the army payroll another twenty thousand dollars light. We gifted it to a Southern woman who very kindly and generously donated her care and costly personal resources to us three times: in the care and protection of Keeley—a Union soldier, no less—in his amnesic state after the battle of Trevilian Station, in aiding our flight back to Union lines to obtain Keeley's honorable discharge from our regimental surgeon, and in fulfilling our duty to you. For the latter, especially, without her arming us with horses, accessories, sustenance, and, most significantly, intelligence to track Fuji and Jed, we might've failed to recoup the stolen treasury as quickly as we did—if at all. You may also take our gift to her out of our commission."

The president shook his head in amazement. "It is a credit to your kindness and compassion, Miss Brady and Mr. Cassidy, to forego a portion of your commission to others in need. Nevertheless, I decline your offer. You shall receive your full commission prior to your departure from Washington"—he glanced at Leanne and Charlie—"and you shall each receive twenty thousand dollars for your participation." To their gasps, he said, "Overall, it is a minor expense the federal government can manage, given we expected the treasury could be lost to us forever."

Jana, Keeley, Leanne, and Charlie burst out in unison, "Thank you, sir."

"Furthermore," the president said, "I shall grant your request to absolve our Rebel allies from imprisonment and allow them their reward, but first they must take an oath of allegiance to the United States. Will you act as my emissaries in delivering my terms to them?"

"Aye, sir." Keeley chuckled. "I'm sure yar concessions will guarantee ye at least two former Rebel votes come yar re-election in four years—that is, if the state of Virginia is readmitted into the Union by then."

President Johnson sighed. "I will need millions more than that." Slapping his palm against the tabletop, he said, "Now, is there anything else you need?"

Jana leaped to say, "How about supporting the *woman's* right to vote? Imagine the number of votes that would yield you."

"My opinion on the matter will not be palatable to you, Miss Brady, as I stand firmly behind 'a government for white men.'"

Jana stiffened in her chair. "I appreciate your candor, President Johnson, and I realize we're here for another matter, but I hope I'll have another opportunity to persuade you otherwise. However, I will leave you with this question upon which to ruminate: Why did you think of *me* first over a man for your assignment if you don't think we women are capable?"

Clearing his throat, President Johnson said, "Yes...well...an exception was made because of your investigative prowess, but back to your concern over the consignment of heroics and fate of the KGC. Please, allow me a minute to think it through." He fell silent, scratching his clean-shaven squared jaw as he stared up at the plaster ceiling.

Keeley, Leanne, and Charlie sat stiller than statues while Jana nervously chomped on a sugar cookie.

The clock on the fireplace mantel ticked louder and louder with each second of the president's self-allotted minute.

After what felt like an eternity to Jana, the president re-focused upon them. "Forgive my lengthy deliberation of your lofty requests. They are not to be entered into lightly."

Lofty? That doesn't sound promising, Jana thought, swigging her lemonade to swallow the cookie crumbs caught in her throat before she choked on them.

"You will understand if I must confer with my cabinet first." The president glanced at the west wall, his expression anchored in gloom. "Although, I can think of only one man who might oppose naming the KGC."

The president's diplomatic position forbade him from outright naming the *one man*, and Jana knew better than to ask. Nonetheless, his scowl in the general direction of the War Department had betrayed his antagonist. Did President Johnson suspect Edwin Stanton of association with the KGC? Jana would probably never know the answer, unless President Johnson one day amassed proof against the Secretary of War for the world to see.

As he'd done a couple of times in Jana and Keeley's first meeting with him, he glimpsed the clock, its hands encroaching upon 1:00 p.m. Rising from his chair, he said, "If I am to expedite your answer, I must hasten away to have my private secretary call an emergency meeting of my cabinet. Where shall I contact you with the verdict?"

"We prefer to stay at Willard's Hotel, close to here, just in case you need us to testify before your cabinet," Jana said.

"Aye, and now that our charade as husband and wife is over, me Jana lass and meself will check into separate rooms. So, ye may direct yar message to Jana's room box," Keeley said.

"I just thought of something, sir," Jana said. "We have no accommodation for Tracker. I doubt the luxurious Willard's would appreciate a large dog roaming through their establishment. Do you know where we could board him?"

"Where is our furry hero now?" the president asked.

"Outside, waiting with our security detail, of whom he's grown fond," Jana said.

"When do you plan to depart Washington?"

"Early tomorrow morning, unless you have no answer for us yet," Jana said.

Pivoting about, the president retreated to his pigeon-holed desk. "I intend to have an answer for you by suppertime." He scratched out a note and handed it to Jana. "Will that do?"

Jana read the order for their cavalry escort to take up comfortable lodging with Tracker at a nearby boarding house and to deliver him at the train station the next morning. "That will do very nicely. Thank you, sir."

President Johnson ushered them to the door. Before opening it, he said, "I will also have the army payroll deposited immediately at the Treasury Department, and you may collect your commissions within the hour or at your convenience." He grinned at Jana and

Keeley. "Perhaps you will consider a trifling portion of it a princely wedding gift?"

Surprised by his remembering her fleeting mention of her and Keeley's intended marriage during their introductory meeting, Jana fell speechless.

"Aye, but more kingly than princely," Keeley said, beaming with jubilation.

The president smiled and then hooked right out of his office to the end of the waiting area.

After President Johnson disappeared into another room, most likely belonging to his private secretary, Leanne pumped her fist at Jana and Keeley. "Thanks to ya both, me and Charlie got us a king's ransom for quick work."

Charlie pushed his spectacles up onto the bridge of his nose, and his eyes twinkled at Jana and Keeley. "Thank you for your faith in me and Leanne to help you in your caper."

"I'm sure this won't be the last time Keeley and I press you into service. As a matter of fact"—Jana smiled as she tapped her index finger against her chin—"Keeley and I need a best man and woman for our wedding."

"Aye. What do ye say, Charlie, Leanne? Will ye do it?"

"We'd be honored," Charlie said along with Leanne's exuberant nod.

"Wonderful! Now, let's get out of here before we've overstayed our welcome," Jana said and waved them on. In retracing their route to the cellar and outside, Jana had a sudden premonition that she'd come face-to-face with Andrew Johnson another time in his capacity as president of the United States.

After checking into Willard's, Jana, Keeley, Leanne, and Charlie hastened to the Treasury Department to collect their commissions. They were shocked when the secretary presented each an additional gift: A small wooden case containing four twenty-dollar gold coins, which were recessed in navy-blue velvet and laid out to make the corners of a flag-like rectangle. The two pieces in the upper left and right corners displayed identical obverse liberty head designs, but one was minted in 1850, the other in 1861. In flipping over the two pieces in the lower left and right corners, displaying identical eagle designs, Jana found that each was the reverse for its correlational 1850 and 1861 coin.

In a dull voice to match his gloomy expression, as had been rumored of his character, Secretary of Treasury McCulloch said, "President Johnson had them assembled immediately after he received word of your success in recovering the army payroll. He wanted to celebrate your efforts on behalf of him and our country in some special way besides your commissions."

Leanne held the 1850 Liberty Head Double Eagle up to the window light. "This could be worth something someday."

While the group gazed at the shimmering liberty head in awe, knowing they could possess the first of its kind minted at Philadelphia, Keeley said, "Aye, especially given the future uncertainty o' coin production with the four mints in Philadelphia, North Carolina, Georgia, and Louisiana closed down and the United States solely dependent upon the San Francisco branch for striking coinage."

"This one could be worth even more someday." Jana ran her fingertip over the reverse of the 1861 Liberty Head Double Eagle with the heading *United States of America* and a shielded eagle holding a double ribbon, which symbolized twice the face value of the ten-dollar Gold Eagle. "We know, by the mint mark *O*, this piece was struck at New Orleans. What we don't know is whether it was struck by the United States, state of Louisiana after it seceded from the Union and seized the mint, or the Confederacy when it took over production for a brief time."

Maintaining his apathetic tone, Secretary McCulloch said, "The historical significance of both twenty-dollar coins—especially the 1861 coin, owing to its having been minted by three different governments within the borders of the United States, as you inferred, Miss Brady—is precisely why President Johnson chose them for your collection."

"No matter their future value, they will always be priceless to me as a perfect memento of our mission." Charlie pushed up his spectacles, and his eyes shone like the buffed coins as he continued, "More so now that our participation in finding the army payroll will forever be silent in the annals of history."

Jana, Keeley, and Leanne echoed Charlie's sentiment, and Jana expressed a wish to thank President Johnson personally for his thoughtfulness.

"I will be certain to pass along your gratitude to President Johnson as I must hasten away to an emergency meeting he has called of his cabinet." The secretary hooked up a balding brow, correlational to his profoundly receding hairline. "I believe it has something to do with your recovery of the army payroll."

Jana gave him a tight-lipped smile, and then she, Keeley, Leanne, and Charlie began busily stowing their pay, mostly in large denominations for ease of toting, and cushioning their chests of gold in their personal travel bags before taking their leave ahead of Secretary McCulloch. They made their way out to the street, giddy with their new fortunes and still in disbelief that their financial futures were secure.

For the next couple of hours, Jana, Keeley, Leanne, and Charlie occupied themselves purchasing new clothes in the shops along Pennsylvania Avenue. Jana, Keeley, and Charlie easily found their sizes, but Leanne's men's trousers, shirt, and coat required tucking and stitching at the seams. President Johnson would've been impressed with the tailor's diligent and seamless work. Afterward they freshened up and rested a spell in their rooms before meeting in the lobby around suppertime. Eager for word to come from President Johnson, Jana drummed her fingers against the dark wood armrest of her upholstered chair while Leanne leaned against a colossal granite column, snapping and unsnapping her holster, and Keeley and Charlie paced across the plush and colorful rugs. They had only to wait very few minutes when, around 5:00 p.m., a dapper young man glided through the front door and up to the registration desk. He delivered a letter to the clerk, who stuffed it into Jana's room box.

Springing from her chair, Jana retrieved the wax-sealed note written on plain, ivory paper rather than on White House stationery. She motioned for Keeley, Leanne, and Charlie to join her in a corner, away from the eyes and ears of those loitering in the lobby. Taking a deep hopeful breath, Jana tore open the communication and noted it was written in code as: *wpcpkoqwu citgVIIogpv vq jgtqkeu cpf MIE. oqtpkpi pfyu. Rtgukfgpv Lqjpuqp.*

"I'm impressed," Charlie said, "with President Johnson's continuing regard for our anonymity."

"Aye, and I'm itching to hear the word o' our leader."

Jana held the paper out where all could read the cipher, and they worked together to decipher it.

Careful not to draw onlookers, the foursome shared whoops, audible only to each other, when it decoded as: *Unanimous agreement to heroics and KGC. Morning news. President Johnson.*

Jana wished she'd been a fly on the wall to see Secretary of War Stanton's reaction. If he'd balked at it, as President Johnson feared he would, he'd certainly capitulated under pressure from his peers.

Immediately afterward, Jana and Keeley telegraphed Louisa Court House to give Fuji and Jed the good news and to receive confirmation from a grateful Versella, who'd received her reward.

That evening, in the dining room of Willard's Hotel, Jana raised her glass of claret to Keeley, Leanne, and Charlie. "A toast to the best of friends and to our gold, guts, and glory!"

"Aye, short but sweet praise, me lass," Keeley said, smiling.

With their glasses still held high, Leanne said, "Here's hopin' to lots more adventures with the four of us to come."

Before they clinked their glasses, Charlie added, "My ma would say Jana and Keeley are about to embark upon some lively adventures: marriage and raising a child. I wish you both the very best in your endeavors."

How did I get so lucky in finding the love of my life and lifelong friends? Jana wondered, with tears welling in her eyes.

The foursome received validation of their success the next morning. Like ants clambering for crumbs on a picnic blanket, the hotel's guests were elbowing their way to the newsstand in the lobby to snatch up their copy of a Washington daily.

When Jana, Keeley, Leanne, and Charlie checked their room boxes for messages, the registration clerk handed them each a reserved copy of the *Daily National Intelligencer*. He studied them, and, with a disbelieving shake of his head, he scampered away to register other guests.

Jana wondered about his odd behavior until she finished reading the editorial on the cover page. In it, President Johnson was credited for spearheading the search in sending out four of his trustworthy, competent, and nameless field agents to recover it. *Ah*, Jana realized, *the reason for the desk clerk's scrutiny of us, given our party of four and our reserved copies of the rag.* Obviously, they had shattered his allusion of the stereotypical detective, outfitted in his wide-brim hat, long canvas coat, scuffed boots, dusty trousers, and holstered revolver with Jana back in a dress, Leanne's gender clear even in her men's garb, and Keeley and Charlie dressed in tidily pressed trousers and waistcoats. Shame on him! All of the female spies, detectives, and soldiers coming to light post-war ought to have given him pause to think. Either way, Jana was glad this same clerk had failed to compare their detective-like deportment upon their check-in yesterday to their dapperly and gendered one today.

The article also praised Fulton Jibbs and Jedediah Fernsby, formerly of the 13th Virginia Infantry Regiment, for having—in Jana's exact words to the president—willingly put aside their hostilities toward the Union to help President Johnson's four field agents recoup the treasury and sew the tattered seams of the country back together again. The buzz all around the lobby:

> Southern Rebels Fulton Jibbs and Jedediah Fernsby were heroes for having put their lives at risk in their triumph over the KGC!

Jana hurried to snag three extra copies of the newspaper to mail to Versella, Fuji, and Jed as mementoes. Then, she said to Keeley, Leanne, and Charlie, "If John Woodcock and his goons know what's good for them, they'll never dispute the flaws in the story."

Leanne smirked. "Ya can bet that's already been bashed into their brains."

"Aye, and, hopefully, the news o' the KGC's deception will permanently snuff out their flame," Keeley said.

Wriggling his nose and cheek muscles to push his spectacles up onto the bridge of his nose, Charlie said, "At the very least, the repossessed Union-Army payroll can't bolster the Confederacy's treasury, which continues to be missing." His eyes narrowed behind his glass lenses. "You don't think President Johnson will ask us to hunt for it?"

"Good Lord, we'd need a company of Union soldiers supporting us for such a search." Although intrigued by the idea, Jana was more eager to get home and marry her soldier-sweetheart and build their hearth and home around Alex and Tracker. She caught Keeley's eye, and his smile told her that he was wishing the same. "Let's skedaddle before there's any notion of it."

They all laughed.

"Actually," Leanne said, "me and Charlie are stickin' 'round for another day. Charlie wants to visit Matthew Brady's art gallery to git some tips on settin' up his own studio."

The foursome bid each other goodbye, and Jana and Keeley checked out of the hotel and hopped a streetcar to the *Baltimore & Ohio Railroad* depot, where Tracker came sprinting toward them with his tail wagging.

Although reluctant to give him up, the cavalrymen handed him over with a written order from President Johnson to the various railroad conductors along Jana and Keeley's route home, allowing Tracker a ride in the passenger car with them as opposed to a baggage or freight car.

Jana and Keeley plopped down on the upholstered bench of their train car, and Tracker curled up in a ball between their feet.

Laying her head upon Keeley's shoulder, Jana gazed up at him with a world of love and adoration. "I couldn't be more pleased with our trip. We worked through situations, which, I think, enhanced our similarities and differences. It strengthened our union and made it everlasting. Don't you think, me lad?"

Keeley leaned in close and pressed his lips against hers, holding them there until Jana pulled away to catch her breath. "Does that answer yar question, me lass?"

Jana felt his love for and devotion to her wrapping around her heart and soul in one big bow. They were the greatest gifts he could ever give her. She could hardly wait another second to bind their love in marriage.

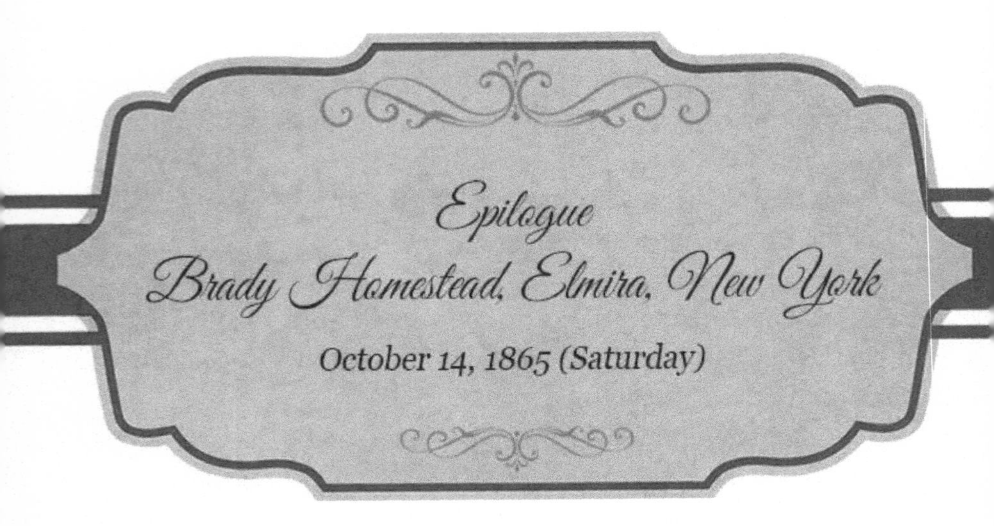

Jana clung to Pa's arm as they stood to one side of the barn's opening, she in her Garibaldi dress, he in his newly tailored white-collared shirt and black cravat and suit.

Rocking on her heeled boots, Jana stared at the outer frame of the barn's double doors, adorned in an autumnal garland of spruce boughs overlaid with an alternating pattern of dried corn cobs dyed burgundy with their yellow husks peeled back and splayed, freshly cut orange and yellow wildflowers, and bunches of brown wispy-hatted field grasses. She yearned to sail through the threshold, down the aisle, and up onto the makeshift altar, where Keeley awaited her. She quelled her impatience with a glance at the resplendent blue sky, picking out the perfect cottony cloud upon which she pictured Keeley's mam, da, and sisters seated to watch over and bless her and Keeley's union. It meant the world to Jana for them to see that their son and brother, who'd been left wanting of family at a young age, was about to be formally attached to another he could call his own. Since Jana and Keeley had chosen to delay their wedding until their house and barn were completely built, they decided to marry on

Keeley's twenty-fifth birthday in special tribute of his mam and da's having brought Keeley and the man of Jana's dreams into the world. She promised the Cassidys two things: She and her family would safeguard Keeley's health and happiness the rest of his earthly life, and she'd never forget that their sacrifice in death from the Great Famine of Ireland had—as Jana truly believed—predestined her and Keeley's hearts to unite in eternal love.

Jana tilted her head back into the cheerful Indian-summer breeze. It fanned the herbaceous and earthy scents of her fresh bouquet of orange and yellow wildflowers overflowing from the hollowed-out bell of a small green warty gourd. It brought the familiar lowing of Herefords from the distant pastures. And it dipped the ostrich feathers of her top hat against the nape of her neck in a delightful tickle. There was no better place in the world for their wedding than on the Brady farm. Her elation with both bloomed warmer upon her face than the radiant midday sun. Absolutely positive her own natural blush would last the entire day, Jana had told Rachel and Rebecca that it was redundant for them to dust her cheeks pink with rouge.

The cameraman, who finished readying his camera to snap a picture of her and Keeley as they exited the barn blissfully married for the front page of the Elmira *Gazette*, slipped past her and Pa and into the barn.

Smirking at the camera, Jana thought, *My facial color is definitely a moot point for the black-and-white photographs you produce.* But they would be splendid for capturing Jana and Keeley's occasion and notable guests, including friends Susan B. Anthony, Elizabeth Cady Stanton, and Frederick Douglass; Jana's nursing mentors Clara Barton and Dr. Mary Walker; and, much to Ma's exultation, the poet Walt Whitman. The photographs would also serve as souvenirs for the scores of people who couldn't be accommodated with an invitation to what had become christened the most-anticipated wedding around Chemung and surrounding counties—maybe even the United States—of a cavalrywoman to her cavalryman.

Jana peered up into Pa's dewy eyes, a reflection of her own in hazel color and ovular shape. "This is the happiest day of my life, Pa. Nothing can possibly spoil it." She'd barely finished her breathless utterance when the echoes of some conveyance clattering down the valley splintered her private moment with Pa.

Dabbing his tear ducts with a knobby knuckle, Pa spun around with Jana to see a cyclone of dust rising beyond the crest of the Brady lane. "Oh, boy, here we go again."

Jana patted his arm. "Don't worry, Pa, nothing's going to stop me from marrying Keeley today. We promised each other that any outside adventures are suspended until after we've spent significant time at home, especially with Alex."

With a swish of her pantalettes and petticoats, Ma appeared beside Jana, her medium-sized hoops swinging into Jana, who'd forsaken wearing a crinoline. Ma was stunning in her burgundy silk dress. It enhanced her fairer complexion, the rosiest ever. When Jana had remarked upon it, Ma averred it was the shine of a mother about to give her eldest daughter of five away. "I've cued Corporal Wallace to blow his bugle upon my. . ." Ma's voice trailed off when she saw company coming at a speedy clip, and her expression dimmed along with the sun ducking behind a cloud. "Who on earth could it be? Not Duke and Kate this time; our Pinkerton agents are here and seated. And the Barneys and Miss Lizzie were adamant about their inability to attend with ongoing tensions between the North and South making travel difficult from Virginia."

Pa whistled at the sight of a shiny black brougham, drawn by two finely groomed white horses and escorted on three sides by mounted sentinels. "Whoever's in that buggy is mighty important."

"I'll say," Ma said, touching her pins to assure her stylish burgundy top hat with a black band was still tightly bound to her sandy-colored hair and centered on her head.

"The only person I know who could lease or own such elegance is Wyatt McGriffin," Jana said, recollecting her ride in her former lecture-circuit patron's luxurious carriage when she was conveyed to her speech in Buffalo.

Ma's face rumpled in bafflement. "And he's here."

Actually, Jana thought, *we Bradys can afford to ride around in such splendor with my and Keeley's newfound and shared wealth.* She suppressed a giggle when she recalled the manager's shock upon her and Keeley's one-hundred-thousand-dollar deposit into the Elmira bank. Not at liberty to disclose where they'd gotten the money, Jana hated to think the manager was wondering if she and Keeley had robbed a bank. Ironically, they'd been occupied with the business of robbery. Only, like the mythical outlaw Robin Hood, they'd robbed the bad guys to give to the good guys.

A mustachioed coachman, wearing the badge of U.S. Marshal over his coat, reined in the horses, yanked the brougham's brake, and tipped his hat to the Bradys before climbing down. While he opened the door of the coach to release his occupant, his three badged-deputies kept a tight rein on their horses and keen eye to their surroundings.

Helping himself down the iron step of the coach, a gentleman in polished boots smoothed out his well-tailored coat and straightened his bow tie before he removed his short top hat, which had been pulled low over his face.

Jana, Ma, and Pa gasped.

First to regain her senses, Jana reached out to shake the hand President Johnson offered her. "To what do we owe your visit, sir?"

"I hope you and Mr. Cassidy will forgive my intrusion upon your wedding, but I thought a commander in chief of the United States Army ought to have a presence at a highly celebrated national event to do with the cavalry and one second only to the Grand Review of the Armies in Washington to reign in the end of war."

Jana wondered if the president had seized a chance to show himself in order to stump for votes in a region where he might be unpopular. Grimacing, she said, "I must warn you, sir, that there are some in attendance who might be uncordial toward you, given your inclination against universal suffrage."

Lifting his broad shoulders, President Johnson harrumphed. "I would certainly hope those persons, to whom you refer, would have the good sense to put aside their political differences for the sake of making your affair a happy one, as I wish to do."

Pa cleared his throat, snagging Jana's attention.

"Allow me to introduce my ma and pa to you," Jana said.

Extending his hand to Ma and Pa, in turn, the president said, "Pleased to meet you, Mr. and Mrs. Brady. I commend you for having raised a brave and patriotic soul in your daughter. I pray our countrymen sow more seeds like her."

Jana puffed up with pride, and her parents pumped her up more with their laudatory smiles.

"How kind of you to say, President Johnson," Ma said.

"It seems I am a bit tardy in my arrival," the president said. "Please, forgive me for this oversight."

Ma clasped her hands. "Think nothing of it."

Pa added, "Actually, your timing is impeccable. We were just about to start."

Looking to Jana, President Johnson said, "Martha regrets her inability to have accompanied me." He sighed, reminding Jana of his solemnity from their first meeting at the White House. "Like you, Miss Brady, I fear she sacrifices too much of herself to the health and welfare of others, especially me and her mother."

Leanne's familiar voice cracked the air. "I've been sent out to see what's holdin' ya—," she cut herself short as she skidded to a stop, scattering hay that Pa had spread out before the threshold into the barn to keep the dust at bay. Stretching to her full height of five feet three inches, she saluted the president.

President Johnson returned her salute. "Greetings, Miss Watson." After inspecting her from head to toe in her kepi, neatly pressed yellow-trimmed dark blue shell jacket, light blue trousers, and spit-shined boots, he eyed Jana and said, "By your Garibaldi dress and Miss Watson's uniform, I am pleased to see that your wedding is a military affair."

Given his former trade as a tailor, Jana wasn't surprised that he'd noted her fashionable military-style dress, but she was impressed that he'd deduced their military wedding.

Tugging the hem of his coat, the president continued, "Well, in my current role as commander in chief of the army, I believe I have arrived in the nick of time to officially cap your ceremony."

Keeley sprung out the barn. "Y'are not having cold feet, me lass, about—," he cut his teasing short and his eyebrows arched high up, almost to the rim of his kepi. "I don't believe me eyes. What brings ye here, sir?"

President Johnson reached out and shook Keeley's gauntleted hand. "Your and Miss Brady's wedding, of course." To Keeley's gawp, he said, "Is there really a more important place for me to be right now than the wedding of a cavalryman to his cavalrywoman?" He chuckled and his playful expression filled with intrigue. "Besides, I wished to deliver some gifts in person. In the coach, I have certificates signed by General Ulysses S. Grant, which make you, Miss Brady, and Mr. and Miss Watson Honorary Majors of Cavalry. Although it is purely ceremonial, it is a glorious accomplishment to pass down through your generations."

Keeley and Leanne blinked their eyes in disbelief.

"I...I...I'm stunned, sir," Jana stammered and thanked him for his thoughtfulness behind it and his previous gift of gold coins, which Keeley and Leanne echoed.

A uniformed Charlie bustled out of the barn, and his azure eyes grew big behind his spectacles upon his sighting of the president.

Ma threw up her arms and said half-jokingly, "Why get married in the barn when the wedding party is out here?" She fixed her welcoming cocoa-colored eyes on the president. "We'd be happy to adjourn a little bit longer if you'd like to get the kinks out of your legs or freshen up."

Bowing, he said, "I appreciate your generosity, Mrs. Brady, but I am more than ready. Please, accept my apology for any delay."

"What about your coachman and guards, should we invite them in?" Pa said.

"Since this wedding is of national interest, you never know what maniacs might turn out seeking to assassinate a former female soldier and contemporary activist or"—his eyes darted nervously around their property—"a president with Southern roots. They will take up posts around the barn to secure the premises."

"Well, then, shall we begin?" Ma said, holding out her arm.

Circling his arm around hers, President Johnson said, "Lead the way, Mrs. Brady."

"I'll be right back, Jana and Thomas," Ma called out over the shoulder of her puffed sleeve as she ushered the president inside to cries of shock followed by applause, which greatly allayed Jana's worry over his reception. Although, she suspected the applause was out of reverence for his position as president of the United States since there were many in attendance who mistrusted that he'd have the best interest of freedmen in mind and that he'd support universal suffrage.

Leanne and Charlie followed them inside with Leanne engaged in an excited whisper, and Jana was pretty certain she was telling Charlie about their honorary titles.

Lagging behind and looking handsome in his cavalry uniform, Keeley wrapped his gauntleted hands around Jana's white kid gloves. His eyes filled with love so deep Jana could've drowned in them. "Don't keep meself waiting long, me lass."

"If I have anything to do with it, she won't," Pa said.

"And if my heart has anything to do with it, I won't," Jana said.

The trio shared a laugh before Keeley took his leave.

Noting Pa's dip in joviality as he gazed down upon her, Jana said, "What is it, Pa?"

Dewiness reappeared in his eyes. "Before the arrival of our distinctive guest, I wanted to tell you, my darling daughter, how beautiful you look."

To brighten his sobriety, Jana brushed imaginary lint from the shoulder of her navy-blue dress, which she'd had specially made in Washington City, on her way home from war. As she'd hoped it would, it had impressed upon Ma and Pa that, ironically, disguised as a soldier, she'd matured into the young woman they'd wished for her when she'd run away from home. And it had helped soften her lie that she'd been playing the role of a *female* nurse at the battlefront the entire time she was away. Afterward, its military style and dichotomous presentation between femininity and masculinity had suited the message of her lectures about her wartime experiences around New York State: Women ought to be granted the same rights to tackle anything a man can if she has a mind to it. And, now, it symbolized the equality that Jana knew would grace her and Keeley's love and marriage. With giddiness, she said, "I wanted to wear my cavalry uniform, but we both know Ma would never have tolerated that."

Pa grunted in amusement.

"You've seen me outfitted this way before, Pa, and I don't ever recall your calling me beautiful in it. Maybe patriotic. Definitely not beautiful. What's so different today?"

"Before, you spoke in it about your army successes. Today, Ma and I are giving you away in it." He sighed. "Where does the time go? Seems only yesterday you were twelve and hunting with me."

Bumping Pa, Jana said, "You still have Eliza, and now you have Alex. Even when he moves in with us, he'll be available to you, unless he's busy with chores or school."

"Not the same. Neither have the dead-eye you do."

"Under your skilled training, they'll catch on quickly. Besides, I'm not giving up hunting with you." Jana sobered. "Don't you want to see me married, Pa?"

"You bet I do!" Pa strapped his strong hands around Jana's puffed sleeves. "I meant what I said. Ma and I are proud of you for not shying away from the tough tasks in fighting for our country and, as President Johnson said, a few times at the near cost of your own life."

Casting aside the memories of war, Jana felt her own tears beginning to well. Softening her voice, she said, "Are you pleased that I'm marrying Keeley? I've never had the chance to ask you and Ma outright."

Pa guffawed.

"What's so funny, Pa?"

"Who'd have thought you'd find a mate who'd put up with your tomboyish ways?" Pa clicked his cheek. "Not to mention a man who fell in love with you while you were dressed as a cavalryman."

Jana rolled her eyes. "For the umpteenth time, Pa, you might think twice about saying that to Keeley, unless you intend to chase him off."

Grinning broadly, Pa said, "Is that all I have to do to get rid of him?"

"Very funny, Pa. Do you *really* like Keeley? Or do you favor him because you want me to be happy and because you know in the long run, whether you like him or not, I'll still marry him?"

"We Bradys, especially you, struck gold the day you happened upon Keeley. And, of course, he struck gold with you too. Ma and I couldn't be more thrilled with your union. Keeley's the son we would've wished for, and your sisters are stark-raving mad over gaining him as their brother." He tightened his squeeze around Jana's arms. "You have our full blessing, and we're glad you're settling here on our land."

Jana reared on the tips of her calf-high boots and pecked Pa's cheek.

Ma reappeared. "I've cued Corporal Wallace to give me two minutes before he calls us in."

Gazing lovingly at each parent, Jana said, "I wish Walt Whitman were out here to poetically translate the depth of my gratitude for all you've done to give me and Keeley a wonderful beginning to our marriage. You've encouraged our love, made our wedding the best ever, and gifted us a parcel of land. I challenge the world to prove there are parents who can emulate your greatness."

Ma and Pa swept Jana up in a tearful embrace.

Sniffling, Ma said, "You don't need Walt Whitman. Your words are music to our ears and carry their own heart-renderings." Ma cupped Jana's face in her gloved hands. "Pa and I are proud of the woman you've become, and we're overjoyed with the man you've chosen as your mate. Keeley has enriched the life, love, and spirit of our family, and we're grateful to the gifts we have in you both." Leaning in, she pecked Jana's cheek.

In her kiss, Jana felt Ma's bottomless well of love for her. She returned a kiss on Ma's cheek, hoping it carried as much depth.

Two of Jana's hometown cavalry comrades popped out of the barn and posted themselves on each side of the entryway.

A slow, gentle melody of "Boots and Saddle" floated out of the barn. Contrary to Corporal Wallace's bugle calling for Jana to don her riding boots, saddle her horse, and ready herself for drills or battle, it was summoning Jana to her new life with Keeley.

From the pasture behind the barn came the high-pitched whinny of Maiti, Jana's battle maiden who'd answered to the bugle's call plenty of times during war. Not to be left out, Jana's childhood stallion, Commodore, whinnied, and Tracker, who spent his days frolicking with his furry friends when Alex was tied up elsewhere, bayed.

Shivers of delight ran up and down Jana's spine to have her horses and coonhound with her and Keeley in spirit.

"It's time," Pa said, batting his eyes to fight back the tears.

Ma and Pa linked arms with Jana and guided her to the threshold.

Unexpectedly, Jana's comrades saluted her.

Jana, Ma, and Pa inhaled a sharp breath at their show of respect toward her, and Jana was humbled by it. Her eyes searched the crowd until they landed on President Johnson. His benevolent smile told her that he'd commanded the noble gesture, and she nodded at him in gratitude.

As the final notes of the bugle's call faded, a beaming Alex and Molly stepped out from just inside the barn and took their places at the head of the aisle.

Jana gaped at her youngest sister in her replica Garibaldi dress and Alex in full cavalry uniform.

"Surprise," Ma gleefully whispered. "I hope you don't mind, but I thought it would be nice for them to partake in your ceremony as your ring bearer and flower girl."

"Oh, Ma, I love it!"

"Your ma burned the midnight candle sewing their outfits," Pa said in a whisper and flashing Ma a look of love and adoration, such as Jana was confident would everlastingly grace her and Keeley's marriage.

Alex glanced over his shoulder, aiming his shining gray eyes and a smile that stretched from ear to ear at Jana. When he turned back to face the front, he began bouncing from foot to foot.

Upon Jana and Keeley's return home from their mission, they'd told Alex about their wish to adopt him after they were married. He was ecstatic over it and began counting down the days to the momentous occasion. Jana suspected his current zeal had more to do with his adoption than his part in the ceremony.

When all had quieted, a violinist seated himself rearward of the altar on the groom's side and took up his instrument, nestling the lower bout between his jaw and collarbone. He drew his bow across the strings and began playing the "Wedding March," composed by Felix Mendelsohn for *A Midsummer Night's Dream*—a play by Jana's favorite author William Shakespeare.

A rustle of skirts and coattails filled the air as the crowd rose from benches hewn by Pa and Keeley with Alex's help.

Holding a pillow embroidered with two joined hearts and carrying Jana's Claddagh ring and Keeley's plain antique gold band, Alex led the processional, and Molly followed, plucking petals of wildflowers from her wicker basket and strewing them onto the floor.

To Jana and her parents' slow methodical march down the aisle, lined with candles flickering inside plump, topless pumpkins, which she, Ma, and her sisters had fun gutting, carving with heart shapes, and assembling and arranging, Jana glued her eyes to Keeley.

His eyes were already glued to her.

Jana felt a powerful gravity pulling them and their love together.

And he must've felt it too. Alex and Molly had barely cleared the aisle on their way to climbing the low platform to stand beside Charlie and Leanne, respectively, when Keeley hopped down and took two long strides toward Jana. Thrusting his hand out to her, he said, "I thought ye'd never get here, me lass."

His rare exhibition of impatience elicited good-humored heckles from the audience.

To the red-hot flames assaulting his cheeks, Keeley gave Ma and Pa an apologetic smile for trying to snatch Jana away from them prematurely, against wedding protocol.

Pa patted his back and Ma blew him a forgiving kiss. Before they withdrew to their front-row benches on the bride's side, they pronounced to the preacher their joy and blessing in giving their daughter away to Keeley.

Hiking her skirts up above her ankles with one hand while still holding her bouquet in the other, Jana stepped up onto the altar along with Keeley and the help of his steadying hand beneath her elbow.

The wedding party of six turned to face the minister.

When only the drop of a pin could be heard, Reverend Hayes splayed his palms outward toward the congregation and began his very brief sermon, as requested by Jana and Keeley:

> Welcome, everyone!
>
> We gather today to witness the wonder of love, which has entwined Jana Brady and Keeley Cassidy.
>
> The secrets of marriage are to:
>
> > love and trust,
> >
> > want only the best for each other,
> >
> > see the inner beauty that makes each special and unique to the other, and
> >
> > accept a difference in personalities and physical endowments, which diminishes neither, but enhances both.
>
> Marriage is:
>
> > an adventure in the sharing of experiences and an intimacy of human relationships, and
> >
> > a union of two people whose camaraderie and mutual understanding have flowered in romance.
>
> Marriage takes dedication to:
>
> > learn and grow with each other through the good and the bad, and
> >
> > forge onward together without knowing what the future deems for each.

Upon Reverend Hayes' request for Jana and Keeley to face one another, Jana handed her bouquet to Leanne and was amazed when she accepted the feminine object without a show of repugnance. Then, Jana turned back to Keeley.

Reverend Hayes announced:

> Now, Jana and Keeley would like to proclaim their love and commitment to the world through their own special words.

Sweeping both of her hands up in his, Keeley began:

> From the very first moment I saw ye, me Jana lass, I fell in love with ye. Contrary to what some might think otherwise. . .

He shot Pa a dimpled grin.

> . . .me eyes were wide open to yar disguise as a man.

The audience tittered.

When all quieted, Keeley sobered to say:

> From then on, I prayed to walk beside ye every day and keep ye safe from harm. I believe in fate, and I know me mam and da. . .

He looked heavenward.

> . . .brought us together. Though, it was up to us to choose each other. I want ye to know, me lass, I'd choose ye every time.

He winked at Jana.

> I think that's obvious since I've already done it twice—the second time through me amnesia.

After a united, “Awwwww,” from their audience, Keeley continued:

> I promise to:
>
> always give ye all o’ me heart,
>
> always keep things equal between us. . .

“Here, here,” everyone chanted, and Jana swore she heard the voices of Susan B. Anthony and Elizabeth Cady Stanton chiming above all.

Again, Keeley continued:

> And I promise to:
>
> never disappoint ye in me love for ye.
>
> I will always be grateful to ye for sharing yar family with meself. . .

He cocked his head slightly toward the front-row pews and stared down each and every member of the Bradys and Alex as he addressed them:

> . . .and, as the most important people in our lives, I promise never to disappoint ye in me love for all o’ ye too.

The sound of sniffles rose to the rafters.

Loud enough for everyone to hear, Jana said, “How can I possibly top that?”

“Y’are the speechmaker, me lass,” Keeley replied, producing a healthy dose of laughter.

When the merriment subsided, Reverend Hayes invited Jana to proceed with her part.

Jana wriggled her hands out of Keeley’s grasp and wrapped them around his in a tight squeeze. Then, she began:

> From the very first moment I saw you, my Keeley lad, I fell in love with you too.
>
> I was blessed the day you strolled into my life. No mate could possibly appreciate my oddities and accept my whims the way you fully do, and I thank you for rounding me out as a person.
>
> You are my best friend and my sweetest of hearts, and I hope never to disappoint you in my love for you.
>
> I promise to always:
>
> > have your back,
> > support your will—that is, if in the end, I've failed in my attempt to persuade you elsewise. . .

Evoking her own dose of laughter, Jana waited for their guests to settle down before continuing:

> And I promise to always:
>
> > put your happiness above mine.
>
> I yearn to hold your hand every chance I get, Keeley, and for us to laugh together every day of our eternal and loving life together.

She gazed heavenward.

> Lastly, as the most important people to always remember, I promise never to disappoint your mam, da, and sisters in my love for you.

Lowering her eyes, Jana smiled at Keeley while Reverend Hayes signaled for Alex to pass him the rings.

The minister waited for Jana to remove and hand her gloves to Leanne and for Keeley to drape his gauntlets over his belt between the *US*-stamped brass buckle and his revolver before he held the rings up for all to see and said:

> Jana and Keeley have chosen to bind their marriage with these rings.

Passing the bride and groom each other's rings, Reverend Hayes continued on:

> Keeley now places on Jana's finger the Claddagh ring he has gifted to her from his late mam and da, and Jana reciprocates with a matching antique gold band for Keeley.

With their rings on, Jana and Keeley joined only their left hands, and Reverend Hayes placed his hand over them and said:

> May these rings, a sign of your love and devotion, be eternally blessed and may the peace and unconditional love of God surround and remain with you now and forevermore. Amen.
>
> I now by the authority committed unto to me as a minister declare that Keeley Cassidy and Jana Brady are husband and wife.
>
> You may consummate your nuptials with a kiss.

Jana and Keeley entwined in a short but sweet embrace and kiss, and everyone clapped and some whistled.

When they separated, Reverend Hayes nudged them around to face their guests. He splayed his arms toward the congregation and loudly proclaimed:

> Allow me to present Mr. Keeley Cassidy and Mrs. Jana Brady Cassidy. Rejoice now with and for them as they embark upon their life's journey as one.

Everyone shot to their feet, and, following another round of applause, Ma and Pa motioned for Alex and Molly to join them in leading their guests outside.

Surrendering Jana's flowery gourd and gloves to her, Leanne congratulated Jana and Keeley with an uncharacteristic hug and Charlie followed suit. Then, Leanne and Charlie proceeded a short distance up the aisle and lined up opposite one another, each completing the tail end of their respective column of four fully-uniformed troopers from the Tenth New York Volunteer Cavalry Regiment.

Corporal Wallace deferred the lead to President Johnson and positioned himself next in line. Unsheathing his saber from its scabbard looped to his belt at his left hip, he raised it high and pointed the blade's sharp tip toward the floor of the barn's loft overhead. "Forward march!" he commanded his small detachment.

His troopers lifted their knees high as they marched in cadence out of the barn on the heels of their commander in chief and superior officer.

Holding their re-gloved hands and glowing to their special tribute, Jana and Keeley trailed behind. When they reached the threshold, where just beyond Corporal Wallace had halted his cavalrymen, they stopped and waited.

A hush befell the crowd outside as they anticipated the next part of the ceremony.

Corporal Wallace ordered his two columns to turn and face each other and join him in raising their sabers high and skyward. "Cross sabers!" his voice boomed.

Slowly the troopers lowered their sabers and gently crossed the tips, softening the clash of metal.

Jana and Keeley stood in awe of the saber arch until the photographer called out, "Smile for the camera, Mr. Cassidy and Mrs. Brady Cassidy."

A split-second after the cameraman snapped his picture, Corporal Wallace motioned the bride and groom through the arch to a resounding cheer from their onlookers.

Hand-in-hand, Jana and Keeley sailed through to the opposite end, meeting a shower of rice as they emerged into the open. Giggling, they ducked and sprinted to the sanctuary of their parade coach and wedding present from Wyatt McGriffin.

Corporal Wallace opened the door, and he and President Johnson assisted Jana aboard. Then, they stepped aside to allow Keeley's mount up the iron step. While the corporal waited for Jana and Keeley to cozy up to each other on the plush velvet bench, the president moved into the crowd next to Susan B. Anthony and Elizabeth Cady Stanton.

Jana was relieved when the trio struck up a civil conversation, evident by their polite expressions and measured gestures.

Retreating to his driver's seat, Corporal Wallace ordered his eight cavalrymen to form up around the coach: two trotted their horses forward, two flanked the sides, and four brought up the rear.

Jana and Keeley had expressed a wish for Leanne and Charlie to lead their procession, but they'd insisted upon riding where they could be closer to Jana and Keeley.

As Leanne and Charlie maneuvered their nickering horses into position directly behind the carriage, Leanne said to Jana and Keeley, "Ya see, this spot is much better for me and Charlie. We can watch yer backs best from here."

Charlie echoed her sentiment, adding, "It was a far greater honor for me and Leanne to be the first to welcome you out into the world as husband and wife at the start of your passage through your saber salute."

Their heartfelt words caressed Jana's heart. She felt blessed to have lifelong friends in Leanne and Charlie, and she called over her shoulder, "I'm glad you're right where you are too."

Keeley shifted on his seat, craned his neck over the folded canvas top, and flashed Leanne and Charlie a toothy grin. "Aye, as long as ye aren't offended if I steal a few kisses from me wife along our route."

With a roll of her eyes, Jana elbowed Keeley.

"Kiss away," Leanne said, laughing along with Jana, Keeley, and Charlie.

In keeping with the colors of the cavalry, Ma and her sisters had cut strips of finely netted tulle of yellow and blue and woven them together to make four gigantic double bows. They were fastened to each side of the coach, and Jana hoped their long flamboyant tails flapping in the gentle breeze would further help to detract attention away from Leanne in case her pa was amongst the spectators.

The royal red interior of the carriage made Jana feel like a princess, and she blurted, "Pinch me, my prince."

Keeley hooked a quizzical eyebrow at her.

With giddiness, she refined her request. "Am I only dreaming that we're husband and wife?"

Touching her nose with the tip of his, he whispered, "How about a kiss instead o' a pinch, me love?" Without waiting for her reply, he swathed her lips in his.

Jana broke out in a desirous flush and reciprocated his ravenous kiss.

Their guests, including President Johnson, shouted praises, parting them before Jana swooned from basking in Keeley's spicy cologne and their love.

To further deflect her flush, Jana stood up, balanced her flowered gourd in her palms, and gently tossed it up and into the crowd.

She and Keeley were thrilled when Rachel, the next oldest Brady sister, only five minutes older than her twin Rebecca, caught it. But they were shocked when she aimed her blushing cheeks at Charlie.

After Jana sat back down and snuggled up against him, Keeley signaled for the procession to start.

"Forward trot," Corporal Wallace called out to the lead cavalrymen to spur their horses on as he set the carriage in motion with a flick of his reins over the fuzzy, black rumps of two identical Morgans. It was one of two treks Jana and Keeley's cavalcade would make in a matter of hours—now for Jana and Keeley's parade, later for their honeymoon at the Elmira Hotel.

Leaning into Jana, Keeley whispered, "Might we have missed something blooming between yar sister and Charlie over the past few days?"

Jana squealed low enough to avoid Charlie hearing her. "Wouldn't it be wonderful? I think I'll nudge that along."

"And who might ye have in mind for Leanne, me little cupid?"

Grinning impishly, Jana whispered, "We've witnessed a few flirtatious moments between her and Pinkerton detective Duke Tanner. I think they'd make a perfect match. I might have to nudge that along too."

Keeley snorted with amusement. "A new occupation or, might I say, preoccupation for ye, me lovely wife?"

Through their sniggers, Jana and Keeley waved goodbye to their guests, who were already making their way back inside the barn to assist in moving the benches around the emptied and cleaned stalls to make a reception hall and room for a dance floor.

True to her vow of holding it every chance she got, Jana wrapped her hand around Keeley's. "I'm so proud to call myself your wife," she said, feeling her happiness bubbling over.

"Aye, as I am to be yar husband." Aiming a kindly, sympathetic smile at her, Keeley said, "I vowed to make all things equal in our marriage, and ye'll always be Mrs. Jana Brady Cassidy to meself, and I'll make sure everyone else knows to respect yar independent designation as opposed to calling ye Mrs. Keeley Cassidy." He scooped her up in his arms. "This is the happiest day o' me life, and

I can't believe me good fortune in our union."

Brushing her hand down his clean-shaven cheek, she said, "Our best is yet to come, my darling husband." The depth of adoration and love in his sparkling emerald eyes, which roved over every nook and cranny of her face, confirmed for Jana that she was forever his. He was definitely forever hers.

THE END

In writing historical fiction, the author sometimes takes liberties in sketching historical places, events, and people and especially where the facts are vague or silent. The paragraphs following the first are those exceptions as they pertain to *Gold, Guts and Glory* (Book 3 of *Glory: A Civil War Series*).

I must qualify that I have honored the following in the writing of my story: First, just as early advocates of woman's equal rights used the singular form of their sex in reference to their crusade, so do I. Second, just as Northerners used War of the Rebellion or Great Rebellion in reference to the American Civil War (1861-1865), so do I. Last, just as the people of Civil-War times called Washington, D.C., "Washington City," so do I.

It is fact that an estimated average of 750,000 deaths for all male soldiers in the American Civil War occurred. This is a contemporary figure, which includes post-war deaths from complications of battle wounds or disease, and it could rise as more on this subject comes to light. Of the total deaths, a staggering two-thirds succumbed to disease as opposed to death in battle or later from wounds. Interestingly, the ratio for women soldiers is just the opposite. Out of the very conservatively estimated 750 Yankee and Rebel women who fought in the Civil War, for each one who died of disease, two were either killed in action or died from battle wounds. None were executed for desertion or failing to do their duty. This evidences the courage and tenacity of women soldiers to stand at the forefront for their respective cause. A few examples: Sarah Rosetta Wakeman (alias Private Lyons Wakeman of the 153rd New York Infantry Regiment) died in 1862 of typhoid fever, and it wasn't until the late 1900s that her true identity was unveiled to her hometown (Afton, New York) and the nation, after her letters home to her family were discovered. Frances Clayton (alias Francis Clalin of the 4th Missouri Artillery) was wounded twice in Tennessee at the battles of Shiloh and Stones River. Another woman soldier was discovered by a Union burial detail amongst the Confederate dead near Cemetery Ridge after the battle at Gettysburg, Pennsylvania. For those who have not yet read *Sweet Glory* and *Train to Glory* (Books 1 & 2 of *Glory: A Civil War Series*), please know that my primary protagonist, Jana Brady of Elmira, New York, is fictional, but she represents an amalgamation of the truths about many women soldiers, nurses, spies, suffragists, and other pioneers. Her soldier-sweetheart, Keeley Cassidy of Ireland, is also fictional, but he represents all males of Civil-War times who would have encouraged women to break out of the norm and into roles traditionally reserved for men.

It is fact that typhoid fever, from the ingestion of food or water contaminated by a form of Salmonella, was the second cause of deaths for soldiers during the American Civil War. Two notable persons who died of it as well: Queen Victoria's forty-two-year old husband, Prince Albert, in December 1861 (near the time my Jana Brady enlists with the real Tenth New York Volunteer Cavalry Regiment as Johnnie Brodie), and President Abraham Lincoln's beloved eleven-year-old son, William "Willie" Wallace Lincoln, in February1862. NOTE: Dysentery (a brutal intestinal infection, causing diarrhea with blood or mucus) was the leading cause.

Although my Jana and Keeley, as well as the rest of the country, might not have known this precise breakdown, they would have been aware that disease fronted the fatalities for soldiers—both Yankee and Rebel alike.

It is fact that, in 1856, recently widowed Kate Warne became the first female detective in the United States and for the Pinkerton Agency; she participated in foiling a plot to assassinate Abraham Lincoln on his way to his first inaugural as president of the United States in 1861 and then escorted him in disguise to Washington (making her the first presidential guard and prototype for the Secret Service); and she was entrusted by Allan Pinkerton to supervise and train a staff of female detectives. Because, post-war, Kate was most likely tied up in training and all other agents were recalled from spying in the South to new or previous duties (Pinkerton detectives to safeguard the railroads from labor strikes and train robberies and United States Treasury agents to investigate counterfeiting and other financial crimes), and because, during the war, President Lincoln hired his own personal field operatives, President Andrew Johnson could have assigned persons with reputations for investigative prowess, such as my Jana Brady and Keeley Cassidy, his operatives in recouping a stolen army payroll.

It is fact that a coal and a prisoner train collided in Shohola, Pennsylvania, on July 15, 1864. However, the research surrounding this tragedy is conflicting because records were far less meticulously kept compared to today. Two examples: The number and type of cars comprising the prisoner train and the number of guards and prisoners aboard the train and how many of them died in the wreck. So, the oft-quoted descriptions and figures were used.

It is fact that President Abraham Lincoln ordered payrolls sent to Union soldiers fighting in the fields, and there are plenty of legends in circulation about stolen Confederate and Union treasuries. In one such legend, President Lincoln ordered a cavalry escort to take a load of gold bars, tagged to be made into coins to replenish army payrolls, on a circuitous route from Wheeling, West Virginia, through the woods of north-central Pennsylvania, and to the Philadelphia Mint in order to avoid confiscation of it by lingering Confederate-Army scouts in retreat after the battle at Gettysburg, Pennsylvania; the gold and the detail, except for the cavalrymen's dubiously delirious guide, went missing. That President Lincoln ordered an army payroll for the soldiers fighting around the Mississippi River to take a circuitous route around the Rebel Army retreating from the July 1864 battle at Fort Stevens, Washington, D.C., and then have it secreted aboard the prisoner train of the Shohola-tragedy is pure fiction. However, President Lincoln was savvy, and he could have conjured up this brilliant scheme.

It is fact that five unknown Rebels are believed to have escaped from the prisoner train in the aftermath of its collision with the coal train in Shohola, Pennsylvania, and that two of them remained in the area to help out on local farms. Although the two Rebel thieves, Jedediah "Jed" Fernsby and Fulton "Fuji" Jibbs of the 13th Virginia Infantry Regiment herein my novel, are purely fictional, soldiers of this unit were aboard the prisoner train. It was also fortuitous to the writing of *Gold, Guts and Glory* that some of the 13th Virginia were recruited out of Louisa County in which Trevilian Station and Louisa Court House were located and where scenes within my story fit perfectly.

It is fact that Willard's Hotel of Washington, D.C., was in existence during Civil-War times. However, research for its courtyard, sandwiched between F and 14th Streets, was scant; thus, its description was pieced together based upon a reference to a fountain with mint leaves garnishing its water and typical florals of Washington, D.C., and landscapes of hotel courtyards.

It is fact that, in 1865, a governor could temporarily fill vacancies in the United States Senate during recesses of his state legislature. However, both John Woodcock and his temporary seat for a

Pennsylvania senator who would have filled the seat during that era are purely fictional.

It is fact that the Knights of the Golden Circle (KGC) was a powerful secret military organization, born in the 1800s, for the purpose of creating its own independent economic and political "circle." If it had been successful, it would have extended its reach beyond the eleven seceding states through border and western states and territories of the United States and down and around Mexico, Central America, and the West Indies, including Cuba, and it would have been supported by the growth of cotton, rice, sugar, indigo, tobacco, and coffee on slave labor. Because there is scant information recorded by or about this organization, due to its highly clandestine nature, it is believed that the upper echelon of the KGC had a hand in monumental events, such as igniting the American Civil War with the firing upon of Fort Sumter (April 1861) and the assassination of President Abraham Lincoln (April 1865). It is also believed that the KGC continued to operate well into the 1900s, including planning the rise of the Confederacy and a second Civil War. The all-seeing KGC's involvement herein my story is purely fictional; however, as its goal was to scrupulously and unscrupulously amass wealth to support their lofty agendas, it could have been on the lookout for an opportunity to seize a Union-Army payroll within its grasp. Also, it is fact that the KGC carved symbols, such as snakes and arrows, into trees, boulders, and other natural formations as compasses to their hidden treasures, but their geographical maps were far more elaborate and prolific than that portrayed within *Gold, Guts and Glory*.

It is fact that there are many theorists who believe Secretary of War Edwin Stanton was linked to the KGC and involved in the assassination of President Abraham Lincoln. The opportunity to enlighten readers about their logic in this regard was capitalized upon; however, this does not necessarily reflect the opinion of this author.

It is fact that the tracks of the *Erie Railway* and other railroads followed the routes depicted herein my story. However, as it was difficult to reconstruct exact train schedules, which were constantly changing around Civil-War times, arrival and departure times were based upon approximate train speeds, miles between places, and layovers at primary, secondary, and *whistle stops to calculate the overall time it would have taken to travel between destinations. *(Small platform or shed in a remote area from which passengers flagged down a passing train).

It is fact that a stagecoach route ran between Fredericksburg and Clayton's Store, Virginia. However, as it was difficult to reconstruct exact departure schedules, one was manufactured. Also, the time it took to travel between the two points was estimated based upon the miles between them, the average speed of a four-horse-drawn coach, the required number of stops and layover times at *relay and swing stations, and the condition of the road, which is assumed to have been roughed up with two armies traipsing over it for four years during war and with war having barely ended upon the writing herein. *(Relay: for passenger dining and repose; Swing: for a change of horses).

It is fact that, starting in 1892, pensions were awarded to women employed by the federal government for their Civil-War work as nurses. Sarah Edmonds Seelye (alias Private Franklin Flint Thompson of the 2nd Michigan Infantry Regiment) was bestowed a pension for her deeds as a Union soldier, nurse, and spy; she fought the entire duration of the war with her sex unknown and without injury. It is also fact that a full military pension was awarded by the state of Massachusetts to Deborah Sampson (alias Robert Shurtleff) who fought with the Continental Army from 1782-1783, in the War of Independence or Revolutionary War. Thus, President Andrew Johnson could have assured that my Jana Brady was awarded a pension for her soldiering, nursing, and spying during the Civil War and earlier than it actually materialized.

It is fact about United States coinage: 1. There were four mints in existence at the outset of the Civil War, one at Philadelphia (Pennsylvania) and the remaining three in the rebellious states of

North Carolina (Charlotte), Georgia (Dahlonega), and Louisiana (New Orleans); 2. The closure of the mints in the South, a lack of coinage in operation at Philadelphia, and a shrinkage of coins in circulation because of their hoarding by the general public forced the United States Treasury to start printing *greenbacks in 1861 to fund the war; and 3. With all four mints closed at the end of the Civil War, the United States had to rely solely upon the branch in San Francisco for coinage. That President Abraham Lincoln earmarked a $2,000,000 shipment of greenbacks to pay the soldiers fighting out west around the Mississippi River in 1864 is pure fiction herein my story, but he could and might have ordered this since greenbacks were the staple currency then. *(Paper currency/ dollars dubbed as such owing to the bright green printing of their backs; their depreciation against gold during the war made a recovery post-war).

It is fact about United States coins: 1. The first gold Liberty Head Double Eagle, valued at $20.00, was struck in 1850 at the Philadelphia Mint; and 2. The gold 1861 Liberty Head Double Eagle, also valued at $20.00 but with the mint mark *O* (signifying the New Orleans Mint, which was the last of the three Southern mints to be in operation), was struck by three different governments within the borders of the United States—first by the United States, then by the state of Louisiana after it seceded from the Union and seized the mint, and last by the Confederacy—the latter two for very brief times within the first quarter of 1861. Because all three 1861 coins were made from the same proofs and are identical, it is impossible to distinguish from which of the three governments each derives. Throughout the war, the United States Treasury would have likely had 1850 and 1861 Liberty Head Double Eagles in stock, as well as it would seem 1861 Liberty Head Double Eagles struck by the state of Louisiana and the Confederacy, which would have been in circulation and accessible for confiscation by the Union Army stationed in and around Louisiana. Thus, President Andrew Johnson could have gifted my characters both an 1850 and 1861 Liberty Head Double Eagle, no matter the latter's origin.

It is fact that Susan B. Anthony, Elizabeth Cady Stanton, and Frederick Douglass are three of the most well-known persons for their work in the abolition of slavery, universal suffrage, and equal rights, and they require no special introduction here. Since in *Train to Glory*, they invite my Jana Brady to travel across Upstate New York speaking about her time in uniform to prove women ought to hold the same rights to juggle everything a man can if they have a mind to it, and each attend one of Jana's lectures, it is plausible that they would have made every effort to attend the wedding of a cavalrywoman to her cavalryman. Such an event was bound to be a nationwide spectacle, especially from the standpoint of baring women's strengths, skills, and intelligence beyond their roles inside the home as wives, mothers, and homemakers and outside the home in the few roles acceptable for women as teachers, governesses, laundresses, and maids. In this same vein, it is plausible that Nurse Clara Barton, Dr. Mary Walker, and Poet Walt Whitman, who befriend my Jana Brady and Keeley Cassidy in *Sweet Glory*, would also have made every effort to attend Jana and Keeley's nuptials.

It is fact that Andrew Johnson championed the common man and, as president of the United States, he vowed to be strict in restoring especially the voting rights of Southern aristocratic planters and politicians, whom he blamed for inciting the American Civil War. Yet, he rushed to pardon thousands of this class of Confederates during the summer and fall of 1865, allowing them to return to the helms of their state and local governments, become eligible to run for federal office in the next elections, and pass "Black Codes" or laws, which restricted the movement of freedmen, practically re-enslaving them by forcing them back on plantations to work for reprehensibly low wages. Historians speculate that President Johnson reversed his post-war edict to be tough on the South, in part, to return Democrats to the 39th Congress of the United States before it convened in

December 1865, confident of their support in crushing the Republican-dominated legislature's Reconstruction plans to enforce military rule over the rebellious states and to continue providing for millions of impoverished freedmen, especially in granting them Southern lands confiscated or abandoned during the war. It is also fact that upon Andrew Johnson's first public scrutiny of him (in March 1865 at Abraham Lincoln's second inaugural as president and Johnson's first as vice-president), former slave Frederick Douglass noted "bitter contempt and aversion" in Johnson's expression followed by "the bland and sickly smile of a demagogue." This brought Douglass to conclude: "Whatever Andrew Johnson may be, he is no friend of our race." Lastly, it is fact that President Johnson once said: "This is a country for white men and, as long as I am president, it shall be a government for white men," and he could have uttered a version of this to my Jana Brady in reply to her request that he support women's suffrage. In light of these particulars, it is likely that, by October 1865, President Johnson's white supremacist and chauvinistic convictions and doggedness to get his way were shining through. Two noteworthy examples that evidence his latter lifelong characteristic: In 1866, President Johnson embarked upon a speaking tour in an attempt to persuade American voters to elect representatives to Congress who supported his lenient Reconstruction policies, which backfired due to his riotous speeches and confrontations with naysayers. In 1868, he dismissed Secretary of War Edwin Stanton (the most-vocal-and-persuasive Radical Republican in favor of military Reconstruction) from office against the 1867 Office of Tenure Act, which required Senate consent before a president could relieve a member of his executive cabinet. Thus, as depicted herein my story, my Jana Brady and Keeley Cassidy would have omitted inviting President Johnson to their wedding out of concern for their own comfort as well as that of their guests, all who staunchly stood behind universal suffrage and equal rights. But, from this discourse on President Johnson's fearlessness and determination and, given his authoritative position as commander in chief of the United States Army, a case can be made for his having no compunction in crashing the military ceremony of a cavalrywoman to her cavalryman—again, bound to be a nationwide spectacle and chance for him to elevate his popularity in and garner future presidential votes from a region of New York State weighty with Republicans in 1865, such as was then reflective of Chemung County and its surrounds.

It is fact that the real Tenth New York Volunteer Cavalry Regiment, in which my Jana Brady, Keeley Cassidy, and friends enlist, assigned buglers at the rank of corporal to call the actions and movements of its troopers in camp, for training, on the march, and during battle. However, Corporal Wallace, who partakes in Jana and Keeley's wedding, is fictitious. Although it was easy to find buglers of the Tenth New York who were mustered out of service at the end of the war in 1865, it was cumbersome tracing if they were still alive at the time of Jana and Keeley's wedding in October 1865, and this could not be assumed.

Rather than turn this section into an essay, I will briefly state that more information can be learned through my "Bibliography" and/or "Webliography" herein about the following persons, who were real to Civil-War times but were only touched upon in *Gold, Guts and Glory*:

Clara Barton: Nurse & Organizer of Charity for the Relief of Union Soldiers, Founder of the American Red Cross, & Suffragist

Maria Isabella "Belle" Boyd: Confederate Spy & Captain and Honorary Aide-De-Camp (Bestowed by Confederate General Thomas J. "Stonewall" Jackson)

Matthew Brady: Photographer

James B. McCaw: Surgeon-in-Chief of Chimborazo Hospital, Richmond, Virginia (1861-1865)

Martha Johnson Patterson: Eldest Child of President Andrew Johnson, Hostess of the White House During Her Father's Term (1865-1869), & Wife of David T. Patterson, U.S. Senator (1866-1869)

Phoebe Yates Levy Pember: Nurse & Administrator at Chimborazo Hospital, Richmond, Virginia

Thomas Franses Pendel: Doorkeeper to the White House for Thirty-Six Years (From Presidents Abraham Lincoln to William McKinley—Both Assassinated in Office)

Noble D. Preston: Commissary Officer & Historian of the Tenth New York Volunteer Cavalry Regiment. (See More about Him in My "Acknowledgments")

Chauncey Thomas (alias Uncle Chauncey): Owner of the Shohola Glen Hotel in Shohola, Pennsylvania, & Local Philanthropist

Elizabeth "Miss Lizzie" Van Lew: Socialite of Richmond, Virginia, Abolitionist, & Union Spy

John Vogt (of Shohola, Pennsylvania): Farmer & Eyewitness to the 1864 Tragic Train Collision

Mary Edwards Walker: Surgeon, Prisoner of War, Abolitionist, Suffragist, & Prohibitionist

Timothy Webster: Pinkerton Detective (Executed in April 1862 by the Confederacy for Spying)

Walt Whitman: Poet

I thank:

All women of American Civil-War times who bravely and tenaciously challenged the injustices of traditional feminine standards by busting out of their norms and into roles traditionally reserved for men. Their interminable gift once again gave me exciting material around which to craft *Gold, Guts and Glory* (Book 3 of *Glory: A Civil War Series*).

Karen Knowles, teacher, writer, editor, and friend who always teaches me so much about honing my writing when she coaches me through revisions of my novel draft and encourages me to keep writing through tough times.

All participants of my character-naming contest for *Gold, Guts and Glory*, which I hosted at www.facebook.com/LisaPotocarAuthor and www.facebook.com/LisaPotocar, especially the winners for coming up with some fun names. They are (in alphabetical order): Brynn Hlozansky who named kindhearted German Tobias Müller; Colleen Schwartz who named English thief Jedediah "Jed" Fernsby; Judy Fernbach Simon who named English thief Fulton "Fuji" Jibbs;

and Linda Zuckowski who named kindhearted German Franz Wilheim.

Civil-War Veteran Noble D. Preston who recorded a regimental history that I believe can be surpassed by none. From it, I extracted almost everything I needed to know about the personality of the Tenth New York Volunteer Cavalry Regiment and its movements throughout the war.

Ron Matteson who, through his book *Civil War Campaigns of the 10th New York Cavalry*, bolstered my research where Noble D. Preston was vague or silent.

All of my family and friends who have supported *Sweet Glory* and *Train to Glory* (Books 1 & 2 of *Glory: A Civil War Series*) and have urged me on throughout the writing of *Gold, Guts and Glory*. I must specially acknowledge the following: my mother, Patricia, who tirelessly searches for new venues in which for me to expose my research and writing; my mother-in-law, Anita, for her tireless efforts in marketing and promoting my books—she could most definitely give anyone in the business a run for their money; my twin sister, Lita, who constantly cheers me on during creative spurts and blocks, reads and edits my materials, and led me to the highly subversive Knights of the Golden Circle for some great story fodder; my niece, Cara, who allows me to chew her ear off about my writing progress and provided me valuable insight into the Treeing Walker Coonhound; my nephew, Brandon, who came to my rescue with historical research and guidance with many computer concerns; my nephew, Brent, who kindly participated in my character-naming contest and is always interested in my writing journey; and my older brother, Doug, who labors to keep the wheels of my online marketing-and-promotion platform rolling along its tracks.

Both my late maternal grandmother, Versella, and great-aunt, Iva, who allowed me the liberty of using their names for my characters.

My dearest author friend Leslie Ann Sartor (www.lasartor.com), of whom I'm eternally grateful, led me through the maze of self-publication when my publisher closed its door and I was forced to learn the business side of writing in order to find a new home for *Sweet Glory* and *Train to Glory*. She also set me on a course to Christa Holland (www.paperandsage.com) and Cindy Jackson (www.whenweshare.com). Both women were extremely kind, patient, and understanding as the former tackled the work of designing *Gold, Guts and Glory's* cover while the latter designed and formatted the interiors of *Gold, Guts and Glory's* digital and print editions and then uploaded the files to each of my distributers.

Just like Civil-War regiments had mascots, I had my cuddly keeshonds Fuji (Yama-San) and Kili (Man-Jaro) to spur me on through their boundless energy. Bless them for understanding those times when I was too engrossed in my writing to play with them.

Last, but definitely not least, my husband, best friend, and hero, Jed. Once again, he summoned the rain during my more frightening creative droughts and let me be (even took over my chores) when he noticed that my writing engine was running in high gear. He is the greatest person in the whole wide world!

Alden, Henry M., and Alfred H. Guernsey. *Harper's Pictorial History of the Civil War: Contemporary Accounts and Illustrations of the Greatest Magazine of the Time*. New York: The Fairfax Press, 1866.

Angle, Paul M. *A Pictorial History of the Civil War Years.* Garden City, New York: Doubleday and Company, Inc., 1967.

Blanton, Deanne, and Lauren M. Cook. *They Fought Like Demons: Women Soldiers in the Civil War*. New York: Vintage Books, 2003.

Campbell, Susan Bartoletti. *Black Potatoes: The Story of the Great Irish Famine, 1845-1850.* Boston, Massachusetts: Houghton Mifflin Company, 2001.

Chemung County Historical Journal: A Civil War Anthology. 1964; rpt. Elmira, New York: The Chemung County Historical Society, Inc., 1985, 1993.

Chemung County Historical Journal: Elmira Prison Camp. 1964; rpt. Elmira, New York: The Chemung County Historical Society, Inc., 1990, 1997.

Colman, Penny. *Elizabeth Cady Stanton and Susan B. Anthony: A Friendship That Changed the World*. New York, New York: Henry Holt and Company, LLC, 2011.

Dann, Norman K. *Cousins of Reform: Elizabeth Cady Stanton and Gerrit Smith.* Hamilton, New York: Log Cabin Books, 2013.

Davis, William C. *The Civil War.* 3 vols. 1990; rpt. London, United Kingdom: Salamander Books Ltd., 1999.

Elmira City Directory, 1860. Elmira, New York: Chemung County Historical Society, Inc.

Fluhr, George J. *The Shohola Civil War Train Wreck: The Great Prison Train Disaster in Pike County, Pennsylvania.* Shohola, Pennsylvania: Shohola Railroad and Historical Society, 2013.

Forrest, Tim. *The Bulfinch Anatomy of Antique Furniture: An Illustrated Guide to Identifying Period, Detail, and Design*. Piccadilly, London: Bulfinch Press, 1996.

Garrison, Webb. *Amazing Women of the Civil War.* Nashville, Tennessee: Rutledge Hill Press, 1999.

Hill, Thomas E. *Never Give a Lady a Restive Horse; A 19th Century Handbook of Etiquette*. 1873; rpt. Cleveland, Ohio: World Publication Company. First Edition 1969.

Janowski, Diane L., and Allen C. Smith. *Images of America: The Chemung Valley*. Charleston, South Carolina: Arcadia Publishing, 1998.

Johnston, Lucy. *Nineteenth-Century Fashion in Detail.* 2005; rpt. South Kensington, London: V&A Publishing, 2009.

Kagan, Neil, ed. *Eyewitness to the Civil War: The Complete History from Secession to Reconstruction.* Washington, DC: National Geographic Society, 2006.

Loomis IV, Frank Farmer. *Antiques 101: A Crash Course in Everything Antique*. Iola, Wisconsin: kp books, 2005.

Lossing, Benson J. *Matthew Brady's Illustrated History of the Civil War.* New York: Gramercy Books, 1994.

Matteson, Ron. *Civil War Campaigns of the 10th New York Cavalry: With One Soldier's Correspondences*. Lulu.com, 2007.

McCutcheon, Marc. *The Writer's Guide to Everyday Life in the 1800s.* Cincinnati, Ohio: Writer's Digest Books, 1993.

McGovern, Ann. *The Secret Soldier: The Story of Deborah Sampson.* 1st Edition Trade Paperback Edition. New York, New York: Scholastic Paperbacks, 1990.

Morton, Virginia Beard. Marching Through Culpeper: A Novel of Culpeper, Virginia, Crossroads of the Civil War. Orange, Virginia: Edgehill Books, 2001.

Preston, Noble D. *History of the Tenth Regiment of Cavalry, New York State Volunteers, August 1861 to August 1865.* 1892; rpt. Salem, Massachusetts: Higginson and Company, 1998.

Stanchak, John. *The Visual Dictionary of the Civil War.* New York: DK Publishing, Inc., 2000.

Stanton, Elizabeth Cady. *Eighty Years and More; Reminiscences 1815-1897.* Elizabeth Cady Stanton: A Public Domain Book.

Starr, Timothy. *Early Railroads of New York's Capital District*. Rock City Falls, New York: Timothy Starr, 2011.

Starr, Timothy. *Railroad Wars of New York State*. Charleston, South Carolina: The History Press, 2012.

Towner, Ausburn. *A History of the Valley and County of Chemung: From the Closing Years of the Eighteenth Century*. 1892; rpt. Elmira, New York: The Chemung County Historical Society, 1986.

Van Doren Stern, Philip. *Secret Missions of Civil War.* Second Printing. United States: Rand McNally & Company, 1960.

Varhola, Michael J. *Everyday Life During the Civil War: A Guide for Writers, Students, and Historians*. Cincinnati, Ohio: Writer's Digest Books, 1999.

Varon, Elizabeth R. *Southern Lady, Yankee Spy: A True Story of Elizabeth Van Lew, A Union Agent in the Heart of the Confederacy.* New York: Oxford University Press, Inc., 2003.

Ward, Candace, ed. *Walt Whitman: Civil War Poetry and Prose*. Mineola, New York: Dover Publications, Inc., 1995.

Whitelaw, Nancy. *Clara Barton: Civil War Nurse*. Berkeley Heights, New Jersey: Enslow Publishers, Inc., 1997.

Williams, T. Harry, and the editors of *Life*. *The Union Sundered: 1849-1865*. 12 vols. 1963; rpt. New York: Time-Life Books, 1969.

Williams, T. Harry, and the editors of *Life*. *The Union Restored: 1861-1876*. 12 vols. 1963; rpt. New York: Time-Life Books, 1969.

Woodhead, Henry, ed. *Echoes of Glory*. 3 vols. Alexandria, Virginia: Time-Life Books, 1998.

"Abraham Lincoln, 1861-1865." The White House Historical Association. www.whitehousehistory.org/bios/abraham-lincoln.

Ackerman, Angela, and Becca Puglisi. *The Emotion Thesaurus: A Writer's Guide To Character Expression*. E-book, Angela Ackerman and Becca Puglisi, 2012.

"American Civil War." Wikipedia, The Free Encyclopedia. Last Updated 2 August 2020. en.wikipedia.org/wiki/American_Civil_War.

"Andrew Johnson (1808-1875)." Biography. Last Updated 17 December 2019. A&E Television Networks, LLC. 2020. www.biography.com/us-president/andrew-johnson.

"Andrew Johnson, 1865-1869." The White House Historical Association. www.whitehousehistory.org/bios/andrew-johnson.

"Andrew Johnson, History & Culture." National Historic Site Tennessee, National Park Service. Last Updated 22 June 2020. www.nps.gov/anjo/learn/historyculture/index.htm.

"Andrew Johnson Suite." U.S. Department of the Treasury. Last Updated 4 January 2011. www.treasury.gov/about/education/Pages/johnson-suite.

"A New Look On An Old Railroad That Helped Build A Nation." The New O & A RR. thenewoanda.weebly.com/.

Bee. "'All Aboard!': The Train Crew and Their Responsibilities." CivilWarTalk. 1999-2020. civilwartalk.com/threads/all-aboard-the-train-crew-and-their-responsibilities.141621/.

Borch III, Fred L. "The Conspirators: Tried by Military Commission." ABAJOURNAL. 1 April 2011. www.abajournal.com/magazine/article/the_conspirators_tried_by_military_commision.

"Brandy Station." American Battlefield Trust. 2020. www.battlefields.org/learn/articles/brandy-station.

Brewer, Bob, and Warren Getler. *Shadow of the Sentinel, One Man's Quest To Find The Hidden Treasure Of The Confederacy*. E-book, Simon & Schuster, 2003.

Brooks, Rebecca Beatrice. "Women Soldiers in the Civil War." Civil War Saga. 2011-2020. civilwarsaga.com/women-soldiers-in-the-civil-war.

Brownstein, Elizabeth Smith. "The Willard Hotel." The White House Historical Association. www.whitehousehistory.org/the-willard-hotel.

Buffalo as an Architectural Museum. Buffalo Architecture and History (Chuck LaChiusa). 2016. www.buffaloah.com.

Bummer. "Lincoln's Assassination Mystery or Stanton's Secret Agents." 14 January 2019. Civil War Bummer. www.civilwarbummer.com/lincolns-assassination-mystery-or-stantons-secret-agents.

Bummer. "Lincoln's Spy That Never Slept...Allan Pinkerton." Civil War Bummer. 11 January 2019. www.civilwarbummer.com/lincolns-spy-that-never-slept-detective-allan-pinkerton.

"Bureau of Military Information." Wikipedia, The Free Encyclopedia. Last Updated 9 February 2020. en.wikipedia.org/wiki/Bureau_of_Military_Information.

"Calendar for year 1865 (United States)." Time and Date AS. 1995-2020. www.timeanddate.com/calendar/?year=1865&country=1.

"Carriage Museum Library: Types of Vehicles." Carriage Museum of America. No. 4075. carriagemuseumlibrary.org/home/library-archives/types-of-vehicles.

"Carriage Showroom." Todd Andler's American Carriage Company, LLC. buggy.com/index.html.

"Coins of the Civil War." GovMint.com. 19 July 2018. www.govmint.com/coin-authority/post/coins-of-the-civil-war.

Conroy, James B. *Lincoln's White House: The People's House in Wartime*. E-book, Rowman & Littlefield, 2017.

Coski, Ruth Ann. "John Singleton Mosby (1833-1916)." Encyclopedia Virginia. 1 March 2014. www.EncyclopediaVirginia.org/Mosby_John_Singleton_1833-1916.

"Crusade for the Vote." National Women's History Museum. 1996. www.crusadeforthevote.org.

DeFerrari, John. "The Willard Hotel in the 19th Century." 9 July 2012. Streets of Washington, Stories and Images of Historic Washington, D.C. www.streetsofwashington.com/2012/07/the-willard-hotel-in-19th-century.html.

Distance Between Cities. 2020. https://www.distance-cities.com/.

"Eliza Johnson, 1865-1869." The White House Historical Association. www.whitehousehistory.org/bios/eliza-johnson.

"Erie Railroad." Wikipedia, The Free Encyclopedia. Last Updated 29 July 2020. en.wikipedia.org/wiki/Erie_Railroad.

"Erie Railroad: 'Serving the Heart of Industrial America.'" American-Rails.com. 2007-2020. www.american-rails.com/ererr.html.

"Etiquette." All Things Victorian, Collected & Arranged by Angel's. http://www.avictorian.com/etiquette.html.

"Female Soldiers in the Civil War." American Battlefield Trust. 2020. www.battlefields.org/learn/articles/female-soldiers-civil-war.

"Frederick Douglass (c. 1818-1895)." Biography. Last Updated 9 July 2020. A&E Television Networks, LLC. 2020. www.biography.com/activist/frederick-douglass.

Friends of Raccoon Ford, Virginia. Friends of Raccoon Ford,

Virginia: Preserving and Sharing the History of Raccoon Ford on the Rapidan River. raccoonfordhistory.org.

Fuoco, Michael A. "Union gold legend lives on; Treasure hunters say Civil War bullion lies buried in Elk County." *Pittsburgh Post-Gazette.* 6 April 2008. www.post-gazette.com/frontpage/2008/04/06/Union-old-legend-lives-on/stories/200804060265.

Gasbarro, Norman. "Shohola Train Wreck." Civil War Blog, a project of pa historian. Series of posts, 2014. civilwar.gratzpa.org/page/4/?s=shohola+train+wreck.

"Graffiti House – Brandy Station, Virginia." Colonial Ghosts. 15 August 2017. colonialghosts.com/graffiti-house.

Gugliotta, Guy. "New Estimate Raises Civil War Death Toll." 2 April 2012. New York Times. 2020. www.nytimes.com/2012/04/03/science/civil-war-toll-up-by-20-percent-in-new-estimate.html.

"Historic Offices of the Secretary of the Treasury. U.S. Department of the Treasury. 25 August 2017. www.treasury.gov/about/history/exhibition/Pages/Historic-Offices-of-the-Secretary-of-the-Treasury.aspx.

"History." U.S. Department of the Treasury. 25 August 2017. home.treasury.gov/about/history.

History.com Editors. "Andrew Johnson." Last Updated 21 August 2018. A&E Television Networks, LLC. 2020. www.history.com/topics/us-presidents/andrew-johnson.

"History, Lincoln and his Marshal." U.S. Marshals Service. Excerpt from Frederick S. Calhoun, *United States Marshals and Their Deputies, 1789-1989*. U.S. Department of Justice. www.usmarshals.gov/history/lincoln/lincoln_and_his_marshal.htm.

Holzer, Harold. "Abraham Lincoln's White House." The White House Historical Association. www.whitehousehistory.org/abraham lincolns-white-house.

Hopp, Michelle. "Transportation in the 19th Century." Literary Liaisons. 2001. literary-liaisons.com/article033.html.

"John S. Mosby." Wikipedia, The Free Encyclopedia. Last Updated 19 July 2020. en.wikipedia.org/wiki/John_S._Mosby.

"Ladies Dressing from the Inside Out." C&C Sutlery. www.ccsutlery.com/store/ladies-dressing-layers.html.

"Ladies Traditional Clothing." Historical Emporium. www.historicalemporium.com/ladies-victorian-clothing.php.

Lambert, Tim. "The Meanings of Some Old English Sayings." A World History Encyclopedia. www.localhistories.org/sayings.html.

lelliott19. "Raccoon Ford, Virginia in the Civil War." CivilWarTalk. 1999-2020. civilwartalk.com/threads/raccoon-ford-virginia-in-the-civil-war.159062/.

Marker, Jonathan. "The Spies Behind Lincoln's 'Secret War to Save a Nation.'" National Archives. 8 August 2019. www.archives.gov/news/articles/douglas-waller-lincolns-spies-civil-war.

"Married Women's Property Act." Wikipedia, The Free Encyclopedia. Last Updated 30 August 2020. en.wikipedia.org/wiki/Married Women's Property Act.

"Martha Johnson Patterson, 1865-1869." The White House Historical Association. www.whitehousehistory.org/bios/martha-johnson-patterson.

"Mary Lincoln, 1861-1865." The White House Historical Association. www.whitehousehistory.org/bios/mary-lincoln.

McNamara, Robert. "Edwin M. Stanton, Lincoln's Secretary of War." ThoughtCo. Updated 13 April 2017. www.thoughtco.com/edwin-m-stanton-lincolns-secretary-of-war-1773486.

"Men's Costumes: 1855-1875." History in the Making. www.historyinthemaking.org.

Mills, Charles A. *The Civil War Wedding*. E-book, Apple Cheeks Press, 2009.

Mr. Lincoln's White House. The Lehrman Institute. 2002-2020. www.mrlincolnswhitehouse.org.

"New York Central Railroad." Wikipedia, The Free Encyclopedia. Last Updated 27 July 2020. en.wikipedia.org/wiki/New_York_Central_Railroad.

New York Central System Historical Society, Inc. "NYC Railroad History." 1970-2011. nycshs.blogspot.com/2008/05/nyc-railroad-history.html.

"Nineteenth Century Fashion and Beauty." Mimi Matthews. 2020. www.mimimatthews.com/19th-century-fashion.

"Northern Central Railway." Wikipedia, The Free Encyclopedia. Last Updated 9 July 2020. nycshs.blogspot.com/2008/05/nyc-railroad-history.html.

Norton, Roger J. "The Route of Abraham Lincoln's Funeral Train." Abraham Lincoln's Assassination Site, 29 December 1996. rogerjnorton.com/Lincoln51.html.

"Orange and Alexandria Railroad." Wikipedia, The Free Encyclopedia. Last Updated 24 June 2020. en.wikipedia.org/wiki/Orange_and_Alexandria_Railroad.

"Paymaster-General of the United States Army." Wikipedia, The Free Encyclopedia. Last Updated 27 June 2020. en.wikipedia.org/wiki/PaymasterGeneral_of_the_United_States_Army.

Pendel, Thomas Franses. *Thirty-six Years in the White House*. E-book, Thomas Franses Pendel, originally published in 1902.

"Pinkerton, Our Story, Our History." Pinkerton Consulting & Investigations, Inc. 2020. www.pinkerton.com/our-story/history.

"Potomac River." Wikipedia, The Free Encyclopedia. Last Updated 21 July 2020. en.wikipedia.org/wiki/Potomac_River.

"Proctor & Gamble." Wikipedia, The Free Encyclopedia. Last Updated 4 August 2020. en.wikipedia.org/wiki/Procter_%26_Gamble.

"Richmond, Fredericksburg & Potomac Railroad (RF&P): '*Linking North & South.*'" American-Rails.com. 2007-2020. www.american-rails.com/rfp.html.

Rietveld, Ronald D. "The Lincoln White House Community." *Journal of the Abraham Lincoln Association*, vol. 20, issue 2, summer 1999, pp. 17-48, hdl.handle.net/2027/spo.2629860.0020.204.

"Scottish Rite." Wikipedia, The Free Encyclopedia. Last Updated 14 July 2020. en.wikipedia.org/wiki/Scottish_Rite.

"Secretary to the President of the United States." Wikipedia, The Free Encyclopedia. Last Updated 24 May 2020. en.wikipedia.org/wiki/Secretary_to_the_President_of_the_United_States#Private_Secretary.

"Shop Civil War Era." Recollections. 2016. recollections.biz/clothing/CivilWar.html.

"Stagecoach." Wikipedia, The Free Encyclopedia. Last Updated 1 August 2020. en.wikipedia.org/wiki/Stagecoach.

"Stagecoaches." TombstoneTravelTips.com. 2016-2020. www.tombstonetraveltips.com/stagecoaches.html.

"Stagecoach History." Genealogy Trails. 2020. Genealogytrails.com/main/stagecoaches.html.

"Steamboats of the 1800s." Encyclopedia.com. Updated 1 September 2018. Publisher Siteseen Limited. 7 September 2014. www.american-historama.org/1801-1828-evolution/steamboats-of-1800s.htm.

Stephenson, Eve. *Pinkerton's Belle: Kate Warne, America's First Female Detective*. E-book, Eve Stephenson, 2013.

Steven. "B&O Railroad Station, New Jersey Avenue and C Street NW." Civil War Washington. 4 October 2011. Civilwarwashingtondc1861-1865.blogspot.com/2011/10/b-railroad-station-new-jersey-avenue.html.

Thayer, Ella Cheever. *Wired Love: A Romance of Dots and Dashes*, transcribed from the 1880 edition by Andrew Katz. E-book, Ella Cheever Thayer, 2012.

The Knights of the Golden Circle. "Albert Pike, Free Masonry and the KGC." 10 December 2011. knights-of-the-golden-circle.blogspot.com/2011/12/albert-pike-freemasonry-and-kgc.html.

"The Lost Confederate Treasure." Southern Sentinel. southernsentinel.wordpress.com/the-lost-confederate-treasure.

"The Military Staff." American Battlefield Trust. 2020. www.battlefields.org/learn/articles/military-staff.

The Victorian Shoppe. The Victorian Shoppe: Step Back in Style. 2020. thevictorianshoppe.wordpress.com.

"The Wells Fargo Stagecoach." Wells Fargo. 1999-2020. www.wellsfargo.com/about/corporate/stagecoach.

"Town History." The Official Website of the Town of Louisa, Established 1873. www.louisatown.org/community/town-of-louisa-rich-in-history.

"Traditional Wedding Ceremony." MyWeddingVows.com. www.myweddingvows.com/wedding-ceremony/traditional-wedding-ceremony.

"Treeing Walker Coonhound." American Kennel Club. www.akc.org/dog-breeds/treeing-walker-coonhound.

"Trevilian Station: Driving Tour." Trevilian Station Battlefield Foundation. 2020. trevilianstation.com/tour.htm.

"Trevilian Station: The Battle." Trevilian Station Battlefield Foundation. 2020. trevilianstation.com/battle.htm.

"Union Pension Records." Family Search/Wiki. Last Updated 28 December 2019. www.familysearch.org/wiki/en/Union_Pension_Records.

U.S. History.org. "Reconstruction." *U.S. History Online Textbook.* 2020. par. 35. www.ushistory.org/us/35.asp.

Vergun, David. "150 Years ago: Army takes on peacekeeping duties in post-Civil War South." U.S. Army. www.army.mil/article/153230/150_years_ago_army_takes_on_peacekeeping_duties_in_post_civil_war_south.

"Victorian Clothing and Victorian Dress." Victoriana Magazine. 1996-2020. www.victoriana.com/Victorian-Fashion.

"Victorian Menswear." Historical Emporium. www.historical emporium.com/mens-victorian-clothing.php.

"Virginia Railroads at the Start of the Civil War." Virginia Places. www.virginiaplaces.org/military/7civwarrr.html.

Visit-Gettysburg. Visit-Gettysburg: Everything About Gettysburg. 2020. www.visit-gettysburg.com.

"Why the Civil War Actually Ended 16 Months After Lee Surrendered." History. Last Updated 1 September 2018. A&E Television Networks, LLC. 2020. www.history.com/news/why-the-civil-war-actually-ended-16-months-after-lee-surrendered.

"Woman's Suffrage Timeline." National Women's History Museum. 1996. www.womenshistory.org/resources/timeline/womans-suffrage-timeline.

Wongsrichanalai, Kanisorn. "Potomac River During the Civil War." *Encyclopedia Virginia.* 27 October 2015. www.EncyclopediaVirginia.org/Potomac_River_During_the_Civil_War.

Wright, Catherine. "Richmond, Fredericksburg, and Potomac Railroad during the Civil War." *Encyclopedia Virginia.* 27 October 2015. www.encyclopediavirginia.org/Richmond_Fredericksburg_and_Potomac_Railroad_During_the_Civil_War.

Young, Bob. *The Treasure Train: The Story of the Confederate Gold.* E-book, Eagle Veterans Services LLC, 2012.

Zezima, Katie. "People used to be able to walk into the White House. Legally." *The Washington Post.* 23 September 2014. www.washingtonpost.com/news/post-politics/wp/2014/09/23/people-used-to-be-able-to-walk-into-the-white-house-legally/?utm_term=.18e380efafdc.

Note: Although not required, it is encouraged to record dates of access for electronic sources. These specific dates for the writing of *Gold, Guts and Glory* are lacking; however, all sources cited above were generally accessed between 2017 and 2020, and they were re-accessed in 2020 for the recording of this "Webliography."

Please!

Consider a review on Amazon, Barnes & Noble,
D2D, Smashwords, Goodreads, and/or
anywhere else you find a home in reading.

A simple statement,
so critical to author feedback and exposure, will do.

I will forever be grateful to you,

Lisa Y. Potocar

Made in USA - Kendallville, IN
20413_9780999048849
12.06.2021 1858